JANE'S AWAY

CLARE HAWKEN

Copyright © 2021 by Clare Hawken

All rights reserved.

No part of this book may be reproduced in any form or by any electronic or mechanical means, including information storage and retrieval systems, without written permission from the author, except for the use of brief quotations in a book review.

All the characters in this book are fictitious, and any resemblance to actual persons, living or dead, is purely coincidental.

1

On the morning of Roger Kurmudge's retirement in late September 2016, his wife, Jane, told him he looked rather too pleased with himself as he sat reading the paper over breakfast. He gave his usual reply: 'And you should be pleased with me, too – you lucky, lucky girl!'

In time-honoured tradition, she tapped him playfully with her copy of *The Guardian* as she cleared the dishes; he responded with his best Sean Connery-esque eyebrow-raise over *The Telegraph*. Afterwards he thought, as he always did, 'Why wouldn't I be pleased with myself?' He was well off, healthy and happily married, with sons who were making their own way in the world. He considered his life to be a great success by any measure. And things were about to get even better now that he was retiring.

After Jane had cleared the dishes, ignoring his running commentary about the headlines – Historic England listing gay heritage sites merited his particular attention – she gathered up her things and set off for the hospital in a taxi. After waving her goodbye, Roger gathered his own things and took the short, familiar journey to Karter's Biscuits Ltd. for the last official time.

The morning passed very pleasantly, with a stream of smiling people coming to his office to reminisce about high jinks at conferences or that time he'd managed to trick – 'Convince, surely?' Roger protested – a customer into delisting one of their products, Karter's Krinklies, which had in fact been losing them money hand over fist. Later, as Roger sat in the boardroom waiting for his farewell speech, he wasn't thinking back over his career or assessing its highs and lows. Instead, he was wondering what he would have for lunch.

Outside, the wind was picking up, making the loading team pull their hi-vis jackets around themselves as they scurried between the articulated trucks parked up next to the warehouse. A glance out of the window showed Roger that the warehouse manager was staring at some paperwork on his iPad while the driver of the nearest artic shrugged at him. Roger really needed to get this kind of confusion sorted out. His performance targets were going to be missed if ...

But no. He no longer needed to do any of that. It would be Tom's problem. Tom Bradshaw, currently waiting to make Roger's farewell speech. The man always made Roger feel a little on edge. Tom was younger, of course – fifty-one. With three-year-old twins. Ludicrous and Ridiculous. Or at least that's what Roger called them. After a brief mental struggle, he brought their actual names to mind – Ludo and Ricardo, thanks to Tom's younger and very glamorous Italian wife, Elena. Obviously the second Mrs. Bradshaw. Roger always felt rather smug about the fact that he'd married so well the first time, he hadn't had to marry again.

He shuddered lightly at the thought of having young children now, at his age. Tom was constantly talking about what joy the twins brought him, how much he was looking forward to seeing them grow up, how he wished he'd had them when he was younger. 'Like you, Roger,' he'd said more than once. 'Sensible choice. Having your kids young.' Roger hadn't wanted to admit Jane had made the decision that the time was right to have Andy, then Sam, and not him.

Instead, he'd smiled at Tom as though he had indeed had great foresight and said, 'Yes, it's a young man's game! I'm a grandad now.' Little Alfie – Roger winced every time he heard the name – certainly kept Jane busy. She looked after him a couple of days a week while Andy was busy as an accountant and his wife, Sarah, did something clerical in an office; it worked pretty well for everyone. Although now that Roger was retiring, he'd want Jane to spend her time with him. Alfie would need a new babysitter.

Tom stood and welcomed everyone to the boardroom. Tall, lean, with thick wavy hair greying at the temples, a crisp white shirt and tailored 'casual' trousers, he had been sent from Central Casting to play CEO. It wasn't that Roger envied him the thick hair, the lean physique, or the charisma. He would just have preferred Tom to be *either* thick-haired, lean, *or* charismatic. Roger's mother had once described her younger son as all nose and ears. He'd grown into his features but had never possessed Tom's good looks. Not that it had held Roger back, of course. He ran his hand through his thinning hair and sat up straighter to ease the pressure on his shirt buttons.

Tom's speech turned out to be just what Roger had expected. A few stats about how well the company had prospered during Roger's tenure as CEO (true, and could have done with a bit more fleshing out, in Roger's opinion); and then far, far too long on what the future for Roger might look like. Spending time with the family, summers in France in his 'idyllic holiday home', tooling around in his classic Jag, and plenty of time on the golf course where Tom 'hoped he might get to reconnect with Roger'. Golf was something Roger enjoyed. The last thing he wanted was to hear more about Ludicrous and Ridiculous for hours on end. No, he'd golf with Frank. At least the man had a long line of dirty jokes and could re-tile the bathroom for him.

Roger registered that everyone in the boardroom was staring at him expectantly. He stood, and took his place at the head of the familiar table. For once, he wasn't quite sure what to say. One of the new graduate trainees, Mohammed, had his notepad in his hand, as though ready to take note of his words of wisdom. Tom coughed lightly.

'Sorry!' Roger laughed his heartiest laugh, the one that always made everyone else laugh too during board meetings. He'd assumed he had an infectious chuckle. This time, though, no one joined in.

Tom cleared his throat. 'I thought you'd like to say a few words, Roger, after years of toiling away here to raise Karter's from sixth place in biscuits to third. And from fifth in savoury added-value crackers to second. Thanks to that huge promotion we agreed with Sainsbury's on the last hole of our golf day!'

There was a smattering of light applause.

Roger smiled broadly. 'Thanks, Tom. Yes, we have much to be proud of. When I first started here, my objective was to help Karter's become market leader. Now we are well on our way to challenging the two biggest brands. Wiping the smiles off their faces by swiping their *heaviest* consumers – excuse the pun! – with our multi-buy strategy.'

The frizzy-haired girl from Accounts who was quite overweight and always had a packet of Karter's Chocowheels open on her desk was wincing, and the attractive account manager from Sales – Samantha? Sandra? – pulled a face. He wasn't getting his usual reception. What could he talk about without a presentation full of charts and bullet points to analyse?

He squared his shoulders. Success in corporate life, he had always found, was a question of masking his sinking sense of being an imposter – he'd had no connections to help him, nor had he been Oxbridge-educated, unlike many of the graduates he started work with – and pretending to be flashily confident. People always preferred that to dull competence. 'As Tom said, I'm sure I'll enjoy golfing, perhaps going to France to build up my wine cellar. Enjoying the good things in life ...'

He could almost hear Jane's calm, low voice in his head. *Choose your audience, Rodge. Do you think they want to hear this?* Indeed, all the young faces in the room looked surly. Samantha/Sandra was whispering something to Mohammed, who for once wasn't taking notes. His hand was very still as he stared at Roger and his face wasn't showing the usual eager idolatry that Roger rather liked. Instead, he wore an expression that would have put paid to any chance of him getting a job at Karter's Biscuits Ltd. if he'd worn it at interview. He looked now like a man who might organise a strike. Or a march to protest outside Parliament. If not worse. He did, now Roger thought about it, always carry a black backpack ...

Roger paused. The room was still and stuffy. Through the window, he could see that the damn artic still hadn't moved. He brought his attention back to the people in front of him. Time to wrap this up and get to lunch. 'Anyway, as I was saying, it's been a pleasure to work with you all. I'm sure we'll stay in touch! And I will think of you all as I enjoy my retirement.'

Tom blathered on for a few moments more before handing Roger a box with an engraved watch in it. Roger did his best to sound grateful but knew it would not replace his Patek Philippe or his IWC. After a few more moments, the crowd started to drift back to their desks. He caught Mohammed's muttered comment to Samantha/Sandra: '... such a knob.' They really didn't like Tom much, clearly. Roger was rather pleased. It was never good to be replaced by someone more popular.

'I've arranged lunch at the Jetty,' Tom said. 'A few of the team will be joining us.'

'Great,' Roger said. He checked his new watch. 'Mustn't forget to pick Jane up from the hospital later. She's having day surgery.'

'Everything's okay, I hope?' Tom asked.

'Oh, yes,' Roger said, 'just a mole being removed. Jane's always proactive about these things. But she said she'd definitely be home in good time to celebrate my retirement. I'm looking forward to seeing what she's going to make for dinner.'

'You married well, Roger,' Tom said, slapping him on the shoulder.

In spite of the too familiar slap, Roger smiled. He'd always had good taste as well as good sense. 'She married well, too, Tom,' he said. Ignoring the insidious memory that threatened his mood – *what if she ever found out?* – he said heartily, 'Jane knows how good she's got it.' He picked up his jacket and briefcase. 'Right, let's be off, then. I want to order the soufflé. Can't be late for Jane.'

Retirement would be a chance for him to make up to his

wife for his past misdemeanours. Even if she didn't know about them.

NAVIGATING THE HOSPITAL, with its long corridors and oblique signs, was a tad tricky after all the wine. Roger hadn't intended to drink quite so much but he'd been forced to, as a coping mechanism. Sitting next to Tom hadn't been part of the plan. Samantha/Sandra would have been far more fun. Or that Australian girl, Kate, from Consumer Insight. Dark, curvy, laughed a lot, lovely teeth. Bit of a stunner, in fact. Although girls like that usually left on maternity leave at inconvenient times and went on to have three children at great expense to the company. He'd always preferred to recruit men. But sitting next to Kate for lunch would have been a pleasure.

Instead, he'd been forced to listen to Tom bang on about the twins until he'd retaliated by bringing up Alfie. He didn't really know much about Alfie, but it hardly mattered. He wouldn't be seeing Tom again. So after the first bottle had gone down, he'd announced that Alfie was a champion swimmer. Already in a swimming squad.

'How old is Alfie?' Tom had asked.

'He's ... er ... two and a half,' Roger said. 'And age is just a number, Tom. His swimming teacher says he's an absolute prodigy, can do all the strokes already –'

'Including butterfly?' Tom looked doubtful. 'Wow.'

'Yes, all the strokes. Lengths. Diving. From the high board. A prodigy, I tell you.'

Tom wanted to know more. Where did Alfie swim? Had he had private lessons? And wasn't diving a separate sport for older kids? How was it that a young child was on the high board? Wasn't that a health and safety issue?

Roger shook his head. 'Not, Tom,' he smiled over his wineglass, 'for a prodigy.'

Telling inconsequential fibs was something Roger considered his 'superpower', as his sons would say. He thought of himself as essentially truthful and law abiding, but he really rather enjoyed spinning tall tales, especially if they got him out of boring situations. In this case, his strategy worked.

Tom stopped discussing children, but moved on to Jane. It was impressive how much he'd noticed about Roger's wife on the three or four occasions he'd met her. How wonderfully capable she was. Charming, talented, attractive. His praise was so excessive it was almost as though he didn't think Roger was good enough for her. *And maybe,* the sly voice in Roger's head said, *you aren't.*

'You must be looking forward to spending a lot more time together,' Tom said.

'Of course.' He was. Jane was far and away Roger's favourite person, and he had agreed to retire a year early to please her and to salve his conscience. But on the whole he expected life to go on much as before. He would be golfing, lunching, taking the E-Type out of storage for a spin, while Jane managed the house, the garden and (occasionally, he hoped) Alfie. Obviously, they'd travel to the Bordeaux property a few times a year, and perhaps take a couple of long-haul trips. But he didn't expect too much upheaval in the way they lived their lives. It had always worked so well for them. He'd explained this while finishing the bottle of Muscat in front of him, while Tom nodded in a way that suggested deep reservations over Roger's words. By the time lunch had ended, Roger never wanted to see the man again.

Marching unsteadily towards the Outpatients department, having consulted with a woman on the reception desk whose Eastern European accent he had found difficult to understand, Roger was looking forward to seeing his wife. She would scold him for drinking so much, ask him what Tom had said about him, and no doubt tut about his invention of Alfie's swimming prowess. They'd go home, enjoy dinner together, and he could perhaps get away with another glass of wine in front of some sport on TV, as it was, after all, his retirement day, while Jane dealt with the cheese soufflé stain on his shirt.

At Outpatients, he couldn't see Jane in the waiting room. He retrieved his phone from his briefcase and called her. No answer. He sent a quick text and waited for a few minutes but she didn't respond. He joined a small queue of people waiting at the reception desk. The wide-faced, grey-haired woman behind it was very brusque. Each person needed to be clear about their enquiry and good at communicating it. Yet so few of them could do it. By the time Roger stepped forward, he was fed up with waiting.

'I'm here to collect Jane Kurmudge after day surgery.' Roger was proud of his brevity.

The woman tapped at her keyboard. 'Not here.'

Perhaps, Roger thought, they had both been a bit *too* brief. 'What do you mean, not here?'

'She's not here.'

'Is she somewhere else in the hospital?' he asked.

'I can't say.' Her tone was even less friendly than before.

'Well, what can you say?' He felt a tension in his head that wasn't just due to the wine.

'I can say that no Jane Kurmudge is on any list for day surgery here.'

Roger gaped at her. He pulled his jacket lapels together

to hide the stain on his white shirt. Perhaps he wasn't looking as groomed and deserving of respect as he usually did. Behind him, feet were shuffling in a get-on-with-it way. Coughs were getting less polite. 'That can't be right,' he said. 'Please check again. I can spell our surname for you.' He did so.

More tapping on the keyboard. 'No. Not here.' The woman looked past him to the young man next in the queue, whose glare Roger could now feel searing his back.

'But where else could she be?' he said. 'She left this morning with a suitcase and said she was going for day surgery. Here. At this hostiple.' He wished he wasn't slurring his words. 'And she told me to meet her here. Outpatients.' He repeated his question. 'Where else could she be?'

'I've no idea,' the receptionist said, cold-eyed, 'but she's not here.'

'You're wrong. She said she was coming here, to this host – hos – hospital!'

'Sir, I'll have to ask you to move aside. Have you been drinking?'

'I've had a glass or two. It's my retirement day.' Roger couldn't see the relevance of his drinking habits and was suddenly overcome by a wave of outrage at the question. 'I demand to see someone else.'

'Fine.' She tapped at her screen. 'Please step aside so I can deal with the next person.'

Roger felt relief replace the outrage. Someone senior, someone powerful, would soon be with him to explain Jane's temporary absence and retrieve her for him. He duly moved aside, ignoring the dark look from the young man who eagerly stepped up to the desk and unleashed a torrent of unintelligible words.

Roger scanned the corridor for the arrival of someone

senior. A few moments passed before he saw a stocky figure marching purposefully towards him. In uniform. The word *Security* emblazoned across one side of his chest.

'I hear you've been causing a disturbance, sir.'

Roger looked around for the person causing the disturbance. He was feeling woozy now, and regretting the Muscat. Time was passing very slowly. But the scowl on the man's face cut through his fogginess.

'Oh, come on,' he said. 'You can't mean *me*. I'm just here to get my wife, Jane, who's here for day surgery, and this person,' he jabbed a finger in the direction of Brusque Woman, 'has been most unhelpful. She's here, somewhere in this hospital, and I can't find her. You just need to help me find her.'

The man took his arm and began leading him towards the exit. 'Time to go home, sir.' The tone was less respectful than the words. 'She might be at home – your wife.'

'She said she'd be here,' Roger said, starting to resist the man. How dare he drag him out as though he was a hooligan or a troublemaker? 'She left home with a suitcase! Where else could she be?'

'I couldn't say, sir,' the man said. 'But she isn't here.' He was much, much stronger than Roger. Twenty years younger and very muscular. He pushed Roger through the heavy swing doors and into the corridor. Before Roger could turn back to have the final word, the door shut with a final-sounding click. The man stared at him expressionlessly through a porthole window.

A surge of emotion hit Roger, a visceral panic that he couldn't contain. He found himself pounding on the door with both fists, his briefcase swinging from his arm. 'Let me in! You've got my wife in there. I'll call the police. It's a conspiracy. Let her go or I'll ... I'll ... You'll regret this, I promise you!'

A young nurse, wholesome in her blue uniform, approached him. She had a kind face that was currently registering the appropriate level of concern. 'Sir? Are you all right? Can I help you?'

Finally. Someone respectful and helpful.

'Yes, you can.' He tried to calm down. The back of his neck felt sweaty. The shouting wasn't good for his blood pressure. Jane would be furious. He pointed at the door. 'They've got my wife. In there. They won't release her to me. They're lying to me and telling me to go home. That woman was rude, and then *he* dragged me out here and shut me out; but she's in there, Jane is, and I need to get her back. They've ... they've *kidnapped* her.'

The nurse was staring at him with pity and comprehension in her face. 'Sir,' she patted his hand, 'I'm going to help you, okay? Just come with me and I'll find someone to help you.'

Roger followed behind her as she trotted briskly down the corridor. It was a maze of intersecting hallways, each with complicated sounding departments – Obstetrics, Neurology, Cardiothoracic, Diagnostic Imaging – but he wasn't looking at the signs in detail. His head was pounding. He followed doggedly in the nurse's wake and wished he'd drunk more water with lunch. Jane had told him he was drinking too much and as he refilled his Villeroy & Boch wine goblet with a rather nice Châteauneuf-du-Pape, he'd told her he was fine. Perhaps, he thought, he should cut down a bit.

At last they arrived at another department and the nurse gently guided him towards a seat. She released his arm and went forward to the desk, where she had authority to jump the queue. This was more like it. It was busy in here, and everyone looked a bit 'banged up', as Andy would have said. Roger hoped they wouldn't be here for long. In fact, the conversation the nurse was having with the receptionist was already taking far too much time. How long did it take to say 'we need to find this gentleman's wife, send out an urgent announcement'?

He got to his feet unsteadily and approached the desk. His eyesight was still a bit fuzzy but his hearing was fine. Which allowed him to hear his rescuer say:

'Come on, Lyn, I know we're jammed. But that old bloke needs help. He reeks of booze, and just got thrown out of Outpatients for making a scene. Totally delusional. Thinks we've kidnapped his wife, was shouting at Simon from Security. I had to rescue him. We can't just throw him out onto the street, can we? Who can you get to take a look at him?'

Roger bolted. Clutching his briefcase to his chest, he stumbled out of the hospital, into the car park and out onto the road. Opposite was the large Tesco, and coming out of it was a taxi. Roger threw his arm out. The driver stopped and Roger got in. He gave his address and fell back against the seat. He wanted to go home. Jane would be there. She'd be so sorry to hear about his horrid experience at the hospital.

The taxi dropped him off at The Grange, his Grade II listed house in the large village of Much Overton on the outskirts of Guildford. The house was dark. It took him a minute to get his key in the lock and when he opened the front door he felt a chill. The heating wasn't on. The warmth and light and odours of cooking he associated with Jane being at home were absent. As was his wife.

He switched on lights and the heating and sat in the sitting room to call her. It went to voicemail. He hung up and tried again. And again. The fifth time, he left her a message.

'Jane, it's me. I'm very worried, I went to the hospital and you weren't there, it was – well, it was most unpleasant. Please call me right away. I'm home now and I'm very concerned.'

She'd call him shortly (Jane always phoned back promptly), and once she got home they could celebrate his retirement. Maybe she'd popped out to get champagne or a bottle of something special. He'd have a quick glass of wine while he waited for her.

Glass in hand, he went back into the sitting room and put the TV on. He couldn't focus on anything except the phone on the coffee table. An hour later, he tried her again. Straight to voicemail. It was almost eight o'clock. He was hungry.

'One more time,' he said aloud. 'She'll pick up this time.'

She didn't.

At eight thirty, alone in his huge, silent house, Roger was forced to conclude the alarming fact.

His devoted, charming, ever-present wife had disappeared.

2

Until the morning she got the message, Jane had never really minded Roger looking a little too pleased with himself. She found his utter delight at the pleasantness of their life, tinged with smugness though it was, quite endearing. After all, their generation was arguably the luckiest in history, and surely it was better to look pleased about it than to be one of the entitled baby boomers who seemed grumpy all the time about the tiniest inconveniences – like some of their friends. She was looking forward to his retirement, which was just a week away.

She indulged her husband, she knew, but she loved him dearly. He still reminded her of the outwardly brash, inwardly rather insecure young man she'd met at a party so long ago and she still enjoyed his company after almost forty years of marriage: they liked to do similar things with their free time, she very much appreciated the lovely home and beautiful garden his career had provided, and he always made her laugh with his ability to tell the most outrageous, pointless fibs at a moment's notice. She just hadn't realised he could apparently tell enormous, life-altering ones, too.

After unloading the dishwasher that morning, she stopped to drink her coffee, leaning against the kitchen counter and casually scrolling through Facebook to see if Sarah had posted any new photos of Alfie. She saw she had a message. From someone she didn't know. The message had a photo attached.

Puzzled, Jane read the message first. Then read it again, her eyes jumping along the lines of words, her confusion growing, her mind unable to make any sense of what it was seeing. She scanned it for a third time, before looking properly at the photo. It was horribly, wordlessly convincing. Reaction kicked in: her knees buckled and she slid slowly down the counter to the floor. The dog trotted across to sit next to her and she fondled his ears as her mind raced.

Time passed. She stood up when the floor became too uncomfortable and went to lie on the sofa. Her mind was busy updating the record of what she'd thought had happened, with this new and utterly devastating information. She thought back. Had there been clues? Perhaps. An avoidance of certain topics. A glance away from her when she'd asked a perfectly innocuous question. But there had been so much else going on at the time. She had been too busy to pick up on it.

Through the French doors, she saw a woodpecker land on the bird feeder as a light breeze ruffled the leaves of the hydrangeas. A car went past in the distance. A totally normal morning, except she didn't feel normal any more and wasn't sure when she would again.

Jane tried to find the right word to describe how she was feeling. Shocked, dazed, distressed. They seemed too small, somehow. Devastated, destroyed. Traumatised. She tried the words on for size. Imagined them on her friends' aghast, yet slightly gleeful, lips. 'Poor Jane ... Did you hear? She's just devastated. *Traumatised*.' These words felt bigger, a better fit for the situation, but Jane couldn't say she was actually feeling them. Right at that moment, lying on the slouchy sofa in the sitting room, the clock ticking softly on the mantelpiece and the dog snoring next to her, she felt nothing at all.

After a few more minutes, she got up from the sofa and continued her morning tasks: tidying away the newspapers, changing the bed sheets, putting the washing on, emptying the dryer and updating the Ocado order that was to be delivered in a couple of days' time. She went ahead with her car insurance quote from the AA and refilled all the bird feeders. She'd planned to clear her studio and paint after months of not feeling inspired. She'd actually set aside most of the day to do so – painting wasn't something she'd ever managed to squeeze into the gaps between chores – but now she felt too strange to even attempt to pick up a brush.

The numbness lasted until lunchtime. She ate a toasted cheese sandwich and felt so tired she needed to lie back down on the sofa. The soft chime of the hideous clock – the square face set into a lump of quartz, a present from Roger's mother that Jane had put up with for many years simply because she was too kind to throw it out – striking one p.m. coincided with her feelings resurfacing as though an anaesthetic had worn off. They smashed into her like an unexpected wave knocking her over. She felt molten with rage and bitterness.

As she lay on the sofa in the house where they'd had so many happy times, the house she'd chosen and renovated and furnished and tidied for almost quarter of a century while her husband relaxed and watched TV and ate the food she prepared and wore the clothes she'd chosen and drank the wine she'd ordered and smiled and *smiled* at her –

More than once, she was ready to have the blazing row, to show him the evidence – 'Look! Look at that photo and tell me it isn't true. I will *never* believe you' – but each time, he was suddenly distracted by something else he needed to do before his last day in the office and he'd stride off, leaving her alone, staring at her reflection in the rain-splashed kitchen window opposite the sink.

So she made her plans. Organised what needed to be done.

Roger swallowed the 'mole removal appointment suddenly available' story without even asking where this supposed mole was on her body. Her anger was now white-hot. On the day she left, he made his usual smug comment over *The Telegraph* and she tapped him as usual with *The Guardian*; it took all her strength not to scream hysterically and beat him about the head with it until the paper disintegrated around his ears like ironic confetti.

She smiled with the bottom half of her face, her eyes implacable, while she got into the taxi and waved goodbye.

He had no idea of her plan. But when she came back with all the unarguable evidence, Roger would have to face the consequences of his lies for the first time in his entire life.

Jane confirmed her destination with the taxi driver, sat back, and, for the first time since receiving the message, quietly wept.

3

The debilitating fog of Roger's hangover made it hard for him to believe Jane's disappearance was real until the following afternoon when Andy, Sam and Alfie turned up to discuss it. His sons were tall and they took up space as they clumped into the hall, instantly shrinking it. They resembled him very little, with their straight noses, wide foreheads and Jane's thick, dirty-blonde hair. Strangers often found it hard to tell them apart but Sam was taller and Andy had a constant pinch of anxiety between his eyebrows. They both had sensitive-looking faces. Too sensitive, really. It would have been fine for a daughter, of course, but not sons.

Now their appearance reminded him of his wife, although their blank shock at Jane's absence reflected his own. They stood in the kitchen surveying the chaos and Roger saw judgment in his sons' expressions. (Which was a bit rich, given the state of their bedrooms when they were growing up.) Alfie's face registered only glee at finding the open packet of chocolate biscuits spilling crumbs onto the usually pristine kitchen counter. The burnt casserole dish on top of the hob smelled terrible, and Roger wished he'd tried to clean up the night before, but he'd stumbled to bed and hoped that the following day would reveal that it had all been a bad dream. It hadn't.

'Wanna biccit!' Alfie said.

'No, Alfie. We don't eat biscuits, remember? They aren't good for us.' Andy's voice was calm.

'Woger eats biccits,' Alfie said. 'I wanna biccit.'

Roger eyed the boy with dislike. Why was it Alfie insisted on using his name when he couldn't even say his 'r's?

The biscuit battle went on for a few more minutes and Roger started to regret the call he'd made to his elder son the night before.

Andy had been panicky at first – 'Dad, you sound weird! Are you having a heart attack? A stroke?' – before a patronising note had crept in. 'Dad, you need to calm down. You sound a bit ... Have you been drinking? Mum must have stayed in overnight. Perhaps her battery's dead. I'll try her now.' He had rung back a few minutes later to say he'd had no more success than Roger had. Finally, he'd promised to come over the following day, as it was a Saturday. He hadn't mentioned bringing Sam. Nor Alfie, who had won the biscuit war and was scattering crumbs all over the kitchen.

'Tell me again,' Andy said. 'What happened? What did Mum actually say?'

Roger searched his memory. 'She said she needed something removed; think it was a mole? I offered to meet her at the hospital after my lunch around five. She said Outpatients. That's it.'

'Do you think she's missing?' Andy said. 'Did something happen to her on the way? I heard this podcast the other day, where this woman –'

'Where's Gwamma?' Alfie said, scowling at Roger. 'Want Gwamma.'

'Alfie, buddy, Grandma's not here,' Andy said, kneeling next to him. Roger had heard a little too often about the 'right way' to speak to children. Apparently you had to get down to their level and speak in gentle tones straight into their faces. It didn't make the little bastards behave any better.

Alfie started wailing. 'Want Gwamma!' The noise made Roger's head hurt even more.

'Another biscuit?' Roger said, offering him the packet.

'Dad!' Andy protested, but Alfie produced a turn of speed across the kitchen that made Roger wonder if perhaps, instead of inventing a bright swimming future for the boy, he should have opted for athletics. Alfie's chubby hands snatched two biscuits and he scuttled to the far end of the kitchen to scoff them down.

Sam was glued to his phone. Just as Roger was about to tell him how fed up he was of this generation's obsession with technology, he said, 'I've checked on the *Find My iPhone* app. Can't find Mum's anywhere. She could be offline.' He clicked his fingers absently for a few minutes. 'What did she take with her?'

'A suitcase,' Roger said. It hadn't looked too large to him as it sat packed and ready in the hallway; Jane hated to be without exactly what she needed.

'How did she get to the hospital, Dad? Did she drive?'

'No. Taxi.' Her Range Rover Evoque was still in the garage.

'I listened to a podcast once about that taxi driver. You know the one. I think we should call the police.' Andy looked grim-faced. He was a big fan of true crime documentaries and Roger wondered now if he hadn't lost perspective.

'Someone might have taken Mum. They might know you're loaded, Dad, and perhaps they want a ransom. Let's hope it's just that.'

'*Just* that?' Roger said. He got himself a glass of water and gulped it down. He usually found it easy to ignore Andy's rather bleak view of life but today he couldn't.

Andy said, 'I need a coffee. Anyone else?'

Another obsession of this generation. Roger liked coffee, but anything basic in a plunger would do. Nothing less than Jamaican Blue Mountain beans from Fair Trade estates, ground extra fine and lovingly made into a flat white with organic milk using equipment that looked hi-tech enough to produce jet engines would do for his sons. Jane humoured them and had bought a fancy machine last Christmas. It sat gleaming smugly on the marble island. Roger found it tricky to use.

Sam strode over to the cupboard and, after a moment of examination, announced in a flat tone, 'Only Essential Waitrose coffee beans.'

'Nothing better?' Andy sounded more concerned than he had about Jane's disappearance. He went to check for himself, as Alfie surreptitiously took the biscuit packet off the counter and cantered back to the far end of the kitchen.

Roger was still reeling at the thought of Jane being kidnapped. Surely not – Andy was just being his usual pessimistic self. *But if he was right* ... How would he raise the ransom? There was a hundred grand that was reasonably liquid, but everything else was largely tied up. The bank would of course fall over itself to give him a loan. Although a short-term loan to pay a ransom would attract extortionate interest rates. Extortion to pay for extortion. It struck him as funny. Was he still drunk?

Andy and Sam were still agonising over the lack of 'decent' coffee beans.

'It's not like Mum,' Andy said. He opened the fridge door. 'There's nothing in. When do you usually get your Ocado order, Dad?'

'No idea,' Roger said. 'Your mum takes care of that.'

Andy sighed. 'Okay, then. I think we should phone the police.'

Sam cleared his throat. 'What about other hospitals first? I mean, no offence, Anders, but I don't think the police are our first port of call?'

Hope leapt in Roger's chest. 'I assumed it was the Royal, but of course it could have been the private place. Stupid of me.'

'Fine.' Andy frowned and chewed a fingernail. 'But, like I say, that taxi driver ... These things do happen.'

'I'll call the other hospitals.' Sam was on his phone immediately.

For the next few minutes, Roger listened to his side of the conversations with dwindling optimism: '... date of birth 25th February 1953? I'll wait. No? Could you ...? Oh, I see. Right, thanks for your help.'

Sam hung up. 'No Jane Kurmudge anywhere that I can find. She's not at the private hospital. She's not at that new clinic.' He sighed. 'Wherever Mum is, she isn't in hospital. Not around here, anyway.' He rubbed his eyes. 'I need coffee.'

Andy filled the coffee machine while engaged in some highly nuanced discussion with Sam about the best bean-to-cup machines currently on the market – 'But just how good do you think that grinder really is, Sammo?' – and after some serious fiddling around, produced two cups of coffee which he and Sam dispatched in less than a minute.

As though the caffeine had woken Andy up, he shivered lightly and checked his phone.

'Sarah's been calling me. Better text her.' He started to thumb the screen. 'Shit! I mean, shoot, where's Alfie?'

A brief panic-stricken search later, they found him in the sitting room on the sofa, surrounded by biscuit crumbs, thumb in his mouth. He was watching TV. Andy sighed with relief until he realised Alfie had somehow found an episode of *Embarrassing Bodies* on playback and was absorbing a large Glaswegian man talking about his issues with his loose foreskin.

'Alfie! Not suitable for you, buddy,' Andy said, switching the TV off and sweeping him back to the kitchen. He put Alfie down on the flagstone floor. 'I'll get you a snack. Maybe some ... crisps?' He opened the snack cupboard and found a packet. 'Don't tell Mummy, okay? Our secret.' He held a finger to his lips but Alfie was already ripping the crisp packet open. 'God, Dad, it's such a mess in here.' Andy picked up the casserole dish and winced. 'How the hell did you burn this so badly?'

'I must have put the oven on the wrong setting,' Roger said defensively. He'd pulled something labelled boeuf bourguignon out of the freezer and, in using the range for the first time without Jane, had inadvertently put on the grill instead of the oven. The smoke alarm had woken him from his stupor on the sofa and he'd had to open all the windows and the sitting-room French doors and waft at the oven for ten minutes with a tea towel before the alarm stopped. It was just as well they had no close neighbours. The beef had been inedible. In the end, he'd eaten half the packet of chocolate biscuits before stumbling to bed. He wasn't sure he'd ever fancy a Karter's Chocowheel again.

Andy slammed the casserole dish into the sink and ran

hot water on it. 'Leave it to soak. Or let Mum sort it out when we work out where the hell she is. Could she have gone to stay with anyone?'

'Who?' Roger asked. Jane's mother had died three years earlier, having long outlived her father; and her sister, Anne, had emigrated to Australia decades earlier and barely stayed in touch. All of Jane's friends – their friends – lived locally, so she never stayed with them. She came home to him and their lovely house.

Andy shrugged. 'Maybe she fancied a girls' night.'

It didn't seem likely after day surgery, but Roger could at least find out. 'I'll go round and see them tomorrow,' he said. He really couldn't face anyone today. Not hung-over, unshaven, shaky.

'Dad, don't you think you should go today?' Sam asked. 'Or send us? What if something's happened to Mum?'

Roger just couldn't believe something could happen to Jane. This was Guildford, after all. It must be a misunderstanding. She must have said something else to him as he was finishing breakfast. Was it possible she'd said 'I'm off for a spa weekend with friends/trip to Paris/New York/Edinburgh'? Hadn't he listened properly? He hunted through his sketchy memories of his last words to Jane. What had she said? She had mentioned the hospital and getting a mole removed. Hadn't she?

Alfie was crawling around on the floor as though conducting a fingertip search of the area, and muttering something. Really, the child was a menace.

Andy squatted down next to him. 'What's that, buddy?'

'Where's he?' Alfie said.

'She, buddy. You mean where's Grandma? I told you –'

Alfie sat up, clamped his pudgy hands on either side of

Andy's face – Roger quite admired the forcefulness of this approach – and said loudly, 'Where's HE? Where's Killer?'

KILLER REAPPEARED AN HOUR LATER, with the dog walker, Hannah. She was an uptight sort of person, Roger thought. Tightly curled black hair that didn't move, a broad face with small features all squashed into the middle of it, and astonishingly few social skills. Perhaps she didn't need them as she spent the majority of her time with dogs. She thrust the lead and dog bed at Roger and said, 'Twenty-five quid a night. One night.' She held up a finger as though teaching a class of five-year-olds their numbers. 'Plus a walk today. Eleven pounds. Thirty-six quid.'

Roger said, 'Did Jane tell you where she was going?' That day's *Guardian* was lying forlornly on the porch behind Hannah on top of his *Telegraph*.

Hannah took less than a second to reply: 'No. Didn't ask.'

From the hall, Alfie said, 'Killer!' He squeezed past Roger's legs and grabbed the dog in an embrace worthy of a Hallmark card. Killer licked his face several times until Roger snapped, 'Killer! Stop that! Alfie, go and wash your face.'

Hannah said, 'Having a dog builds strong immune systems in kids.'

'Letting them lick your face is most unhygienic,' Roger said, as Alfie ignored him and allowed Killer's tongue free rein across his face and neck, giggling madly. 'I'll get my wallet.'

Andy appeared on the step. 'Hey, Hannah. How are things?'

'Can't complain. How's your building work going?'

Hannah said as Roger went to the kitchen to get his wallet. In the background, he could hear an animated conversation going on and by the time he returned they were on to the intricacies of council planning regulations.

'Took us ages,' Andy said. 'Well, you know.'

'Two years for me. But it was worth it. My kennels are now fit for a king. Just ask Killer.' Hannah's smile faded as Roger returned. She took the money he handed her without a word. 'Anyway, Andy. See you.' She bent down and tickled first Alfie, then Killer, under the chin. 'Be good, you two.' She turned on her heel and marched down the drive.

'Miserable bit–' Roger stopped himself as Alfie stared up at him. 'Alfie, let go of the dog and go and wash your face.'

'No!' Alfie roared up at him. The volume such a small boy managed to produce quite shocked Roger.

He turned to Andy. 'I hope you're not going to let him speak to me that way.'

'Of course not,' Andy said. He knelt down in front of Alfie and said gently, 'Now, Alfie, buddy, that's not nice, is it?'

'Woger not nice.' Alfie turned to give Roger one of the coldest, hardest looks Roger had ever received. Worse than old Garth Retton at the AGM last year. Really, the boy was insufferable. He had half a mind to pick him up and sort him out.

As though Andy had read his thoughts, he picked Alfie up himself and hugged him firmly. 'No, Alfie. Grandad loves you very much and you're hurting his feelings.'

Alfie turned his head towards Roger and, after a moment of very clear deliberation, stuck out a tongue still covered in mushed-up chocolate biscuit. 'Don't like Woger.'

'Feeling's mutual,' Roger said in his clearest, most disdainful voice.

'Dad!' Andy looked shocked. He hugged Alfie even more tightly. 'That's a terrible thing to say. He's only little.'

'I really don't expect to be spoken to like that,' Roger said. His head thumped. His wife was missing. He'd only had biscuits to eat for the past twelve hours. His lunch at the Jetty, the twice-baked cheese soufflé followed by the rib-eye steak on the bone served by servile waiters, seemed to have happened years earlier to someone else.

Where the hell was Jane? She would usually deal with family visits while he sat in the snug reading the newspaper or watching Sky Sports. He'd saunter out for a quick chat with the boys if he felt like it, but he knew they didn't mind if he didn't appear. He was beginning to realise how exhausting it was to spend time with them.

Andy said flatly, 'I'd better call the police. Dad, you still seem a bit ... off.'

The call wasn't a success. To judge from Andy's responses, the person on the other end sounded incredulous that police time was being wasted to report the disappearance of a sixty-three-year-old woman with no financial worries, no health problems – 'Tell him about the mole!' Roger had interrupted – no domestic violence issues, indeed no worries of any serious kind at all. Andy put the phone down and informed Roger that until she'd been missing for at least twenty-four hours and unless any signs of a struggle or violent coercion were found, the police were not concerned.

'Why do I pay so much tax? My wife's disappeared and I pay a fortune in tax for public services.' Roger waved his wallet in the air. 'And when I need them, they're nowhere!'

Sam sighed. 'We'll contact the police again if Mum doesn't turn up. Tomorrow, you're going to get in touch with her friends to ask if they know where she is. You do have all their addresses, don't you?'

Roger wasn't sure. He had a vague idea about a couple of them but would have to try to find Jane's address book for the rest. 'Of course!' he said.

Sam was a software engineer. Now he looked at Roger as though he was a piece of software that needed an urgent upgrade. 'Have you eaten today, Dad?'

'I had some tea and biscuits.' Roger couldn't really remember when. He'd been expecting Jane to come home at any minute, full of apologies, and make him something. 'There's not much in the fridge.'

'Maybe we should get some food in,' Sam said. 'Do you want me to go shopping?'

'That would be great,' Roger said. He hadn't been to a supermarket for years.

'Okay,' Sam said. 'Make me a list, Dad, and I'll get what I can.'

'But I don't know what your mum would usually buy,' Roger said.

'Mum cooks everything from scratch, doesn't she? I'll get you some stuff that's a bit easier.'

DOWNSTAIRS, Roger slumped onto the sofa as Sam let himself out. Alfie was sitting at the other end playing with Andy's phone, and Roger vaguely registered how crumb-crusted he was. Did the boy have to eat so many biscuits without using a plate? It was going to take Jane hours to clean this all up when she came home.

Andy was staring at him appraisingly. 'So what's the plan?'

'Well, tomorrow I'm going to contact her friends.'

'Using Mum's address book?'

'Yes.'

'Have you found it?'

'No.' He shut his eyes and registered Andy getting up and scuffling around in the sideboard drawer.

'Here, Dad.'

Roger opened his eyes.

Andy thrust a leather address book at him. 'Found it.'

'Great.' Roger shut his eyes again.

'What else?'

'Nothing. We've told the police –'

'*I've* told the police –'

'We've contacted all the hospitals –'

'*Sam* contacted the hospitals –'

'What else can we do?'

Andy said to Alfie, 'Buddy, I need my phone back for a moment.'

Alfie set up a wail of protest and a tug of war ensued, which only ended when Andy reached with his free hand for the TV remote and put CBeebies on. Instantly Alfie relinquished the phone, put his thumb in his mouth and gazed at the screen.

Honestly, Roger thought, *why does everyone else always give in to him? If I had time alone with the little bastard, I'd sort him out in ten minutes.* As though he could read his grandfather's mind, Alfie's eyes slid from the screen to him, iced over instantly, and returned to the underwater cartoon creatures with large heads. *Yes*, thought Roger, *I'd tame you, you little –*

'Have you checked your emails?' Andy asked.

'Your mum never emails me.'

'If she's been kidnapped, the kidnappers might have

emailed you. They're getting very tech savvy these days, criminals.'

'Kidnapped? In Guildford?' Roger said.

'Not everyone's well off in Guildford, Dad,' Andy said. 'There are some mean streets out there.'

Self-pity welled up in Roger. 'I just don't understand. Why is this happening? Everything was going so well, especially with me retiring. We're so happy.'

Andy made a sound. The kind of nondescript 'mmm' noise that indicated non-agreement in a non-specific sort of way.

'What does that mean?' Roger asked.

'Well ...' Andy hesitated. 'I mean, honestly, do you think Mum was really happy?'

'Of course she was!' Roger felt outraged again. 'Look at her life!' He threw out an expansive arm and felt a twinge in his shoulder. 'This house! The one in Bordeaux. Plenty of trips and holidays. I never asked her about her spending. That time she went to London and spent ... well, more than most people earn in a month. She has whatever she wants!'

Andy wiggled his head from side to side in another non-specific yet very judgmental kind of way, indicating complete disagreement. 'Not everything in life is about money, Dad. She never had a career, even though she was such a promising artist. She stayed at home with us, and I'm really grateful, and now she helps with Alfie, which is amazing of her, but I think she feels she hasn't achieved much.'

'Why do you think that?' Roger demanded.

'Because she told me,' Andy said. 'And the rest of it, the taking care of the houses and the garden and the bills and insurances and food shopping. None of it's very exciting, is it? She paints a bit but painting properly needs loads of free time and she doesn't get much.'

'She has a cleaner and a gardener!' Roger protested.

'Even they need a bit of managing,' Andy said. 'Making sure the money is there for them, directing what they're doing. This place is huge and needs loads of work, and so does the garden, and I don't think it's what Mum saw herself doing with her life. And, well, you ...' He stopped abruptly.

'What about me?' Roger said.

Andy picked at some invisible fluff on his sleeve. 'Well, you just haven't been very involved, Dad. Not in any of it. Not in bringing us up, not in all the house stuff, even when you were renovating, she did all of it. Chose the builder and the tiles and the kitchen. All of it. It was such a mess, too, while the extension was being built. *And* she had to deal with all the problems with the conservation officer. You were always at work. And when you came home, you didn't really engage with any of us. You went to your study or watched TV –'

'I was exhausted after work!'

'– and Mum did it all. And now she does it for Alfie, and thank goodness, because we couldn't have afforded lots of childcare, and I know she loves him so much.'

There was an unspoken 'and you don't, Dad' bristling in there somewhere, Roger thought.

'And for someone with Mum's ambition and talent,' Andy said, 'what a waste.'

Roger was reeling. Only a day earlier, he'd told Tom how good Jane had got it, and now here was their son telling him how unhappy she was. A sudden thought ambushed him. 'Do you think your mum's been having an affair? With that sleazy Italian landscaping guy – what was his name, Tomasso? I'll *kill* him.'

'No, Dad. No way. She'd never find the time.' Andy shook his head. 'But you still haven't checked your emails. I don't have anything.' He held up his phone screen at Roger.

'I'll have a look.' Roger fetched his phone. Getting into his Gmail account, he felt his heart rate rising and felt light-headed and unsteady on his feet. Could a kidnapper have possibly sent him something? He scanned his inbox.

There was a new email. From an address he hadn't seen before.

From: Janes Away Hurray
To: Roger Kurmudge
Subject: To Do
Feed Killer.
Take Alfie for the day on Monday. Buckle up. It's hard work.

4

The shock made Roger's knees buckle. He dropped abruptly onto the sofa, bouncing Alfie up into the air at the other end.

'Dad? Dad!' Andy's breath reeked of coffee as he leaned over him. 'Did you get an email?'

'Are you okay?' Sam was back, carrying two large shopping bags.

'No.' Roger shook his head.

Alfie was leaping around. 'Again, Woger, again!'

'Alfie, buddy, no bouncing on the sofa,' Andy said.

'Again! Again!' Alfie chanted.

He wouldn't give the little shit the satisfaction, Roger thought. He shot Alfie a steely look.

'What happened?' Andy asked. 'What did you see? Has Mum been kidnapped? Is there a huge ransom for her?'

'Worse than that,' Roger said. 'She's lost her mind.'

'Wanna snack,' Alfie said, pulling at one of the bags Sam was carrying.

'Well,' Sam said, 'I did get you something, Alfie. Hope you don't mind, Anders – just to keep him occupied.'

'Desperate times,' Andy said, nodding and putting CBeebies back on.

Sam handed Alfie a Kit Kat and Roger said sharply, 'Get a plate, please.'

Roger could sense that his sons thought they had bigger problems than crumbs as Sam fetched the plate. But now it was clear to Roger that Jane wouldn't be returning very soon to clean up. Silently, he showed his phone screen to Andy.

'Wow. Oh. I don't know what to say, Dad.' Andy read it, then showed it to Sam, who frowned.

A heavy silence fell.

'Why would she do this?' Roger asked, when the silence grew too much.

'People usually go missing if they're not happy,' Sam said quietly.

Roger's head was spinning vertiginously as he tried to understand. 'But she can't have been that miserable ... can she?'

'Well, I mean, I did have that chat with you,' Sam said. He lowered the shopping bags onto the carpet and Killer trotted into the room and sniffed appreciatively at one of them.

'What chat?' Roger couldn't remember any chatting.

'You know? At your garden party in August? I told you she looked really fed up and you said you were off to France the following week and she'd have plenty of time to relax and I said she wouldn't because the house there needed some work and you said it was fine, and I said it was only fine because Mum kept sorting it remotely but it would need Victor to go in and fix the entire heating system because honestly, now you're retiring you might want to go over there in winter for a few months and you really can't rely on just a few fireplaces to heat it all, and you said it wasn't like Mum had to actually fix the heating herself so what was the drama, and I said even Victor needed managing to make sure he didn't just go off-piste doing stuff you didn't need that costs a fortune, and you said –'

'Oh, that chat.' Roger did remember it. He hadn't registered it as a chat about Jane, though. It had been a chat about the French house, surely? And rather a dull one.

Killer was easing a packet out of the largest bag of shopping. He moved very slowly and Roger admired the cunning of the beast as he took two tiny steps backwards with the packet in his mouth.

'Oh no, not the ham,' Sam said, grabbing it. A brief tussle took place before Sam won. He said, 'Have you fed the dog, Dad?'

'No.'

'I guess that's why Mum sent that email. To remind you. It's six o'clock, he usually eats at five thirty.'

Roger shrugged.

'I'll feed him,' Sam said, heading back to the kitchen with the bags. 'I got you some ready meals, Dad, to tide you over while Mum's away. I'll put them in the fridge.'

'Thanks,' Roger said. 'How much do I owe you?'

'Don't worry about it.' Sam's voice was muffled. Roger heard him open the fridge.

'So you think that's definitely Mum getting in touch?' Andy asked him.

Alfie said, '*Andy's Dinosaur Adventures*! Like Daddy!' and sprayed bits of Kit Kat onto the sofa.

Roger gave a half-nod back to his son's question. Who else could it be? Half-finished thoughts sizzled in his mind. Jane was obviously not half-dead in A&E somewhere, or kidnapped.

Sam came back into the room. 'Have you checked Mum's passport?'

'I'm sure it's still valid,' Roger said. Realisation dawned. 'You don't mean ...?'

'Has she taken it?' Sam said.

'I'll check.' Roger took the stairs two at a time, which made his head pound, and charged into his office. He threw open the drawer to the bureau that held all their official paperwork and rifled through it quickly: their birth certificates, marriage certificate, solicitor's documents from the house purchase, and their wills. At the bottom he found his passport. But not Jane's. He held his up at Andy and Sam, who'd followed him upstairs. 'Just one in here.'

'She did take it.' Andy sighed. 'Where do you think she went?'

'But it makes no sense,' Roger said, sitting down heavily at his desk. The room seemed so empty without Jane in it asking him what on earth he was doing ferreting around and did he want to watch *Gardeners' World* with her. 'I was the one who wanted to go to lots of new places. She liked Europe, on the ferry, perhaps ...'

'She'd still need her passport for that.' Andy bit his lip. 'And money? Had she been spending lots on her credit card?'

Roger felt the hallucinogenic quality of the day thicken around him. He logged on to his banking website and checked the current account and the credit card. 'No sign of your mum spending anything at all here since Thursday.'

'But she has her own account too, right?' said Sam.

'Of course. Granny Day left her plenty of money.'

'And you wouldn't necessarily know if she was spending it?' Andy said.

'But why would she do that?' Sam asked.

'To hide her tracks,' Andy said. 'This is how people disappear. Like that case, you know, where was it? Somewhere in the States.'

'I know that, Anders,' Sam said, 'I meant why would Mum want to leave *and* hide her tracks?'

Both his sons turned to stare at Roger, waiting for his answer. He felt a rush of blood hit his face.

'I've no idea!' he said. 'It's beyond me. Why on earth she'd do this is a mystery!'

'She must have gone to Bordeaux,' Andy said. 'Mustn't she? Let's call Victor.'

'I'm not asking that man if your mother is there,' Roger said. 'Why don't I just go and get her?'

Sam rubbed the back of his neck. 'Well, look, I mean, don't you think it's weird she's gone?'

'The strangest thing that has ever happened to me,' Roger said.

'So out of character,' Andy said.

'But the email looks real,' Sam said. 'Like, she's not in danger or kidnapped.'

'No,' Roger said, reluctantly.

'I'd give her a day or two before racing over there. In case she just needs a break.'

'A break from what?' Roger said.

Sam hesitated. 'Well, maybe she wanted a rest or a change of scene from the house and the dog and ...' He trailed off.

'Me?' Roger said. He felt weakness wash through him – *Jane wanted to get away from him?* – and was grateful that he was sitting down. But the thin, reedy worry that had been threading its way through his head – *Does she know?* – was now replaced with another thought. How had he missed the fact Jane wasn't happy?

It was, on balance, perhaps a better problem, one he could fix.

'I'm sure she'll be back, really soon,' Andy said. 'Perhaps she just needs a day or two on her own, relaxing. The weather's nicer over there at this time of year. Maybe she's swimming a lot and chilling out.'

Alfie appeared at the doorway. 'Hungwy. Wanna snack.'

The boy was already covered in crumbs and hadn't stopped eating since they'd arrived, Roger thought. Honestly, where was the discipline with kids these days?

'Shoot, I'd forgotten you were still downstairs,' Andy said. 'Listen, buddy, we're going to get off home now. You can have a proper snack there.'

Alfie started a low grizzling noise that set Roger's teeth on edge.

'There's a bit of an urgent issue with Mum being away,' Andy said, slowly. 'Monday.'

'Monday?' Roger said.

'Well, Mum usually takes Alfie on a Monday, Wednesday and Thursday. She's not here.'

'So?' Surely Jane and Andy couldn't actually expect *him* to step in?

'So ... you'll have to take him, Dad. At least for Monday and Thursday. Wednesdays Sarah's at home but Mum gives her an extra Alfie-free day to do household stuff. You won't need to do that one. Alfie, spending time with Grandad will be fun, won't it?'

Alfie's sharp scream sent a bolt of pain through Roger's head.

'Come on, buddy, you'll have a lovely time with Grandad.' Andy perched on the desk and pulled his son onto his knee. The toddler was bucking and writhing in fury, hitting Andy in the face with his fists.

'No Woger! No WOGER!'

'I can't possibly have him. What do I know about looking after toddlers?'

'Dad, come on. It's two days. Well, maybe a few days over the next couple of weeks, until Mum comes home.'

'Out of the question, Andy! Look at the boy!' Roger pointed at Alfie, who was trying to bite Andy's arm to get free. 'He's like a wild animal. And there must be other options, surely?' He raised his voice above the screeching. 'Nursery?'

'Oh yeah, sure, nursery.' Andy threw his hands in the air, releasing Alfie. 'No worries, I'll just saunter into the nearest one on Monday and ask them to take Alfie for us.'

'Great, that's sorted. You can calm down, Alfie,' Roger said.

His grandson was rolling around on the carpet, still shouting his new mantra – *No Woger!* – like a miniature activist on a picket line.

'I was being sarcastic!' Andy said. 'You have to go on waiting lists, Dad, for nursery. For months, if not years. Not to mention the expense.' Andy took his phone from his pocket and held it out in front of Alfie. 'Here, Alfie. Do you want the *Peppa Pig* app?'

As though someone had switched him off, Alfie stopped screaming. He sat up, grabbed the phone and started scrolling with a practised finger.

Roger felt a wave of relief that the noise had stopped. 'Well, what about getting a babysitter? I'll pay if money's a problem.'

'Sarah won't hear of it,' Andy said gloomily. 'She won't leave him with a stranger on his own; says at least with pre-school, once he's a bit older, there will be lots of people watching out for paedos and weirdos.'

'If Sarah is so concerned,' Roger said, 'perhaps she should stay at home and look after her son herself.'

Andy hunched his shoulders. 'She would stay at home. If we could afford it. But the building work still isn't finished and the mortgage needs two incomes and ... Look, she just can't. I really think you're being unfair, Dad. It's just a couple of days and you're retired now, for God's sake.'

Both his sons were looking at him in a deeply unfriendly way. A way that suggested they saw him as weak, or a failure; someone not up to a difficult task. It galled Roger. He'd never been a man to shy away from a challenge. Looking after a toddler couldn't be that hard, after all.

He'd have him tamed in no time.

'Fine,' Roger said. 'Count me in for Monday. When do you need me?'

5

Tall, long-nosed and skinny, with narrow feet and hands, Andy's wife, Sarah, exuded frostiness. She was the most emotionally distant person Roger had ever met and it often puzzled him why his anxious, kind-faced son had married her. She wasn't even especially warm to Jane, who most people took to instantly, but her coldness was particularly marked whenever she saw Roger. On Monday morning, she opened the door to their three-bedroom semi, smoothed her dead-straight mid-length brown hair behind her ears and said, 'He doesn't want to see you.'

'Andy?' Roger said.

'Alfie.' She snapped the word out. 'He says he doesn't like you.'

'No problem.' Roger turned and walked back down the path. He felt deep relief. The thought of spending the day with that little horror was not appealing. He wanted to go home and see if Jane had replied to any of his emails. Truth be told, he regretted sending a couple of them. After he'd eaten a ready meal on Saturday night and drunk a few glasses of a decent Merlot, his initial email asking where she was and if she was okay seemed a bit *lame*, as Andy and Sam would say. So he'd beefed up his second one, demanding she come home to her responsibilities and accusing her, perhaps a little aggressively, of leaving him in the lurch with Alfie. There had been no response yet, but fortunately he'd been too busy to keep checking. There was a great deal to do now that Jane was away.

For a start, he had to make his own breakfast, lunch and dinner. He'd quite enjoyed the Tesco Finest lasagne on Saturday night after the boys had left. On Sunday, he'd had toast for breakfast, and had made ham sandwiches for his lunch, adding some of the Tesco Mixed Leaf Salad, with Tesco French Salad Dressing drizzled over it. In the evening, he'd microwaved a Tesco Finest Creamy Fish pie, and added the rest of the salad. Not the same as Jane's roast dinners, but not bad. He was slightly startled that Tesco suggested it could serve two. Perhaps Jane was right to say that his portion control wasn't what it should be.

He'd have to start shopping for himself soon, in addition to stacking and unloading the dishwasher, tidying the dry dishes away and disposing of the rubbish and recycling. He was very much hoping Jane would return before he needed to do a weekly shop, because shopping online was bewildering. There were so many choices, and, without her, no one to cook them.

Relieved of the task of caring for Alfie, he wanted to lie on the sofa and watch TV to get rid of the lingering headache he'd had for several days. Just picking up the car from work the day before had been challenging enough; he'd wondered whether he was still over the limit as he'd driven home. But any plans to head back to the house and relax were scuppered, as Sarah was shouting after him.

'Roger! Don't be ridiculous. We have no other option. Please come inside.'

With a sigh, he complied.

'I just meant that because he's not your biggest fan you might want to try winning him over,' Sarah said, striding ahead of him into the kitchen. Strapped into a booster seat at the dining table was Alfie, still eating breakfast. It was a messy business, Roger thought, surveying the chunks of porridge that were stuck to the table, the floor around it and Alfie's face. The boy's hair was of the wild, spiky variety that could not be usually be tamed, but one strand was weighed down by a dollop of porridge. A half-finished kitchen extension jutted out into the garden, taking up half of it. There was dust everywhere and it was cold, thanks to the plastic sheeting in place of walls and windows.

'Almost finished, sweetie?' Sarah cooed. 'Look who's here to take you out for the day!'

Alfie smacked his laden spoon down on the table and a large lump of porridge sailed through the air, narrowly missing Roger's head. He heard it splat on the wall behind him.

'Sarah, if Alfie really doesn't want to come with me, I honestly don't –'

'Alfie would love to spend time with Grandad, wouldn't you?' Sarah grabbed a wipe from a packet and scrubbed Alfie's face clean, then laboriously wiggled his rigid body out of the booster seat. Rubbing another wipe across his hair, she placed him firmly on the floor in front of Roger. 'He's ready to go!'

Alfie started to back away. His cold blue eyes never left Roger's.

'Grandad will take you to the park!'

Would he? He hadn't been to a park in years.

Alfie paused to consider it. 'Wiv Killer.'

Roger never took the dog with him: Jane took care of the dog walking. The idea of picking up after Killer made Roger shudder.

Sarah was bustling around the kitchen, wiping the porridge off the wall, stacking plates and mugs in the dishwasher. 'Right, better go! Coat's on the rack. Change bag's over there if you need to take it. Not that he's in nappies any more, he's so advanced, but you do need to keep an eye on the toileting, ask him if he needs to go, that sort of thing. But don't let him take Bingo with him. That's a no-no.' She held up a hand like a policeman ordering a motorist to stop. 'Bingo Bear cannot leave the house under any circumstances in case we lose him, or Alfie won't sleep at night. And we can't find another bear that's exactly the same. Mandatory detention for Bingo!' She dropped her hand and checked her watch. 'Okay, then. Have a lovely day, you two!'

'But wait!' Roger was flabbergasted. 'I don't know anything about looking after a toddler.' He'd imagined they would spend at least half an hour discussing how to go about it.

Sarah laughed, a musical tinkle of genuine amusement. 'Oh, Roger, it really hasn't changed in the last thirty or so years. Entertain him, feed him, make him nap at midday. Entertain him again, feed him again. That's it!'

'Feed him what?'

She frowned. 'Anything. Beans on toast. Fish fingers. Mashed banana. Not all together, of course. Give him some peas, he loves those. Plenty of stuff in the fridge. No sugar whatsoever. He never, ever has sugar. Only for birthdays and very special events. Carrot sticks for snacks.'

The words 'plenty of stuff in the fridge' sounded

tempting to Roger. He could manage beans on toast. 'Should I stay here with him?'

She shrugged, grabbing her car keys from the hook. 'Whatever suits you.'

'I want Killer!' Alfie sang out.

'Killer's not here,' Roger pointed out. The child really wasn't the brightest. It was just as well he was a great swimmer. Only, wait – he'd made that up, hadn't he? The boy had no future at all.

'WANT KILLER!'

Maybe he could be an opera singer. Those lungs were powerful.

Sarah was patting the air with her hands. 'Darling, don't worry! Grandad will take you home to his house, get Killer, and then take you to the park.'

Alfie's chest swelled as he sucked in air for another yell.

'And!' Sarah held up one witch-like finger. 'And! Grandad can buy you an ice cream at the park! A small one. As a very, very special treat indeed.'

The change was instant. Alfie gave a sweet smile, showing a couple of tiny white teeth. 'Coat!' He ran past Roger.

'You see?' Sarah said to Roger, as though she'd managed something clever, rather than a simple act of bribery. 'I'll be home at six. Take the buggy from the hall.'

Six o'clock? It was only eight thirty and Roger was already exhausted. Sarah dropped some keys into his hand and before he could protest she was out of the kitchen door. A second later, she poked her head back round it. 'Alfie, get the car seat for Grandad. And Roger? Just watch out for the blue breath-holding spells. Try to avoid those!'

A moment later, the front door slammed shut. What did the woman mean? Was this a reference to some kind of magic? Something he'd find at the park? Surely he needed proper briefing notes: something written down to guide him. Before he set off for a park he'd never been to with a child he'd never spent time with alone.

Alfie came back holding a seat covered in stains. He thrust it at Roger. How would this fit in the Range Rover? Surely it couldn't be hard to work out. Total simpletons had children and managed perfectly well. Alfie dashed off again and returned holding a dejected-looking stuffed toy. Although 'stuffed' was a bit of a misnomer, Roger thought. *Formerly* stuffed, perhaps. It drooped over Alfie's hand, sad-faced.

'I be taking Bingo!' Alfie said.

Sarah had said something about Bingo staying at home. It irritated Roger. Surely he could manage a soft toy accompanying them. He took the boy's hand. 'Right, then. Let's go.' He sounded far firmer and more confident than he felt. He found the buggy in the hall, and after a few minutes grappling with it, released the brake. He motioned for Alfie to jump into it, but instead the boy ran ahead down the hall and opened the door for him. This was rather helpful. Roger decided to ignore the defiance.

He shut the front door behind them and locked it, walked down the short path pushing the buggy, and pressed the key fob to unlock his car. Alfie scrambled in and helped Roger position the car seat. After a few minutes of fiddling, Roger worked out that the seat belt needed to loop through the curved plastic bits on either side. Alfie encouraged him – 'Like dat, Woger!' – and for the first time ever Roger felt a grudging admiration for him.

'How old exactly are you, Alfie?'

'I almost fwee.' Alfie held up two fingers and a thumb. He stuck the thumb in his mouth and sat back, Bingo in the crook of his arm, like a celebrity waiting for his driver to take him somewhere.

Roger shut his door and eyed the buggy. It was quite large. Could he fit it into his boot as it was? He tried. No, he couldn't. He walked around it, taking a moment to work out how to collapse the thing before finding a lever that made it fold into itself.

Roger heaved the buggy into the car and drove home, acutely conscious of his passenger in the back, particularly as Alfie needed to comment on everything that went past.

'Police car! Bus. Cat! Woger, cat!'

Roger soon realised he needed to keep up and respond, or Alfie would simply repeat the word in a rising tone until it was a shout.

'Yes, Alfie, I see the cat. Oh, yes, and the bus. And the man.' It was exhausting. He preferred listening to Radio 4, which didn't require him to say, 'Yes, I hear you, Jim Al-Khalili. I hear your words about dark matter. Yes, and the question of whether time is just another dimension.' In spite of constant demands on his attention from the back seat, they arrived home safely and Alfie scrambled out of his seat.

'Killer! Want Killer.'

The dog burst out of the front door and leaped all over Alfie, licking his face again. Roger tried in vain to stop them both and then gave up. After all, Andy hadn't seemed too worried, why should he? Now they were back at the house, he felt very reluctant to leave it. He had Sky. Alfie had CBeebies. There was food and beer in the fridge. Roger was certain they could manage the whole day here.

'Park!' Alfie said, shaking Bingo at him as Roger bent to remove his shoes.

'Alfie, why don't we stay here? I'll find you a movie, or

that show about the cartoon underwater thingies? And some biscuits?'

A strange keening noise was coming from the boy's mouth. High, shrill, unending. It rose and rose before breaking with a guttural sound into the most emphatic sobbing Roger had ever heard.

'Park! *Ice cweam.*'

This was ridiculous. Who was the boss here? Surely he, Roger Kurmudge, recently retired, didn't have to put up with this nonsense? Did he not deserve a day at home to relax and enjoy his new-found freedom? He wasn't going to be forced into anything by this sobbing.

Roger pulled out a chair from the hall table and sat down on it. He crossed his arms. In just such a way he'd dealt with the strike from the warehouse team three years earlier, and they'd caved to him in the end. Alfie didn't know who he was dealing with.

Alfie exhaled deeply and Roger braced himself for the next scream. But it didn't come. As though his diaphragm was stuck, Alfie froze. No sound emerged from his mouth. A second ticked by, then another and another. And now Alfie's face was changing colour. Less puce; blue around the lips. Was he choking on something? Should Roger pat him on the back?

He remained where he was, with his arms crossed. Unease trickled up his spine. It was he who cracked, as five seconds turned into ten. 'Alfie? Alfie! Breathe.'

Alfie's eyes were rolling in his head and he tottered slightly.

Really. Roger wasn't putting up with this. He was being played. The boy was, it had to be said, quite the actor. Perhaps RADA …

Alfie hit the hall rug in a huddled heap on top of Bingo, and Roger sprang from his chair.

Was the boy dead? He crouched down next to him, the floor painfully hard on his knees, staring intently at the boy's face. Killer nudged him with his nose and whined softly. Alfie didn't seem to be breathing at all. The enormity of the situation hit Roger. The headlines: *Neglectful Grandfather Kills Toddler; retired CEO in court over death of innocent angel Alfie*, next to a photo of Alfie looking frail and vulnerable. Those were rare, but the media would find one, he was sure.

'Alfie? Alfie! Can you hear me?' Nothing. No sign of life. Roger put his hand on Alfie's arm in its soft cotton jumper and tried a gentle shake but Alfie didn't move. A shaft of sunlight illuminated the ends of his tufts of hair and blanched his face.

Roger stabbed at his phone. What was that thing Sarah had said? *Blue breath-holding spells*, she'd called them. He googled it and scrolled madly through the NHS advice. There was a checklist:

1. *Stay calm.* He muttered the words in the hope it would help.
2. *Lie the child on their side.* Roger pushed Alfie onto his side gently.
3. *Stay with them.* Where the hell else would he go?
4. *Make sure they cannot hurt themselves on anything nearby.* Roger ordered Killer to go back to his bed and placed cushions from the sofa around Alfie.

The advice said the child would start breathing again in one to two minutes. Roger wished he'd checked his watch as soon as Alfie had stopped breathing. The seconds ticked by.

He wanted to shout and shake the boy, anything to rouse him, but it said not to in the checklist of Don'ts.

Should he call the ambulance? By the time they arrived, Alfie would be dead. Should he do CPR? The checklist didn't say to do CPR. Perhaps it was even too late. Roger rocked back on his heels and then curled into a ball, head in hands. *Christ!*

He'd go to prison. Andy would never forgive him and Sarah would have an actual reason for her hatred. He'd never go to France again or take the Jag to Goodwood or ... How could Sarah not have warned him that Alfie could *die* on his watch? And this was all Jane's fault! If she'd been here, it would all be fine: he'd be in his snug watching sport and could just have popped out to say a brief hello. If this was karma for his past sins, it was pretty brutal stuff.

He felt overwhelmed with terror as the moments ticked past. In the distance, a faint police siren made him curl even further into himself. Would he have to wear overalls, as they did in American prisons? Those unflattering orange ones? Andy would know. He lay down next to Alfie, screwed his eyes shut and wondered who to call first. Andy or the police?

'Woger? You be on the foor too.'

Roger opened his eyes to find Alfie staring at him. Their faces were very close together. He could smell the dust on the rug.

'Alfie! Are you okay?' Roger gripped his arms.

'Sometimes I cwy and fall down.' Alfie gave a happens-to-the-best-of-us shrug.

Roger savoured a few moments of relief then got to his feet.

'Park!' Alfie shouted again, picking up Bingo.

'Park it is,' Roger said.

6

According to Google Maps, the nearest park on the outskirts of the village was only seven minutes from the house, so Roger decided to walk. Which turned out to be quite a mistake. It took Alfie, Killer and Roger twenty-five – after quarter of an hour spent at home, debating, of all things, whether to take the damned stuffed toy.

'I be taking Bingo Bear to the park.'

'It's not a bear, it's a sloth,' Roger said, automatically. 'Look at those arms.'

'Dat's a bear.'

'*That's* a sloth.'

Alfie planted his hands on his hips and jutted his jaw at Roger. 'Bear.'

'Sloth.' Roger could hear Jane's voice in his head again. *Seriously? You're going to argue with a toddler over something this pointless?* Why was the child so pig-headed and convinced he was right? Such an unattractive trait; Roger wondered who on earth he'd inherited it from.

He took an enormous breath to calm himself and said,

'Let's just go to the park. Bingo Whatever can come. In my backpack.'

Alfie refused to take the buggy. Roger couldn't understand what the point of the thing was if the boy wouldn't even use it. But at least Alfie was moving more or less in the right direction.

Whereas Killer had to stop and sniff at something – a patch of moss, a cracked paving stone, someone's abandoned sandwich carton, sometimes just a scent – every three or four metres. He couldn't be hurried, and violently resisted any attempt to drag him in the right direction. Roger was astonished by the strength of such a relatively small dog. He planted his feet on the ground and leaned back hard against the lead, and when Roger tried shouting, Killer lifted a lip to reveal a few sharp teeth. For the first time, his name seemed apt.

It was undignified, Roger decided, tussling in the street with an animal so much smaller than him. Instead, he resolved to wait patiently (after all, he had to look after Alfie until six p.m. Six p.m.! They had time) while Killer's nose travelled, sniffing hard, in small circles around a spot before he lifted his head and trotted off again.

The moments that Killer spent exploring the traces of some small nocturnal rodent allowed Alfie to also stop and explore whatever he found. Leaves. A snail. A pile of something disgusting that didn't bear too much examination.

'Look, Woger. Look!'

If Roger didn't look – and looking alone was not sufficient, he also had to make a relevant comment – Alfie would stop dead and ask again and again with a rising inflection that was heading towards a tantrum. It was easier to simply develop a range of expressions Roger could trot out – what a pretty leaf; we should move that snail; feathers are dirty, don't touch – in order to keep Alfie happy.

By the time they arrived at the park, Roger wanted nothing more than to sit down and read the paper for a few minutes while the dog lay next to him and Alfie played on the slide. Surely that would be possible? He might even take a photo of how well it was all going and send it to that *Janesawayhurray* email account. Perhaps she would realise how much she missed them all and come home.

The park was half-full of people, almost all women with young children, and all of them wearing the same uniform: dark puffer jackets, some with fur around the hoods, skinny jeans and boots. True, at the far end of the park was an elderly man walking briskly with his dog, but he crossed the grass in a few minutes and rejoined the road. Also, his dog was a proper dog. A black Labrador that looked muscular and active yet obedient. An imperious whistle stopped him sniffing at something curled in the grass and made him bound towards the exit and his rapidly vanishing master.

Roger eyed Killer with some dislike. It had been Jane's decision to get a Westie four years ago, pointing out that she would almost certainly be doing the majority of the walking; and the boys had chosen the name one Sunday over roast lunch where a little too much wine had been consumed. Various names had been tested – Buddy, Felix, Max – before they got sillier: Terminator, Fang – 'like *Harry Potter*!' – Killer. They had laughed immoderately over it, pointing at the whiskery little face in the puppy photo the breeder had sent to Jane. 'He just looks like a Killer! Killer Kurmudge!'

Jane had rolled her eyes but Roger had felt that she'd enjoyed his obvious dislike of the name and had gone ahead with it to annoy him. It was now too late to change it.

Roger marched to the nearest park bench not occupied with gossipy women and whining children. He tied Killer's lead to it then sat down and reached into his backpack for the newspaper.

'Woger!' The voice was coming from far away. Past the bandstand was the fenced playground, with its swings and slides, and beyond that was an ice cream kiosk that was open despite the cool weather. Standing in front of it was Alfie, and he was waving madly at Roger. Blast the child, why didn't he stay where he was put? When he, Roger, was little, that sort of behaviour would not have been tolerated. A few of the mothers were staring at Roger now, pursing their lips. Of course, mothers these days followed their children around slavishly, never letting them leave their sight. Really. So uptight. How was the boy to develop his own style and personality and independence if he had to be policed all the time? Roger sat down and snapped open *The Telegraph*. He was halfway through an article extolling the benefits of Brexit when he realised that Alfie was not going to stop yelling.

'Woger! WOGER! WANNA ICE CWEAM!'

He peered over the top of the paper. Killer whined. The mothers were staring at him judgmentally – with, he thought, a whiff of contempt. One of them gave him a black look for several seconds before turning to another woman and saying something that made her laugh. Alfie continued to yell. The man in the kiosk was leaning out of the serving window, saying something to him (no doubt 'please shut up') but Alfie wouldn't stop shouting.

Sighing, Roger stood. 'Stay, Killer,' he said firmly, and set off across the park with his backpack.

At the kiosk, Alfie was stabbing a finger at the board that displayed the selection of ice creams. 'Wanna Feast.'

'Alfie!' Roger was impressed. 'You can read!'

'Nah, mate,' said the kiosk bloke. 'Ordered that one before, ain't he? With the nice blonde lady.'

Roger did not enjoy being called *mate*. He stiffened slightly and gave the man a cool look.

'Whatchawant?' the man said impatiently.

'Alfie, I think a Feast is a bit much for you,' Roger said in his most reasonable tone. 'You're only little. Let's choose something smaller, shall we?' Roger had learned much from the drama caused by his earlier approach to the boy's demands. He wasn't going to be so strict and unyielding this time; he'd try calm rationality instead.

He was therefore unprepared for the ferocious sobbing that burst from Alfie's mouth. The noise was just extraordinary. In the background, Killer started howling in unison, a wolf-like noise that set Roger's teeth on edge. He didn't want to look around, knowing that every eye in the park was fixed on him in silent grim judgment. Alfie's tantrum was horribly reminiscent of the blue breath-holding spell. Roger couldn't go through another one. Although Google had assured him that once consciousness was regained there were no ill-effects, the thought of it happening in the park with an already hostile audience was too much. Google had also insisted the spells were involuntary. A likely story, Roger thought.

'One Feast, please!' Roger promptly said to the kiosk man, and handed over the money. As though the sun had come out, Alfie stopped sobbing. He took the Feast from Roger in the way that a woman very much in love might accept a large diamond engagement ring (or so Roger imagined: Jane's ring hadn't been that big) and tried to rip open the packaging, his tongue between his teeth with the effort.

'Shall I help you with that, Alfie?'

'I do it by my own,' Alfie said firmly. A few more seconds went by. It was obvious to Roger that even if Alfie managed to open the packaging, the force he was using would shoot his ice cream into the nearby hedge.

Roger wrenched the Feast away from his grandson, who gave a sharp scream and stamped both feet. His shoes lit up with flashing coloured lights like warning signs.

'Look, Alfie, it's open, take it.' Roger handed it to Alfie's grabbing hands.

Alfie proceeded to devour it in less than a minute, cramming it into his mouth as though he hadn't eaten for weeks, dropping bits of hard chocolate casing onto his jumper and his shoes. In the background, Killer was still howling, and Roger took Alfie by the sticky hand to start leading him back to the bench. But Alfie resisted.

'More,' he said.

'No,' said Roger with what he considered to be extreme self-control.

'MORE!' Alfie roared and took a deep in-breath.

'No. Way.' All of Roger's calm resolve melted like ice under Alfie's blowtorch hot-headedness. He crossed his arms and gave Alfie his best I-don't-negotiate-with-terrorists expression.

Alfie started crying again. He let out two operatic, diaphragm-expanding sobs; Roger could see he was gearing up for another epic breath-holding moment. He was acutely conscious of all the eyes. In the background, the dog had started howling again.

'Christ. You win,' said Roger. He pushed a tenner towards Kiosk Bloke, who was frowning at him.

'Think that's wise, mate?' he said.

'Take the cash,' Roger said tightly.

'It's your funeral.' Kiosk Bloke took the note, handed

back some change and another Feast was shortly in Alfie's hand. He ate it in large bites once again.

'There. Satisfied?' Roger asked.

'More,' said Alfie, but without conviction.

'I don't think so,' Roger said. 'We need to get back to Killer, don't we?'

Alfie ran back across the park, whooping and jumping on the leaves that had started to fall from the trees. 'Look, Woger, look!' He stomped enthusiastically with both feet on the ground for a few metres, lights flashing, and then hopped erratically until he reached Killer, who licked his Feast-covered face vigorously.

'Chocolate is toxic for dogs,' a stern voice said behind Roger.

He turned to see an auburn-haired woman in her thirties (clearly a maverick, as her puffer jacket was purple), holding the hand of a little girl with red hair and freckles, who looked a little older than Alfie.

'Hello, Alfie,' the little girl said in a composed tone.

'Woberta, I be having two ice cweams!' Alfie said, holding up all his fingers.

'Two?' said the woman in disapproval.

Roger felt he needed to 'take back control', as Theresa May kept saying. 'And you are?' he asked in his most imperious tone.

'I'm Vanessa,' she said. 'Roberta and Alfie do swimming lessons together. Where's Jane?' Something in her tone suggested that perhaps Roger shouldn't be on his own with Alfie. Roger entirely agreed with her on this if nothing else, but felt his mind go blank. The last thing he wanted to do was explain to this *stroppy* woman where Jane was. Especially as he didn't actually know.

'Jane's ... Jane's ... Jane's away.' The answer came to him in a flash.

'Oh,' Vanessa said. 'So you're looking after Alfie, are you? And you are?' She echoed Roger's words back to him.

'Dat's Woger,' Alfie said, pointing up at him.

'I'm Roger,' Roger said firmly, rolling the 'r's a little. He held out a hand, which she regarded with suspicion. 'I'm Alfie's grandad.'

Vanessa took his hand with what looked like revulsion and shook it for a brief moment before dropping it.

'First time looking after him?' she asked with a patronising smile.

'Lord, no,' Roger said. 'Regularly do it. At the weekend, usually. But now I've retired so can do it more often.'

Fortunately Alfie was too busy twirling round on the spot, shouting, 'Watch, Berta, watch!' to comment.

'I've never seen you down here before,' Vanessa said.

Good grief, the woman was like a terrier. Why couldn't she stop asking questions?

'Well, Alfie and I come here a bit,' he said, airily, 'but we mix it up, too. Sometimes I take him into London to go to the Natural History Museum, or the Planetarium or Cirque du Soleil, or we take a day trip to Paris ...' Perhaps he was getting carried away. He must remember not to boast about Alfie's swimming, too; Roberta actually did lessons with him.

Vanessa was open-mouthed and Alfie stopped twirling long enough to say, 'Gwamma likes fowers.'

'Wow,' Vanessa said. 'I had no idea. I only ever see Jane here with him and she always seems so tired. Like she's the only person who looks after him.'

'No, no,' Roger said, 'I do my share! I suppose we do go

to other parks a lot, too, perhaps that's why you haven't seen me.'

'Like where?'

'Well ... like ...' He stopped. What other parks were there locally? He had no idea. He didn't need to go to parks, he had plenty of outdoor space at home.

'It's just we're always looking for new options.' Vanessa widened her eyes at him and waited.

'We prefer parks that are further afield, don't we, Alfie?' Roger said. 'And sometimes I take him – oh, all over the place.'

Alfie was jumping over Killer in an attempt to impress Roberta, who regarded him expressionlessly. 'Berta, look at me!'

Having got no response, Alfie then tried a handstand. It was a wobbly effort, and as though he knew he hadn't performed it well, he tried again. Then again. Then once more. Roger had to admire the persistence. 'Look. Look!' Failing at handstands, Alfie twirled around on the spot wildly for a few seconds before whirling in the opposite direction. He staggered to a halt and fell over. When he regained his feet, he looked faintly green. 'Woger, my tummy ...'

The undigested Feasts exploded out of Alfie's mouth and for the first time Roger fully understood the phrase 'projectile vomiting' as the trajectory of the chunks hit Roberta, spattering her tights and coat.

She shrieked loudly. 'Mummy! Yucky!'

'Bloody hell,' Vanessa said, pulling Roberta away. 'I hope it's not a bug.' As if she realised she might have sounded unsympathetic, she added, 'Oh, Alfie, poor you.'

Poor Alfie? Roger felt outraged. The greedy little pig

shouldn't have eaten two Feasts, should he? It would be a learning experience for him.

Vanessa glared at Roger. 'You'd better get him cleaned up.'

Alfie was moaning gently. 'My mowf ...' He threw up again and Vanessa took this as a sign that she should leave, towing Roberta behind her across the park.

Alfie looked down at his soiled clothes and burst into tears. 'Wanna go home! Want Mummy!'

If only Sarah *was* here. Roger patted his pockets helplessly. It was at this point he remembered the change bag. Why hadn't he brought it? He had one tissue in his inside coat pocket, but dabbing the small crumpled rectangle against the devastation of Alfie's face and clothing quickly showed him the futility of the gesture. 'Bugger.'

Alfie stared up at him, lips trembling. 'Woger? Wanna go home now.'

Across the park, Roger could see that everyone was looking at them. The scorn on all the faces was making him feel something. He searched his mind for the emotion's name. He'd felt it before, he was sure, but not for many years. It came to him in a lurch: embarrassed. He felt deeply embarrassed. And now he had the difficulty of getting Alfie home.

LATER, when he thought back to the rest of that day, it took on a nightmarish quality for him. Could the events possibly have occurred to him, Roger Kurmudge, (former) CEO of Karter's Biscuits Ltd.?

He imagined the email he'd send Jane:

We walked home and people actually held their nose passing us. I stripped Alfie of all his clothes on the drive to avoid contaminating the house, only to be accosted by an elderly gentleman drawn by the appalling noise, who accused me of child cruelty. Me! Shortly after lunch (a very messy and conflict-filled process), I received a visit from two police officers to check on Alfie's welfare. Policemen! In our home! Can you imagine? I wanted to ask them to help me find you, but I think they'd have started digging up the garden.

He definitely wouldn't be sending *that* to Jane.

The policemen had had to track down a naked Alfie, as he'd hidden in Roger's bedroom, and then there had been a difficult conversation about why Alfie called Roger 'Woger'. They'd been very sceptical until Roger had grabbed a photo of the whole family together from the mantelpiece and taken it to show the officers. Alfie was clearly recognisable, sitting on Sarah's lap with one finger on the way to his nose. Roger was in the background. The policemen had given him some terse advice as they left: no more naked children on the lawn – and two Feasts would make most children 'hurl'.

After that, the tedium of the day continued: in the long process of trying to remove the vomit from Alfie's clothes, he'd shrunk them by at least fifty per cent, so had to go and buy new ones, leaving Alfie alone in the car wearing one of Roger's jumpers. Returning home, Roger realised they still had three hours left to fill; after some frantic googling, he and Alfie made coloured rice in the kitchen, which was the messiest process Roger had been involved in since he himself had been a child, resulting in a smashed bowl, food-dye stains all over the kitchen and bits of rice underfoot in every downstairs room. Afterwards, he'd given up and put the TV on.

It was, Roger considered, the longest day he'd spent in

his life. Was this what Jane had gone through every time she looked after Alfie? He'd had no idea. He drove Alfie home at ten to six and when he turned the engine off he briefly leaned his head back against the car seat and shut his eyes before turning to face his grandson.

'Alfie? Perhaps don't mention ...' *Feasts. Vomiting. Policemen. Watching* Desperate Housewives *while Roger did the washing. Eating an entire packet of Lindt Balls while the re-washing took place. Being left alone in the car while Roger went clothes shopping for him.* So many banned topics. And Alfie couldn't keep secrets. He'd told Jane two weeks before her last birthday that Andy had bought her a new bird-feeding table and then put his finger to his lips and said 'Shush! It's a seecket.'

Alfie's eyes were very large and blue as he stared at Roger. Roger felt another unfamiliar emotion surge in his chest. Was this one ... shame?

'Never mind.' Roger got out of the car and helped the boy down with the car seat. He took the buggy out of the car and rang the doorbell.

'Alfie! Sweetie, I missed you!' Sarah knelt down to hug her son and then drew away from him. 'New clothes!' She checked the label at the back of the coat and her eyes widened. 'From that new children's shop in town! Wow, thanks, Roger. I love that place, but Andy says it's too expensive.'

'Well, I'm afraid we got his clothes dirty at the park and then I shrank them. Sorry about that.'

Sarah hugged Alfie again. 'Did you have a nice day, Alfie?'

'Look, Mummy, wed wice.' Alfie held out the container.

'How lovely!' Sarah beamed at Roger. 'If he wasn't too

much trouble, could you possibly do it again on Thursday? If Jane's not back?'

'I'm sure she will be. But if not, of course!' Roger said. He could have hugged Alfie. Never had he seen so much approval in Sarah's face.

He drove home. On the threshold of the kitchen he stopped and surveyed the chaos. He closed the door on it and went to the sitting room. Realised that looking at the Lindt wrappers was unlikely to relax him. Went back to the kitchen and got a beer out of the fridge. Killer was sitting at his feet, staring at him imploringly.

'Hungry?' Roger asked. Killer grinned up at him. Roger opened the fridge again. The effort of scooping tinned dog food into Killer's bowl was just too much. Instead, Roger took a packet of beef slices and threw the dog two lunches' worth (three slices). They were gone in seconds. 'That's your lot, dog. I'm going upstairs. Don't step on the broken bowl pieces.'

In his study, he turned on his PC and cracked open the can of beer. He drank half of it and sat down heavily in his chair. 'What a day.' He wanted someone to talk to about it. Someone who would empathise. Agree it had not been his fault that Alfie had been sick. That he'd been right to strip Alfie on the lawn. That it had been an outrageous violation to have heavy-handed policemen tramping through his house suspecting him of the most heinous of offences. Not that they'd actually accused him, of course. But he knew. Oh yes, he knew what they'd been thinking. He and Jane had watched a harrowing BBC drama about paedophiles a few weeks earlier. The idea that anyone could find children attractive in that way – or indeed any other – was mystifying to Roger.

A ring tone from his phone interrupted his thoughts.

'Dad? Where's Bingo?'

'Bingo?'

'Alfie can't sleep without Bingo. And he's not here.' Andy sounded furious. 'Sarah says she told you not to take him.'

'The boy insisted, Andy. And you can calm down, it's here.'

'You'll have to drop it round. Right now. Alfie's in bed crying and Sarah's livid.'

'Of course.' Heat rose in Roger's face. It had been a long time since someone had told him off like this. What a fuss. 'I'll be ten minutes.'

He went back into the sitting room. No Bingo. He checked the kitchen in case the sloth had been discarded there. No. A rising sense of panic gripped him. He should have said no to Alfie, weathered the tantrum. Sarah was not the only one furious with him, Andy was, too. He'd undone the good work of the day. And what if he couldn't find the damn thing?

Heart racing, he moved from room to room, looking for Bingo. Another call from Andy buzzed on his phone but Roger ignored it. Ten minutes went by, then another ten. He ended up in the kitchen, leaning on the island, head in his hands. He was exhausted and felt another unfamiliar sensation. Failure. He felt like a failure.

One of the deep drawers in the island was slightly open. He kicked at it petulantly but it wouldn't shut. There was a scrap of fabric stopping it. He bent and pulled the drawer open. There, draped across the saucepans, was a sad-faced Bingo. How had he ended up in the kitchen? And why on earth would the child have put Bingo in the drawer? It could have taken Roger days to discover the thing in such a daft place. Especially since he currently had little use for saucepans.

'Andy?' This time his son answered the call. 'I'm on my way.'

'About time, Dad. Alfie is beside himself.'

He dropped the sloth off. Andy met him at the front door, took the toy and shut the door firmly in Roger's face.

Roger drove home. He wanted to talk to Jane. He missed her kind good sense and ability to find the funny side of life. He checked his emails. His heart lifted for a moment, then plummeted.

From: Janes Away Hurray
To: Roger Kurmudge
Subject: To do
Cleaner (Morwenna) comes tomorrow at 9.30 for three hours. Make sure house is tidy. Have £36 in cash ready.

7

'Sonly me, Jane! Hope you're decent!'

The sound of Morwenna letting herself in alarmed Roger. He hadn't realised she had a key to his house. He'd been rushing around tidying but there were still sweet wrappers under the sofa and rainbow splashes of food colouring on the kitchen countertops and laundry flagstones. He had swept most of the broken pieces of bowl up but had left some rice on the counter. What was the point of a cleaner if you had to clean up before she arrived?

He greeted her as she stopped at the door to the kitchen. 'Morning, Morwenna.'

Her face was vaguely familiar, although Roger wouldn't have liked to pick her out of a line-up. The best word to describe her was *fierce*. Even her hair looked ferocious – jet-black, very short, aggressively tapered around her ears and neck. Her lips were painted a very vivid shade of red and pressed together as though she didn't much like him. She seemed very *abrasive*, he thought, which was perhaps a good thing in a cleaner. If only Jane was there to laugh at his little joke.

'What the 'ell 'appened in 'ere, then?' she said, hands on hips.

'Alfie came round yesterday. I looked after him.'

'Where's Jane?' There was something accusatory in her tone, as though she suspected Roger had done something to her.

'Jane's away.' Such a useful phrase.

'She never said nothin' to me about goin' away.'

'Well, perhaps she doesn't feel the need to apprise you of all of her movements in advance,' Roger said before he could stop himself. Fortunately, she was frowning at him as though she had no idea what he meant. 'Where do you usually start, Morwenna?'

'In 'ere. I need my money first.'

'Right away?' Roger hadn't had time to go to the bank; he'd been too busy tidying.

'Yeah, Jane always gives it to me as soon as I arrive, like.'

'Can I just do a quick bank transfer to you?'

'Bank transfer?' She blinked at him. 'Nah, I need cash.'

Roger had half a mind to tell her what he thought of people like her, not paying tax on their earnings. Disgraceful. On the other hand, he did rather want the house cleaned. 'Right. I see. I'll have to pop out to the cashpoint.'

Her face was dark. 'How long will that take, then?'

'Only a few minutes. Perhaps you could make a start while I'm gone?'

After a bit of muttering, Morwenna went over to the sink and opened the cupboard under it. She got out the multi-surface spray and used it vigorously, in the manner of an American actor on a police drama shooting the baddies – outstretched arm: *bam, bam, bam,* take that, germs! – on every surface she could see. The countertops got blasted, then the sink and draining board, then the hob. Grabbing a sponge, she started to scrub viciously at the food-colouring stains on the countertops. She stopped and glared at Roger. 'You goin', then?'

He went. It seemed like a good opportunity to pop into Tesco Express after the bank and get some more food supplies, so he did.

When he got back, the vacuum was on. Roger located Morwenna by the sound and handed over the money. She took it, checking the amount as she did so.

'Thanks.' She put it in her pocket. He backed out of the room.

Upstairs, he took stock of his options. He didn't really want to get caught watching sport while she cleaned. He felt somehow guilty about it. What else could he do? He went into the bathroom. The laundry basket was bulging. With Jane away, his dirty clothes were building up. After the previous day's disaster, he wasn't confident in his ability to get them washed and retain their current dimensions. Could he ask Morwenna? The thought was appalling. He couldn't give her any justification for her all-too-apparent contempt. While he was dithering, she appeared behind him.

'I need to do in 'ere.'

'Of course!' Roger said heartily. 'I'll move.'

He scuttled off to the snug and put Sky Sports on quietly. So quietly he could barely hear it, in fact; but it was women's rugby and he didn't need to hear much. He settled back in his armchair, watching slack-jawed as the exhaustion from the day before caught up with him. Only when Morwenna swung open the door in the middle of a replay of a scrum that focused unnecessarily closely on the thighs of the prop-forward did he think about the picture he might be presenting. Staring at – no, *ogling* young female rugby players. He sat up straight and smiled at her weakly. She sniffed.

'Need to do in 'ere now.'

'No, don't worry. Really. It's fine in here.'

'I always do in 'ere.' She glanced around. 'I can see the dust.' She swiped a finger across the side table and held up it triumphantly to him. 'See?'

He could. 'I'll move.'

He went to the sitting room. Could he face putting Sky Sports on in here? Even thinking it made him feel furious. This was his house. He was paying her to clean it. He could do what he liked. It was none of her business what he did while she worked. He, Roger, had worked hard for many years and had now retired. The whole point of retiring was to do what he liked, for once. Vindicated in his own mind, he picked up the remote.

He couldn't therefore really explain to himself why, half an hour later, when Morwenna came barging in with the vacuum, he felt so shifty to be caught watching the end of the rugby game. Yet again he was watching a replay, this time with the camera focusing quite lasciviously on the bouncing bosom of the wing woman as she thundered down the pitch towards the end line. The slow-motion didn't help. The rise and fall of her astonishingly large breasts was mesmerising, and perhaps his mouth had been open as he took it all in. Roger was forced to admit that if he had been a female cleaner, working in the house of a sixty-something man whose wife was away and had caught said man watching women's rugby slow-mo replays with his mouth open, he too might have muttered 'perve' under his breath. He stood with as much dignity as he could muster and said, 'I'll leave you to it.'

Outside the snug, he was tempted to pop back in and

just see if Big Boobs had managed to get the try. The mere thought seemed to conjure up Morwenna. She stumped back up the hall towards him, and he bolted. Christ! The woman was everywhere. Like she was spying on him. Why did she clean in this random manner? Although, as he went into the kitchen, he could see that the house did look significantly cleaner than it had before she'd arrived.

To stay out of her way, he went into the garden. Leaves were starting to turn yellow. The beds looked a little untidy now, after the magnificence of the summer months when they'd been full of flowers. They had a gardener once a week. He couldn't remember his name. But someone came in to help.

The bird feeders were empty. Jane would hate that. She was forever filling them up. He summoned Killer from his bed in the kitchen and went to the scruffy shed that backed onto what the boys had always called the 'wild bit' of the garden. He pulled open the warped door with some effort. The shed had definitely seen better days. It smelled of damp, mould and rodents. He found the fat balls, peanuts and seeds, turning a blind eye to the signs of gnawing on the packaging.

Refilling the feeders took two minutes while Killer ambled around sniffing at invisible trails. Roger sat down on the bench and watched a mass of blue tits arrive to feed. Shortly afterwards they were joined by the great tits, a woodpecker and some doves. There was a chill in the air. Roger wondered if he could bear going back in to make some tea, but he could see that Morwenna was back in the kitchen. He decided it wasn't urgent. In fact, it was rather pleasant out here.

He was usually too busy to enjoy the garden, but it had been one of the main selling points of the house for Jane.

She'd loved the luxuriant main garden, with its country-garden flowerbeds crammed full of blooms of every height and colour imaginable, and the acre of unstructured woodland with a little stream that was a haven for birds and insects. He'd told her not to show the estate agent how much she wanted the house, but her face had given her away and they'd paid the full asking price.

Even now, when the lawn needed cutting and with autumn underway – all the summer flowers were gone and the plants were overgrown and browning – the garden was a very lovely spot in which to pass the time. If he'd had some company apart from Killer, it would have been positively enjoyable. Where on earth was Jane? She was the one who'd wanted him to retire, moaning about him not being around. Now he was at home, ready to spend time with her, and where the hell was she?

On impulse, he decided to ring Victor. If Jane was in Bordeaux – and it was the obvious spot for her to go to – Victor might know, since he was paid to pop in once a month to check the house when they weren't there. A trim man with jug ears and a strong smell of tobacco hanging over him, Victor had taken an instant dislike to Roger. When he and Jane were in France, he left Jane to deal with him. The man had been looking after their house and garden for them for years, since they'd first bought it from his estate agent son, Frédéric. Jane's French was much better than Roger's and she liked practising, so she always took the lead.

Roger had heard Victor laughing with her about his tendency to disappear as soon as the Frenchman arrived. His French might not have been great but Roger knew quite well that Victor called him '*Monsieur Pas Là.*' Mr. Not There. Whenever Victor arrived, and asked for him, in the classic

French chauvinist way, Jane would respond, '*Monsieur n'est pas là,*' and Victor would laugh, a deep hacking laugh that always ended in a chesty coughing fit. '*Monsieur Pas Là!*' he would respond. '*Ben ouais, che bien! Il n'est jamais là!*' He is never there.

Roger had to steel himself to make the call.

'*Ah, Monsieur ... Kemuge? Ouais. Je vous écoute.*' I'm listening.

'*Oui, bonjour.* I ... Je ... Look, can we speak English? *Anglais?*'

'*Bien sûr.* Of course. Eengleesh.'

Roger just knew the man would be looking smug. 'Thank you. I wanted to speak to you about the heating work. Is it all really necessary at the moment?'

'*Nécessaire? Mais oui.* But yes. It is. The costs are ... how you say, acceptable. I know Nicolas. He is a good worker.'

'You can't get some more quotes?'

'More quotes?'

'From other people? Not just Nicolas?'

A long silence on the end of the phone. '*Je peux essayer ...* I can try.'

'Please do.' Roger was exhausted. 'Two more, at least.' Bracing himself, he asked, 'Victor, is Madame Kurmudge there? At the house in Bordeaux?'

'Madame?' Another long silence, as though Victor was translating what Roger had said. '*Non, Monsieur, Madame n'est pas là.*'

Roger could have sworn the man was laughing at him. He said goodbye and hung up. He'd really have to find someone else to be their caretaker. Someone much less irritating and more respectful.

He returned to the kitchen and picked up the paper again at the kitchen table as Killer forlornly dropped into his bed. Roger was starting to feel positively sorry for himself.

The feeling only intensified after Morwenna left. She had grunted something at him – perhaps *see you next week?* – and had slammed out of the house. He was relieved to be able to have the run of the place again, but wandering through the rooms, he also felt bereft of any purpose. The house was clean. He had no plans. No one was likely to pop round.

He got himself some late lunch and ate in front of the TV. It was only one thirty. What would they be doing in the office? Should he call Tom and ask how sales were? No, of course not. But he could ring Frank and set up a golf day.

Frank answered after several rings. 'Who? Oh, it's you, Rodge. I didn't expect to hear from you during the week.'

'I've just retired, remember?'

'Oh yeah. Forgot that. Hang on a sec, I just need to ...' There was some banging in the background and then Frank came back on. 'Sorry. Tricky bit of pipework here. Actually can't talk now. Can I call you later? Half your luck, is all I can say. Retirement, hey? Kicking back, enjoying life. Speak later, okay?' And Frank was gone.

He spent the rest of the day watching sport. Made himself a lasagne, ignoring the fact it was only five p.m., and had finished a bottle of Burgundy by eight. And when he logged on to his emails ten minutes later, he found this:

From: Janes Away Hurray
To: Roger Kurmudge
Subject: To do
Remember to organise flowers for your mum. It's her birthday next week. On Friday the dog is due at the vet's for his annual vaccinations. Buy some more flea treatment and apply it (to

Killer, of course). Oh, and get Hannah to groom Killer next time she takes him for you.

Tight-lipped, he responded:

From: Roger Kurmudge
To: Janes Away Hurray
Re: To do
Jane,
I think you've made your point! I'm not quite sure what it was but I think it's that I don't appreciate how much you do. Or maybe that I don't know what your life is like. Or perhaps that I don't know what effort it takes to look after Alfie. (I do now, I assure you. That boy is seriously hard work. Why didn't you tell me about the blue breath-holding spells?) Anyway, the point is, you've made your point. Time to come home. This is ridiculous. The past few days have given me time to think and I now know what your life is like. I can sympathise. Even empathise. But only if you come home.
Roger

An hour later, with no reply from Jane, he made a decision. Something about Victor's response to his question had sounded a little off. The man would have no compunction about lying to Roger about Jane's whereabouts; and he lived half an hour from their house, so he might not even know if Jane was there.

Roger logged onto the Eurostar website and booked a ticket in first class to Bordeaux the following day. He could just make it a quick trip if Jane wasn't there. If she was, he'd change his ticket and stay longer – until he'd convinced her to return with him. If by some incredibly unlucky stroke of fate she had indeed found out what he'd done, he'd have to work out what to say to her; but this was ridiculous. Her place was with him in Guildford and he knew he could persuade her of that if only he could see her in person.

He texted Hannah to ask her to pick up Killer using the key he'd leave in the porch and to look after him for a couple of days and to groom him at the same time. He also texted Andy to say he couldn't take Alfie on Thursday as he was going to Bordeaux. He'd expected Andy to be thrilled that his father was being so proactive: instead, Andy seemed grumpy that he would have to take a day off work to look after his own son. Why couldn't Sarah do it? Roger thought. Who wore the pants in that relationship, anyway?

He fell asleep on a surge of relief that finally he was *doing* something, rather than responding passively to events. He'd always talked Jane around in the past. He could do it again.

8

Roger was up at four thirty a.m. to get the earliest train out of Guildford station. At London St Pancras, he picked up a paper, a coffee and a Danish pastry before boarding the Eurostar and settling himself into his first-class seat. He felt tired and a little hung-over, but once the train had departed the station he let his thoughts drift along pleasantly as he considered all the things he and Jane would be doing once she was back.

At the Gare du Nord he disembarked and took the métro to Gare Montparnasse, where he settled into another seat on the Bordeaux train and shut his eyes. He ran a few scripts in his head. What was the best approach? Anger? Laying the guilt on thick? He might have to be nimble about it and change tack if what he said wasn't working. Should he buy some flowers before he turned up at the house? Maybe he would.

Three and a half hours later, he left the train at Bordeaux-Saint-Jean station and allowed himself to be bustled along towards the exit with the crowd. He had only brought a small overnight case and he was grateful that he didn't have lots of luggage as he walked to the nearest florist and bought the largest bunch of yellow roses he could. He then walked back to the taxi rank, where the queue had dispersed, and took the fifteen-minute journey to the Saint Augustin area where they'd bought their house ten years earlier. And the place was only going to increase in value, he congratulated himself, with the TGV link going into Paris.

The French house was smaller than The Grange, but somehow still seemed as hard to maintain. However, there was no doubt the pretty stone exterior, with its pale blue shutters and symmetrically placed windows, had what estate agents would call 'street appeal'. He pushed open the side gate and walked up the front path, half expecting his wife to come out of the front door to greet him. Their French city runaround was in the gravel driveway next to the house; his heart lifted. She was here, he was sure of it.

He put his key in the lock and opened the door. He sniffed the air in the hallway. He couldn't smell Jane's perfume but he called out, 'Jane! Are you here?'

Silence greeted him and he felt a wave of weariness. The week since he'd retired had been the most emotionally draining of his entire life. A thought rallied him: maybe she was just out. He put his suitcase down and placed the flowers on the hall table. It felt as though someone had been here, he thought. The shutters were open, for a start, and it didn't smell as musty as it usually did when they arrived.

He wandered about downstairs, trying to work out if his wife was in Bordeaux. The open shutters in the sitting room suggested yes; the fact that the fridge was switched off, its door left slightly ajar, whispered no. And it was cold. True, the house was hard to heat, hence the need to sort out the heating system. But usually if Jane was staying here she'd have pulled out some of the plug-in heaters, and he couldn't see any sign of them.

He tried calling his wife's number but it rang out, as it had every time since he'd waved her off in the taxi all those days ago. It felt as though a decade had passed.

A slump of disappointment hit him but he fought it off. Jane might still be here, in Bordeaux. Maybe she'd only just arrived, too, from wherever she'd gone after leaving home, and had opened the shutters before heading off to get provisions. The thought reminded him that he was hungry. He had only had a baguette at Gare Montparnasse and now his stomach was grumbling.

In the kitchen, he checked the cupboards but there was nothing to eat apart from some rice and a few tins of tomatoes. He returned to the sitting room and sat down heavily on the sofa. It smelled dusty and made his nose itch. He shut his eyes. It had been a long day.

The sound of a key in the door made him sit upright as delight surged through him. 'Jane?' He sprang to his feet.

But it was Victor. He looked almost as shocked to see Roger as Roger was to see him. Perhaps Roger's enormous smile in greeting was also a bit of a surprise. Usually, on the rare occasions that they met, Roger scowled at him and Victor scowled back. Although Roger's scowl returned in very short order as he fully absorbed what Victor's presence meant. Maybe he, rather than Jane, had opened the shutters.

'*Monsieur Kemuge? Je* ... I didn't know that you were coming?'

Roger's words were clogging up in his throat. His brain was totally taken up with processing yet another piece of information about Jane, even though it was a negative one. She wasn't in Bordeaux.

After a long pause, Roger said, 'I thought maybe Jane was here. I wanted to surprise her.'

Victor took in the roses on the hall table and made a hacking noise in his throat. A laugh? A hair ball? Roger wanted to punch the man's bad teeth down his smoke-furred throat. 'As I did tell you, *Madame Kemuge n'est pas là, Monsieur*.' Madame is not here.

'I see that,' Roger said. He needed to regain the upper hand. 'While I'm here, do we need to talk about the heating system?'

Victor made a classic French face, puffing a breath of air out of his pursed lips. 'Maybe. There is a lot of work that must be done.' He started to talk about the different options, using words Roger simply didn't understand, and there was something about the Agence de l'environnement et de la maîtrise de l'énergie. So many French words that would usually be dealt with by Jane.

'Victor, just send me some quotes. For the different options.'

'Oui, Monsieur.'

'I'm too tired to discuss it now.'

'No problem. I came to shut *les volets*, ze shutters. Sometimes I open them to make *les voleurs*, ze teeves, think someone is 'ere.'

'I can do it, thank you, Victor.'

'*D'accord, Monsieur*.' He nodded and left.

ROGER WENT to buy some milk. Returning home, he made tea and sat drinking it. The house felt unwelcoming, almost hostile, with echoing rooms and cobwebs in corners. Wandering upstairs, he saw that the beds were unmade.

That was always one of Jane's first tasks, along with opening shutters and windows to air the house out, plugging in the fridge freezer, and popping to the shops to get essentials, including wine. Roger sometimes went along but had often insisted he needed to check his emails. Which he would do by the pool, enjoying the sunshine while Jane sorted the house out until it felt like home again.

He now sent a text to his sons:

In Bordeaux. Your mum's not here.

Andy texted straight back:

When will u be back?

Sam sent:

Hope ur ok

Neither response seemed quite satisfactory. Roger mulled them over for a few minutes before he got it: Andy seemed more interested in when he would be back to take care of Alfie, and Sam's text seemed faintly patronising, with a hint of *poor old Dad* in it.

Roger's rage took him by surprise. He'd had it with traipsing around looking for his wife. He'd go home tomorrow and bloody well show her how easy her life actually was. He'd *smash it*, as the boys would say. In the meantime, he wasn't going to sit in an empty dusty house alone. He was going to pour the rest of the milk down the sink, book himself into the Intercontinental and have the most slap-up dinner he could.

His rage burnt itself out shortly after he checked into the hotel. He hadn't been able to reserve at such late notice for Le Pressoir d'Argent Gordon Ramsay, so he'd eaten at Le Bordeaux. In spite of the elegance of his surroundings and the food – oysters, beef with roast potatoes and seasonal vegetables, followed by Meringue Lemon Tart – which had been an order of magnitude better than Tesco Finest Fish Pie, dinner alone was a lonely business without Jane to twinkle across the table at him and suggest perhaps they didn't need a glass of port to finish: surely a decaf would be a better idea.

Afterwards, he fell asleep easily enough in his luxurious room and comfortable bed after the long day of travel, but woke up, hand to his racing heart, ears straining to hear something in the dark. In the distance, there was the sound of a heavy door shutting, and someone had laughed, a merry burst that only underlined Roger's solitude.

Watching TV didn't make him feel sleepy. He leaned across and switched on the bedside lamp. The best he could hope for was to read a book for a bit and then try dropping off again. A few minutes later he gave up. He couldn't concentrate at all. An hour passed with him staring up at the ceiling, trying to imagine where his wife could be and why she would have left in this way.

The journey home was much less pleasant than the outward trip. He had no hope of seeing Jane at the end of it, and he found the noises of other people talking, eating and making phone calls almost intolerable. Reading was still impossible; he stared out of the window instead. Arriving back at Guildford station in drizzling rain, he'd got into a cold car and gone to pick up a rather shorn-looking Killer from Hannah's kennels. He needed company at home.

For the second time in as many days, he opened the door to an empty silent house. He fished a pizza out of the freezer and ate it in front of TV before trudging upstairs to bed where, again, he struggled to sleep well. A rustling from the roof cavity woke him just as he was about to drop off and he spent two more hours awake, alternating between fury and depression. Where was his wife? If she had found out – the idea shot adrenaline through his system and made his heart pound – why hadn't she just confronted him? Fought about it? Given him a chance to convince her it hadn't happened?

He went downstairs to get some water and was glad he'd fetched Killer. It was nice not to be entirely alone. The dog yawned and then followed him back out of the kitchen, placing a questioning paw on the first tread of the stairs.

'No. I'm not that desperate,' Roger said. 'Back to bed, Killer.'

The dog slunk back to his bed, looking as depressed as Roger felt.

9

Get up
　　Make coffee
　　Take Killer out
Feed Killer
Fill Killer's water bowl
Unload the dishwasher
Work out when Killer needs to be at the vet. And which vet to take him to

WHEN ROGER TRUDGED DOWNSTAIRS the next day, he had a mental list running through his mind. Had Jane lived like this, constantly thinking of what she needed to do next to keep things running smoothly? He usually awoke to the sound of the dishwasher being unloaded and the coffee machine being filled with water. By the time he got downstairs, a coffee was always waiting for him in his favourite *World's Best Dad* mug (a Fathers' Day present from Andy years earlier) while the *Today* programme examined the issues of the day. Perhaps, he thought, he had taken such things far too much for granted. He certainly missed them now. He was almost looking forward to Morwenna coming to clean next week, just to hear someone else in the house.

Making his own coffee this morning, he contrasted it with life when Jane was here. He'd never thought of her as a noisy person, she was too contained and efficient for that, but he now understood that she was always busy. Tidying. Washing. Measuring for new blinds in the laundry. Doing some light gardening. Sorting out bags of clothes for the charity shop. Baking for a Macmillan coffee morning. Emailing the local soup kitchen to offer to help one evening. Chatting to people – dental receptionists, the GP – on the phone as she organised their health checks. Such tasks brought with them a certain amount of noise, along with the ubiquitous Radio Four, which had been the background to Roger's life with Jane for as long as he could really remember.

He sat down at the kitchen island and sipped his coffee. The dog was whining and pawing at him. Sighing, Roger stood up and went out of the house. He and Killer walked quickly around the lawn, where Killer did what was necessary, before returning to the house. Roger fed him and then returned to his coffee.

He needed to 'maintain the rage', as the Aussies would say. He'd show Jane how competent he was without her. What did he need to do today? She'd sent an email about the dog – something about vaccinations. But she hadn't been very clear about what time Killer's appointment at the vet was. Surely if she was going to insist that he honour her appointments, she could have told him the exact details? He made some toast, managing to burn it, and was swearing to himself when his phone rang. At last.

But it was Andy.

'Just wanted to check you got home okay. Everything all right, Dad?' He sounded apologetic.

'Not really. Still no word from your mum. Honestly, I don't know what she's playing at, I really don't. It cost me a fortune, that trip to Bordeaux. I'm livid, in fact –'

'Yeah, look, sorry to interrupt, but I think I should pop over tonight so we can discuss it. Are you around?'

'Yes.' Where else would he be? 'What sort of time?'

'I'll finish work at six thirty, pop home to say goodnight to Alfie and then come over. Say eight-ish?'

'Fine. You could have dinner here, if you like?'

Andy hesitated. 'That's ... will you cook, then?'

'Well.' Roger thought about it. He hadn't factored in Andy coming for dinner with his ready-meal purchases, and the fish pie really wasn't big enough for two. 'Take away?'

He wasn't imagining the relief in Andy's voice. 'Great! Maybe an Indian? I'll see you at eight. What are you up to today?'

'I've got to take Killer to the vet, according to the blunt email I got from your mother a few days ago. But she didn't tell me when.'

'Ring the vet's?' Andy's voice was gentle yet slightly patronising.

'Well, of course I thought of that!' Roger snapped. 'But which vet's?'

'Mum takes Killer to the Pet Practice. Google the number.'

THE APPOINTMENT WAS for two o'clock. He might as well grab some lunch in town first and then do the appointment. Killer was lying in his basket looking depressed. Roger wasn't imagining it. Actively depressed. Jane used to take him out several times a day, just for short walks here and there, and always took him with her when she went out. Perhaps Roger should do the same, to save coming home to get the dog for the vet's appointment. He could get some lunch in a café, to make what he had in the fridge last longer. He showered, changed into the only clean trousers he now possessed, and found the lead.

'Come on, Killer!' He didn't have to ask twice. The dog leapt out of the door, tail wagging manically. There was excitement in the dog's eyes for the first time in days.

What Roger had forgotten was that dogs were prone to embarrassing situations and that one needed to carry small bags for such moments. The first thing Killer did when he jumped down from the car was to curve his rump towards a small piece of grass at the edge of the car park.

There were three people getting out of cars nearby and they all turned to stare at Roger.

He rummaged through his pockets. No bags. Why hadn't he remembered this? And why were there so many bodily functions involved in dealing with children and dogs? Was this what Jane's life was like? He felt increasingly stressed, turning out his trouser pockets and muttering to himself.

His panic must have been evident, as one of the people, a middle-aged man with an earring and a small moustache, crossed the car park and silently handed him a black bag. There was judgment in his face. Roger murmured a thank you and bent to do what was needed, holding his breath. Killer panted up happily at him. Bloody dog. Roger tied the bag up and looked for a bin. Nothing around.

Judgment Man was still standing there. 'There's a bin near the High Street. Take it there.'

In town, and bag disposed of, Roger considered his café

options. His favourite eateries were not dog-friendly. Killer seemed to be heading somewhere, trotting determinedly along in a clear direction. Roger allowed him some leeway. After all, he, Roger, was in charge, and this direction was fine, for now. It was nice to be out and about, part of society again. He felt quite cheerful for a few moments. Until he remembered: where was his wife?

Past Trailfinders (could she have booked a trip through them?) then Hobbs, which was one of Jane's favourites. She also liked The Body Shop. Should he pop in and ask them if they'd seen her recently? He would have liked to stop and think about it, but Killer wouldn't let him.

After a series of shops of no interest to either Jane, Roger or Killer (why were there so many phone shops so close together?), the dog darted down a small side street, dragging Roger with him. Now he was really tanking along, tongue lolling, breath sawing in his throat, desperate to get somewhere. Passers-by were laughing at them, the large man being pulled along by a small dog. Roger tried to hold Killer back but the dog was insanely strong. Just as Roger was about to get really irritated, Killer stopped dead outside a small café. Roger eased his fingers from the lead. He would have liked to shout at the dog but there were too many people about. The kind who looked as though they'd take the dog's side.

Roger peered through the window. It looked a bit, well, vegan. Healthy and worthy. Not somewhere he'd ever choose. Lots of green in the décor and on the menu. He was more of a red meat person.

'We're not going in here,' he said firmly to Killer. 'Let's go back to the high street.'

Killer planted all four feet on the pavement and stood

stock-still. He wasn't smiling at Roger. Roger tugged the lead. Killer's body leaned backwards, resisting.

'Come on, you stupid animal!' Roger tugged harder. Killer's lean became more extreme. He sat down on the pavement and did the lip thing again, showing a few teeth.

The café door opened. A solid young woman with short orange hair and a small silver hoop through her nose popped her head out. 'Killer! Hey, sweetie! So lovely to see you.' She bent down and stroked Killer, who was whimpering with excitement. She looked up at Roger with deep-set grey eyes. 'You must be Jane's husband! Is she coming, too?'

'No,' Roger said, 'she's away. I'm just in town to get some lunch –' Before he could say 'somewhere else', she interrupted him.

'Of course! Come in! We've got a great vegetable frittata on the specials today, you'll love it.'

Would he love it? He was far from convinced but it was too late to back out now: Killer was halfway into the café. He followed the dog, shut the door behind him and looked around. It was a small space, with about ten tables in all, of which three were taken. Of the remainder, there was a nice round one in the window – technically for four people, but the café wasn't busy – or some less pleasant ones right at the back of the room. Killer was dragging at the lead, pulling him towards the back. Roger resisted.

'We're going to sit here,' he said firmly, heading for the window table.

Miss Nose-Ring said, 'Oh, you can't.'

'Why not?' He knew he sounded haughty, but couldn't help himself. 'It doesn't say reserved.'

She laughed, a spontaneous sound, loud and unrestrained. 'Oh, I didn't mean that! No, you can't sit at anything but Killer's usual table.' She pointed towards the back of the café. 'That one. He likes to sit under the bench.'

Killer's usual table? The dog wasn't the customer. Roger tried harder to pull the animal towards the window table. Killer started to reverse stockily, sitting on his bottom, jerking on the lead. The occupants of one of the tables, a middle-aged mum and two daughters, were giggling, and cooing over how sweet Killer was.

Miss Nose-Ring came over to him and put a gentle arm on his sleeve. 'I'm afraid it really isn't worth it,' she said. 'Jane sat at that table the first day she came in to the café and Killer found half a sandwich under the bench. The next time she came in, she tried a different one, but Killer wouldn't have it. He did that to her, too,' she pointed at Killer's jerky backwards movements, 'and the second she sat down at a new table and took her hand off the lead, he ran back to the other one. It was a right old battle, and in the end Jane lost. She just sits there now. Unless there's someone else at that table – and they soon move.'

This was ridiculous. He'd only come into the café to suit the dog and now he couldn't even choose his seat. He wasn't being dictated to by a Westie.

'Come here, Killer,' he ordered. Killer sat down hard and looked away from him. His muzzle looked mulish. 'Now!' Roger clicked his fingers, uncomfortably aware of everyone watching him. 'Okay, then, you asked for it.' He took a step forward and scooped Killer up. The dog bared his teeth again and gave a low growl but Roger ignored him. He strode over to the nice window-table and sat down, plonking Killer by his feet. He tied the lead to the chair leg and sat back to look at the menu.

The first howl was a warm-up, a muted sound like the

string section of the orchestra tentatively putting bow to strings. The second was stronger, more vibrato. The third had a small child at the nearest table putting her hands over her ears. The fourth made all the adults in the room wince, and the middle-aged mum shook her head. Roger could see the vibrations in Killer's throat muscles as he threw his head back and howled at the ceiling. It was very difficult to concentrate on the menu. Or indeed anything else. In desperation, he glanced at Miss Nose-Ring. She pointed at the table at the back, shrugging her shoulders. A shrug that said: *Give up. You're dealing with forces stronger than yourself.*

Gathering the tattered shreds of his dignity around him, Roger stood up and untied the dog. The howling stopped instantly and Killer trotted to the back of the café, with Roger at his heel. He sat down as Killer settled himself under the bench and sighed deeply.

'What can I get you?' Miss Nose-Ring said, appearing with a notepad.

'I'll have ...' Roger hadn't looked at the menu. He now couldn't face it. 'I'll have the special you mentioned, the –'

'Frittata?' she said, beaming. 'Great choice! Coming right up! And I'll get Killer a dog biscuit.'

Roger hardly thought the bloody dog needed a reward for his behaviour but allowed her to feed two treats to Killer. He picked up a copy of a newspaper that was sitting on an adjacent table and read for a few minutes. The frittata, when it arrived, was surprisingly good. It would have been better with some chunks of meat, he thought, but nevertheless not bad.

When Miss Nose-Ring came back to get his plate, he asked, 'So how does Killer get people to move from this table if they're already there?'

'Easy.' She grinned at him. 'He stares at them and does

that howling thing. Jane can't stop him. Works every time. No one can focus on eating, or drinking, or talking with that racket going on.'

As he paid the bill, she said, 'See you next time!'

No chance, Roger thought.

10

'What's the name?' the receptionist at the vet's asked.

He'd never been to the practice before. It was clean, comfortable and had a surgery at the back that looked quite high-tech. Roger wondered darkly about euthanasia for badly behaved pets.

'The appointment was for Jane Kurmudge.'

'Oh, no, I mean your pet's name,' the fifty-something woman said. She had a perky little face like a bird and tilted it at him as she spoke.

'Killer.' He said it quietly.

'Killer?' She started to laugh. She stood and peered over the counter at Killer, who panted up at her. 'Oh, look at you. You're too cute to be called Killer, aren't you? Daddy has a sense of humour!'

Daddy? Was the woman quite mad? The other people waiting were murmuring with amusement, too. It was all very well for Andy and Sam to choose silly names for his pet — they weren't the ones at the vet's being ridiculed.

She found his appointment and told him to take a seat.

Barely a minute later, an absurdly young blonde woman called, 'Killer Kurmudge?'

Really? Did they have to use his surname? What if someone recognised him?

He stood and started in the direction of the vet, but Killer wouldn't move. He cowered under the seat Roger had been sitting in.

'Is he nervous?' the vet asked.

'I don't think so,' Roger said, tugging at the lead. 'My wife usually brings him but she's away.'

'Well, he looks nervous,' the vet said. 'You might need to carry him.'

Roger was getting used to the carrying bit. What he couldn't work out was how to get the damned dog out from under the chair. He tried cajoling but Killer was now shivering in an overly dramatic fashion, so that the ruddy-faced woman across the room from them said, 'Poor little thing!'

The vet stood next to Roger. 'You might have to get down and get him.'

Roger knelt down. He really didn't kneel very often, he realised. His knees felt very stiff. He reached an arm towards Killer and managed to grab his front leg.

'Gentle!' the ruddy-faced woman said. '*Poor* little thing.' Her stern expression reminded Roger that people did shop others to the RSPCA for animal cruelty.

Roger was gritting his teeth. 'Come on, Killer. It's not so bad, come on.' He pulled the dog out from under the chair and grabbed his stocky body before Killer could make a break for it. The dog was writhing around so much Roger was afraid he'd lose his grip.

The vet clearly agreed. She set a cracking pace into the treatment room and shut the door firmly. 'You're just here for his annual jab, is that right?'

'I think so,' Roger said. 'And to buy some more flea treatment.'

'We usually carry out a general check-up at the same time as the jab,' the vet said. She eyed Killer, who was shivering in a corner of the room. 'That might be tricky. But let's try.'

They had to catch him first. He managed to wriggle backwards out of his collar as Roger gripped it, and proved very hard to catch. He was surprisingly nippy and, Roger had to grudgingly admit, fantastic at lightning-fast changes of direction around the high table in the middle of the room. It resulted in several embarrassing collisions between Roger and the vet. Fortunately, they were both too occupied with Killer to make eye contact.

The only sounds were the squeaking of the vet's shoes on the floor and the grunted suggestions – 'Grab him!', 'Quickly, now!', 'Go that way! No, the other way!' – as they raced after Killer. Finally, in a desperate lunge across the room, the vet trapped Killer in a corner with her leg. A trickle of urine slowly leaked from under the dog, found a small indentation in the floor and pooled next to Roger's foot.

'Did you know he behaved like this?' the vet asked breathlessly. 'I could have had my nurse standing by.'

'I had no idea,' Roger said, honestly. Had Jane ever mentioned such antics? He had a dim recollection of her returning from the vet's once with an injury. A sore wrist, perhaps? But he'd imagined she'd done something clumsy rather than it being the result of wrangling Killer. He did recall that vet trips involved Jane talking a lot afterwards, but he'd usually been immersed in the paper and had grunted over it without really taking her words in.

'Can you grab him now? For God's sake, don't let him go!' the vet said.

Roger took a fistful of Killer's neck fur and wrapped his other arm around the animal's body. A violent episode of thrashing ensued while Roger hung on grimly, trying to ignore the spots of urine flying around. Finally Killer gave up. The dog's shivers made Roger's arm shake. He felt sudden sympathy for Killer. He seemed genuinely terrified. 'There, there,' he said. 'It's okay, Killer. We're not going to hurt you. Not for long, anyway.'

The vet took a moment to wipe up the urine and wash her hands. She approached Killer quietly, making soothing noises before she touched him. She looked up at Roger as her hands explored Killer's body, squeezing his muscles and flexing his hips to check the angle. 'Can you keep talking to him? Look, he's relaxing now.'

It was true: Killer was calmer, Roger thought. He was shivering less. The vet moved to the top of the table and said, 'Put your hand around his muzzle for me. I just don't want to get bitten.'

Roger did as she asked, but gently, and kept up a soothing murmur of nonsense: 'There, there, it's okay, you're okay, Killer, soon be over. What a good dog you are.' The dog was relaxing against his arm, which meant that Roger was bearing his whole weight. He was undoubtedly a chunky little beast. Perhaps he was feeding him too much? Jane hadn't told him exactly how much food to give the dog, so Roger had been going on instinct. An instinct that suggested a chubby dog was a happy dog.

The vet did a thorough job of looking him over, checking eyes, ears, looking under his body, examining his feet. Eventually, she even dared look in his mouth, although with Roger holding the dog's jaws apart and from a respectful distance. 'He looks in tip-top shape, actually. Just need to do the jab and then you're off.'

Roger tensed. 'Will that hurt him?'

She laughed. 'Not really. I don't think most dogs feel it.'

She pinched a thick fold of skin on Killer's neck and stabbed the needle in. True to her word, Killer didn't seem to notice. Roger kept his grip tight until the vet said brightly, 'All done! But next time do tell reception he's incredibly nervous; we can have a couple of extra people on hand. And ...' She looked nervous herself. 'I know owners can't always tell but he's a bit overweight. Perhaps less food? And more exercise?'

HE FELT a strange sense of achievement after a quick stop at Tesco to get more ready meals. Obviously Jane was trying to tell him that she did all the work and he didn't understand her life. Well, it turned out he did. He was doing rather well, in fact. He'd managed to look after Alfie for the day (admittedly with a few mishaps). And now he'd taken Killer to the vet. He was looking forward to telling Andy all about it.

In the laundry, he took off his dirty trousers and considered them. How hard could it be? He found a few other things to fill up the machine. The trousers in particular needed a proper wash so he decided it would be best to do a cotton wash for a couple of hours. The material looked and felt like cotton. He threw in generous amounts of laundry powder and put it on.

When he drew the trousers out of the machine a few hours later, they were definitely smaller. Had it been the addition of the excess powder that had made them shrink? Now he felt too worried to make his own washing decisions.

Jane always came shopping with him to buy new clothes, and if he shrank all his trousers he'd have to go without her to guide him. No, he'd have to find another way of getting things clean. He opened the door of the laundry cupboard and found some freshening spray. It promised to eliminate odours without leaving the heavy residue of its own scent. Perfect.

He fetched two pairs of trousers from the washing basket and laid them out on the ironing board before picking up the spray and attacking the trousers in the way he'd seen Morwenna using the spray cleaner in the kitchen. The smell did seem quite strong, but that would dissipate as it dried, no doubt. He just needed to wait for the alchemy of one strong scent removing another to take place. In the meantime, he'd have to dig out the old pair of jeans he kept at the back of the cupboard because Jane hated them. She wasn't here to see them.

Andy arrived on the dot of eight o'clock. He looked ill at ease, Roger thought. With a jolt, he wondered how often he and Andy had been alone in the last few years.

'What do you fancy eating?' Roger said. 'I've got some menus out.' He'd put them on the kitchen counter. They were, he realised, perhaps a little out of date. 'Indian? Or Thai? I'll have whatever you'd like.'

'We'll just do Deliveroo, Dad,' Andy said, taking out his phone. 'Would you prefer Indian?'

'Yes, I think I would.'

Andy showed him his phone and Roger ordered a lamb biryani. Andy ordered chicken tikka masala and then he said, 'Let's grab a beer and go into the sitting room. I need to talk to you.'

Roger fetched two bottled beers. In the sitting room, he sat down and handed one to Andy. Andy drank some, glugging it down. His hand on the bottle was shaking slightly. He swallowed and coughed lightly. 'It's about Mum. It's been days since she disappeared and she's not in Bordeaux, and we're just accepting it, because of those emails.'

'So,' Roger said, 'you think there's something sinister going on?'

'No.' Andy looked uncertain. 'I don't think so, although there was that case where that guy murdered his wife and then hacked into her emails and sent some to their friends to pretend she was still alive. Remember?'

Roger shook his head. For all his faults as a husband, he wasn't the murdering, email-hacking kind.

'But shouldn't we be trying to find her anyway? I mean, if she ran away from home because she's unhappy or upset about something, shouldn't we be trying to find her?'

'She'll be back,' Roger said. 'She's just making a point. That she did a lot around here and wasn't perhaps as appreciated as she should be.'

'And maybe she felt like she was missing out on life. That's what I wanted to talk to you about,' Andy said. He took another slug of beer. 'I know something I should have told you before.'

Roger felt a dull thud in his stomach. 'An affair?' he said.

'No! God's sake, Dad. Not an affair. Mum had a ...' Andy blinked at him, '... a job.'

'A job?' Roger repeated the words. He couldn't understand it. 'Why would she get a job? She doesn't need the money. She got quite a nice inheritance from your granny, and she kept it in her own account, and I've never been mean with her, I hope you know that ...'

'Not everything is about money, is it? Mum felt she needed ...' Andy searched for his words. 'She needed *purpose*.'

'Purpose?' Roger rolled the word around his mouth. '*Purpose?* She had plenty of purpose right here.'

'She could have been a great artist. Don't you think? Those portraits in the hall she did of me and Sam. I mean,' Andy let out a low whistle, 'I know I don't know much about art but I think they're really good. Do you remember that friend of hers who kept asking her to put on an exhibition? What was she called? Sandrine? She runs that gallery in Paris and stayed with us in Bordeaux that time?'

'She's got her studio here,' Roger said stiffly. 'I never stop her using it.'

'No, of course not. But it's quite lonely doing what she did, looking after the house and garden and Alfie and, not being rude, Dad, but you, too. I think she wanted to meet new people and be herself again. Not just 'Mum' or 'Grandma'. Painting on her own wouldn't quite achieve that. And you've seen her studio, right? Not exactly set up for painting, is it?'

'What job?' Roger came back to the point. 'Where?'

'That art gallery in town. You know the one. The nice one just off the high street.'

'She was a saleswoman?' Roger couldn't believe that his wife would be working in a shop.

'More than that,' Andy said. 'She's really good with people, and so I think she gave advice to people who didn't know much about art. She quite enjoyed it, I think.'

There was a silence. A question hung heavy in the air.

'Why wouldn't she tell me?' Roger asked.

'I don't know.'

'How long did she have this job for?'

'Six months?'

Roger stared at his son.

Andy cleared his throat. 'So I wanted to tell you because I felt bad for keeping it from you.'

'Anything else you're keeping from me?' Roger said.

The doorbell saved Andy from replying. He came back with a bag of containers and fetched plates and cutlery from the kitchen before returning again. He sat down with a sigh and started to help himself. The smell of freshly prepared food made Roger's mouth water. He said so to Andy, who smiled.

'Dad, I don't think you always appreciate how lucky you are. Mum's always looked after you so well, hasn't she?'

'Well, I like to think she had a good deal, too,' Roger said, tucking into a chunk of lamb.

'Mmm.'

Roger looked up from his plate. Andy was making one of those non-committal noises again. The sort indicating lack of agreement. 'What do you mean?'

Andy looked uncomfortable. 'I'm a dad too, now.'

Did Andy think he was unaware of this? 'I know – I looked after Alfie the other day.'

'It's just … I think you probably spent more time with Alfie that day than you ever spent one-on-one with me or Sam. Not on one single occasion, anyway. It was all Mum. And she did so much for me with my dyslexia. Spent hours every week at primary school helping with reading so she could support me. And at secondary, she often had to pick me up when I was feeling too stressed to be there. I feel really guilty about taking up so much of her time but I don't know what would have happened to me if she hadn't been around to help. My mental health was pretty bad sometimes.'

The comment felt pointed. 'I was working!' Roger said.

The lamb wasn't quite as good as he'd hoped. And he hadn't expected such a negative conversation.

'I'm not having a go, Dad,' Andy said (when of course, he *was*, Roger thought), 'but I'm trying to show you how much Mum did that you might not have noticed, while you just focused on work and ... yourself.' The last word was very quiet.

Roger loaded some rice and sauce onto his fork and ate it. 'I'm sorry you think I let you down,' he said stiffly.

Andy shrugged. 'It's changed a bit now. Sarah would bloody kill me if I didn't get involved.'

Roger was really missing corporate life. Colleagues were so much nicer to him than his family was. Why had he retired at all? As though sensing this, Andy leaned across and patted his hand once before saying gruffly, 'Dad, I just mean that I really want you to get to know Alfie. And him to know you. You can add so much to his life, with your life experiences.'

Andy was obviously sucking up to him but Roger liked it. He nodded slightly sulkily and ate the rest of his takeaway while Andy chatted about the football. As they cleared up, Roger said, 'I'm very happy to look after Alfie, you know. I can do the days your mum used to do until she comes home.'

Andy grinned, showing the straight teeth that had cost Roger a fortune at the orthodontist. 'Cheers, Dad. We were kind of counting on you, thanks for volunteering.' He checked his watch. 'I'd better make tracks, but Sarah will see you Monday morning? With Killer, perhaps?'

Roger nodded. 'I'll be there at eight thirty. I'll take them to the flower shop to order flowers for your gran's birthday. Alfie might enjoy that.'

As he got ready for bed, he checked his phone.

From: Janes Away Hurray
To: Roger Kurmudge
Subject: To do

Remember: on Monday the gardener is coming for three hours. She's called Gail and you'll need cash to pay her (£15 an hour). And time to clean Killer's teeth. It's quite tricky.

11

From: Janes Away Hurray
To: Andy Kurmudge;
Sam Kurmudge
<u>Subject: None of your dad's business</u>
Dear Andy and Sam,
First: I'm fine. Please don't worry about me. I'm just fucking FURIOUS with your dad. I left without telling you both because I wanted your reaction to be genuinely puzzled. DO NOT TELL HIM YOU HAVE HEARD FROM ME! I just need some time on my own to work some things out. And I want him to sweat. To make sure he doesn't wheedle the truth out of you about where I am, I'm not going to tell you either.

I'll be back at some point to sort things out. Look after yourselves, tell Alfie I love him and please check that Killer gets fed and walked.
Love,
Mum

Andy read the email five times before he rang Sam.

'Have you seen Mum's email?' he asked.

'She finally sent an email? Seriously? Is she okay?' Sam often had breakfast at his desk, and it sounded as though he was crunching his way through Weetabix. Or gravel.

'Take a look now. I'll wait.' Andy drummed his fingers on his desk. Around him people were chatting about the TV they'd watched the night before, some detective thing that Andy had found ridiculously far-fetched. He could have pointed out three procedural flaws in the first scene.

'I don't know what to say, Anders.' Sam sounded shaken. 'She sounds okay but really pissed off with Dad.'

'What do you think "sort things out" means?' It sounded ominous to Andy.

'God knows.'

Andy lowered his voice. 'Do you think it's actually her?' He and Sam had sent plenty of emails to their mum, some of them very plaintive, since her disappearance. All had been ignored and this email didn't reference them at all.

'Yeah, of course. Who else could it be?'

'Mum has literally never used the f-word. Not in my entire life. Not even that time you took her car without asking when you first got your licence and you smashed it on Grumpy Golding's gate and he came over to yell at her.'

'Oh, yeah. I'd forgotten that.' Sam laughed for a moment before sounding serious again. 'You're right. Never. Weird. I wonder what he did?'

'But could it be someone else?'

Sam's voice was doubtful. 'Like, a kidnapper? No way, Anders. I mean, it's that new email address she's using, she sends love to Alfie, and the rest of it sounds like her.'

'I'm not sure.' People were getting up from their desks and heading to the nearest meeting room. 'Better go, Sammo, but I'm thinking about getting a private detective involved.'

'To do what?'

'To find Mum of course!' Vivian, the office nosy parker, turned interested eyes towards Andy and he lowered his voice. 'I know she says she's okay. But what if she's actually having a breakdown or needs us? I mean, I've seen enough crime dramas to know that when someone disappears, the only family members who don't actively search for them are the ones who bumped them off!'

'She sounded okay to me,' Sam said. 'But if you want to get someone on the case, I guess you could check her IP address as a start point?'

'Can't you do that?'

'It's tricky but I could probably get there with a bit of time. I'll take a look tonight,' Sam said. 'If the IP address looks like she's somewhere safe, can we assume she's okay?'

'Maybe.' Andy had been looking forward to getting a private investigator on the case. 'Let's chat later.'

ONCE ALFIE HAD FINALLY GONE to sleep after what had apparently been an exciting day at the florist's with Roger, Andy told Sarah he needed to speak to Sam. She huffed slightly, but he noticed she didn't protest too much about sitting down to watch a rom-com instead of the Ted Bundy documentary they'd been watching together. Andy took his phone and stepped into the garden. The temperature was the same as in the house. The fluttering plastic sheet taped to the brickwork reminded him they still had a large builder's bill to pay before they'd be able to get it finished.

Sam answered the phone immediately. 'Okay, so I haven't had time yet. To look at the IP thing, I mean.'

'Not to worry, Sammo. I'm definitely going to get a private eye, so that –'

Sam interrupted. 'Look, Guy wants to go out for dinner and he's making faces at me. I'll call you tomorrow, okay? I don't know what to do next and I feel weird tracking Mum like this when she asked us not to –'

'She actually didn't say don't –'

'And I think she's fine. Mad with Dad, but fine. Let's chat tomorrow, yeah?' Sam hung up.

Back in the half-built extension, Andy wound a scarf round his neck and sat down at the kitchen table, drawing his laptop towards him. His mum had not specifically said not to track her down … well, not exactly. Provided they didn't tell Roger what they found out, it would be fine.

He googled private investigators near him and came up with a screen of options. He scrolled until his eye was caught by an ad.

THE VERY PRIVATE PI.
WORRIED ABOUT A LOVED ONE'S WELFARE OR SUSPICIOUS ABOUT A CHEATING SPOUSE? FAST ANSWERS. ABSOLUTE DISCRETION. RESULTS GUARANTEED! jamie@theveryprivatepi.co.uk

The 'very private' bit appealed, so Andy emailed the address straightaway with some brief details. He asked if they were free to start immediately and how much the hourly rate was. In short order – he was impressed they worked so late – Jamie responded that they were free now to start the search for his missing mother and it would cost £55 per hour. Please could he send across Jane's passport number and a good recent photo? Plus as many details as possible about her movements on the day she disappeared, as well as her date of birth, place of birth and maiden name. A full list of family members and their relationship to Jane. Her email address, and where she banked.

Andy balked at handing over banking information. Nor did he want to speak to his dad about her passport number. His mum had been quite strident about not telling Roger where she was, and if he asked for passport details Roger would ask why. The rest of it would be fine. Andy emailed back with all the information, including both Jane's normal email address and her *Janesaway* one, and asked:

I don't want to give away bank details, I'm afraid. Is the passport number essential?

A response pinged back seconds later:

Nope! Can do without it. Photo is a good one. Laters.

Andy shut down the laptop with a surge of relief that someone – a skilled professional – was now looking for their mum.

12

Roger had passed the florist in the village many times and had always rather fancied going in. Unlike the florists from his youth, full of plastic-wrapped bouquets of lacklustre carnations or tubes containing a single depressed-looking rose, this one had a jaunty striped canopy outside, and inside the small space was full of metal containers crammed with blossoms of all colours, types and sizes, as well as dark green foliage and thrusting ferns. The names of each type of plant were written in chalk on tiny blackboards stuck into the soil. He couldn't identify most of the flowers, which had to be a good sign in a florist. It was an extremely attractive shop that enticed the passer-by to enter.

He had both Alfie and Killer with him. They'd walked from the house: it was going to be a long old day and he needed to fill time. He'd assured Sarah that he would never again take Bingo so much as a metre away from home, and Alfie had accepted it after he'd promised the boy a trip to the florist. Alfie had been keen to see the 'pitty fowers' and

Killer had been keen simply to leave the house. The trio had set off with reasonably high hopes of an enjoyable outing.

These hopes had lasted until they reached the end of the road, at which point Alfie had decided he needed a wee. They'd returned to the house rapidly, and after some cajoling, Alfie had done what was necessary and they'd set off again. This time they'd almost reached the florist before Alfie clutched at the seat of his trousers and declared he needed a poo. The clutching was something Roger found most distasteful and he had never reconciled himself to the p-word, although he did have to admit that the boy needed to be able to explain what was going on.

Roger scanned the street. There was a café up ahead, but memories of the cajoling earlier made him reluctant to go in there to use the bathroom, even if he did also buy something to eat and drink. As he'd discovered that morning, Alfie liked to give a loud running commentary on the toileting process, and Roger suspected it might put other customers off their breakfast. They turned and went back home.

By the time they set off for the third time, Roger had to check his phone to ensure it wasn't three in the afternoon. The day had already been interminably long, yet it was only ten a.m. Was this why housewives in the sixties were addicted to valium? He'd have necked a tablet or two if he'd had any at that moment. Alfie was on good form, though, pointing out all the major landmarks: 'Police car! Big twee! Fat lady!'

The latter glared at Roger as though he'd put the boy up to it, and all of her chins wobbled as she shook her head at him.

'Alfie, we don't make personal comments about people,' he said sternly.

Alfie considered this for a long moment. There was doubt in his eyes.

'I know I said your hair looked like a toilet brush this morning,' Roger said, 'but that's okay. It's fine for me to say it to you.' He took Alfie's hand and hurried him away from the woman.

The florist was part of a small row including the café he'd spotted earlier, a hairdresser and a charity shop.

'Café!' Alfie said, pointing.

'Yes. But we're going to the florist,' Roger said.

'Café!' Alfie's voice was rising. 'Wanna go to the café!'

Roger evaluated the situation. How would Sarah manage this? 'Alfie, we can go to the café later. First, the florist, okay?'

Alfie thought about it and then nodded. 'Okay, Woger.' He started skipping.

They reached the door of the florist and Roger peered in. It didn't look particularly dog friendly, so he tied Killer to a nearby bench.

A silver-haired, earthy-looking woman wearing an apron saying *Bloomin' Lovely!* greeted them. 'Good morning! Can I help?'

'I'd like to order some flowers to send to my mother for her birthday, please, it's on Wednesday,' Roger said. The scent of the flowers filled the shop. Three long low benches in rows were crammed with metal tubs full of vibrant flowers, shrubs and foliage, a visual feast that cheered Roger immediately. Alfie was moving from bucket to bucket on tiptoe, sniffing the blooms and exclaiming loudly, 'Woger! Pitty fowers!'

The woman nodded and said, 'What sort of thing were you after?'

Roger ran his fingers through his hair to buy some

thinking time before owning up. 'I'm not really sure. Can you advise me?'

'Of course!' She smiled. 'What sort of flowers does your mum like?'

'Well ...' Roger had no idea. They'd had peonies in the garden when he was growing up, presumably because she'd liked them. 'Peonies?'

'Lovely.' She pointed to a bucket. 'And these would go nicely with peonies? And some pale pink poppies? With perhaps a few white roses and some foliage?'

'Great,' Roger said, glancing across to check on Alfie, who had a thick streak of yellow pollen across his face.

The woman glanced up from her notepad and smiled. 'He's a lovely little boy. Your grandson?'

'Yes,' Roger said, pleased that Alfie was on his best behaviour.

'What's your mum's address?' the woman asked.

'Her address is ... She lives ...' Roger stopped. Where did she live? In a home, he knew, and he knew how to get to it, but he was damned if he could remember the address. Or the name. Why hadn't he brought Jane's address book? A shadow of a frown crossed the woman's face.

Roger started to try to explain.

'Of course, I d-do know where she lives! It's just she's in a home so although I know how to get there ... and usually my wife deals with this and, well ...'

The woman was staring over his shoulder out of the window. 'Is that Killer? Are you Killer's dad?'

In spite of a powerful aversion to the title 'Killer's dad', which was something he expected to see in a *Daily Mail* headline, Roger said, 'Yes.'

'Oh, so you're Jane's husband! How is she?'

'She's away,' Roger said. 'Oh, and fine. She's fine.'

The woman went back to the counter and started tapping at her computer keyboard. 'I think I've got your mum's address in here, actually. Jane orders her flowers every year through us.'

'Great!' Roger said.

'Evelyn Kurmudge?' the woman asked.

'That's my mum, yes.'

He paid. Sixty quid. Flowers had gone up dramatically since he'd last bought some for Jane. The florist assured him the bouquet would be with his mother by ten a.m. the following morning. He thanked her and turned to look for Alfie. For one panic-stricken second, he couldn't see anything but flowers and leaves. 'Alfie? Where are you?'

'Boo!' Alfie leapt up from behind a bench and shrieked with laughter. 'I be hiding, Woger!'

Roger forced out a laugh. 'That's very funny, Alfie. Time to go home.'

'Café,' Alfie said.

'No, home,' Roger said firmly. 'I want to go home now.'

Alfie sucked in a breath.

'No, I really mean it. We're going home.' Roger had set himself up for failure on his first day with Alfie by giving in to the Feasts. Today, he was going to stand firm. He was conscious of the florist standing nearby watching the proceedings. He didn't want her to think he was completely hopeless, not knowing his mother's address and not able to cope with his grandson.

He grabbed Alfie's arm. 'You need to come home with me, right now!'

Alfie pulled his arm out of Roger's grasp, and too late Roger realised he had hold of Alfie's coat and that his grandson had slipped out of it. He was now racing around the shop, totally out of control.

'Come here, right now!' Roger roared as he almost collided with the florist lady. She retreated behind the counter and watched, huge-eyed, as Roger tried to lunge for Alfie through a couple of buckets. Alfie wrenched his arm away, knocking over the largest bucket, which toppled off the bench. Water gushed all over Roger's shoes.

'Now look what you've done!' Roger yelled. 'Stop right now!'

Alfie stuck his tongue out and backed away.

'Stop!' ordered Roger. 'You're about to –'

Too late: Alfie had already dislodged the bucket behind him. Expensive-looking long-stemmed red roses cascaded over him like a parody of the *American Beauty* movie that Roger had rather enjoyed years earlier. More water slopped onto the floor.

The florist was squeaking at them, 'Please stop! Look at the mess! Can't you both stop?'

'I'm going to get you!' Roger said, and Alfie shouted back, 'Café!'

The pursuit continued. Roger ran past the door just as an elegant woman in a black turtleneck pushed it open. He narrowly missed her but only by dodging sideways and smashing into a row of small terracotta pots filled with pastel flowers; she screamed and beat a hasty retreat.

The florist was shouting something new, Roger realised, as he changed direction and went past her again. Alfie was now scrambling precariously up onto the bench at the back of the shop that was crowded with large plants in pots. They were wobbling dangerously as he wove between them, keeping them between him and Roger.

What was the florist saying?

'Take him to the bloody café! For God's sake!'

Roger stopped. Water was dripping from the benches

and there were flowers strewn all over the shop, some trampled underfoot. As he took stock, a large ficus tree in a pot toppled slowly off the bench Alfie was standing on and smashed on the floor. Soil and leaves scattered.

'Oops,' said Alfie, jumping down.

Roger was going to kill him. But first he had to catch him.

He feinted one way, then instantly went the other. Alfie ran headlong into him.

'Oof!' Roger had forgotten how solid the boy was. 'Gotcha!' He gripped Alfie's waistband with both hands and lifted him clear off the ground, legs kicking madly. His grandson was roaring with fury, bright red in the face, tears streaming down his cheeks. For a second, Roger's triumph felt wrong before he allowed himself to truly enjoy it. 'Ha!' he said into Alfie's face. 'That was very, very naughty! Definitely no café for you!'

Alfie's fury crumpled. 'Pease, Woger, pease!' He started to sob.

'Oh, I really think you should take him to the café!' The florist put her hands on her hips. 'Look at the poor little mite.'

Poor little mite? Why on earth did everyone take the boy's side? Roger surveyed the chaos at the same time as the florist. Their eyes travelled in opposite directions around the shop and met in the middle. Hers were very, very cool, he thought. Given how stressful the experience had been for him.

'I'm afraid you owe me quite a lot,' she said.

'For?' he said.

'For. The. Flowers.' She swept an arm around the shop and he took it in. The floor was covered with trampled petals, soil and leaves; it looked like a posh wedding gone badly wrong. He had to admit, it wasn't going to encourage customers, to see such carnage. Alfie went dead in his arms, as though the effort of racing around and trashing the place had worn him out.

'You don't have insurance?' Roger said.

'Insurance?' Her tone was very heavy. 'And what would I put down as the cause of the accident?'

'Um ... toddler running amok?' he said.

'I don't think that's a category that's recognised by my insurance company.'

'I see.' He thought for a moment. 'How much damage would you say has been caused?'

'Well, I can't even quantify the cost of wear and tear on my nerves,' she said tartly. 'But I'd say that's about three hundred pounds' worth of flowers, shrubs, pots and plants.'

'Three *hundred*?'

'Three. Hund-er-ed.' She drew the word out. 'Since your *wife* has always been a lovely customer, let's call it two-fifty.'

'Thank you.' He struggled to hold Alfie and get out his credit card.

After the payment had gone through, the woman sniffed and picked up Alfie's coat from the floor. She held it out to him wordlessly.

THE TRIP HOME WAS ARDUOUS. It was difficult to restrain the dog and carry a heavy toddler at the same time. By the time Roger panted through the front door, his back was killing him.

He deposited Alfie on the sofa with relief. Killer slunk off to his bed while Roger stood over Alfie and wondered what to do with him. What had Sarah mentioned when he'd picked him up? *Make sure he has a sleep.* She'd obviously worked out that Alfie hadn't, on the previous occasion that Roger had looked after him. As if to prove the point, Alfie opened his eyes, stared up at Roger, sighed deeply, then stuck his thumb firmly in his mouth and shut his eyes again. He was instantly asleep.

Roger stretched his aching back and went to the kitchen for lunch. Looking at the oven clock, he was stunned to realise that it was in fact only eleven thirty in the morning. How could that possibly be true? Would it be wrong to have a beer? Or glass of wine? He drew out a bottle of rosé and looked it at longingly. Only the thought of what might happen if the florist had called the police to protest made him pause. He put the bottle back in the fridge, found a pizza at the bottom of the freezer and put the oven on.

Alfie woke up after forty minutes and polished off half of the pizza, even the burnt bits. While he ate, Roger texted a brief summary of the morning's events to Andy, hoping he'd respond with a heartfelt apology for Alfie's behaviour. He also posed a question.

What did your mum do to stop the tantrums?

Ten minutes later, he received the response:

Mum knew better than to try to get Alfie past the café without going in.

As Alfie powered his way through a chocolate mousse, Roger took stock. He'd need to find something to do with Alfie every single time he had to look after him. Something Alfie wanted to do, in order to minimise blue breath-holding spells, tantrums and vandalism.

'Alfie?' He leaned towards his grandson. 'What do you like?'

'Mousse,' Alfie said, licking the pot enthusiastically. 'More mousse!'

'I mean, what do you like to do?'

'Eat.' Alfie grinned at him with chocolate-stained teeth.

'Apart from eating.'

'Swim.'

Roger shuddered. He hated the public swimming pool. Nothing on earth would induce him to take Alfie swimming, even if it might turn him into a future Olympian. 'Anything else?'

'Twucks.'

'You like trucks?'

'Big ones.' Alfie held his arms out wide.

A thought occurred to Roger. Why hadn't he thought of it before? 'I might be able to help you there,' he said. He sent a text to the warehouse manager at Karter's and then wondered what to do for the rest of the afternoon. He felt very tired; would it be wrong to have a sleep? As he contemplated it, there was a loud bang at the door. He jumped.

'Who's dat?' Alfie said, sliding down from his chair and heading for the front door, with Killer trotting briskly behind him.

'Wait, Alfie, no opening doors without me!' Roger hurried to catch up. At the door was a wiry woman of indeterminate age, with blonde curly hair.

'Gail!' Alfie hugged her legs.

'Ah, you must be the gardener,' Roger said. No wonder Killer hadn't barked.

'That's right. Is Jane not here?' She peered around Roger as though he was physically restraining his wife from answering the door.

'Jane's away,' he said. 'Come in.'

'No, I always use the side gate, I just like to let Jane know I'm here first.'

With a start, Roger realised he didn't have any money for her. 'I don't suppose I could pay you today through bank transfer?'

'I'd prefer cash,' she said, bluntly.

'Right. It's just that the little chap has been out a lot today and is very tired. I don't want to drag him out to the bank with me.'

'Leave him with me,' she said.

'Really?' He wasn't at all sure about this. Was it another potential headline in the making?

'Jane does.' She bent down to speak to Alfie in the Andy-approved method. 'You can garden with me, can't you, Alfie? Rake some leaves!'

'Yes!' Alfie was hopping from foot to foot. 'Find worms!'

'Sure.' She winked at Roger. 'Start 'em young. Grab your coat, Alfie, Grandad just has to go out and get some money.'

If Jane did it ... why not? And he could pop to Tesco Express again and get more food. He could add pizza to the repertoire now.

When he returned to the house, he could see Alfie in the garden with Gail, enthusiastically prodding around in the soil while she neatened up the beds with her shovel, planted some bulbs and raked huge piles of leaves. Killer was sniffing around in one pile and seemed quite content. Roger had decided to ignore the instruction to clean the dog's teeth. If visiting the vet hadn't merited a warning but teeth-cleaning was described as tricky, Roger could only assume it was a task requiring three people and a sedative for the dog. Killer's teeth would just have to survive.

While Alfie and Killer were outside, Roger used the time

to watch some sport. He considered the £45 money well spent on the babysitting, if not the gardening. By the time he returned Alfie home, he was yawning and sleepy-eyed; Sarah said approvingly that Roger had obviously worn him out, and turned a blind eye to the light smattering of soil he was wearing all over his clothes. Which reminded Roger, he still had a washing problem to sort out. The trousers, now dry, smelled very powerfully indeed of a scent Roger would have described as toilet cleaner. He was wearing his old jeans again and would have to do so for the foreseeable future until he solved the laundry crisis.

He drove home with a glow of satisfaction that the day with Alfie had gone rather well. Apart from the £250 tantrum, that was.

There was no email for him that night. He went to bed feeling a sense of anticlimax.

13

Andy had to wait four days before he got an email from Jamie at The Very Private PI at seven thirty in the morning. It informed Andy that he had some results for him and how would he like to receive them? Was normal email okay or did it need to be encrypted? Andy wrote straight back to suggest a face-to-face meeting. This was an opportunity he didn't want to waste, the chance to meet a real private investigator. The response pressed him to accept results on email.

Andy replied tersely that he really wanted to chat in person, and after ten long minutes he received a reply.

Busy most of the day. Can meet you at the café on the High Street at 3.45? Please sit outside. Wear a pink shirt if you have one. Sunglasses if not.

The true-crime fan in Andy thrilled to the details of the message. He did have a pink shirt. And sunglasses. He was sure he could sit outside. He'd have to find an excuse to leave work but he replied instantly:

Fine! See you then.

The day went by very slowly. He wondered what Jamie had found. He had to assume his mum was basically okay, because if not, surely Jamie would have said so? Unless he hadn't been able to find Jane at all, in which case it would surely become a police matter? And the encryption thing started to worry him. Why would he ever need to encrypt details of his mum's whereabouts? Had she somehow fallen in with some Russians? Or stumbled over something corrupt that had meant she needed witness protection?

His anxiety levels started to climb. He gnawed the skin around his thumb as he tapped one-handed at his keyboard and wished his mum was around to help him manage his worrying.

At twenty past three, he picked up his backpack as quietly as he could. Vivian still popped her head above the cubicle divider and said loudly, 'Off somewhere, Andy?'

'The doctor,' he said. 'Bit of a rash. Quite a nasty one, in fact. Do you want to see it?'

She stepped back. 'If you're contagious, you shouldn't be in the office.'

'I know,' he said. 'Trouble is, some people love to snitch on colleagues. Just makes people who are sick come to work when they shouldn't.'

He left the office with a spring in his step and headed for the High Street. The weather was still just about warm enough to sit out, so when he arrived he chose a table under the awning, facing the street, put on his sunglasses and settled himself down to wait.

To pass the time, he amused himself wondering what Jamie would look like. The name sounded dark-haired and tall, broad-shouldered, capable in a crisis. Hunting down people smugglers, say, or busting a drugs gang. Andy hoped he wouldn't have any prominent scars or tattoos. This café was full of smartly dressed women just like his mum, having coffee with friends. Tattoos or scars wouldn't fit in.

A few possible candidates wandered past but no one approached the café. He was just checking his watch when a small blonde girl with very fair eyebrows sat down at his table. Her hair was tied in a demure ponytail and she was wearing a school uniform.

He said, 'Sorry, I'm waiting for someone, actually.' There were plenty of other outside tables free; he had no idea why this child would want to sit next to him.

'Yeah, I know. Andy Kurmudge?' she said. Her face still wore the roundness of childhood and she had braces on her teeth.

He looked past her to see if a parent was lagging behind. 'Yes. And you are?'

'I'm Jamie.'

His look of astonishment made her sigh.

'It's for girls as well as boys, you know. Bit sexist to assume I was a man, if you don't mind me saying. You really look like your mum, I didn't even need the pink shirt! Or the glasses. Although clients who insist on meeting love that stuff. And I'd checked you out on Facebook, obvs, to make sure you weren't a weirdo.' She pulled a laptop out of her bag while he was still trying to understand what was going on.

'It's not that. I mean' – he pointed at her uniform – 'you're a schoolgirl. You can't be a private detective!'

'Why not?'

'How old are you?'

She widened her eyes at him. 'Asking if I'm underage? Don't you think there are more appropriate questions?'

Andy glanced around him. Was anyone watching him sitting alone with a young girl? 'Schoolgirls can't be private detectives,' he repeated.

She opened the laptop and tapped at the keyboard before peering over the top at him. 'Look, Mr. Kurmudge. Here's the thing. Being a private investigator isn't following clues with a magnifying glass or a map, not nowadays, right? It's all about the internet. I don't have to leave my bedroom at all to find this stuff out. It's all right here,' she pointed at the screen in front of her, 'ready to be discovered. I'm quite good with computers. So I guess the question is: do you want to know what I found out?'

A waitress came across. 'Can I get you anything?' she asked, pen poised above her pad.

'I'll have a toasted teacake and a large vanilla frappuccino with that squirty cream stuff and lots of chocolate sprinkles, please,' Jamie said. 'Mr. Kurmudge?'

Andy said. 'I'll have a flat white, thanks.' He took off the sunglasses, feeling foolish.

Once the waitress had disappeared back into the café, Jamie looked at him expectantly. 'So?'

'Yes. I do want to know, of course I do. And call me Andy. I feel bad enough already without feeling like my dad.'

'Rightio, then. Sooo ...' she drew out the word, 'your mum, Jane Kurmudge, DOB February 25th 1953 – wow, that's so old! – left home at around eight thirty a.m. with a suitcase on Friday 23rd September in a taxi, right?'

Andy nodded.

'Well, I've traced her to Sydney.'

'*Where?*'

'Sydney. Like, Australia?' All of her sentences went up at the end as though they were questions. She clarified: 'You know. Bondi Beach, kangaroos.'

'That can't be right,' Andy said. 'Why on earth would my mum go to Australia?'

'I dunno,' she said, smiling with glee as the waitress brought their order, putting the teacake and the frappuccino in front of her. 'But that's where she is.'

'How do you know?' Andy asked. 'Where's the proof?'

He had to wait for a moment while Jamie ate a large teaspoonful of cream that left a deposit of chocolate powder across her top lip. She pursed her mouth. 'So, like, do you really want to know? I mean, in my experience, often people don't.'

'Of course I want to know. Did you hack CCTV cameras? Or passenger manifests?'

Jamie frowned. 'You watch too much TV. Like, that's not where anyone starts, right? Start with the person's emails. You really need to chat to your mum about making her accounts secure. I hacked her emails in eleven minutes flat. Do you want me to give you her password?'

Andy shook his head vehemently. 'No! I'd feel ... weird.'

'Okay. But let's just say old people always use words and dates they know, easily remembered, right? Like their name and birthday. Honestly? It's like she *wanted* to be hacked.' She turned her laptop towards him so he could see an email. 'Confirmation of a British Airways flight to Sydney. And then, with the info in her old emails, like notes to solicitors about her bank account details when her mum died a few years ago, I could ...' She paused. 'Well, how I got into the bank stuff is a bit dodgy, if I'm honest, and I'd rather not go into too many details. It was a bit fiddly and took a bit of

... well, anyway. Just tell your mum not to use the same password all the time and her memorable info needs to be better than Alfie1. She really needs to use an app. All you need to know is that she bought something in Boots in Heathrow, and then in Sydney she bought something when she landed.'

Andy stared at the surface of his flat white. Drinking it might make his anxiety worse. He felt terrible about hacking into his mum's emails and even worse about the bank account. He pushed his coffee away. 'Hang on. Is that legal?'

'I told you.'

'Told me what?'

'That you might not want to know.'

'Listen,' Andy said, 'I've always been very law-abiding. I'm not sure about hacking into stuff ...'

Jamie frowned and bit into her teacake. She spoke around a mouthful of it. 'You know, legal is just what people in power say it is, right? And they're always doing shit stuff behind the scenes, so I figure we should do what's right, not what's legal. She's your mum. I mean, you're not the Mafia tracking her down, or someone dodgy. So it doesn't really matter.'

'I think you'll find,' said Andy, 'that the police would take a very dim view of a young girl hacking into people's emails.'

She nodded seriously. 'They would. They'd also take a really, really dim view of older men contacting young girls and buying them frappuccinos in cafés after school.' She stuck her spoon back into the cream.

Andy gave her a dark look. 'So you could technically move my mum's money out of her account?'

'Not if she downloads the app and uses it properly.'

'But you could.'

She shrugged. 'But I won't. Just tell your mum to change her passwords and memorable info and to make sure she always does the two-step authentication process.'

Andy made a note to do so straightaway. 'So you say she's in Sydney. Any idea where?'

She finished her mouthful before saying, 'I wanted to check with you. I mean, my brief was 'find her' – so is Sydney enough? There wasn't anything in her emails about hotel bookings or anything, which is a bit weird. I can see she's spending money there but just meals, drinks, stuff like that. In a few different places.'

'I don't want my mum stalked,' Andy said. He was beginning to wish he hadn't started this. His dad was maddening: it was more of a mystery why his mum had put up with it for so long than why she'd want to leave him for a break. But instead of going to Bordeaux, she was on the other side of the world, behaving completely out of character, driven by whatever his dad had done to make her angry. Although, on the plus side, she was obviously fine. Maybe she had decided to see her sister in Byron Bay. He wasn't too sure where that was or whether Jane would need to go through Sydney to get there. He'd google that himself, rather than ask this precocious person to check it for him.

'So what do you want to do now?' Jamie finished her teacake and sat swinging her leg.

Andy felt inappropriately disappointed. He'd found his mum, after all. It was just that this wasn't the alcoholic, trench-coated, misanthropic private eye of his dreams. Nor the brilliant oddball who saw things no one else had noticed. There was no way this schoolgirl who drank milkshakes and still had braces could be spun into an interesting yarn for the office or his mates. He'd really be best off never mentioning her again because, honestly, who wanted to confess he'd been contacting teenage girls, even if he hadn't known her age? He felt old and out of touch compared with this girl, and had a pang of sympathy for his dad. Was this how Roger felt sometimes?

'I think that's all I needed to know. How much do I owe you?' he asked. He hoped the bill wasn't too large. The credit card bill for the month was already huge: the builder had come back with some additional costs for work that apparently had to be done and Sarah would be on his case if he spent a lot of cash. It would be hard to hide.

She tipped her head to one side and tapped away at her screen. 'Hmm, fifteen, then eleven, then twelve, then twenty-five, then two ...'

Andy would have to ask Sam to contribute. That many hours at fifty-five pounds a pop was going to be impossible. Did she have a team of feisty, tech-literate schoolgirls working on it? His dad would have paid for it but Andy couldn't tell him without breaking his mum's trust. 'Hours?'

She frowned. 'I'm adding up *minutes*,' she said. 'I think it's about three hours in total. Including this meeting.'

He fell back in his chair with a whoosh of relief. 'So one hundred and sixty-five pounds, then?'

'That seems like a lot,' she said. 'Actually, my mum monitors my bank account so I usually ask for cash.' She tapped her fingers on the table. 'You and your mum seem nice, Andy, so why don't we make it a hundred quid and then that's enough for me to get a new LAN Turtle.'

'A land turtle?'

She frowned pityingly. '*LAN*. It's not an *actual* turtle. It's kit I need to ... Well, I just need it.'

'Won't your mum notice new kit?' he asked.

She laughed. There were little bits of teacake stuck in

her braces. 'Honestly, my mum doesn't have a clue about technology or what I get up to – apart from the bank account. As long as I'm in my room and quiet and I do my homework, it's all good as far as Mum's concerned.'

'I've got enough on me, as it happens,' Andy said. He made a note to himself: if teenage Alfie started to spend a lot of time in his bedroom, Andy and Sarah would need to get pretty savvy about technology to keep up with whatever he was getting up to in there. He handed over the cash to Jamie, who took it and put it in a purple purse with a diamante star on it. 'And listen, Jamie? I am a bit worried about you meeting strangers like this. I mean, obviously I'm okay, but you will be careful, won't you?'

'Oh, totes!' She grinned back at him. 'Over there's my friend Max, she's been watching the whole time. Any messing and she'll call the police.'

Andy jerked his head in the direction of Jamie's finger. A ginger-haired girl built like Roger's American-style fridge with angry acne on her face was staring at them from a nearby bus stop. Andy felt himself blush under her hard gaze. 'How about another tenner for her time, too,' he said, sliding the note across the table.

'Thanks! You're all right, Andy,' Jamie said.

All too aware that he was only salving his conscience, Andy stood and picked up his backpack. 'Right, then. I'll just get the bill. You take care.'

'So, just checking: you don't want me to track your mum in Aus?' Jamie said.

'No, thanks. I just wanted to know she was okay and hadn't been kidnapped.'

'Deffo not,' Jamie said, cheerfully. 'No signs of duress, no signs of anything dodgy on her Facebook or bank accounts or email, right? It all looks like she just wanted to have a holiday.'

Andy couldn't believe his mum wanted a holiday in Sydney. Unless her sister had met her there, perhaps?

'One other thing, though,' Jamie said.

'What?' Andy knew this could be the key. This was the final-moment question that unlocked the mystery.

She pointed at his untouched flat white. 'Can Max have that? She's a coffee lover, unlike me.'

'Of course,' he said, deflated.

'Max! Flat white here, untouched,' Jamie shouted, and Ginger Girl unpeeled herself from the bus shelter and crossed over to them.

'Ta,' she said, sliding into his vacated seat. 'Love a flat white.'

He nodded slightly nervously at them both, paid the bill, and went back to the office. After furiously dashing off several work emails to look diligent and holding a totally unnecessary conversation on the phone chasing a report especially for Vivian's flapping ears, he sent a text:

Sammo, Mum's in Sydney, according to the PI. Weird. But I guess she's fine. I'll email her now. CC you. A.

From: Andy Kurmudge
To: Janes Away Hurray
Cc: Sam Kurmudge
Sydney? What is going on?
Dear Mum,
I know you asked us not to tell Dad where you were but you didn't specifically ask us not to find out and, well, let's just say we know you went to Sydney. We honestly don't know why and I just wanted to say I hope you're okay. We definitely won't tell

Dad. Just please tell us if you need anything or you've got a problem. We miss you.
And please change your bank password and memorable information. As soon as you get this!
Love,
Andy

14

The next few days reintroduced Roger to more unfamiliar emotions. One morning, for the first time since Jane had disappeared, the immensity of it struck him like a blow to the heart. He looked through her wardrobe, wondering what she'd taken with her, moving the hangers along the rail with a soft metallic whine – blouses, knitwear, coats, dresses, trousers, all immaculately stored in a way that would instantly have informed a stranger of Jane's meticulous personality – only to realise that he had no idea what was missing.

The scent of her perfume wafted faintly around him and for a moment he expected to turn and find her standing behind him, chiding him for being so nosy. He couldn't tell from what was left whether what she'd taken was enough for a month or a year.

Quite apart from her possessions, what she had left behind her was a huge hole. He felt very ... lonely. He placed the emotion with a stab of surprise. He hadn't realised quite how much of his life was run by Jane. Their friends were largely her friends. Their activities were facilitated by her. Roger might suggest an outing but it was Jane who worked out the best time to go, organised a dog sitter, made bookings if necessary. He could do it – of course he could! – but it took effort. And what was the point, when he'd be on his own? He missed having company, generally, but more than that, he really missed Jane. Her bell-like laugh, when something really tickled her. The way she saw the world differently from him and challenged him on his entrenched views. Her ability to strike up conversation with anyone she met. She smoothed his path.

Without her and without work, he didn't know how to fill his time. He ate ready meals, watched a lot of TV and wandered around the house on Friday. Killer's sad-eyed look made him feel guilty so he took him to the park in the afternoon. Passing the pile of unread papers stacked up in the porch, he wondered if he should cancel *The Guardian*. Somehow that seemed very final, proof that Jane wasn't coming home.

Weekends were the worst. No plans. No one likely to ring him. On the Saturday, he texted Andy to ask him if he'd like to come round and watch a football match in the evening but got a text back explaining they were out for the day and Sarah wouldn't be happy if he went out that night without her. He texted Sam the same question. Sam replied an hour later:

Out w Guy at gig. U cld come 2? LMK.

Once he'd deciphered this, Roger shuddered. He didn't really enjoy live music. And he could feel the half-hearted nature of the invitation. Sam's flatmate, Guy, was perfectly pleasant in a wiry, muscular, health-nut kind of way – fair enough, he was a personal trainer – but they had very little in common. No, he'd stay at home.

But an hour later he was so bored that he had to do something. So he pulled on a coat against the thin drizzle, grabbed Killer's lead and drove into town. Where had Andy said the gallery was? He had mentioned the nice one just off the High Street. Roger knew where that was. He set off with purpose. Killer tried his dive down the side street again but Roger was forewarned this time. He tugged the lead and Killer rather meekly accepted. Or, Roger thought, perhaps the dog knew this route? Had he gone to the gallery with Jane? A horrific thought occurred to him: did the *dog* know more about Jane's life than he did?

The gallery was small but shiny. Glossy black paint on the door and window frame. Inside, he could see minimalist décor and high-wattage spotlights on large canvasses of various artistic styles (and merit, Roger thought). A voluptuous red-haired woman in a well-cut black trouser-suit and crisp white blouse was standing behind a small counter. Roger wondered if he could take the dog in. It was very clear Killer had been here before, and when the woman clocked the dog through the window she clicked briskly to the door in her vertiginous heels and opened it.

'Killer!' Her slightly aloof manner disappeared. 'How are you, you gorgeous little thing?' She bent over and tickled his tummy as Killer rolled over and shut his eyes. She looked up. 'You must be Roger! How are you getting on without Jane?'

'You knew she was going away?' he said.

Her forehead creased. 'Of course!' She blinked heavily mascaraed eyes. 'Did you think I didn't?' She looked confused and slightly suspicious.

'Oh, no.' Roger was damned if he was going to admit to

posh red-haired women whose existence he was previously unaware of that they knew more about his wife's activities than he did. 'It's just that some of her friends don't seem to know.'

'Well, I suppose you don't always tell everyone everything, do you? But obviously, what with working here, Jane had to let me know about her Italian break. Such great luck, winning that competition!'

'Competition?' Roger said. Killer was still lying on the ground, absorbing most of the woman's attention. Roger really wanted to get inside the gallery and ask some more searching questions that somehow wouldn't reveal his lack of knowledge. 'Look, would you mind if I came in? I've never managed to see the gallery and I'd love to; before, I was working and now I'm retired ...'

'Oh, how rude of me! Of course! Come in. You must be dying to see where Jane worked. She's such a wonderful person, you're a really lucky man.'

'I am, aren't I,' Roger said. He followed her into the room and looked around. He murmured rather lamely, 'Lovely ... pictures.' The art on display proved Jane's view that most people had child-like taste in paintings: they wanted something pretty and undemanding on their walls. Opposite him on the widest wall was a large Jackson Pollock knock-off, next to another slightly smaller canvas in a plain white frame that depicted a rather saccharine landscape of fields of sheep, and finally a seaside scene with a distorted perspective, all the seagulls enormous against tiny houses the colours of Neapolitan ice cream.

'We sell what people like,' the woman said. She smiled wryly at him. 'I'm Nina, by the way. I mean, obviously you knew that!' She held out her hand.

He shook it. 'Lovely to meet you. I've heard so much

about you.' The lie dropped from his lips effortlessly. 'Killer, come away from there!' Killer was sniffing madly at the woman's bag, hanging over the back of the chair behind the counter.

'Oh, he always does that! He can smell my sandwich – can't you, you naughty thing!' She bent again to tickle the dog.

'Did Jane always bring Killer with her?'

'I told her to. It was only once a week and customers love him. Such an engaging little character.'

Roger really wanted to go back to the competition she'd mentioned. He couldn't work out how to get to it. Fortunately, she was what Jane would call a Chatty Cathy.

'I'm actually really envious of Jane,' she said. 'I always loved painting but was never good enough to progress much and the idea of three months in Italy with some expert tuition ... well, wow. I'm so glad for her. Who knows, maybe some of her work will be hanging here next year!'

Roger was trying to process the words. But he couldn't get past three months.

Three months.

Three. Months.

He couldn't imagine that far away. He could tell from Nina's slightly bemused expression that he was standing with his mouth open.

'You must be missing her,' she said kindly. 'It's a long time, isn't it? I know if Freya, that's my other half, was away, I'd miss her dreadfully.'

'Yes,' Roger said.

'Well, anyway, I've been so thrilled to have Jane here. She's just got that knack of working out who wants one of these,' she pointed at the Pollock knock-off, 'or who is a serious art collector who might want us to track something specific down for them. And she's so personable.'

'So she's like a consultant?' Roger said.

'Yes. I mean, I don't know why I'm telling you this, you know it all already, of course.' She laughed lightly. 'But sometimes we don't really understand certain things about our other halves' lives, do we?'

'No.' Roger shook his head. 'We don't.'

'Are you going to join her?' Nina asked.

'Join her?'

'In Italy? I'd love to, I really would. Starting in Florence and Sienna, then ending up in Rome.' She looked wistful. 'Can you imagine?'

He wanted to ask her what the competition had been called but decided to google it instead. The boys could help. They were good at tracking things down. They'd track Jane down and insist she came home.

He spent a few more minutes chatting with Nina before leaving. He drove home via a quick stop at Waitrose. He ate some lunch. He sat staring into space. *Three months*. It was October. She wouldn't be back until January.

The dull sensation in his chest was like the beginning of a heart attack. Feverishly, he checked his symptoms on the NHS website on his phone, sliding his fingers apart to make the words enlarge on screen. *Chest pain or discomfort that suddenly occurs and doesn't go away ...* Tick. *Pain that may spread to your left or right arm or may spread to your neck, jaw, back or stomach.* He felt pain everywhere. *Feeling sick, sweaty, light-headed or short of breath.* Tick. He'd better lie down. He carefully got down onto the carpet and put his phone to one side. He concentrated on breathing slowly. Should he call 999? Why wasn't Jane here, she'd know what to do. He *needed* her.

After a few minutes, it was clear he wasn't having a heart attack. Killer crept up to him and licked the side of his face. It was almost comforting. Roger could see now why Alfie liked it so much. Still, when the dog's tongue moved towards his mouth, he sat up.

He picked up his phone and called Andy.

'Dad? Everything okay?'

'Yes. No. I went to your mum's gallery. The one she was working in. I didn't really believe it, so I went to check it out and she said – you won't believe what she said –'

'Alfie! Put the knife down! Right now! Sorry, Dad, go on.'

Roger struggled to get back on track. 'Yes, well, she said that your mum had won a competition and was going to be in Italy for three months.'

'*Three months?*'

Roger was pleased that Andy had zeroed in on the same big issue he had.

'Are you sure, Dad? Wait, what was that about a competition?'

Roger explained that he hadn't wanted to reveal just how little they knew of Jane's whereabouts. 'So I need your help. Working out what this competition is.'

Andy sounded distracted and Roger could hear Alfie start to wail. There was a sharp comment from Sarah in the background: *Get off the phone.* 'Okay, well, I'll try, Dad. Not right now. Maybe tomorrow?'

The disappointment that Andy wasn't getting straight on the case hung over Roger all evening. He ate pad thai from Waitrose (a welcome change from Tesco's range of ready meals) while watching a BBC drama about a missing wife. Roger envied the husband. He wasn't getting snarky messages from *his* wife. She'd been taken by a serial killer who only targeted housewives with dark hair who enjoyed running. It was so much more straightforward than Roger's situation. Once the police had finished interrogating this husband, people were sorry for him. They brought casseroles and lasagnes to his house. And his wife was returned to him at the end of the programme. In fact, even though it turned out she was the key to catching the killer and she had to spend two long days with the police 'debriefing', she'd been back in the kitchen making dinner within hours of her return home.

When the news came on, Roger switched the TV off and took Killer out for his final walk around the garden. Through the kitchen window he could see the washing up piled up by the sink. He had no clean undies. His life felt out of control.

ANDY RANG him the following day. 'Come and meet me at the soft-play place, Dad.'

'The what?'

'Soft play. Alfie wants to go. It's just off the road in from your place. The Magic Kingdom? You know the one?'

'What time?'

They agreed to meet at ten a.m. He looked over his clothes and selected the least dirty pair of jeans and one of his last clean sweatshirts. He put them on and sighed at himself. He was beginning to look unkempt, but there was nothing to be done. He was already late.

The soft-play centre was busy. Harried-looking parents were chasing over-excited children of all ages and sizes who whooped as they ran through the doors. Queuing for tickets was chaotic.

Alfie was jumping up and down with excitement. 'Less go, less go!'

'Hold my hand,' Andy told him. 'Try to stand still for a moment.'

They bought tickets and went through the turnstile gate into the soft-play centre. It looked, Roger thought, like a holding pen for criminally insane children. Padded surfaces, bright colours, huge foam blocks and obstacle courses. Magical it was not.

Alfie said something to Andy, who nudged Roger. 'He wants you to go with him.'

'With him?'

'Dad, he's too little to go in there on his own.' Andy pointed at the entry to what looked like a construction site, multi-levelled, but with nets and foam obstacles instead of scaffolding. On the first level, a chunky older boy was hanging onto the netting and bellowing something down to his mother, who was sitting at a table near the café, lost in her phone. Roger wanted to join her. He wanted a coffee, a slice of cake and a chat with Andy about the three-months thing. But Andy's face told him that being requested by Alfie was a compliment and that he should be flattered. (Rather than feeling somewhat 'played', as the boys would say.)

Alfie grabbed Roger's hand. 'Less go, Woger!' He tugged Roger towards the opening in the nets.

'You need to take your shoes off,' Andy said.

Roger hadn't been able to find matching clean socks that morning. He'd only been able to find one of his socks (Paul Smith, rather natty-looking, navy blue with red spots), and one of Jane's. She had unusually long feet and so it had just fitted him. Unfortunately, it was a delicate shade of pink and purples stripes. Definitely not a match for the Paul Smith. He wanted to protest but Alfie was yanking at his arm.

'Come on, Woger.'

Roger looked back up at the netting. The chunky boy was leering down at them. It was a jungle in there, Roger realised. The large ate the small. Or at least thumped them, denied them access to the cool stuff, got in their way, mocked them. He could tell all of this from the gleeful malice in the chunky boy's face. Someone needed to defend Alfie. He might be a little shit, but he was Roger's little shit.

He nodded to Andy. 'Here, can you look after them for me?' He took off his shoes and could see Andy suppressing a smile. 'Yes, I know, I know. I haven't done any washing since your mum ... went away.'

'Right.' Andy took the shoes.

Glancing behind him as Alfie led him away, Roger was deeply envious. Andy dumped his backpack on a chair and went to order a coffee. How exactly had Roger managed to end up here? He looked down at Alfie.

'Come on!' Alfie let go of his hand and ran through the entrance. They rounded a corner and found their way barred by two cylindrical foam rollers, horizontal, parallel to each other and with only a small gap between them. Roger stopped.

'Go foo, Woger! Like dis!' Alfie threw himself between the two foam rollers, wriggled frantically and dropped onto the other side.

Roger looked at the gap. It was tiny. This wasn't dignified. A shuffling noise behind him made him realise there was a queue forming. A line of impatient children. Taking a deep breath, he strode forward, bent down, thrust his arms and head through the gap and then pushed off with his feet. For a second, he was suspended across one of the rollers, acutely conscious of the giggling behind him. He was damned if he'd get stuck here. He grunted, and wriggled, and fell through the gap. Ahead was a similar set-up, but this time the rollers were vertical. Alfie was nowhere to be seen. He squeezed through the rollers and found a series of huge steps that he had to scramble up.

He was now on the first level. Chunky Boy level. Where was Alfie? He could go left or right. A girl with pigtails and a very red face was hauling herself up the steps behind him. She side-stepped him and ran left and around the corner. He followed her and found a tunnel ahead, which the girl disappeared into head first.

Roger peered into the opening. 'Alfie?' An echo came back at him, along with high-pitched squeals. It was obviously a slide. Gingerly, he put his legs into the tunnel's opening and sat down on the lip. He hadn't been on a slide for a very long time. Again there was a queue building up behind him. He pushed off hard and felt his body slip down the slope. Steeper than he expected. A vertiginous rush. His heart in his mouth. In the dark with a spot of light rushing towards him. A giddiness to the experience. As he slowed to a halt at the bottom, where several parents were milling around, he felt something fizzing in his chest. Another unfamiliar feeling. He stood and brushed himself down, trying to place it. He couldn't see Alfie anywhere, and Andy was lost in his phone.

There was another direction Roger could take to get back into the construction zone, so he did. He had to weave between large mirrors that distorted him so he was either monstrously tall and thin or enormously fat and short. Roger chortled to himself. He then climbed up some nets that gradually ascended, hooking his feet into the gaps in the netting and finding the right spot to put his hands. It was hard work. Small people were making nothing of it, scrambling upwards without pausing or panting. It took Roger a lot longer.

At the top, he stopped to catch his breath and look down. No sign of Alfie. He strode to his right, stepping over the instruments-of-torture obstacles and found more foam blocks that he had to climb over. On the other side was a dead end, a wall of red plastic sheeting blocking off the end of that section. It was a corner point. On the same level, diagonally across from him, Roger could see Chunky Boy. And – with a gasp of breath – Chunky Boy's hand gripping Alfie's belt loops at the back of his jeans so that Alfie couldn't run away.

Roger gripped the netting. 'Everything okay, Alfie?'

Alfie squeaked. Tears were running down his face. He wore the look of someone who felt wronged and scared. 'Help, Woger!'

Chunky Boy grinned. The evil grin of someone who was going to end up in Borstal. Or on the *News at Ten*. It made Roger want to kill him. With a gun, if only he had one. Why didn't he live in the USA where presumably it would be just fine, given such provocation, to waste the little creep with his handgun, or pistol, or piece?

'You!' Roger used the voice that carried across the warehouse. The tone that made people flinch and scurry down the corridor away from him.

Chunky Boy sneered at him. 'Wha'?'

'I'm a ... an undercover policeman. Let go of that boy. Right now.'

'Gonna make me?' Chunky Boy yanked hard on Alfie's jeans and Alfie squealed.

'Yes.' Roger tried to make his voice as calm as possible. 'Well, not me. The sharp-shooter that's currently got his red dot on your nasty little forehead.'

'Ha! That's crap!' Chunky Boy said. But he glanced up and around.

'You can't see it,' Roger said in his most authoritative tone. 'It's infrared. The naked eye can't see it. But you have a large red dot of death right on your evil little face.'

'Policemen don't shoot kids,' Chunky Boy said. His tone, for the first time, was a little hesitant. His eyes darted around the play centre, searching for the shooter.

'Oh yes, they do. Conservative government, right?' Roger said. 'Brutal. They've decided to start young. Get rid of boys like you. Boys who will grow into troublemakers later.' It was handy, he realised now, to have a wife whose political leaning was so different to his own. They'd had many a debate about the callous nature of the Conservatives; he hadn't expected it to be so useful.

Alfie's eyes were huge in his frightened face.

'You live on the estate, right?' Roger said. Reasonable guess: it was close by. 'We know you. We've been watching you.' He pointed a menacing finger towards Chunky Boy. 'You're the reason I'm here.'

Behind him, Roger could hear a noise. He had an audience. He couldn't turn to see who it was. 'Let go of that kid and we will let you go, too. But we're watching you. Make no mistake. If we see you doing this again, you're toast.'

'How d'you know where I live?' Chunky Boy asked.

'We. Know. Everything.' Roger dropped his voice. 'Where you live. Where you go to school.' He emphasised the final word of each sentence. 'Or don't, often. We own you, you little shit. Let go of that boy right now, or I'll give the order.' He touched his ear and spoke into his palm. 'Stand by. Repeat, stand by. On my mark.'

Chunky Boy looked around wildly. He gave Alfie's belt loop another tug.

'Okay, on my mark, shooter one,' Roger said loudly, with his finger still on his ear.

'Shit!' Chunky Boy let go of Alfie and dived to the floor.

Alfie took off like a terrified rabbit, scorching away from Chunky Boy.

Roger turned to go back past the instruments of torture. He had to push past a small crowd of both parents and kids. Their faces were stunned. One dad pulled his son tightly into his side and muttered, 'No idea they watched us like that. Flippin' surveillance, bloody invasion of our rights!'

Roger smiled to himself. He'd take the slide down, he thought. It was rather fun.

He found Alfie huddled in Andy's lap.

'Dad, what happened?' Andy said, stroking Alfie's hair.

'Nothing,' Roger said, sitting down.

'Weren't you keeping an eye on him? He seems really upset.'

Alfie sniffed and looked up. He slipped off Andy's lap and came over to Roger. He hugged him fiercely, pushing his face into Roger's chest.

Roger felt strange. Emotional. He patted Alfie's back.

In the background, he could hear a commotion. He turned to see Chunky Boy pointing vigorously at him and saying something vehement. A small, tired-looking woman next to him was trying to calm him down. Focusing in on the words, Roger heard 'nutter', 'shoot me' and 'fuckin' crazy'.

Andy frowned. 'What on earth happened? That boy is going bananas over there. He's pointing at you.'

'Ignore him,' Roger said. 'Now, about your mother.'

A light cough from behind him made Roger turn around. He saw a small, tired-looking woman with a nervous expression.

'About what you said to my boy,' she said.

'Ah,' said Roger. 'Well, look ...' He let go of Alfie and stood up.

She leaned forward and spoke in a hushed tone. 'Thank you,' she said. 'He's been out of control since his dad left and no one helps and it's just me. He's actually a bit scared of you. So could you just look really mean, now, so he sees?'

Roger glanced over her shoulder. Chunk Boy was staring at him, with a gleeful smile. Roger gave him a gaze full of icicles and looked back at his mother.

'Of course,' he said, stabbing a finger towards her face with a malevolent sneer. 'Like this?'

'Oh, yes, just like that, thanks,' she said.

'Listen, tell your boy –'

'Grant.'

'Tell Grant if he steps out of line again, we'll deal with him in accordance with the 2015 Evil Boys Act, section 2, Public Order, paragraph 2.1.5, Bullying in Soft-Play Centres. Tell him we're watching the whole time,' Roger stabbed his finger in the air at her again, 'and we'll know.' He grimaced in as menacing a fashion as he could manage, lifting his top lip off his teeth just as Killer did.

'Thanks again,' she said. 'That was *perfect*. I really appreciate it.' She scuttled off and Roger watched her update Grant on the conversation, her eyes wide with faux concern. Grant blanched a little and his sturdy shoulders slumped. The woman turned and gave Roger a grin and a surreptitious thumbs-up.

Andy was staring at him. 'What the hell, Dad?'

'Honestly, it's nothing. It's fine, isn't it Alfie?' Alfie gave him a broad smile. 'I want to talk about your mum. Perhaps we can get Alfie a biscuit, to give us a minute?'

'Well,' Andy said, 'I suppose just this once.'

They sorted out a biscuit for Alfie – whose grin at Roger was now full of complicit glee – as well as a cup of tea for both of them, and went back to their table.

'So, run it by me again,' Andy said, stirring his tea. 'Mum won a competition?'

'Apparently.'

'Where?'

'Nina from the gallery said Florence. And Sienna. And Rome, I think.'

'I really don't understand.' Andy looked lost in thought.

'Nor do I! What is she thinking of?' Roger felt corrosive guilt roiling around in his abdomen. 'You're good at googling things. Can you look? I'm more worried about the time factor.'

'Three months.' Andy sounded gloomy. 'Nightmare. You realise what this means?'

'Yes. She's away for far too long. I mean, how much artistic input does she even need?'

'No.' Andy leaned across and wiped some crumbs off Alfie's mouth. 'It means Mum's away for Christmas. *Christmas.*'

15

Roger took a moment to control his panic. Christmas. Without Jane. It was unimaginable.

The presents. The food. The decorations. The tree. The wreath. The music. The smells. Everything about Christmas in their house was controlled by Jane. It was her day. Planning started in in August and filled several pages of her notepad, in addition to the file on her laptop that she would update with the new additions for that year.

The presents were bought and wrapped by October. The food order was booked as soon as the slots became available, with just a few surgical strikes required for last-minute fresh items such as meat, fruit and vegetables, and the bird, of course. Ocado would turn up in good time and Jane would start the process of making all the family favourites (Christmas pudding, Christmas cake, mince pies, chocolate and brandy mousse, shortbread biscuits with ginger). Roger and the boys would plough through all her offerings as though they were in training, building up to the over-eating final itself: Christmas Day.

The tradition was turkey, a beef joint and a ham, with all

the trimmings. Three types of stuffing: sage and onion, pork and chestnut, hazelnut and apricot. Yorkshire puddings. Roast potatoes in duck fat. Roast parsnips, roast pumpkin, roast Brussels sprouts with bacon lardons; roast anything else Jane could think of. Cauliflower cheese. It was a struggle to get everything on the table. The main course followed a seafood starter with prawns, smoked salmon, scallops, dressed crab and oysters. It was, Roger had to admit, gluttony writ large.

Plus there was a colour theme every year (rotated, because how many different colour themes were there, in fact, for Christmas?). Red and gold. Silver and blue. White and silver. White and blue. The bit that kept such themes alive was the addition of something spectacular and new each year such as the intricate wooden Christmas decoration from last year with rotating baby-blue sheep and silver wise men that she'd imported from Germany and which Alfie had found mesmerising. The year before that, the red and gold had been freshened up by colour-themed fireworks in the early evening just after they'd finished eating, which had frightened Killer into conniptions and which they'd agreed afterwards over glasses of port might have been a step too far. Especially for Tristan Golding next door.

It was *impossible* for Jane to be away for Christmas.

Roger stared at Andy in dismay, which was reflected right back at him. Roger found his voice first. 'She'll be back before then. Of course she will. She's just making her point and by then it will have been well and truly made.'

Andy shook his head.

'I'll email her,' Roger said. 'I'm actually pretty annoyed about it all. I take her point, that I wasn't perhaps as involved as I could have been. But now she's just neglecting her responsibilities, and I'm not at all happy. I mean, she has a family. She can't just leave.'

'You did,' said Andy.

Alfie stopped crunching his biscuit and stared at Roger.

'What does that mean?' Roger demanded. 'I've never walked out on you all!'

Andy pushed his phone across the table to Alfie. 'Here, buddy, a special treat! Daddy's phone for a few minutes, okay?' He picked up his spoon and started to trace patterns on the table, as if he couldn't look at Roger. 'Well, except you sort of did, Dad.'

'What on earth are you talking about?' Roger said.

'Remember in 1993? When I wouldn't go to school because of anxiety, and Granny Day had that car accident and broke her leg, and Sam was bullied all the time for … well, he was being bullied?'

'Yes,' said Roger. Which wasn't strictly true. He had a vague recollection of some of those things, but he'd been very busy at work.

'Well, you went on secondment, remember? To Australia? For six months.'

'That wasn't leaving,' Roger protested. 'I had to go. And thanks to filling in at such short notice for the Aussie head of sales after his heart attack, I was able to come back here as 2IC to the sales director and then get that job when Henry left. It was for my career.'

'And it left Mum doing everything here.'

'She could have come with me.'

'She really couldn't. *We* couldn't.' Andy gave a scoffing laugh. 'No way would I have agreed to change schools. And Granny Day needed her here. She had to move Granny Day in with us and wait on her hand and foot until she was better. She couldn't have left her on her own to go to Australia. And it wasn't long enough to uproot all of us.'

Now that Roger thought back properly, he did remember his marriage going through a very sticky patch in the 90s. The kind of patch you aren't sure you'll get through at all. But he took great exception to being told he'd 'left' his family, and told Andy so.

Andy shrugged. 'I don't see how this is different. At least Mum waited until you were available to help us before she left.'

'For a competition! Not for a job.'

'Well, she can't get a decent job any more, can she? She's been out of the work force for too long, looking after all of us.'

From his son's mulish face, Roger could see he wasn't going to win the argument. He needed to focus on the priority: the fact that they needed to track Jane down and insist she came home. 'We'll have to agree to differ on this one,' he said stiffly. 'But can you try to find the competition your mum won and work out where she is, so we can get her back home?'

'Did Mum never want to go to Sydney to see it?' Andy said. 'Not when we were kids, but after we'd left home?'

'No,' Roger said. He felt the conversation was moving in entirely the wrong direction. He could hardly admit that he really didn't want to go back to Sydney with Jane once he'd left. 'She likes Europe.'

'I do wonder ... I mean, maybe she'd think it was poetic justice to go.' Andy seemed lost in thought again.

What on earth was his son talking about? 'I have no idea what you mean,' Roger said. 'Care to explain?'

'Hmm,' said Andy. 'There's a bloke over there waving at you.'

Roger turned around. 'Blast. It's Tom.'

'Tom?'

'My replacement at Karter's. He has two boys, Ludicr – Ludo and Ricardo.'

Tom was approaching, clutching hands with two identical small boys with shocks of dark hair and button noses. 'Of all the men I never expected to see here, it's Roger! How's retirement treating you?'

'Oh, good, good!' said Roger as heartily as he could. He shot Andy a look. A look that said not to mention anything. Not vanishing wives, not champion swimmer sons. Andy looked puzzled. 'Keeping busy!'

'This must be the champ!' Tom said, looking at Alfie. Alfie was scrolling on the phone with a pudgy finger. He looked extremely un-sporty. The kind of boy who'd grow up to spend all his waking hours on the X-box, possibly wearing elasticated trousers that struggled to contain his considerable girth.

'Do you come here a lot?' Roger said.

'Yes, the boys love it.' Tom was still staring at Alfie as though he was about to ask for a demo. Maybe a dive into the foam-ball pit, to show how he managed the high platform.

'Have you been down the slide?' Roger asked. He needed to stop Tom from posing some searching questions to Andy.

'Slide?' Tom laughed. 'Not recently, Rodge!' He turned to Andy. 'So, about Alfie's swimming lessons –'

'No, listen, Tom, you really should! I'll show you. Come on, it'll be fun.' In desperation, Roger looked down at Ludicrous and Ridiculous, who were both looking excited at the prospect. 'Alfie, you'll come with us, won't you?'

Andy wore the look of a man with amnesia who had

been told that the clown in full make-up was in fact his strait-laced father. 'Dad? Are you sure?'

'It's such fun!' Roger picked Alfie up, ripped the phone from his grasp and pushed it back to Andy. 'Come on!' He set off across the play centre with a stunned Alfie in his arms. 'Come on, you two!' he shouted over his shoulder at the twins. At least now if he had to answer questions about Alfie's swimming chops, it wouldn't be in front of Andy.

Half an hour later, Roger had to admit to himself that he'd actually had fun. Tom had not enjoyed the swooping sensation of descending the slide, so Roger had taken over with all three boys and had even managed to go down the slide gripping onto all of them. He slid to a halt to hear, 'Goodness, what a hit you are!'

The softly accented voice made him look up. Elena was regarding him with huge eyes. 'You must be Roger, yes?' She held out a manicured hand to help him up. The tips of her nails were white, he noticed, and she smelled of something light and spicy, a welcome change from the sweat and stale-crisp odour of the play centre. Her cloudy dark hair was swept away from her face and she was wearing a lot of make-up. She couldn't have been more than thirty-five, Roger thought, and was flattered by her slightly parted lips and flared nostrils.

The three boys were jumping up and down on the spot, yelling, 'Gain, again, again!'

He smiled down at them. 'One last time, okay? Otherwise, I might have too much excitement for one day!' He took the twins' hands and checked that Alfie was following them.

He felt ten feet tall as he went through the maze again and down the slide for one more go. They got off the slide and Roger said firmly, 'Right, time to go, Alfie. Shall we get lunch? Boys, I'll take you back to your mum and dad.'

Elena's fluttered eyelashes as he dropped the twins back made him wonder again about Jane. She lived a life full of women, with almost no male interaction from anyone except her family. Did that perhaps make her more likely to indulge in a flirtation with someone – a giggle at the gallery, perhaps, with a wealthy art collector? He wondered. And Andy's comment about him, Roger, leaving the family still rankled. He hadn't left. Not like Jane had.

Back at Andy's table, his son was still lost in his phone.

'Ready to go home?' Roger said. He leaned across him to sip the last dregs of his tea.

Andy wrinkled his nose. 'Dad? I hate to say this but you ... well, you smell a little.'

'Smell?' Roger felt like a schoolboy.

'Didn't you say you were behind with your washing, earlier?'

'I need to do quite a bit. It's just I was hoping your mum would be back soon.'

There was something in Andy's face that Roger didn't easily recognise. He had seen that emotion before, he was sure, but not directed at him. Was it ... pity?

'I was thinking perhaps you need to find someone who can help with some cooking and washing, that sort of thing,' Andy said. 'Maybe even some shopping. You could afford to pay for it, couldn't you?'

Alfie was tugging at Andy's hand. 'Lunchtime, Daddy!'

Roger had to admit he probably could do with someone to do some of the tedious stuff for him. 'But who?' he said.

'I think you need to prove to Mum that you can help a lot more than she thinks,' Andy said. 'But you'll need some help to get there. What about Morwenna? She's already cleaning for you, maybe she could do more?'

THE THOUGHT MADE Roger quail a little. The Sky Sports episode still made him flinch inwardly. But that night, after he'd sent a clarification email to Jane – he asked if she was really going to be away for three months; her silence indicated she was – he realised it was going to be a very long time. He'd have to wash, shop, cook and tidy, as well as chase after Alfie and walk Killer.

So when Morwenna arrived later in the week, he hung around in the kitchen making small talk until she put down the spray cleaner, put her hands on her hips and said, 'Something you want?'

'Yes, actually. Well ...' He tried a smile. 'Yes ... I was wondering if you'd have more time during the week to help me around the house? Maybe some shopping, cooking and washing? Jane is going to be away now until January' – she looked as dismayed as he felt – 'and I'm not very good at this stuff. I can obviously pay you.'

She was already shaking her head. 'Not me. I'm fully booked.' She turned away and he was about to leave the room when he heard her say, 'But my niece. She could do it.'

'Niece?' He turned back.

'Mel. She's a good girl. My sister is a bit of a one. Not great at cookin', cleanin', shoppin'. So Mel's been doin' it for a while now.'

'How old is Mel?'

'Sixteen. Nah, seventeen, now.' She glowered at him. 'Problem?'

'Isn't she at school?'

'Yeah, obviously. This would be after, like. She can cook stuff and organise your shoppin'.'

'How is she at washin' – I mean, washing?'

She eyed him suspiciously. She picked up a sponge and ran it under the hot tap for a few seconds. 'Washin's no problem.'

'Right, well, perhaps you could ask Mel to pop over and see me one afternoon?'

'When?'

'As soon as she can?'

'Tomorrah?' Morwenna picked up the surface spray.

'Tomorrow would be good for me.' He bowed out of the room, wondering what he'd got himself into.

HE RETIRED to his study and found Jane's sister's email address in her address book. Anne had always been a prickly character. When he'd gone to Sydney for work, Jane had asked him if he planned to see her sister. He'd told Jane he was too busy to fly up to Byron Bay. Now he composed Anne an email.

From: Roger Kurmudge
To: Anne Halton
Subject: Jane
Dear Anne,
I hope you're well. The Australian weather seems to be getting rather hot, but you must be used to it by now. I'm emailing you on the off chance you've heard from Jane lately? She hasn't been herself and I wondered if you knew why?
Apart from that, we're all fine! Andy and Sam are quite grown up now, of course, and Andy's son Alfie is quite the character! I

think Sam's a confirmed bachelor, still sharing a flat with his friend Guy, and no signs of girlfriends or children. Probably just as well – we're busy enough helping with Alfie!
Hope to hear back from you soon re Jane.
All the best,
Roger

He wondered if he should email his brother, Arthur. They'd never been close. Arthur was older, lived in north London and had become a barrister after making it to Oxford. His success wasn't the only reason Roger didn't get on with him – they'd fought like cat and dog as boys – but it added to Roger's injured sense of being the lesser brother. Arthur was now very much part of what Roger had seen described as the 'metropolitan elite'. His son, Charlie, had been born a year after Andy and had gone into the City after doing an English degree at Bristol. Had done *extremely* well, in fact, according to the annual Christmas letter they'd received for several years from Arthur's wife, Rachel. But last year he had made a rather sudden decision to become a teacher. Roger was pretty sure that meant something had gone badly wrong and found he was just a little bit ecstatic to hear it. No, Arthur wouldn't know where Jane was and would return Roger's glee at Charlie's downfall. Anne was his best bet.

Just before he went to bed, he checked his emails.

From: Anne Halton
To: Roger Kurmudge
Re: Jane
Dear Roger, how very strange to get an email from you. You never showed the faintest interest in Jane's family so I can only assume something quite dramatic has occurred! She hasn't

been quite herself, you say? Sadly, she and I lost touch after I pointed out your flaws to her one too many times. Jane always was loyal to a fault. So I'm the last person she would have contacted to discuss anything that was worrying her, I'm afraid. Perhaps you should talk to her yourself? Instead of expecting everyone else to do everything for you?
Regards,
Anne

16

Through the stained glass panels in the front door, Roger could see a bulky, distorted figure with huge hair. A burly delivery man? Or worse – a policeman again?

'Hello?' he said cautiously through the half-open door.

The figure that greeted him was much less strange now he could see her in the flesh. The bulk was mainly from a large navy-blue puffer jacket (she would fit right in with the park mums). The hair was a huge Afro and it was also blue. Bright blue, not a subtle navy colour. Roger blinked. Who was this person and what was she doing on his porch?

'My arn' told me to come.' She blinked back at him.

'Your arn? Oh, your *aunt*.' Roger caught on. 'You're Mel?'

'Yeah. I'm Mel.' She looked down at her feet.

'I didn't realise you were …' He trailed off.

'Black?' she said. Not aggressively. In a resigned sort of way. 'My dad's side.'

'I was going to say so young!' He sounded a bit too hearty.

'I'm seventeen. Almost.'

'Right. Come on in, then.' He pulled the door wide open to let her in and stood back. She looked hesitant. It occurred to him that she wasn't keen on entering the house of an old white man on her own, just as he associated young black women with unrest in Brixton. 'I won't bite!' he said.

She gave him a tremulous grin and stepped over that day's *Guardian* and into the hall. 'Do you want me to take my shoes off, then?'

'Please,' he said. 'My wife, Jane – she's away – hates people keeping their shoes on.'

She slipped off well-worn trainers and stood waiting.

'Shall I take your coat?' He held out a hand.

She looked as though no one had ever done that for her before. After some awkward side-stepping, she turned around and he slipped the coat off her shoulders and put it on the hall stand.

'Right. Where shall we start?'

'Up to you, Mr. ... Mr. ...'

'Call me Roger,' Roger said.

She burst out giggling, stifling the sound behind her hand. 'I can't do tha'!'

'Why ever not?' Roger said.

'Cos, like, you're ...' She made a gesture he couldn't quite interpret. Did it mean white? Old? Middle class? Affluent?

'So what would you like to call me? Please not Mr. Kurmudge. That's my dad.' Deceased, but still.

She thought for a moment. 'Mr. R.?'

'If you like.' He smiled and gestured for her to head towards the kitchen. 'After you.'

Her feet were slow and cautious as she made her way through the house, as though she didn't trust the ground under them – or him. Stiff-backed, she walked through the door into the kitchen and stopped dead so that Roger had to squeeze gingerly past her.

'So, here's the kitchen, and through there's the laundry.' He pointed. 'And I suppose what I'm after is someone who can cook for me so I can freeze the meals and defrost them when I need them? And teach me how to do the washing.'

'There's not much to washin',' she said doubtfully, as if it was unclear why anyone would need to be taught.

'Ah!' He raised his hand. 'That's where you're wrong!' He went into the laundry and found Alfie's jumper, which he'd tried to wash the week before. 'See this? Belongs to my grandson.' He held it out to Mel, who took it and wrinkled her nose. 'Exactly! He was sick on it and I tried to wash it, and look how that turned out. And I've shrunk some of my trousers, too.'

She handed the jumper back to him hastily.

'I promise I won't ask you to wash things with vomit on them,' he said. 'I just want my clothes washed. And I'm not good at it. So I want someone who can teach me how to do it.'

She nodded.

'Could you tell me what sort of things you can cook?' he said.

'Everything,' she said. 'Curries, stir-fries, pies, roasts, whatever. What sort of thing are you after?'

His mouth was watering just listening. 'Those all sound good. Anything but lasagne or fish pie. I don't suppose,' he said carefully, 'that you'd be prepared to give it a trial run today?'

'Like, now?' she said.

'Yes. Is that possible?'

'How many hours a week? If the trial works?'

'Maybe two hours a day three times a week? After school?'

'Um, well, what would you pay me?' She was twisting her hands together. Without the large coat, she was slight and very young. The only defiant bit about her was the huge blue Afro.

'I thought £10 an hour? I think Morwenna earns £12, so, as she's older, £10 would be about right?' He'd expected her to quickly agree, but she pressed her lips tightly together.

'Um, well, thing is, my arn' only has herself to look after? And I 'ave Gary and Treen?'

'Gary and Treen?'

'My little brother and sister.'

'Oh, I see!' He didn't, really. Where were her parents? Morwenna had suggested her mother was feckless. But her father?

As though she could read his mind, she said, 'Mum's a bit … And my dad, well, he left a while back. So it's me looking after the kids, really.'

'Same wage as Morwenna, then?'

Still she pursed her lips. 'Mr. R., how 'bout I do it for £12 an hour for a month. And if at the end of that you like my work, you pay me £15.' Her skin was flushing.

'You'll have to do a great job to earn more than your aunt,' he said.

'Easy,' she said, with a small grin. 'Auntie Mor can't cook to save herself.'

He admired her spirit. And if it didn't work out he could easily fire her. 'Fine. Done.'

She crossed the kitchen and opened the fridge. There was a pause as she looked at its contents. 'There's not much in 'ere, is there?'

He had to admit she was right. He'd lost any ability to

plan and shop for meals. He lifted his hands helplessly. 'Is there something you can make from what's there?'

She took another look, then shook her head. 'Nah. But I can nip to Tesco's and get some stuff and then make dinner?'

'Marvellous!' He reached for his wallet.

'What do you want me to make?'

'How about a curry? Chicken? I like to buy organic or free range, if it's there. Apart from that, up to you.'

'Right-oh, Mr. R.' She took the twenty pounds he handed her. 'Next time, if you're 'appy with what I do, I can do a big online shop and they'll deliver it?' She made it sound as though Roger didn't know about online shopping. He was about to protest, then thought better of it. If he did, she'd surely wonder why he hadn't already ordered food. Ready meals were easy. It was ordering basic ingredients for home cooking that defeated him, because he didn't cook. He had to admit it sounded a bit feeble.

While Mel was gone, he re-read Anne's email. He'd managed to resist emailing back – what would be the point? – but if nothing else, it made it quite clear Jane wasn't there. Anne would surely have been unable to resist crowing if Jane had made it to Australia to get away from him.

Mel was back in less than half an hour with chicken thighs, brown rice, some good-quality curry paste and various herbs and vegetables. She handed him the change. He pocketed it and watched her as she moved assuredly around the kitchen. She had to ask for a few items – 'garlic press?' – but most she found quite easily on her own, as though Jane had put saucepans, wooden spoons and olive oil in the most logical positions.

There was no doubt that Mel knew what she was doing. It took her thirty minutes to make the curry and as she slid the plate in front of him onto the kitchen island, she gave him a smile of triumph. She ripped some coriander and sprinkled it over the top before standing back. The smell alone was proof she could cook. He took his first mouthful and shut his eyes for a second. Home cooking. He'd really missed it. When he opened his eyes again, she was staring at him.

'Is it okay?'

'It's bloody good, Mel.'

She blushed.

'Can you start this week?'

'I'll 'ave to move a couple of things. So, like, Monday, Wednesday, Friday, yeah? Is that what you want?'

'Please.' Roger didn't look up from his curry.

'It's just Treen likes me there after school. I'll 'ave to get Gary on it, useless little tick that he is.' Her voice was fonder than her words.

'Well, let me know.' He handed her one of his old cards. 'Ignore the "Karter's" bit. That's my number, okay?'

'I'll get back to you,' she said. 'Do you want me to wash up now?'

'Well, if you do, I'll pay you for three hours,' he said.

She beamed at him. 'I can also put a quick wash on for you, if you like, Mr. R.? Talk you through it?'

'That would be great.' He finished his food while she did the dishes and dried them. Then he fetched several shirts, a pair of jeans and some undies. He hesitated to give them to her – there was something over-familiar about giving dirty clothes to a stranger – but she made an impatient gesture which suggested she'd been handed worse. She led the way into the laundry.

'Right. So this is a mixed load, see? Different colours and textures. So safest is to put it on a 30-degree wash, not too hot.' She pointed out the symbol on the machine. 'And then the other thing to watch is how much laundry liquid you're using. If you use too much, clothes smell too strong and they can dry a bit stiff.'

He nodded, feeling foolish. 'What do you think went wrong with Alfie's jumper?'

She twisted her mouth. 'Honestly? Trying to get vomit out of stuff like that is a nightmare. I know. I've 'ad to do it for my ... Well, I've 'ad to do it. I think you'd better bin it.' She leaned forward and twisted the dial to the right symbol before pressing the large triangle next to it. A rush of water flooded the washing-machine drum.

'There! I put them on a short cycle with a fast spin. Won't take long to dry. You'll 'ave clean kecks tomorrow, Mr. R.!'

He hoped she couldn't tell that he didn't have any clean undies to wear at all.

He placed three ten-pound notes and six pound coins in her hand, which closed over them tightly. With any luck, her mother wouldn't find the money before she'd exchanged it for food or clothing or whatever Gary and Treen – Treen? Short for what, for Pete's sake? – needed. She gave him a hesitant smile, pulled her coat on and left.

WITHIN A WEEK, he couldn't understand how he'd ever coped without Mel. She arrived on the dot of four p.m. on the allocated days and would work tirelessly until one minute after six. On her first official evening she spent almost an hour setting up his online shopping list after dismissing Jane's Ocado account – 'Let's just start again on Waitrose, Mr. R., in your name, like' – which meant that subsequent orders took just a few minutes.

After that, her time was always spent in a well-organised fashion. She would batch-cook a casserole or curry. Ladling the food into Tupperware containers, neatly labelled with handwritten stickers, she would put them into the fridge and then would 'pop a load on', as she put it: sheets or towels or anything he'd left in the washing basket. She would put the cooled Tupperware in the freezer and the washing in the dryer once the cycle finished. The smell of fresh laundry pervaded the house after her visits. She was always smiling and he found her engaging company. The only down side was the radio blaring while she cooked. But it was a small price to pay.

And the days that overlapped with Alfie worked even better. Although not initially. At first, Alfie had eyed Mel with enormous suspicion, his face solemn.

He'd tugged at Roger's hand. 'Woger, why is her –'

Roger stopped him. 'Alfie, this is Mel. She's very nice.'

Mel squatted down in the hallway and held out her hand. 'Hi, Alfie.'

'But Woger –'

'Alfie, ask me later,' Roger said, hastily.

But Alfie wouldn't be contained. 'Blue!' he said, pointing to Mel's Afro.

Roger felt a huge rush of relief.

Mel gave him a quick glance that told him she knew exactly what he'd feared Alfie would say. 'I like blue. Do you want to touch it?' She leaned forward.

Alfie put a hesitant finger on a springy blue coil.

'I'm Mel. You can call me Mel, or Melissa, or Melly-Belly, or Meleficient, or Mel- Mel, or whatever you like, okay? My little sister, Treen, she calls me all them names.'

Alfie considered it. 'Melly-Belly?'

'Sure.' She stood easily. 'If that's your favourite. And I'll call you Halfie-Alfie. Because you're half the size of a person; you're so little.'

'I almost fwee!' Alfie held up two fingers and a thumb, looking indignant.

'Halfie-Alfie. It suits you.' Mel walked off and Alfie looked at Roger as though making up his mind. He followed Mel into the kitchen, where she was starting to prepare arancini balls.

'Do you like arancini?' she asked.

Alfie took a big sniff of the fragrant air. 'Yes?' he said cautiously.

'They're yummy,' Mel said. 'You can try one, if you like.'

Alfie did like, and ate three without any prompting from Roger. After that, he and Mel were firm friends.

Roger often found himself wondering if they should keep Mel once Jane got back. It would take the weight off her and leave her more time to spend with him.

Because it wasn't the cooking, cleaning, washing, shopping Jane he was missing. It was the Jane who talked about the Radio Four podcast she'd just listened to. Or the article she'd read in *The Guardian* about the alarming reduction in insect numbers, and did they want to stop using chemicals in the garden? The Jane who organised theatre trips to London which he had complained about at the office – 'Another liberal play about the evils of capitalism! Not my idea of a good night out, folks,' he'd say, shrugging on his coat and reaching for his briefcase – but enjoyed very much. The Jane who touched his cheek whenever she brought him coffee or tea, a tiny moment of affection that was now automatic but no less affectionate for that. The Jane who was so loving yet familiar to him in bed that he forgot how lucky he was that this – the side of marriage that sometimes died when children and life's trials came along – still worked for them.

He felt at a loss about what to do to get her back. He alternated between acceptance that she wasn't returning for another ten weeks, and outrage that he couldn't drag her home, kicking and screaming, to her place. Here, with him.

The idea that she wouldn't be there with them at Christmas seemed impossible. Surely she would come home before that. One morning, as he was drifting towards wakefulness, he dreamed that she did come home. On Christmas Day. Her present to him was to be present on Christmas Day. The joy made him smile sleepily to himself. Except that then, in the dream, they had the most fearful row about the lack of Christmas lunch, the complete absence of presents, decorations, a tree; anything, in fact, that indicated this was the peak of the festive season.

He jolted awake with a hand to his chest. It was November. *Mid*-November. He'd need to find out where she was in the planning process. Once he'd eaten breakfast and had a coffee, he sat down at the computer. In clean clothes and underwear. The house felt under control with Morwenna and Mel sorting their various areas out. He was rather proud of how he'd managed that.

His email was short.

From: Roger Kurmudge
To: Janes Away Hurray
Subject: Christmas
Jane, if you persist in staying away, please let me know what the plan is for the boys' presents. And what the plan is for Christmas lunch. I assume you'll order from Ocado. I am very much hoping you will return before then to help.
Roger

He didn't expect a response until the evening but he got one at eleven a.m.

From: Janes Away Hurray
To: Roger Kurmudge
Subject: Ah, yes. Christmas
The presents are in the shops. I haven't planned anything. Over to you. Get cracking. Maybe take advantage of Black Friday, that's coming up.
As for Ocado, no, I won't be ordering. Perhaps you should? And you should plan with the boys who will cook, etc?
Give my love to Alfie and Killer. I do miss them.

17

Christmas was coming. Like a dental appointment, or surgery, or a court date.

The sense of impending doom made him speak to Andy the following evening, as he dropped Alfie home. Andy looked spent. He'd clearly just got home himself, loosening his shirt collar and cricking his neck to get the kinks out as he opened the door to them.

'Hi, Dad. Has he been good?'

Alfie marched past, saying, 'Snack!'

'I just fed him,' Roger said.

'I know, he's an eating machine at the moment. Do you want to come in?' The words were inviting but the face was less so. Andy looked like he needed a beer and a sit-down, not a heart-to-heart with his father.

But Roger accepted and stepped into the hallway. 'I wanted to talk about Christmas. Do you know, your mum said she isn't coming home for it?'

In the untidy sitting room, Andy dropped onto the sofa. He yawned and put his head back on the cushions. 'I sort of assumed not. I can do the maths. We heard about the three-month thing in October.'

'So who's going to cook?' Roger demanded.

'We could always go and have Christmas with Sarah's family, Dad.' Andy ran his hands through his hair and cricked his neck again. 'If it's too much for you.'

'It's not too much for me,' Roger said, registering that somehow he was not only volunteering to host but was doing the cooking, too. He wasn't sure how he'd arrived at this juncture. But he didn't want to spend Christmas day alone, and if they went to Sarah's family, he might be. Would Sam come without Andy being there? It would be fine, he thought. He'd get Mel to do it.

BUT MEL, when he asked her, shook her head instantly. 'Can't, Mr. R. I mean, I can get stuff ready, maybe. Help you shop a bit and everything. But I need to be with Treen and Gary. I can't be 'ere on Christmas day.' He was paying her £15 an hour now and he knew she needed the money. If she said she couldn't come, she meant it.

'When you say, "get stuff ready",' Roger said, 'what do you mean?'

She thought about it. 'I can do some veggie prep and obviously get the turkey and stuffing ready and everything. I suppose we could pre-cook the turkey, maybe? Get it ready and you could just heat up slices? We could deffo do that with the ham.'

Now it was Roger's turn to think about it. Pre-prepared food sounded like a lot less hassle. He could even go to Marks & Spencer and get the whole thing: there'd been an ad on the TV the night before suggesting that very idea. But an image flashed into his head of silver foil trays full of food being decanted into dishes and presented to his smirking family. And murmurs of 'Told you Dad wouldn't be able to do it' stifled behind hands. Comparisons with how Jane did it over mulled wine, while he sorted out mounds of recycling in the kitchen. He felt anger rising. He'd damn well show them all. He could easily cook one bloody dinner. He'd been CEO, for God's sake, of a major multinational business. Overseeing hundreds of millions of pounds. How hard could it be?

'Don't worry about it,' Roger said. 'I'll do it. I mean, it would be great if you could help sort out ordering it all in and everything. But I'll cook it.'

'Right,' Mel said after a pause. 'No worries, Mr. R.'

She handed him a list two days later. He took it from her, realising as he did so that it covered two sides of A4.

'What's this?' he asked.

'What you need for Christmas. Lunch, with starters, like – seafood stuff. An' desserts an' crackers an' two types of stuffin', two types of meat an' a turkey, cranberry sauce an' bread sauce, champagne, olives, chocolates …' She took a huge breath in and before she could continue, Roger said:

'Really? Seriously? This is what the Christmas list looks like?'

'Yeah. I mean, not at my 'ouse. But 'ere, yeah.'

Roger looked at her. 'So how did you know what should be on my list?'

She looked a bit bashful. 'I watched a couple of cooking shows about getting ready for Christmas. Saw an online article about it. An' this is what they said you need.'

'Blimey.' Roger read through the list slowly. 'And you'll get this all delivered?'

'Yeah. Better crack on, though, Mr. R., I reckon most of the slots for Christmas delivery 'ave gone.'

He was panic-stricken. 'Order it now, could you? I'll pay you double time if you stay till you have.' He still was hesitant to order anything more complex than a ready meal online. The person who knew how to cook should order the food, he thought.

She pursed her lips, then nodded and made a quick call. He tried not to overhear but couldn't avoid it.

'... jus' for once, Gary? Please? It's worth it, okay?'

She came off the phone and followed him into his office, where she logged on to the Waitrose website and with rapid efficiency got all the items, with a few minor exceptions, checking with him as she went.

'You'll be wanting the best welfare turkey, am I right, Mr. R.? How big? Enough for eight, maybe? And which champagne? Veuve do you? What about some choccies? How many bottles of the red?' A silence after his answer. 'Okay.'

As the process went on, he felt more and more ashamed of the clear contrast between his Christmas and hers. It was so awkward to sit with this girl listing the gluttony he'd be indulging in when her Christmas was going to be so different. He wondered what they would have for Christmas lunch. Finally, she sat back and took a final look at the screen of items. 'There! Got everything. Happy, Mr. R.? You just need to pay. I've sorted out delivery for two days before Christmas. It's a rubbish slot, late at night, but at least I got one.' She stood up and stretched.

Roger slid into the seat and got out his credit card. 'Thanks, Mel. Now, as well as paying you for your time, I'd like to order Christmas lunch for you, too. If there's a spare delivery slot.'

She gaped at him. 'You can't do that.'

'I can.' He was sharply aware that he was paying to reduce his discomfort levels.

A huge tear welled up in her eye and dropped down her cheek. 'That's so ... so *nice* of you. But honestly, I can't let you. And ... I mean, if I'm honest, I'd prefer ...'

'Prefer what?'

'The money. We're a bit behind on the rent and stuff.' She was twisting her hands together, and scowling now to stop the tears.

He looked away to give her a chance to compose herself. 'Of course. I totally understand. How about, though, for Gary and Treen, I order just a simpler list? And give you some money? Like a bonus?'

'A bonus?'

'A Christmas bonus.'

'I dunno what a bonus is.'

'It's a payment you receive to reward you for working hard and going the extra mile. A payment that you're not really counting on.' *Although, of course, he'd always counted on his.* 'To help with Christmas expenses.'

She looked incredulous. 'Really?'

'Really.' He put his credit card details into his order, and once it had finished processing, he said, 'Come and sit here,' he stood up and vacated the chair, 'and order what you'd like for your family, please. Whatever you'd like.'

She looked so deeply uncomfortable, he wondered if he'd made a mistake in suggesting it. But eventually he was able to lead her through it. Yes, she'd love a turkey, just a little one: they had a small kitchen with a tiny oven. Maybe some sage and onion stuffing and some cranberry sauce and some crackers and some Prosecco (she refused to order champagne), and some chocolates and various vegetables, and gravy stock.

'Anything else?' he asked.

'My mum really loves Baileys,' she said. 'An' it's the one time of the year that she's 'appy when she drinks, so I don't mind.'

'Baileys it is,' he said.

She put in the address and he realised it was in one of the poorest areas of Guildford, a street he'd never driven down despite living in the area for many years. She stood up for him to put in his credit card details. He finished, and heard a muffled sound. He turned to see that she had her hands over her eyes.

'Are you all right?' he asked.

'Yeah, I'm fine. Thanks, Mr. R. This is … the nicest thing ever.' She broke down and sobbed.

Roger didn't quite know what to do next. Where the hell was Jane when he needed her? This conversation was women's work. 'Are things that bad?'

The sobbing intensified. It turned out, when he coaxed the information out of her, that things were really very bad. That she and Gary and Treen were often hungry in the holidays, when school dinners weren't available. That food was expensive and there were bigger priorities, such as rent. She couldn't stop crying once she'd started; her chest heaved and her nose ran.

'How often have you had Christmas lunch?' Roger asked as the tears slowed.

'Maybe once. Before my dad left. I seen pictures. I don't remember it. I 'ad a party hat an' everything. A paper one.'

Jane would know what to do. She'd know how to help this girl without it seeming like charity that didn't make Mel feel good about herself. What Mel needed was a plan. To lift her out of this and into something better than helping Roger, much as he hated the thought of her leaving.

'What A-levels are you doing?' he asked.

'Chemistry an' biology an' maths.'

'Maths?' He was impressed.

'Yeah. I like maths.'

'And after you finish A-levels? Then what?'

'Dunno. It's a problem. I need to stay close for Treen an' Gary. Mum's not good. They need me. And I need a job. Like, a proper one.'

'Maybe I can help after Christmas? Give you some advice? Help you look at options?'

She sniffed vigorously and he tried not to wince. He held out a box of tissues and she took one and blew her nose for a few seconds. 'Thanks, Mr. R. I'm okay really.'

He found some cash and paid her generously and watched as she left, pulling her coat around her, a dejected figure apart from the defiant hair. He'd have to think how to help her.

At least Christmas was sorted.

It took an hour for him to remember that in fact it wasn't.

The presents were in the shops, Jane had said. Which meant he needed to buy them.

Two days later it was Black Friday, which created a tsunami of greed and panic combined, if he was to go by reports on the news showing queues everywhere. He thought about wandering around Guildford in the cold, trying to make decisions while other people talked loudly about their own choices. No, he'd do it online. It would be easy. He just needed to think about what the boys and Alfie would like.

And Mel? And as for Morwenna and Gail, surely just money in an envelope would do?

He pulled a piece of paper towards him and put the names down.

Andy
Sam
Alfie
Jane
Mel
Killer???

What could he get the boys? Roger thought for a few moments, then smiled to himself. He had the perfect gift for them. They'd be impressed. They'd realise he was just as good at this as Jane. He logged on to the John Lewis website and found the bean-to-cup coffee machine with the best reviews. He was a little startled to see the price point – surely £1,499 was rather a lot for a coffee maker? Even with £100 off, it seemed a lot – but the boys would be thrilled. He stuck two in the online basket. He found a large Lego Duplo set for Alfie – £89. Now for Jane.

What did his wife want? He grimaced to himself. Who knew? The woman was becoming a mystery. But gazing around the room, his eye was caught by her portrait of Andy when he was ten. It was really rather fine. It captured Andy in some essential way. She was very good at faces, although not great at hands, as she herself would freely admit. They were all too large and they looked a little warped. She almost never painted now. The room above the garage, which had been allocated as her studio when they first moved in, had never been properly used for painting. It was full of overspill from the garage and he couldn't see that changing.

True, there was an easel in one corner, but it was almost hidden by skiing equipment, a four-man tent that the boys had taken to festivals a few times, two boogie-boards and two wetsuits from a summer holiday in Cornwall fifteen years ago; three mountain bikes which hadn't been ridden for years and weren't good enough for the boys to take with them when they moved out, a gas stove, and sundry miscellaneous clutter.

But when she got back from this competition, she'd want to paint. Of course she would. Through the window, he could see the bird feeders shaking a little in the breeze. A thought struck him: Jane loved the garden. She would adore something like that cabin David Cameron had got for himself after resigning. (But a bit less expensive, Roger hoped.) He idly clicked through to the John Lewis garden section. There it was. He sat up straighter. A *garden studio*, it was called. Two of Jane's favourite things slapped together. They would assemble it for you. It looked marvellous. She'd love it. It was a punchy price point, he had to admit, but it would make her so happy. He put it in the basket.

When he came to check out, he had to suppress a small gasp at the total. Almost twenty thousand pounds, most of which was the garden studio. The website flagged up that he'd need a concrete base to put the studio on in the garden, and that it wouldn't be delivered until after Christmas. He thought for a second. It wasn't a problem. At this rate, Jane wasn't going to be delivered home until after Christmas either. He clicked on the button and got the confirmation email.

Mel fell into the same category as Morwenna. She needed money more than stuff. And help longer term, he thought. To get out of the life she was trapped in. He tapped his pen on his teeth as he thought about it. There had to be more he could do. Jane would know how to help. In the meantime, he would give her the most useful thing he could: cash towards the rent problem she'd mentioned.

Killer was his final issue, and the idea of a dog present was more for Alfie than the dog. He found a website selling dog Christmas stockings full of treats and clicked a couple of times to finalise his purchase. He sat back. Christmas was done. He'd smashed it, as the boys would say. Even Jane would be impressed.

His feeling of deep satisfaction lasted until his phone pinged.

Dad, just a quick text to say I'm off to Italy to find Mum! Took some time off work. Will text you when I find her. Andy x

18

Andy had always found it difficult to sleep, and in the weeks following his mum's departure his insomnia got worse. Now he wasn't just lying in bed fretting over bills, work, Sarah's desire for another child (could they afford one, though?), Alfie's potential schooling costs in the future and an insidious concern that life wasn't quite working out the way he had thought it would. Now he was worrying about his lies to his dad about where his mum was.

The weeks since she had been gone had brought about rather a startling change in Roger. He was a much nicer person to be around, and Alfie was getting positively fond of him. They had fun together these days, and certainly Killer looked happy enough. While this was a good thing, it meant Andy felt increasingly guilty about lying to his father. Sometimes when they talked about Jane, his dad's eyes reminded him of Killer's when the dog was after some bacon. It was true Roger was no better at putting that yearning into heartfelt words than Killer would have been, but his eyes did it for him. Roger's need for Jane to come back was so raw at times that Andy felt awkward witnessing it.

One evening after three beers instead of his usual weeknight limit of two, he tossed and turned until Sarah said sharply, 'Oh for God's sake, bloody move if you can't sleep. I'm shattered!'

He pulled on his dressing gown and went down to the kitchen. Opening the fridge, he stared into it for a snack, but nothing appealed. He wandered into the sitting room and put the TV on. He needed something bland to watch to put him to sleep. *A Place in the Sun*, maybe. Maybe not. It might remind him that his mum was currently sunning herself on the other side of the world.

He opted instead for a new episode of a true crime series he was enjoying. This one was about a man who decided to fake his own death to claim insurance money. Andy could have told him it would be harder than he thought with modern technology. The man seemed quite indignant when he was caught, and very keen to tell his side of the story.

'I told my wife not to tell anyone I was going to South America,' he said plaintively. 'Just in case she couldn't keep her trap shut, I left Brazil after a few weeks cos it was actually not my cup of tea; I went to Majorca instead, then. I had a fake passport and everything, cost me a couple of grand. It's this surveillance society we live in. A man's not free any more!'

Andy sat up as a thought hit him. He was assuming Jane was still in Sydney. But what if she'd moved? Come back to England, or to Bordeaux? He couldn't fly to Australia to find his mum. Not just because of money or annual leave – although those things were also a problem – but mainly because he was terrified of flying. But Bordeaux was easy.

He could do a trip over two days, like his dad had. He could persuade her to come home and make things normal again.

He went back to the kitchen and got his laptop from his work bag, which was hanging on the back of a chair. He decided it would be worth getting Jamie back on the case, and pinged off a quick question.

THE FOLLOWING MORNING, he checked his emails.

From: Jamie Private PI
To: Andy Kurmudge
Subject: Too easy, mate!
That's what the Aussies say on *Home and Away*. And this really was. Because you could have done it, honest you could. First, I checked her emails and she left Aus on a flight to France about a week ago. I was hoping to try my new IP address-finding app or my facial recognition software but didn't need them. She's got some connection with an art gallery in Paris. I did a Google search and I found information about her on their website and her photo. She never even changed her name! (Basic mistake if she wanted to disappear. Honestly, you need to talk to her about this stuff.) It's Galerie LeBlanc. Owner is Sandrine LeBlanc. Your mum doesn't seem to have a hotel booking anywhere though so perhaps she called someone to sort that out? Best way to find her is at that gallery. I feel a bit bad taking your money, but I want to get a Blunder Bug. (It's not an actual bug, ha ha!) My fee is £55, please. Could you meet me at the same place and give me cash? Let me know what day suits you after school. Not a Tuesday, I've got chess club.
Laters!
J

A GOOGLE SEARCH? Andy couldn't believe how easy finding his mum had been this time. Paris was totally possible. He could go and get her and bring her home. He'd tell her how improved Roger was and persuade her to return to their lives and make it all normal again. Breathing a sigh of relief, Andy shut his laptop and went back to bed.

He announced over breakfast that he had to go to Paris to get his mum back, and although Sarah was clearly irritated, she could see the benefit of having Jane returned to them. He made a 'family emergency' excuse at work – ignoring Vivian as she asked him loudly, 'Taking the day off to sort out the rash, Andy?' – and got on the Eurostar two days after receiving Jamie's email.

On the train, he clicked through on his phone to Sandrine's website. There it was: an oil painting of Sydney Harbour, from an unusual angle so that the perspective looked distorted. There was a white smudge where the Opera House should be. Andy vaguely remembered a term his mum used: 'anamorphic perspective'. Maybe this was that? Where you only saw the Opera House if you stood next to the painting in exactly the right spot because it was painted on a slant? He wasn't sure but as far as he could tell, his mum really did have talent.

There was a picture of his mum on the website with a brief biographical statement: *Jane Kurmudge est anglaise. Ses oeuvres reflètent ses passions: ses voyages, sa famille et le beau paysage près de sa maison.* Jane Kurmudge is English. Her work reflects her passions: travel, her family and the beautiful countryside near her home.

Andy was relieved to hear that his mum was still passionate about her family. Especially as he was defying her request to give her some space and leave her alone. He just hoped she'd forgive him for turning up. A gnawing thought nagged at him all the way to the Gare du Nord: what if she'd left? What if she'd moved on again?

He had been to Paris often enough to feel comfortable although his French was rusty. It was nice to be back in the city after two years of taking child-friendly holidays in Bordeaux that largely involved hanging around the pool all day and making sure Alfie didn't drown. Andy breathed in the smells of fresh croissants as he passed a bakery and enjoyed a svelte Frenchwoman berating her boyfriend about his inability to park closer to the pharmacy.

He had decided to walk to the gallery to avoid catching the métro, which would trigger his anxiety about being underground – and, if he was honest, to delay the moment of discovery or disappointment. He hadn't told Sandrine he was coming. He didn't want to frighten his mum off. (Not, of course, that there was any *reason* to frighten her off. She wasn't a fugitive, was she? Although she had told them a version of 'keep your trap shut and don't tell your father where I am'.)

He started to feel increasingly anxious as he approached the gallery. His French really was a bit rusty and he very much hoped whoever he spoke to at the gallery would be kind, helpful and excellent at English.

The gallery itself was in the Marais district, down a narrow street. Andy had assumed it would be sleek and glossy like Nina's gallery in Guildford where he'd visited his mum one day, but this had an edgier, more urban vibe to it. The industrial glass door was heavy as he pushed it open, and he let it swing to behind him as he took in the space.

It was a long rectangle with a whitewashed ceiling and polished concrete floor: so far, so normal for a gallery. But what set it apart was the profusion of canvases: they hung with almost no gaps between them at all and covered all styles of painting and all manner of subject matter. It didn't have the stark pretentiousness of the galleries he'd been in previously, and Andy thought it was all the better for it.

In the near corner was a small counter with a young woman standing behind it. The name badge pinned to her high-necked blouse said Elodie. She greeted him cheerfully: 'Bonjour, Monsieur!'

He greeted her back. '*Bonjour! I, er, je cherche la peinture de ma mère.*' I'm looking for my mother's painting.

The young woman looked a little startled. '*Monsieur? Je ne comprends pas. Quelle peinture?*' I don't understand, which picture?

He'd known he might have a language problem. '*Est-ce que tu,* I mean *vous,* er, *parlez anglais?*' Can you speak English?

'I can try.' Her accent was enchanting.

'I think you have a picture here my mum painted. Can I look?'

She swept an arm around. '*Mais bien sûr!* Of course!'

He glanced around, looking for the picture he'd seen on the website. He couldn't see it so he walked the length of the room, darting quick glances at each painting and the small card fixed beneath it with details of the artist. It was only when he was returning to the desk on the other side of the room that he finally found her. He was grateful for the name cards, as he would never have recognised the angry orange sky brooding over a raging bushfire bleeding sparks as something his mum could have produced. It seemed full of rage or angst. 'This is her. Jane Kurmudge.'

'*Ah oui!* Madame Kemuge. She is ... how do you say, very talented, *non?*'

'She is. Although this isn't really her usual thing,' Andy said. 'It's a bit ... bleak.' There was a carcass of an animal in the distance, now that he looked closely at the painting. Maybe a dead kangaroo, with wizened, blackened paws. It definitely wasn't a hopeful picture that he'd like in his house. More like a warning about apocalyptic climate change. 'She did another one? Showing Sydney Harbour?'

'Yes. It only came in a few days ago and we sold it. We had it in the window. Someone came in the same day and,' she snapped her fingers, '*poof!*'

'Do you know where she is?' Andy said. 'I came to surprise her.' He wasn't lying, after all. He'd definitely surprise her.

'*Ben ouais,*' she said, nodding. 'She is having *un p'tit café,* a coffee, with Sandrine this morning. Sandrine wants to do an *exposition* with her. More like the Sydney painting, you know? Less ...' She stopped and gestured at the bush fire. 'Very interesting, *mais ...*'

'An exposition?' Andy said. 'Do you mean an exhibition? Of lots of paintings?'

'*Oui.* Lots of paintings.'

Um, where is she having this *café*? I mean, coffee?'

'*Juste là bas,*' she said. 'Over there.' She pointed to an awning in the distance at the opposite end of the street.

'Thank you so much – *merci bien,*' Andy said. '*Bonne journée.*' Have a nice day.

She smiled at him and went back to staring at the brushstrokes licking the canvas and the dead kangaroo.

The café was larger than it had looked from outside. It was quintessentially French, to Andy's eyes. A display counter of elaborate patisserie behind a glass screen, with flat boxes piled on the shelves behind for takeaways. A woman with glasses was clearly waiting to take his order, but he was scanning the tables. Half were occupied, mostly with tourists, but at the back was Sandrine, an exuberant Frenchwoman whose full figure testified to her love of good food, and opposite her, with her back to Andy, was his mum. Andy felt a lump in his throat as he took in her neat grey-blonde bob and straight back.

Sandrine was in full flow: '... the most important thing for you will be to produce enough work for us to show your range and ...' She broke off and looked up as Andy stopped at their table. 'Andy! *Quelle surprise!*' She stood and kissed him on each cheek. 'You are so grown-up and handsome now!'

Jane was staring at him as though he was a ghost. 'How did you find me?' she said.

Sandrine frowned. 'Find you?'

'I didn't tell anyone I was coming,' Jane said. 'I just fancied a break.'

He sat down next to her and kissed her cheek, inhaling her familiar perfume. She looked well, he thought. Not ill or too stressed. Maybe there was an edge there that hadn't been part of her in Guildford, but apart from that she was just Mum. 'It's a long story. And I hope you've changed your email passwords.'

She frowned. 'Is everything okay? Alfie's all right?'

'We're fine. I just ... missed you and thought I'd take a day trip. See your paintings.'

'Yes, aren't they amazing? I always told her that she was too talented to stay at home with you boys!' Sandrine said. 'I was so happy when she rang me to say she was coming and I am so delighted to have the chance to show her work. Did you meet Elodie? At the gallery?'

'I did. I hear you've already sold something?' Andy said.

'The same day!' Sandrine said, flapping a hand at him. 'Can you believe it?'

'It was a wonderful piece,' he said.

Jane smiled. 'It's very nice to be painting again.'

'I heard you talking about an exhibition,' Andy said. 'Won't you need to paint a lot to have enough paintings to exhibit?'

'Yes,' she said, 'I will.'

'But you're coming home, right?' Andy said. 'You've had a break and restarted your career but now you're coming home?'

Jane's face grew stony. 'Not at the moment.'

'But what will I tell Dad? He thinks you won a competition. I told him about Nina and the gallery because, well, you didn't tell me *not* to, right?' He was beginning to sound like Jamie. 'So he went to see her and she told him you'd won a competition to paint in Italy.'

'Yes. That's what I told her when I needed time off work. And don't tell your dad anything at all.' There was no emotion at all in her voice.

'So,' he tried to muster his thoughts, 'in three months you'll be back. That means you won't be home for Christmas.'

'I know.'

'But you're always there for Christmas.' He knew he sounded childish, but even after he married Sarah they'd always spent Christmas Day with his parents. Her family wasn't very interested in Christmas or indeed Alfie, and Jane always made the day such a delightful experience that Sarah didn't even complain about going to his family every year. It was inconceivable that Jane wouldn't be there.

'Not this year. Your dad will need to get organised if he's hosting.' She sipped her coffee while Andy searched for words. Something that would bring his mum to her senses. She was acting so strangely. It was clearly his dad's fault.

'What exactly did Dad do?' he asked. 'You seem really angry with him.'

Sandrine coughed lightly. 'I'll get back to the gallery, I think.' She stood and said, '*Je t'invite* for the coffee, Jane. My treat.'

'*Merci.* I'll get the next one,' Jane said.

There was a long silence after Sandrine had paid and left.

Finally, Jane spoke. 'Andy, I don't mean to drag you into this.'

'I'm already in it, Mum. And honestly, you know that I'd always be on your side ...'

'Except?'

'Dad's much nicer now. I don't know if it's the fact he's got more time or what, but he's so much better with Alfie. I think Alfie is actually quite fond of him. And he misses you so much. Dad, I mean. Can't you forgive him being grumpy and selfish and come home?'

Jane drank the rest of her coffee, tipping the cup up to get the dregs. 'Roger and I have been married almost forty years. Do you really think grumpiness and selfishness are the reasons I left? Our marriage wouldn't have lasted two weeks if that was the case.'

There was only one thing his dad could have done that would make his mum react like this. 'He had an affair, didn't he?'

She tilted her head.

'Who with? How did you find out? Do we know her? Is it over, or still going on?' Andy had so many questions.

'A long time ago, and with no one we know, and does it matter how I found out?'

Andy fell back in his seat. He wished he'd ordered a coffee now, although it would make his heart pound and his stomach clench, so maybe it was better that he hadn't. 'Are you sure it's true?'

'The evidence was extremely compelling.'

Andy wanted to ask about the evidence but something about his mother's expression stopped him. He chose his words carefully. 'Mum, I know it's very upsetting to find something like that out, but honestly, if it was a long time ago, why don't you just come home and have a blazing row and make him grovel and offer to do whatever you want?' He leaned forward again and took her hand. It felt cold in his. 'If it was going on now, I'd get it, but it isn't. Surely that would be worse?'

'I don't think it would,' Jane said. 'If he was having an affair now it would almost be a relief, especially with retirement looming. I mean, if he disappeared every day for a couple of hours and left me in peace at home, it wouldn't be the worst thing.' For a second, her tone held a glimmer of humour. 'But he had the affair ages ago when I thought we were happy.' Her face looked suddenly old. 'And yes, I was angry that he was going to Sydney, and don't forget, this was before the internet and easy communication, and you were really challenging at the time. I understand why you were, but it was difficult to deal with on my own. And apart from that, I thought we were totally happy together.'

'He had an affair in Sydney?' Andy said. 'You went there to find out what happened?'

She nodded.

'He must have been lonely there, on his own. And that was ages ago, Mum,' Andy said gently. 'Such a long time ago, I bet he regrets it bitterly.'

'He would if he knew ...'

'Knew what?'

'How angry I am,' Jane said after a pause.

'So what are you going to do? Are you going to get divorced?' As a child, he'd worried constantly about divorced parents, along with other things that hadn't happened: missing a critical homework deadline, losing control of his bladder in class, being forced to speak to a popular girl in front of his sniggering classmates. He hadn't realised he still needed to worry about his parents divorcing.

Jane said, 'Do you want another coffee? I do.'

'No, thanks.'

She got up and ordered more coffee and a mille-feuille. Andy noticed a sharply dressed bald man with a neat beard having a coffee and a croissant at a nearby table and giving his mum an appreciative stare. Andy coughed loudly, and when the man looked over at him, Andy glared back. The man dropped his gaze.

His mum returned to the table and sat opposite him in the seat Sandrine had vacated. Her shoulders drooped a little. 'I don't know what I'm going to do, to return to your question. But at the moment I'm just staying here and painting and taking some time.'

'So I can't tell Dad anything?'

'No. I want him to sweat.'

'He's definitely sweating,' Andy said.

'Good.' Jane smiled at the waitress who delivered the coffee and the mille-feuille. 'You're young, but when you get to my stage in life, time's running out. I thought there'd be years for me to do the things I dreamed of. But I was tethered to Roger and the house and you boys,' she smiled to take some of the sting out of the words because *tethered* wasn't good, 'and I didn't mind. Well, not too much, anyway. The only good thing about that message is that it has set me free. I want to make something of what's left of my life. Do something I want to do when I want to do it. I mean,' she stuck an elegant little fork into the mille-feuille and cut off a corner, 'I'm still the bloody fool that sends him emails to keep him on track. I should have left him to sink.'

'But that would affect other people, too,' Andy said. 'Me and Alfie, and even Morwenna.'

'I know; that's why I do it.' She ate the mille-feuille, her eyes distant. 'Maybe I should cancel the direct debits. And redirect our mail. The bailiffs would arrive before he'd notice.' She focused back on Andy. 'Share this with me, please, it's huge. And tell me about Alfie. How is he? Does he still call your dad Woger? I do miss him.'

Before Andy could answer, the sharply dressed man approached their table, heels clicking on the tiled floor. This man – Andy struggled for the right description of him before coming up with *suave*, or worse, *dapper*, a word that no self-respecting Englishman of a certain age really aspired to be – was definitely a threat. On a good day, Andy's dad looked neat and presentable. But not suave. Never dapper. Andy's phone buzzed in his pocket. No doubt his dad was texting him yet again.

The man said something to his mum in French too rapid for Andy to follow. His mum was giggling – *giggling* – back and chatting equally quickly, then she handed him a small business card with Sandrine's gallery logo on it, and Andy said, 'What's he saying, Mum?'

'He's saying you're a lucky man to have such a beautiful wife. *Merci,*' she said coyly back to the man, who said to Andy, '*Chapeau!*' before leaving the café.

'And why the card?'

'Oh, he said he'd seen me around and did I live locally, and I just told him where I work – you know, at the gallery.'

Andy picked up his spoon and stuck it into the mille-feuille. 'But he actually thinks you're married to *me*. You didn't set him straight, did you?'

'No, what would have been the point? And here in France, with a president who's married to a much older woman, it's seen as perfectly normal.'

'Like affairs are?' Andy said.

Jane sipped her coffee, a small private smile on her face. 'You know, I'll have to stop at a *tabac*. I really fancy a cigarette.' Her expression was soft and nostalgic. 'Or maybe even a joint. I used to really enjoy a joint from time to time. When I was younger, of course. Perhaps I should try LSD. It's supposed to enhance your creativity.'

Andy had intended to return home that evening. But clearly there was no way he could. His mum was being approached in cafés by random blokes, handing them cards, and talking about *joints* and LS bloody *D*. After all those lectures when he was growing up about drugs and smoking. She was going completely off the rails. He'd have to stay a little longer and do his absolute best to make her come home before she decided that smooth-talking Frenchmen were the future, instead of grumpy, selfish Englishmen.

'Tell me more about the paintings you've been doing,' he said. 'I mean, you could do those at home, couldn't you? Still do an exhibition here, but paint everything at home?'

'I could,' Jane agreed. 'Or I could stay in lovely Paris with Sandrine and paint in her studio and enjoy myself.'

'You know, I think I'll stay for another day or two,' Andy said. 'You can show me where you're staying, and the studio.'

'Of course,' Jane said, 'if Sarah can cope without you?'

'She's fine. Dad's helping with Alfie,' Andy said. He didn't mean his tone to sound so pointed but he'd never seen his mum so fixed on something that didn't work for the rest of the family. Perhaps, he thought, he too was guilty of never quite seeing her as a person in her own right.

'I should hope so,' his mum said. 'About time he helped someone. Have the last piece of mille-feuille, sweetie. Then I'll show you Sandrine's studio and we can book you a hotel room.'

19

Any news? Let me know if you find your mum. Love, Dad

Roger sent several texts to Andy that day, and as the hours wore on he couldn't stop himself sending a plaintive message asking why he hadn't invited him along to Italy. He found himself asking Killer the same question that evening after a long, boring day.

Killer panted up at him.

'Why?' Roger repeated. 'I could have helped.'

Outside the light was fading. The days were short, and the dusky light in the room made him feel as though it was an omen, a reminder that his life was getting shorter, closer to the end. He shook himself slightly. He'd never been prone to introspection, but retirement had revealed that the reason wasn't simply his positive personality. Spending all day in a brightly lit office with the hum of conversation and machines and people moving about made it much harder to wallow in thoughts or emotions for very long. Working life had kept him moving along at a brisk clip.

Being home alone made it much harder. It was easy to start looking through photo albums, running a finger across Jane's face beaming out from a mane of blonde highlights. They'd been somewhere in Greece, in their late twenties. She looked like a woman with everything ahead of her. The boys must have been with them on the holiday, but there was no sign of them in this photo or the next one, which was of him and Jane together, his tanned arm slung around her shoulder and her slim hand on his leg.

They both looked so happy. His career had been on the up, she'd seemed very content being at home with the boys, who'd both been easy at that stage, not showing any signs of dyslexia or the anxiety that would plague Andy's teenage years. Or the bullying that had marred Sam's.

He turned the page. Andy and Sam in the pool on the same holiday, batting an inflatable ball to each other, with Jane in her bright red bikini reading in the background. For the first time, Roger noticed that the waiter delivering a drink to Jane was staring at her as though he was starving and she was lunch. Had Roger realised at the time how attractive she was? Had he enjoyed the male attention she received? Or been annoyed? He couldn't remember.

The next album: photos of them moving into the house. A removal truck on the driveway, and Jane in baggy jeans walking towards the house with a large box in her arms. They'd stretched themselves to buy the place. She'd been worried that he might lose his job or be demoted. Instead, he'd been offered the role in Australia and had jumped at it. He scanned the photos. He'd left a month after they'd moved in, when they still had boxes around. Now that he'd put the timing together, he could see tension in Jane's face. She looked thin and tired, worry lines around her mouth.

A photo of her with her mother, the latter in a chair with

her leg in a cast, brought back the faxes he'd got from Jane at the time. He'd felt she was moaning, always telling him about how fragile her mother was, how much she had to do for her, what a terrible time Andy and Sam were having at school. He, Roger, was on his own in Sydney, trying to make his name at work during the week and trying to find people to spend time with at the weekend. He wasn't perhaps as sympathetic as he should have been. And now his guilt was made even worse by nostalgia. What wouldn't he give to go back in time and enjoy their youth again, this time with the full understanding of just how lucky they were.

Another page and he was looking at his own face at Heathrow when he returned, tanned and smiling. Next to him, Jane, looking in the other direction as he aimed a kiss at her cheek. Her posture was taut. Now he remembered. She'd taken weeks to thaw. He'd been thoroughly irritated that she hadn't shown much interest in his experiences – the ones he'd been happy to share – such as trips to the Blue Mountains and snorkelling on the Great Barrier Reef. He wondered now what life would have been like if she'd come with him for the secondment, brought the boys. Would they still be there? Would they be happier? Would she be with him now, rather than in Italy? For a start, he wouldn't have had the affair. He wouldn't have been lonely and stupid.

He turned a final page. Her mother's funeral. Andy had had a new camera for Christmas just before Jane's mother had died, and Roger remembered telling his son that no one took pictures at a funeral. This one had somehow made its way into the album. Jane in the foreground, with suspiciously shiny-looking eyes. In the background, he was shaking hands with someone and laughing, mouth stretched wide, head back. He didn't even recognise the bloke he was acting so matey with. Jane would know who he was. Something stirred in his memory, a wisp of a fight they'd had afterwards; something about him networking while she buried her mother. He shut the album and sighed.

THE FOLLOWING DAY, he checked his phone constantly for a message from Andy: as he was eating, when he put the TV on, before he sorted out the dishes. Was this what modern dating was like? From the reality TV shows he'd glimpsed, he thought it might be. He didn't enjoy it at all.

Even Mel caught him at it. She'd been talking to him about how to prepare Christmas lunch and he'd glanced at the phone, convinced it had vibrated slightly. It hadn't.

'Mr. R.? Are you waitin' for a call?'

'No, no, carry on.' He stared at the PC screen, where she'd set up an excel spreadsheet of all the actions required to prepare a magnificent lunch.

'So like I was saying, Mr. R., I'd get that turkey out early, like, so it's not too cold. Slows the cookin' up. Cos timin' will be everything on the day, Mr. R. Can't stress that enough.' She peered at him. 'Let's go over it another time, yeah?'

'Yeah,' he said, already looking back at the blank phone screen. After all, surely Andy would find Jane and persuade her to come home in time for Christmas and Roger wouldn't need to do lunch. He'd be sitting with a glass of champagne, watching his beautiful, capable wife make it as she always had.

He wanted to keep texting Andy to ask him if he'd found her, spoken to her, told her how much they all missed her. How much *he* missed her. She could go back to finish her art course afterwards, of course, but surely she could come home for Christmas? He'd ordered a case of her favourite champagne, Bollinger. To show her how sorry he was for taking her for granted. They'd keep Mel on, at least for the next year or so while she finished school. He and Jane could take Killer and Alfie out together once she was home permanently. It would be much more manageable with both of them. They could do those trips to London to see Cirque du Soleil, and maybe Roger could even take them to Paris. Not Killer, of course. Hannah for him.

TWO DAYS after Andy had departed, a delivery truck pitched up with two coffee machines and a large box of Lego and he put them in the spare room cupboard, ready for Jane to wrap when she came home. Suddenly, as he shut the door on the boxes, the lack of texts seemed like a good omen. Andy must have found her. Convinced her that she could paint at home, that she didn't need to stay in Italy. Yes, Andy would bring her home. He had no need to text his dad; he'd just bring her back, and present her to him like a prize, straight from the airport.

From that moment, every knock at the door, each ring of the doorbell injected adrenaline into his bloodstream. He had to control his reaction after the postman asked him, 'All right, Mr. Kurmudge? You look like you've seen a ghost.' He'd taken the post and tried to nod cheerfully. Disappointment had drained all the colour from his face. He had to trust Andy, that was all. Andy would sort it out. He just had to wait.

In the meantime, Christmas was drawing ever closer. Mel had finished her spreadsheet for timings; she printed it off and pinned it to the noticeboard in his office.

'If you just stick to that, Mr. R., you'll be sorted,' she said.

She then took him through it again, reminding him of all the steps required to go from raw materials to a fully cooked Christmas lunch. He asked her if she would teach him to cook something every week once Christmas was over. When Jane came back, he'd be able to help cook from time to time.

'That's a good idea, Mr R. I'm teaching Treen, too; maybe she can come 'ere and you could learn together?'

Once Mel had gone home, he read the plan carefully again. This was manageable. It would be a great day, he knew it would. Jane would be back and grateful that so much of the planning had been done for her. He'd bought everyone thoughtful presents. There'd be delicious food, organised by him to great acclaim from everyone.

Something about the planning gave him an idea. Perhaps he could throw a party. For their fortieth wedding anniversary in June. She'd be back then, and he wanted her to know how much he loved her and – perhaps more importantly – appreciated all her hard work over the years to help him build this life. Their life.

Hard on the heels of this first thought came a second. Jane had wistfully suggested certain elements for their wedding that he'd vetoed at the time because of cost. The nicest hotel nearby, Watney Manor, which had two Michelin stars, for the reception. A three-tier wedding cake with a chocolate layer in the middle. Champagne for the toasts. Those chairs that always looked 'gussied up' with large bows.

She hadn't had any of it. They'd gone to the local registry office and had a few people at the pub for a long lunch. None of it had been very flashy.

Nor had she had a really nice ring. Her ring was a thin gold band with a chip of diamond in it; it had still cost him the better part of a month's salary at the time. Over the years, he'd wondered if he should upgrade it, but she'd never hinted at wanting something better and he'd convinced himself that the original ring would be full of sentimental value for his wife. Like the time she'd swung around in the kitchen of The Grange when they were viewing it, with her arm at shoulder height to show him how high she'd want the new cupboards to be and had caught him near the eye with the ring. He still had a tiny scar. Now he found himself looking at jewellery online and considering a rather significant upgrade.

After a bottle of good burgundy, he made an online enquiry at Watney Manor and received an enthusiastic response the following day. Why, yes, they did have availability in June. On a Saturday. A cancellation. The rough quote for hiring the room and hosting an anniversary party made Roger wonder if the cancellation was due to another couple deciding to use the money for a house deposit instead. Or else having such a ding-dong row about the cost that they'd called the whole thing off. But he paid the deposit and reserved the day. Gussied-up chairs were, at least, included.

Three days after Andy went to Italy, with no Alfie that day and with no text from Andy either, Roger took himself and Killer off to Guildford to look at rings. At least it would kill time. There were several jewellers in Guildford but only one that he'd seen Jane linger at when she passed. The window displays at Malfields were so shiny that he almost needed sunglasses in spite of the gloomy weather. He tied Killer up and entered; inside, the glass cabinets were staring-at-the-sun bright. A smartly dressed woman of around forty with smooth blonde hair in an upswept style approached with a discreet smile.

'Can I help you with anything?' She gave him an

appraising look. He was certain she'd clocked his watch and the Range Rover key fob he was carrying and would calibrate her offerings to him accordingly.

'Yes. It's our anniversary soon and I wanted to give my wife something rather special.'

Her eyes sparkled almost as much as the window displays: Roger assumed she was on commission. 'Oh, how lovely! I'm quite sure we can find something truly delightful to give your wife. Her name is?'

'Jane.'

'And for Jane, are you thinking … earrings? A necklace? Bracelet?' She spoke the words lasciviously, wrapping her tongue around the vowels.

'I rather thought a ring,' Roger said. He followed her as she crossed the room briskly to a cabinet. 'Perhaps a diamond? Princess cut?' He'd heard Jane once say something about princess-cut diamonds, and when the woman held out a ring to him on a velvet cushion, reverently, as though it was a thing to be worshipped, he saw that it was a square shape. Why on earth, he thought, didn't people just say that? Although – he squinted at the price tag – you couldn't charge ten grand for something you simply described as square.

'This sort of thing?'

'Yes, perhaps.' He scanned the line of perfect, dazzling rings. 'That one?' He pointed.

'Oh, you have excellent taste,' she said. She lowered her voice. 'That ring really is exquisite.' She carefully opened the sliding door behind it and removed the ring. Up close it was rather large, Roger thought. He was trying to remember Jane's hands. They were quite small. Dainty. This ring was not something that would be described as dainty. Roger searched his mind for the right word. Whopping. Ginormous. Humongous, as the boys had said when they were growing up. It was perfect. As well as the central princess-cut diamond, it had small diamonds on either side. Like a diamond knuckle-duster. If you were scratched across the face with this ring, you'd really know about it. The scar would be something a Mafioso would be proud of.

The woman was telling him something about the Four Cs, its F colour, SI1 clarity and lack of inclusions, which meant nothing to him. But the words 'two carats' got his attention. He'd once had to sit through the boredom of Sarah discussing a friend's engagement and she'd remarked that two carats was a serious ring. Something that signalled real commitment.

'This ring is two carats?'

'Yes. The central diamond. And it's also the best possible quality.' She held it up to the light. 'Can you see? Almost colourless.'

He looked at it. She kept talking. Lots of words about it being reputably sourced and rather rare due to its high quality. Essentially, the only word he was interested in was whopping. Jane would not fail to see how much he'd missed her if he gave her this ring.

'And ...' He coughed lightly. He didn't need to say more. She turned the price tag towards him with a smile as bright as the ring. A man of his calibre, the smile insinuated, would not wince or turn away.

He didn't. But he did gulp quietly. More than the studio. Quite a bit more. The credit card was taking an absolute hammering. He squared his shoulders. 'That's fine. I would need to move some money around. May I come back for it next week?'

'Of course,' she breathed. 'Perhaps a small deposit? And if you could drop in one of your wife's existing rings, we can alter the ring to fit her exactly. For a purchase of this magnitude, we would also want to clean it and check that it's perfect before it leaves us.' She sounded as though she was talking about a much loved child leaving home for the first time. 'Next week would be ideal for you to pick it up. I'm sure Jane will be thrilled.'

The small deposit turned out to be a thousand pounds. A sleek man appeared suddenly to take payment and fawned over Roger, his taste, his elegance of vision. Much as Roger was enjoying it, he couldn't help but wonder what Jane would have made of it all. She was much less susceptible to flattery than he was. Meanwhile, Sleek Man was also trying to persuade him that the gift would be truly complete, would genuinely ensure his wife's total happiness forever, if it came with a wedding band studded with diamonds.

In a move Roger would have described as well-oiled, Sleek Man reached into the cabinet for a band and touched it reverently to the ring on the velvet cushion. The effect was to move the ring from elegantly whopping to utterly vulgar: something a Middle Eastern despot with a crush on an extremely materialistic supermodel might purchase to get her undivided attention.

An expectant pause filled the air.

'I think that might be a bit over the top,' Roger said.

The man nodded, resigned yet gracious, and handed Roger's credit card back to him.

Roger agreed to drop a ring off with them for sizing and left the shop. Stepping out into the thin wintry light, he still felt dazzled, as though he had actually stared directly at the sun. Jane would feel the same, he was certain. He could almost feel how happy she'd be as he slipped the ring onto her finger.

Killer was lying glumly on the pavement.

'Come on, then,' Roger said. 'Let's go home.'

Back at the house, he dug out the address book and the box of generic invitations Jane kept in the stationery cupboard of his office. He sent invites for the anniversary party to all their mutual friends – Benedict and Grainne, William and Elaine, Clive and Rebecca – and several of Jane's single friends. Should he invite Arthur and his family, too? No, why would he? They hadn't seen each other in years. But he'd invite Mel. She was part of his support network. Did that mean he needed to invite Morwenna? He dithered about it, then decided he could invite them later, once Jane was home. She'd know what to do.

20

'Daddy's home!' Alfie opened the front door, hopping from foot to foot.

'He's home?' Roger said. Why hadn't Andy texted him? Rung him? Where had he hidden Jane? Were they going to leap out at him, shout 'Surprise!'? He looked around slightly wildly, as though Jane might be peeking out from behind the coats in the hall. It was early. He'd had too much wine the night before, moving on to a second bottle, which he usually avoided. It had been very cold and there was nothing on TV. He'd felt he deserved more wine. Today he was regretting it.

'Woger, come!' Alfie grabbed his hand and dragged him up the hall and into the kitchen. Sarah was finishing her toast. Andy was making a coffee. He didn't turn towards Roger.

'You're back,' Roger said. The question in his voice was impossible to miss.

'Hi, Dad,' Andy said. 'I meant to call you, but I just grabbed the last flight yesterday and got home late, and I knew I'd see you today.'

'Where's your mum?' Roger said.

'I didn't find her.'

'Woger, look at my picture!' Alfie thrust a smudged piece of A4 in front of him. 'Big twuck. Like we seed at your work.'

'Didn't find her?' The thought hadn't occurred to Roger. There simply couldn't be that many art competitions in Italy. Or attractive sixty-something English women. Surely she could have been found by someone as keen on technology as his sons were. 'Lovely, Alfie,' he said, automatically. 'Why don't you put in a man with a yellow jacket, like the one we saw?' Alfie nodded and turned back to his craft table.

The two of them were mostly in sync now. That's what came of working as a tight-knit team day after day, withstanding regular interrogations about daily sugar intake without crumbling or admitting to eating two mini Kit Kats in one sitting followed by a cupcake. Just one look at each other, now, and they were able to wordlessly convey reams of information under Sarah's searing scrutiny. *Don't mention the Percy Pigs at the park. No one else needs to know about the hot chocolate with marshmallows and whipped cream at Bethany's café. Remember to throw away the wrapper from the Cadbury's Buttons packet when your mum isn't looking.*

Roger had read somewhere that children only learned to lie deliberately at around the age of three, and given that Alfie hadn't quite reached that age yet but could tell whoppers with absolute conviction – replying 'cawots' or 'wice cakes' whenever asked about his treats that day, blue eyes wide with sincerity – Roger was secretly rather proud. Alfie couldn't keep secrets about other people but he could keep his own. The boy was a chip off the Roger block, able to enjoy telling unimportant fibs. Roger wouldn't lie to the taxman, or a policeman, say – he muted the sly voice in his head saying *What about your wife?* – but if lesser matters were involved he felt no qualms. He couldn't explain why he enjoyed lying so much; it just felt as though he was evading scrutiny and control in a way that felt essential to his personal freedom. Alfie clearly felt the same, and it gave Roger a rush of pride in his grandson.

'No. I didn't find her.' Andy turned towards him and sipped his coffee. He looked terrible, Roger thought. He'd obviously tried his hardest to find Jane.

Nevertheless, Roger felt a pulse of irritation. 'Where did you look?'

'Er, Rome, Florence, Sienna.' Andy looked as though he was pulling the names of Italian cities out of thin air. 'I went all over. Tried everywhere I could think of. No one had seen her, or heard of the competition.'

'Where else could she have gone?' Roger said. 'Venice? Maybe we could go back together and have another look?'

'Dad, she's not in Italy. Trust me.' Andy finished his coffee and put the mug down on the kitchen counter, hard. 'I need to get to work. I've been away too long.'

Sarah muttered something. It sounded like 'too right'.

Roger put his hand out in a gesture he'd copied from Sarah. *Stop.* 'But what do we do next?' he said. 'I have to find her. I thought you'd bring her home.'

'Mum'll come home eventually.' Andy picked up his briefcase and stooped to kiss Alfie. 'Bye, mate, see you tonight.'

'Park, Woger!' Alfie said, throwing down the crayon and sprinting to get his shoes.

'But, I mean, *wait*,' Roger said. 'Doesn't that make it even more likely that something bad has happened to your mum? Where is she, for Pete's sake?'

'I don't know. I've tried my best. We'll just have to wait

till she comes home.' Andy walked down the hall and a moment later Roger heard the door slam behind him.

He sat down hard at the kitchen table. Alfie was tugging at his sleeve. 'Park, Woger. Wiv Killer.'

Sarah put her plate in the dishwasher and turned to pick up her bag. She paused. A look of something like sympathy crossed her face. 'Roger, I've had Andy away for the last few days and so I really do see how tough it's been for you. But for what it's worth, I don't think anything bad has happened to Jane. Those emails you're getting: do they sound like her? Or like someone who's under duress to write them? There's been no ransom or anything, has there?'

The emails definitely sounded like she'd written them. *The presents are in the shops ...* Definitely Jane.

'I suppose not,' Roger said. He roused himself. He wanted to go home and crawl under the duvet and sleep for a week. Instead, he had Alfie all day. 'While I remember, can you put 3rd June in your diary?'

'For what?' Sarah said.

'For an anniversary party. For Jane and I.'

'Jane and me,' Sarah said. For a second he wasn't sure what she was talking about. He'd forgotten she liked to pick people up on their grammar. She smiled. It reminded him of a crocodile. 'Yes, of course we will. There. You see? You can't be that worried if you're organising a party. And talking of calendars, can you put 14th January in yours?'

'For what?' Roger said, echoing her words.

She glared at him, all sympathy gone. 'For Alfie's birthday, of course. We're holding his party on the actual date itself.' She swept past him, gave Alfie a kiss, and slammed out of the house.

'Ready to go?' Roger said.

'Yes.' Alfie's eyes brightened. 'Wanna Feast!'

'Not a Feast today,' Roger said, adding hurriedly, 'but we can go to the café if you like?'

Alfie thought about it. 'Café now?'

Roger needed coffee. 'Fine. Café first.'

HE DIRECTED Alfie out of the car and got Killer on the lead. 'What do you want for your birthday, Alfie?'

'A camel,' Alfie said. 'A weal one.'

'Hmm,' Roger said. The old Roger would have snapped, *Don't be ridiculous*. New Roger mulled it over for a moment. 'Have you got room in your garden for a real one? They like sand, Alfie. Miles and miles of it. And you hate it when sand gets in your shoes. Perhaps a toy one would be easier?'

Alfie thought about it. 'Yes. A toy camel.'

'I see,' said Roger. 'A big toy or a small one that can sleep in your bed?'

Alfie's turn to mull it over. 'A *big* one.' He stretched his arms out in line with his shoulders and flipped his hands in to show how long the camel should be.

'Well, I'm sure we can try to find one of those,' Roger said.

They arrived at the café and Bethany greeted them. 'Why, hello! It's my favourite customer!'

Alfie grinned up at her. 'Beff, I be getting a camel for my birffday!'

'Wow,' Bethany said, 'a real one?' She'd swapped her nose ring for a tiny bright green ceramic stud; it looked as though a vibrantly coloured beetle had landed on her nose and decided to stay.

'No, silly!' Alfie said, heading straight for the back table, with Killer behind him. 'A toy.' He climbed onto the bench and Killer sidled under it, shuffled a bit and sighed deeply.

'What colour?' Bethany said, notepad poised in her hand to take their order.

Alfie looked around the café, at the vegan menus and healthy snacks board by the coffee machine. He peered at her nose stud. 'Gween,' he said.

'Good choice,' Beth nodded seriously. 'What will you have to eat?'

'Babycino. And toast with butter,' Alfie said with authority. He swung his legs on the bench and smiled at Roger. 'What you be having, Woger?'

'I be having ... I mean, I'm having a flat white and one of those flapjacks, please. Did you say please to Beth, Alfie?'

'Pease, Beff, pease babycino and toast with butter,' Alfie said.

Beth beamed at him. 'What a lovely boy you are! Coming right up.'

She was back a moment later. 'Can Killer have a dog treat?'

'Doesn't he always?' Roger said.

It was amazing, Roger thought, how quickly a routine was established and how strangely satisfying it could be. Alfie was thrilled to be at the café, as was Killer, and so Roger's day was made easier. He liked the company, too.

While Alfie ate his toast and slurped his babycino, Roger had ten precious minutes to flick through the paper, provided he also mumbled vague responses to Alfie's questions.

'Toast is cwunchy, Woger.'

'Yes. It's the Maillard reaction.'

'What's weaction?'

'It's when something changes, under heat. Makes things crunchy.'

'You like babycinos, Woger?'

'I prefer coffee or tea.'

Broadly speaking, while Alfie's tone was conversational, Roger could get away with 'phoning it in', as Sam would have said. Once the tone changed and a higher note crept in, he needed to put down the paper, finish his coffee and flapjack, and plan their exit. He'd made the mistake of not responding quickly enough too many times and found it hard to navigate the narrow space between tables holding a flailing Alfie under one arm and Killer's lead in the other hand. He now knew the warning signs. And always, *always*, he thought, have a plan for the next activity. Even if it was just walking somewhere. He wondered how many other grandparents were in the same boat, caring for their grandchildren while their children worked.

Idly that evening, to take his mind off the thundering question that occupied his waking hours – *Where is she?* – he googled 'grandparents caring for grandchildren'. He was astonished to see how many articles appeared. Over two million people were caring for their grandchildren. He browsed a couple of articles, one from the local paper, and then noticed a link to a Facebook group. He clicked on it and up popped a page with a photo of a woman he recognised. Round face, with a blunt dark fringe and small square glasses. He was sure he knew her. He leaned back in his chair, swilling his wine around the glass until it came to him. She lived along the road. Back towards town. Her name was Cara Edwards. She'd set up a group called GPPG and he read some details:

... *look after my grandson Mathew when my daughter Emily needed to go back to work. It was quite a shock to my system!*

You can say that again, Roger thought.

I found it very tiring to get used to the rhythm of caring for a toddler, but so rewarding. Mathew and I are now very close after so many hours in each other's company. But the thing that has greatly helped me is spending time with other people in the same situation. Not only do the children benefit from a 'play date', as they call it these days, the adults love the company and the chance to share tips (and sometimes a small moan or two about the difficulties!). If you're a grandparent caring for grandchildren in the Guildford area and can come along to our Grand-Parents Parenting Group (GPPG) support group/play date session, please join us! Thursdays from 10 a.m.-12, at my address. Please email me for details. cjmedwards@hotmail.com

Roger finished his wine and pulled the keyboard closer.

From: Roger Kurmudge
To: Cara Edwards
Subject: GPPG
Dear Cara,
My name is Roger Kurmudge and I live quite close by, I think. I'm currently looking after my grandson, Alfie, and would love to come along to one of your sessions! It's hard work, isn't it? I'll be there this Thursday.
Regards,
Roger

He waited for a response but nothing came. Nothing from Jane either. Killer sighed and turned over heavily. Apart from the dull thump of the boiler lighting, it was quiet in the house. He had to admit, he was lonely. Very lonely. He just wanted his wife back. He tried googling art competitions in Italy but found either beginner competitions that didn't seem likely to have attracted Jane, or holidays with art courses thrown in, which wasn't what Nina had described. Which made him wonder: had Jane made it up? But why? To leave her family behind and trot off to Italy to meet someone? A new man? He was getting worked up. He got up to get some more wine and Killer yawned, stretched and followed him to the kitchen. He was a lovely little dog, really. Such a good companion.

He stopped himself from opening a second bottle and had decided to go to bed when he saw a notification pop up on his phone. He checked his emails.

From: Cara Edwards
To: Roger Kurmudge
Re: GPPG
Dear Roger,
Do bring Alfie along this week. It's been a while since I saw him. How's Jane? Is she not around? You know my address, anyway, don't you? The Old Rectory. Just come along at 10. See you then!
Cara

21

The Old Rectory was just a short walk, even with Alfie, from Roger's house. Its pleasing symmetry and neat tree-lined gravel drive screamed middle-class England and calmed Roger's nerves as he rang the doorbell. He couldn't remember when he'd last met someone socially for the first time without Jane.

'Do come in, sorry it's not very tidy. I've had Mathew all week and honestly, I love him dearly, but the mess! Dear Lord, the mess!' Cara opened the door already talking, as though they'd been mid-discussion and he'd popped outside briefly to get something. He took Alfie's shoes off as well as his own and followed her down the hall. She turned to say, 'Alfie, do you want to head straight into the toy room? Mathew is already there.'

Alfie didn't need to be asked twice. He shot off into a room that looked as though it contained every toy manufactured in the last decade, stacked high around the room on the kind of basic shelving unit that Roger recognised from Andy's house.

Cara was still talking as she walked. 'I mean, I knew children were untidy little beasts but I think in our day we made more of a fuss, you know? About chores and tidying their rooms. Whereas now,' she threw her hands up as they entered a long narrow room with a shabby rug and worn sofas, gesturing around her and managing at the same time to indicate that he should take a seat on the opposite sofa, 'I honestly despair a little.'

She sat down and started to pour tea from the large ornate pot on the coffee table. 'You can't criticise them, or tell them no, or tick them off for being naughty, in case you crush their spirit or reduce their creativity or something. I think the pendulum might have swung too far in the wrong direction, although I wouldn't tell Emily this – do you want milk? And sugar? No? – so essentially I try to follow her rules, and I suppose if I'm really honest, I think the kids are much happier not being told off all the time – except how does it prepare them for work? I can't imagine many bosses being as kind and lenient as we are, can you? What if they get fired on their first day? Will it take until they're fifty for them to finally work it out? Isn't a little grit good for the soul? Isn't it better to get used to a bit of hardship before you're an adult? Is that tea okay?'

Roger wasn't sure which question needed answering, so he sipped the tea, which was too strong and not milky enough, and said, 'It's just right. Is anyone else coming today?'

'No, it's very quiet this week. Lots of regulars can't make it for various reasons, so I was glad you could.'

Roger had time now to properly look at his hostess. Cara obviously didn't care about her appearance. Her hair was what Roger's school friends would have called a bowl cut, with its severe fringe. She wore a baggy, long-sleeved T-shirt that was pilled under the arms, and cargo trousers, with black socks. Most of the women he knew made an effort. Wore clothes that had clearly been designed in the last couple of years. He returned his gaze to her face and realised she knew exactly what he was thinking.

Roger blushed. How embarrassing. He hadn't felt embarrassed for several days. He coughed and searched desperately for a question. 'So, did Jane come to the GPPG meetings every week?'

She frowned. 'Didn't she tell you?'

'No, in fact I'm realising she did – does – all sorts of things I didn't know about. Because I was at work.' He tried a laugh but it sounded forced.

She gave him a wide-eyed look that he wasn't sure how to interpret. 'So where is she at the moment?'

'She's away,' Roger said, sipping his tea.

'Where?' Cara asked.

Roger hadn't had to explain to anyone else. They'd been quite happy to take his one-liner as all the response needed. 'Well ...' He shifted in his seat. 'She won a competition to do an art course in Italy.'

'In December?' she said.

Roger stared at her. Of course. Why hadn't he seen that? Why on earth would anyone do an art course in Italy in the winter? 'I ... don't know much about it,' he said. It sounded, as the boys would say, 'totally lame'. His mind fizzed with questions. Clearly the story about the art competition was just that – a story. He couldn't believe he hadn't seen it before. No wonder Andy hadn't found her. She wasn't there to be found.

'No?' Cara said. She drank her tea, peering at him over the top of her cup. Bone china with tiny flowers on it and an ornate shape with a curly handle. Like something his mother would have used. But her eyes were sharp as tacks.

The single-word question made him blush again. Like she thought it was strange that Jane's husband knew so little about the so-called art course she'd gone on. Which, of course, it was. 'When will she be back?'

'In January, I think.' He was finding it hard to concentrate on anything apart from his wife's absence.

'She's away for Christmas?' Cara said. Her voice was incredulous.

'Yes, well, I mean ... it's fine, I can cope and the boys are grown up now, and although we'll miss her it's no big deal.' He could hear how defensive he sounded.

'I can't believe she's missing Alfie on Christmas Day. She adores that boy.'

'She does.'

'So have you been looking after him while she's away?'

'Yes. It's fine, in fact.'

She pursed her lips. 'That's good. And what about cooking? I thought Jane did all of that?'

He was getting irritated. Time to ask his own questions. 'So apart from Jane coming over with Alfie, did she see you in the week?'

'Well, we did Body Pump together on Tuesdays, of course.'

'Of course,' Roger said. *Body Pump? Just how many secrets had his wife been keeping from him?*

'Signed up together at the Spectrum.'

Roger nodded. He knew where the Guildford Spectrum Leisure Complex was. He just hadn't realised that Jane had not only been inside but had signed up for a class called Body Pump. Hadn't he read somewhere that if your partner suddenly signed up for a new exercise class it was a sign they were having an affair? Perhaps with a sleazy Italian called Tomasso?

'I thought she liked it. She said she did. We used to meet there just before the class started and sometimes went for coffee afterwards.' Cara frowned and poured herself more tea. 'But towards the end of September she stopped coming. I texted her a couple of times but didn't get an answer, so I just assumed she was run off her feet, because she wasn't coming to GPPG meetings either. Wasn't the French house proving a bit tricky?'

'No more than usual.'

'So I haven't seen much of her lately.'

Roger wanted to leave so he could mull over what he'd learned, but he hadn't finished his tea. 'Should we check on the boys?'

'I am,' she said. She flashed up her phone at him; on the screen he could see Alfie and another small boy playing, separately, with some Lego. Alfie was frowning and his tongue was sticking out. A sign of utter concentration. 'I have a webcam in there. If they start to get tetchy, we'll go in.'

Roger was mildly impressed. Sarah wouldn't have approved, but there was no doubt that provided the room was child-proofed and they didn't have access to things like matches (Alfie's latest morbid obsession), there was little reason for two grown people to hover over them. He settled himself back into his seat before realising that in fact he needed a diversion.

He didn't want to be asked searching questions that made him feel inadequate as a husband or grandfather (and therefore, he assumed, also as a father). Or cook, come to think of it. He wanted a pleasant conversation about the kinds of things Jane discussed. Radio 4 programmes. The garden. Their travel plans for the year. The latest book she was reading. Whether or not they should go to the new play by the RSC, or if it might be a little too experimental for their tastes. Which wine to have with dinner and should they invite Benedict and Grainne over again soon?

Such soothing conversation could wash over him while he drank tea, or better still, wine, and just added in comments when he felt like it. He never felt inadequate with Jane. That was, he realised, a powerful statement. He simply always felt good about himself with her. A wave of self-pity washed over him. He wanted to go and watch Alfie rather than dwell on why exactly his lovely wife had deserted him, possibly to run away with Tomasso, leaving him open to unpleasantness of all kinds: domestic, social, familial.

He stood up abruptly. 'I think I should just check on him,' he said to Cara.

'Of course,' she said. 'Bring your tea.'

Alfie had a large box of Lego in front of him and was rummaging through it percussively, obviously searching for a specific piece. In the corner, Mathew was pushing a wooden train around a wooden track, puffing his cheeks out as he *choo-choo*ed. They looked quite happy.

Roger squatted down next to Alfie, feeling a twinge in both knees. There was so much bending down involved in looking after children and dogs; his joints weren't really up to it. 'Can I help?'

'Yes,' Alfie said, without looking up. 'Maffew, dat's Woger.'

Mathew didn't respond.

'My Gwamma's gone,' Alfie said, still rummaging. 'Dat's Woger.'

'Do you miss your granny?' Cara asked. She lowered herself with some difficulty into a small armchair in a corner of the room.

'Yes,' Alfie said.

'Did she say goodbye to you?' Cara asked.

Alfie frowned. 'Woger, need wed pieces.' He held up a piece that was a classic Lego square but with a tapered additional end section.

'I'll help,' Roger said, kneeling stiffly on the floor next to the boy. Anything to avoid the questions. Christ knew what she was aiming for with the 'missing Granny' direction. The woman was a human Rottweiler. He pushed his hand into the Lego. 'Like this?'

Alfie considered it. 'No. Too wound.'

He was right, it was rounded. They needed a more angular one. Roger dragged his hand through the box again. Body Pump? Now that he thought about it, he did remember Jane buying some new sportswear in the summer. He hadn't really taken much notice. It had been during tough trading conditions – Tesco had been threatening to delist a few product lines – so he had had other things on his mind. He was uncomfortably aware that Cara was watching him.

'A-ha!' He brandished his discovery at Alfie. 'Here's one!'

Alfie took the piece and said, 'More.'

'So what sort of career did you have?' Roger asked Cara. Time to get on the front foot.

'I was a journalist. For the BBC. I worked in some pretty hairy spots around the world and loved every minute of it.'

He sat back and looked at her. 'Remind me of your surname.'

'I use Edwards now.' She said it neutrally. 'But the name I used at work was Lewis.'

'You're Cara Lewis? *The* Cara Lewis?' He knew she had looked familiar.

'I'm sure there are others,' she said tartly. 'But I am the Cara Lewis who reported from war zones for a couple of decades. I looked a bit different then. I had to, to be on TV. Many years ago, now.'

'And had children?' Roger said.

She bristled. 'Yes. Why shouldn't I? Men have children and then go back to work, travelling, doing dangerous things. Why not me?'

Roger managed to suppress his instinctive response.

'Only one child.' She softened. 'Emily. I realised quite quickly that another child would be too much for us. And Harry did a good job, along with his mum. They brought her up well.' There was regret in her voice. 'But I always felt the guilt. Perhaps that's why I do so much for Emily and Mathew now. Making up for it.'

If Jane had tried to work full time when the boys were small, Roger thought, how would they have managed it? Not that she'd have gone to war zones, of course. Working in an art gallery, even one frequented by entitled middle-class people, could hardly be called a war zone. But it would still have been hard to manage.

'What I've realised,' Cara said, getting stiffly out of her seat and carefully lowering herself down onto the floor with Mathew, 'is that there's an opportunity cost to whatever mums do. There's always a compromise. Go to work and you miss vital moments with your child. Stay at home and you lose out financially and are bored out of your mind.' She smiled at Mathew. 'Sorry, sweetie, but goodness, it's boring. Jane and I have often discussed the stuck-at-home boredom.' Mathew wasn't listening, which was just as well, Roger thought. Cara added another train to the track in front of his, and said, 'Can they link up? See if you can join them.' She glanced up at Roger with those sharp eyes. 'Mind you, there's an opportunity cost for dads, too, they just don't realise it.'

'What do you mean?' Roger said. He'd found two more red pieces, which again received no thanks at all from Alfie.

'More, Woger,' he said without looking up.

'Well, did you know your kids?' Cara asked. 'Really know them?'

'I certainly did,' Roger said. 'I was very much involved.' *Oh, Rodge!* The words were so clear in his head, he almost turned to see if Jane was behind him.

'You were the exception, then,' Cara said in a tone that made it clear she didn't believe him. 'Most men don't seem to know the first thing about what their children's lives are actually like. What they spend their time doing, or what school is really like, or which after-school clubs are on which day.'

'Well, I'm not most men,' Roger said.

'No, maybe not.' She gave him a face-saving smile. 'I just saw a lot of my male friends, other reporters and journalists, lose custody when their other halves got sick of carrying the entire parenting load. And they ended up lonely. The kids always preferred the people who'd cared for them most, put most in – their mothers.'

'Sad,' Roger said. 'Divorce must be unpleasant.'

'It is,' Cara said.

'Oh! I didn't realise.' Roger felt awkward. This was the sort of conversation he'd never really practised. It was a Jane-style conversation. 'When did that happen?'

'Not long after I decided that working full time was untenable. I was getting older and so was Emily. She needed me more as she grew up, not less. Harry had had enough. He felt pretty bitter.' She smiled without humour. 'He got married again, quite quickly.'

Roger couldn't imagine it. If he and Jane had broken up and she'd married someone else, how would that have worked? Come to think of it, if he and Jane got divorced now – or soon, when she came back and told him that she'd been in Italy with Tomasso, who loved what Body Pump had done for her glutes – how would it work? He swallowed hard.

He wanted that ring to convince his wife that she was appreciated and loved. And the party. He'd better write to her, something really meaningful to make her see how much she meant to him. It was grim without her. Even with the support network he'd started to establish around himself, it was lonely and boring and he felt no one understood him. And where the hell was she, anyway? He wanted to go home and email her right away.

His wish was granted ten seconds later when Mathew grabbed the train Alfie was holding. A tussle broke out and once the boys were separated, Roger said, 'Time to head home, I think. Thanks for the tea, Cara.'

'You're welcome. Come again next week. Meet the rest of the gang.'

BACK AT HOME, he settled Alfie in front of the TV and gave him a snack. Then he headed up to the office and composed a note to Jane.

From: Roger Kurmudge
To: Janes Away Hurray
Subject: Please come home
Jane,
Alfie misses you. Andy and Sam miss you. *I* miss you. I don't think it's unreasonable of me to want to know when you're coming home. I do see that perhaps in the past, I let you down.

Going to Australia was a mistake, I realise. But I can't make up for that if you're not even here, can I? Please come home and we can discuss it.
Roger
PS Body Pump? Really?

Two hours later, he received a response.

From: Janes Away Hurray
To: Roger Kurmudge
Subject: To do
I hope you posted the Christmas cards.

22

Christmas was beginning to loom large in Roger's mind. And everyone else's, it seemed. When he picked Alfie up one morning, he saw that they'd decorated the house and had a small artificial tree up in the sitting room. All the baubles were clustered around the bottom of the tree on one side.

'Alfie really enjoyed decorating the tree, didn't you, sweetie?' Sarah said, ruffling his hair.

Alfie tugged at Roger's trouser leg. 'I did it by my own. You have a twee, Woger?'

Usually Jane organised a large real tree and they'd decorate it together. Roger had no idea where to get one from but Alfie's question made him realise that if the family was coming for Christmas, they'd expect a tree.

Google informed him that he could get one from most of the large supermarkets. He duly drove to Tesco with Killer one Tuesday and bought the largest one he could find. Only when he tried to get it into the boot did he realise that Killer was going to have to sit in the front passenger seat on the way home. He didn't think he was imagining the dog's smugness as he fastened his lead into the seat, but the panting sound as he drove was almost companionable.

He'd managed to get the tree in the car and home without injuring himself. Putting it up was quite another matter. It was spiky. The needles were annoying and itchy, and once up, it looked somehow less impressive than he'd imagined, with an asymmetry to its branches that he didn't love. He went into the attic to retrieve the decorations. He decided that this year's colour theme would be red and gold and spent an hour putting the baubles on the tree, then another hour untangling the lights, then an hour putting them on the tree. He plugged them in and switched them on. Nothing. Much fiddling and swearing later, he took the lights off, drove back to Tesco with Killer on the front seat, bought more lights, went home and put them on the tree. This time they came on.

Roger slumped into the armchair and regarded the tree with deep antipathy. He remembered decorating with the boys and how much fun it had been. Admittedly, his part had been the sitting-on-the-sidelines-drinking-mulled-wine bit, while Jane sorted out the lights and tinsel and directed the boys. But it had been fun. Hadn't it? Now it felt a lot less fun. But when Alfie arrived on the Thursday that week, Roger conceded it had been worth it.

'Woger! Look!' Alfie said, pointing at the tree.

Did the boy think it had simply appeared by magic? Did he not realise that Roger had put it up and decorated it, single-handed? He swallowed his snappy responses and simply agreed that it looked so pretty, and yes, Alfie could take that sparkly red bauble off and keep it, if he really wanted to. But not all of them. To head off the tantrum, he asked Alfie if he'd like to go and choose some outdoor Christmas lights from Tesco. Alfie's dash back up the hall to put on his shoes was answer enough. He was even more delighted to see Killer sitting next to Roger in the front of the car.

'Killer likes dat, Woger.' He smiled and put his thumb firmly in his mouth.

Tesco was very busy and Roger wondered at his decision to bring Alfie, but the enthusiasm of a toddler buying Christmas lights was infectious. Roger got rather carried away. They bought three reindeer, one large and two small, a couple of Christmas present-shaped lights, a sled, a Father Christmas figure and a *Santa Stops Here!* sign. It was hard to get the boxes into the boot but Roger managed it without swearing and they spent an hour back at the house unpacking them, positioning them under the oak tree in the middle of the garden and then switching them on. The glorious winter sunshine made it hard to see the lights.

'Not working,' Alfie said. He glared at Roger and sucked in a breath.

'Wait until this evening!' Roger said hurriedly. 'Wait until teatime when it gets dark. Mel will be here, too, I bet she'd love to see them.'

While Alfie was napping, Roger wrote Christmas cards to the same people he'd sent anniversary party invitations to, and even wrote a short update to each of them. He kept it brief: *My wife has left and I don't know where she is* didn't seem like quite the Christmas spirit. Instead, he wrote: *I hope all is well with you all. Perhaps we can catch up in the new year? Once January settles in, I'll get Jane to call you.*

Now he came to think about it, Benedict and Grainne, Will and Elaine, and Clive and Rebecca were people he only saw when Jane arranged dinners. They never contacted him directly. The wives got in touch with each other and the men came along for the ride. Were they, in fact, even Roger's friends? He wasn't sure.

He addressed the cards anyway – another job done that Jane had challenged him to complete – and put stamps on. He was feeling rather smug when Mel arrived. Alfie danced down the hall to open the door on tiptoe and let her in.

'Melly-Belly!'

'Halfie!'

They high-fived each other and Mel asked, 'What 'ave you been up to, Halfie?'

'I been up to doing Cwistmas lights,' Alfie said. 'Come see, Melly-Belly!'

Daylight was fading from the sky and it was crisply cold as Roger joined them outside, with Alfie's coat. He coaxed Alfie into it and went back inside to turn on the lights. He heard a cry as he flicked the switch and looked out to see Mel with her hand over her mouth.

'Halfie, it's beautiful!'

Alfie nodded solemnly and slipped his hand into hers. Positioning one of the small reindeer on top of one of the presents had been his idea – 'I do it by my own!' he'd said, dragging the reindeer along the grass and onto the present-shaped square light – and although Roger wasn't convinced it quite worked and thought it would come down in a high wind, Alfie was happy. It did make quite a display: Roger made a note to himself that inviting Cara and Mathew over to look at it might kill an afternoon (although Mel quickly reminded him that there weren't many afternoons left to kill).

'Christmas next week, Mr. R.,' she said.

Alfie said, 'My fingers be fashing,' and he made fists followed by widely spread fingers five times. 'Look, Woger, look!'

'Yes, Alfie, I see you!' Roger flashed his fingers back at Alfie. 'And yes, Mel, it's coming round fast.'

'You feelin' okay about all the stuff? Cookin' an' tha'?'

'I think it will be fine,' Roger said. 'Thanks to you for all the notes and tha', I mean everything.' He felt mildly anxious, in fact, but also ridiculous. He was inviting his family over for Christmas. He wasn't hosting the annual AGM. No one was getting fired or reprimanded. How much could go wrong?

The week went fast. Time was speeding up. He woke each morning with a head full of notes to himself.

Saturday: Take Killer into town for walk. Get cash out for Gail, Mel and Morwenna for the week.

Sunday: Take Killer to newsagent's to get paper. Pop in on Cara? Rugby match on Sky at 3 p.m.

Monday: Take Alfie (Soft play?)

Tuesday: Dentist. Ring Victor re French heating quote. Seems <u>outrageous.</u>

Wednesday: Give Killer decent walk. GP appointment for health check. N.B. alcohol allowance per week for men now only 14 units, not 21!

Thursday: Alfie: go to the café again? And find a new park with a decent climbing frame? Waitrose delivery!

Friday: Put the bins out. Walk Killer.

Saturday: Ask Mel to go through Christmas lunch timings again and do veggie prep.

He'd always woken up with a head full of notes, but in the past they'd been a bit more exciting. *Write report for the board pre-AGM meeting. Sit down with HR to discuss exec remuneration – bonus time! Book in annual reviews for the team.* And he was getting very well paid for such activities, too. Now, every waking hour was full of planning and organising and there was no perfumed, pencil-skirted, sweetly indulgent executive assistant to keep him on track. He hadn't heard back from Jane again. He kept hoping that she would suddenly email or, even better, arrive. Perhaps that would be his Christmas present. It would be like Jane to make it a surprise for him.

WAITROSE DELIVERED ALL the food on the 22nd December at ten p.m. It took the delivery driver sixteen minutes to bring everything in, stack it on the kitchen floor, the island, then the boot-room floor, and finally collect up all the plastic trays. He looked a bit fed up and rather sweaty. Roger handed him a ten quid tip and the man quickly pocketed it and grumpily left. It was then up to Roger to try to cram it all into the fridge.

Quarter of an hour later, he was still scratching his head about how to make enough room. He took out a tub of olives and ate them to free up space. Then two chocolate mousses. He felt slightly guilty about eating them after having been told by the GP the day before that he was a little overweight. Roger had insisted he ate very healthily (mostly true again now, thanks to Mel) and had lied as convincingly as he could about the amount of alcohol he drank. From the GP's face, it was clear he hadn't been remotely convinced of Roger's claim that he drank exactly the 14 units that the government now suggested was a man's limit for the week.

He scraped out the remains of the mousse with his spoon. It was a shame it was so late at night, or he could have dropped some of them over to Alfie, who would have cheerfully got stuck in to help.

He scanned the fridge again and removed two cans of something rejoicing in the name *Beavertown Neck Oil Session*

Indian Pale Ale lurking at the back (who'd bought such a thing? Surely it must have been Andy or Sam), and wedged a punnet of raspberries into their place. He couldn't fit the blocks of chocolate in but managed everything else.

The fridge freezer was one of those enormous American things that Jane liked so much but it was struggling to contain everything: a huge ham, an even larger turkey and a joint of beef; a large packet of Scottish premium smoked salmon, a packet of whole frozen prawns and two bags of frozen scallops; a tub of fresh dressed crab; fresh vegetables including Brussels sprouts, parsnips, cauliflower, carrots and two heads of broccoli; two punnets of raspberries, three of strawberries, a bag of oranges, a bag of lemons, and two nets of easy-peeler mandarins; three cartons of cream – two double, one clotted; vanilla ice cream, a Sicilian lemon tart; and three types of stuffing. Two large blocks of cheddar cheese. Two bottles of champagne, eight bottles of beer and three large cartons of milk. There was not a square inch of free space left.

Roger should have felt pleased that he had everything under control, but instead the fridge seemed to be making far too many demands on him. *Chop this. Marinate that. Cook the other. Eat far, far too much in too brief a time period.* If Jane had been there, he'd have felt quite excited about Christmas Day but instead he felt burdened. Had she felt burdened?

The following day he decided to sit at his desk and have a long slow think about Christmas and how to manage it. He took his coffee into the office and switched on his laptop. His first mistake. He looked up an hour later to realise he'd done nothing but read the news: Storm Barbara was approaching; Putin looked sombre at the funeral of a Russian ambassador; a very merry Prince Charles was pulling a cracker with a woman at a hospice in Cheltenham; two new cheetah cubs were outside for the first time at Longleat; and there was a particularly distracting picture of the outgoing US President laughing at a large and jolly-looking snowman through a White House window.

Roger shook himself and shut the laptop. It was the 23rd December, for God's sake. Unlike Barack Obama, he had proper responsibilities. He didn't have a wife and staff to prepare a Christmas Day feast while he had fun with snowmen. He needed to 'crack on', as Andy would say. He checked the time: 9.06 a.m. Better get moving.

It was at this point that he heard the doorbell. He was still in his pyjamas. He looked out of the window and could see yellow flashing lights below. Was it the police to say they'd found Jane? But that wouldn't require flashing lights, would it? Unless a serial killer had taken her. But they'd be blue in that case, wouldn't they? He'd have to ask Andy.

Another ring at the door. Killer was barking ferociously.

Roger dashed to his bedroom, threw on some clothes and bolted down the stairs.

At the door was a young man with dreary-looking hair and droopy eyes. Behind him was the cab of a truck, yellow warning lights rotating on the roof. On the back of it, several pallets. One of them had a picture of the product stuck on it.

'Oh, no,' Roger said. 'There's been a mistake.' He pushed Killer away from the door with his foot. 'Shush, Killer.'

Droopy Eyes peered at him. 'I'm from John Lewis, to deliver your garden studio.' *You over-privileged twit* was implicit in the way he said *garden studio*.

'No, no,' Roger said. 'The delivery was for after Christmas. They said so when I ordered.'

'Yeah.' Droopy Eyes spoke slowly. 'But we managed to bring some stuff forward. For Christmas, like.'

'Wait here, please,' Roger said. He pushed the door shut,

told Killer to go back to his bed and then legged it upstairs and into his office. He was breathing hard and not because of running up the stairs. He went into his emails.

He hadn't realised how far behind he was with them. These days, he only scanned his in-box for emails from Jane. There were two hundred he hadn't read and some of the titles didn't look like they were just offers from Sky. He raced down them and found one from John Lewis that had been sent at seven a.m. He read it with increasing alarm.

From: John Lewis Partnership
To: Roger Kurmudge
Subject: Delivery of 5 x 4m Garden Studio
Dear Mr. Kurmudge,
We are delighted to remind you that you will receive your Garden Studio today. Our driver, Malcolm, will be with you between 8.30-9.30 this morning. Please ensure you are at the delivery address at this time to take receipt of the Garden Studio and show Malcolm where to site it.
We hope you have many happy years enjoying the studio in your garden.
Kind regards,
Will Reston,
Delivery Coordinator, John Lewis Partnership

Ridiculous, was Roger's first thought. He needed to get a concrete base built in the garden for the studio to sit on. Which he hadn't done. Or even thought about. He'd simply have to ring Will Reston and explain that he couldn't take receipt of the studio today. This was John Lewis. They'd understand. Why hadn't they told him about the imminent delivery?

Five minutes later, he was sweating lightly. He'd never

had a conversation with a John Lewis employee quite like this one. He couldn't say that Will Reston had been rude. Quite the reverse. He'd spoken to Roger as though he was used to elderly men not quite understanding how the world worked. Compassionate to the point of patronising. John Lewis had sent him a series of emails regarding the delivery, had he received them?

Roger said firmly that he absolutely had *not* received any such communication, just as his eyes travelled slowly down his screen and registered unread emails from John Lewis. Three of them, one entitled: *Early delivery of your garden studio in time for Christmas!* It had been sent three weeks ago.

Will Reston had then started to query the email address details Roger had left with them until Roger had been forced to admit that in fact, now he came to look at it, he had received the emails. Yes. All three of them. Yes, with details of the delivery time and date – just in time for Christmas! – and very explicit instructions about the concrete base. Also stating that if he didn't reply, they would assume the new date was acceptable. Yes.

There was a very awkward pause on the line. When Will started to speak again, he was talking more slowly, leaving pauses between each word. As though Roger might need time to understand what he was saying. Roger's toes curled in his socks.

'Malcolm is with you at the moment, is that right?' Will said.

'Yes.' He could see Droopy Eyes wandering around the front garden with a cigarette hanging from his lips.

'So I can't ask him not to deliver it today,' Will said, 'as we can't book it back in. It's the last working day before Christmas, as you know.' There was a question in his voice, as though perhaps Roger didn't know that. Or indeed anything.

'It's fine.' Roger sat up straight. 'I'll get someone to build the base later and install it.'

'Right.' Will sounded hesitant. 'But if *we* don't install it, your warranty is null and void.'

Roger paused. This was rather an expensive building and he wanted the warranty on it. 'I'm sorry, I've been rather ... disorganised. It's just my wife usually does this stuff and she's away. So I've been incredibly busy. Doing what she would normally do. Her ... work.' It really was work, Roger thought. Rather hard work, at that. And unpaid. Bloody Barack didn't know how good he had it, laughing at snowmen while everyone else sorted Christmas out behind the scenes. Who'd even built the bloody snowman, hey?

'I see.' Will Reston didn't sound very sympathetic.

'In fact, she's left me.' Roger needed to up the ante a bit. Even if it was humiliating.

'I'm sorry to hear that.' A hint of concern in Will's voice.

'So you see, I've been very distracted and now I have to cook for my whole family tomorrow and I've never really made Christmas lunch before.'

'How many people are coming?' Definite sympathy now.

'Fifteen.' It sounded better than five.

'Fifteen?' A low whistle. There was a long pause then Will said, 'Look, Mr. Kurmudge, you've obviously had a difficult time, and here at John Lewis we strive to give good customer service.' He lowered his voice, as though trying not to be overheard in the office. 'And my wife was ill last Christmas, so I had to do it all, and honestly it was knackering. I feel your pain. So if we can leave the garden studio with you, I'll organise for Malcolm to come back and install it later, if that's okay?'

'That would be brilliant,' Roger said. 'Ideal, in fact.'

'Okay, then,' Will said brightly. 'Have a lovely day and the team at John Lewis hope you get a lot of satisfaction from your Garden Studio. Um, when it's built, of course.'

Back downstairs, Droopy Eyes was still smoking. He dropped the cigarette onto the drive and crushed it with his heel as Roger beckoned him over. He didn't, Roger noticed, pick up his butt.

'I've spoken to head office,' Roger said with as much dignity as he could, 'and agreed to take delivery of the studio.'

'Right-o. Can you show me where the concrete base is?'

'Well, in fact, there's no base.'

'No base? Can't install it then, mate.'

'I know, I've spoken to Will Reston.'

'Who?'

'Will Reston? The bloke who emailed me about delivery?'

Droopy Eyes shrugged. 'Big company, John Lewis.'

'Well, he told me it was okay to leave the studio here and he'll send you and the team back later to build it.'

Droopy Eyes gave him a stare. The kind of stare that said, *You live in a huge house and have spent more than some people earn in a year on some poncy David Cameron-type studio for your garden but aren't savvy enough to have the base ready. A thousand years ago, you wouldn't have survived in the wild.* What he said was, 'Okay then. Will I just leave it on the drive?'

'No,' Roger said. *What cheek.* 'I need it in the garden. I want the drive for cars. For parking. Can you put it in the garden?'

'Sure.' Droopy Eyes shrugged. 'Kills the grass, though.'

Now Roger wasn't sure. The lawn was something Jane

cared about. Did he really want to kill a large patch of it with the studio? He felt at a disadvantage as Droopy Eyes stared at him. He hadn't even had time to shower. Perhaps he smelled.

'Fine. Just leave it on the drive.'

Droopy Eyes made him sign something to the effect of *I'm a total loser who didn't really understand the process of this purchase and will now have a garden studio on my drive for three months while I organise the concrete base.* Roger signed it with as much of an insouciant flourish as he could muster.

Droopy Eyes got back into the truck. Roger noticed that another man was in the passenger seat and that there was some hilarity going on between the two of them. He was glad the windows weren't open. It took five minutes of manoeuvring and lots of action with the crane before the pallets were carefully lowered onto the gravel of the drive. It took up quite a lot of space. Most of the space allocated for parking, in fact.

'Okay?' Droopy Eyes shouted out of his window.

'Great,' Roger said. He gave a small wave and watched as they drove away. He could see their profiles through the back window of the truck's cab. They were definitely laughing.

He walked down the steps and around the pallets. The picture sellotaped on top was appealing. The studio looked well made, like something that a successful person would have in his or her garden. But stuck on Roger's drive, it was simply a reminder that he wasn't organised enough to get it installed properly.

He could imagine it in the back garden, ready for use. The smell of fresh paint. All square corners and flush floors. He would be able to sit in there and read the paper while Jane painted. They could chat companionably together.

Although not if that disturbed the painting. He didn't have to chat. Throw a sofa in there and it would be great for a nap.

He shut his eyes. He imagined the peacefulness of the studio. It would be so quiet. Just as it was now. Just some birdsong (reminding him he needed to fill up the bird feeders), and a car going past on the road. He wanted to go back to bed for a while. Tomorrow was going to be a big day and he wanted to keep his energy going. He could feel himself swaying slightly. This was going to be a very lovely studio. Jane would be thrilled.

A loud cough made him start and open his eyes. The postman was staring at him. Roger hadn't heard him walking up the drive.

'All right, Mr. Kurmudge?'

He felt himself blush. 'Hello, yes, I'm fine, thanks.'

The postman was giving the pallets the once over. 'This is ... nice. Is it supposed to be here? On the drive, I mean?'

'No, no. It was supposed to be delivered after Christmas and then they suddenly delivered it today.'

'With no notice? That's not on. Where did you buy it?'

Roger felt he couldn't in fairness blame John Lewis. He coughed and said, 'I've been waiting for some mail, actually.'

The postman handed over some cards. He was keen to linger, Roger thought. Usually he was off down the drive before the letters had dropped onto the floor.

'So, any plans for Christmas?' Roger said. Once he'd said it, it seemed rather a stupid question.

'Yes.' The postman gave him a look full of meaning but Roger couldn't decipher what it was. 'Okay, then, Mr. Kurmudge, have a good Christmas. And Mrs Kurmudge. A lovely lady. And always very generous. Especially at Christmas.'

'Thanks!' Roger gave him a hearty wave and hoped he wasn't going to linger at other people's houses. Possibly sharing with them the fact that he had seen Roger standing on the drive with his eyes shut. Their previous encounters had been mercifully brief, Roger striding past him in the morning, throwing him a quick yet hearty greeting on his way to the office. Roger would have looked competent, successful, dynamic. Not the sort of man who would go into a trance on his driveway. He really wasn't quite sure how he'd got to this stage in life.

He went back inside and opened the cards. They were all from 'friends' he hadn't seen or spoken to in months. Even one from his brother, Arthur, although there was no letter this year. With a sigh he put them on the mantelpiece.

In the kitchen, he opened the fridge door and took a long hard look at the turkey. He re-read Mel's timing plan. *Get the turkey out first thing on Christmas morning, no later than 7 a.m. Put the oven on at 9 a.m. ready for the turkey to go in at 9.30; set timer for 4 hours, baste occasionally, serve at 1.30 p.m.* Perfect Christmas lunch timing. The family was coming at 12.30; they could all have a drink and then he'd amaze them by serving up a delicious festive feast. He was looking forward to their praise, actually. And their delight when they saw their presents.

He was increasingly sure Jane would come home, too. She'd be on the doorstep in the morning. He'd agree he hadn't always been quite as good a husband as he'd imagined. Or father. She'd agree she'd made her point and they'd go back to the way things had been. Although he'd help more with Alfie, of course, from now on. And even walk Killer a bit. Yes, Jane would be home on Christmas morning.

He couldn't wait. He'd just check his emails again in case she'd sent him something.

She had.

From: Janes Away Hurray
To: Roger Kurmudge
Subject: To do
Remember to tip the postman and the bin men. £10 each in a card (so two tenners in 'Refuse Collection Team' card). It makes them more cheerful and means I (now you) don't have to drag the bins down the drive to the road for them every week. Worth every penny.

23

Christmas Eve was incredibly busy; there was much to do. Roger walked Killer and tidied the house and got out the special Christmas table mats and laid the table, trying to remember how Jane did it. Mel came at four p.m. (special Christmas dispensation for him that she was prepared to work on Saturday) and for two hours she prepped all the veggies and the turkey and talked non-stop about what he needed to do the following day and how thrilled Treen and Gary were with the food that had been delivered to them the day before.

He handed her a Christmas card with £200 cash inside when she finished, which reduced her to tears, and then drove her home as it was raining. The sight of her drab flat in its grim street brought a lump to his throat. Mel hadn't had the same starting point as him on the Monopoly board of life. Her first Chance Card had been *Go To Jail* and she'd no money to buy her way out. Depressed, he headed home to drink a bottle of wine and eat lasagne from the freezer.

At nine p.m., after a whisky chaser, he suddenly realised that he hadn't wrapped the presents. And had no wrapping paper or tags. By then, he was too drunk to drive to a supermarket to get some. He scoured the house before walking over to Cara's and asking her if she could possibly lend him any wrapping paper she had left over. All she had was three rolls of Thomas the Tank Engine birthday paper and some Peppa Pig tags. He was grateful, especially as she'd managed, in a most un-Cara-esque way, not to ask him if he was drunk.

Wrapping the presents took far too long. It was ten p.m. when he started and he felt the effects of the wine impinging on his ability to judge how much paper might be needed. It was just as well he'd bought items in big square boxes. He wrapped Alfie's first, and when he realised there was a gap in the paper, he sellotaped another piece to the box to cover it.

The identical size of the coffee makers meant he was much better at estimating the amount of paper needed the second time around. It was only when he'd finished wrapping them and was imagining the glee on both boys' faces that he suddenly thought about Sarah and Guy. How had he forgotten them? They would be here too. He didn't know why Guy always came along for Christmas Day with Sam, but he did.

He stumbled upstairs to his bedroom. Sarah he could probably fix. Jane had heaps of things that would be suitable. He dug around in her jewellery box and found some earrings that didn't look expensive: small silver hoops studded with multicoloured semi-precious stones. Definitely not from Malfields. Jane wouldn't miss them. He trotted downstairs and wrapped them up for Sarah.

What to get for Guy? Wine? He wasn't sure Guy drank wine. Gin, maybe? Where was Jane when he needed her? She would have remembered both Guy and Sarah and she would be the perfect sounding board now. She noticed people. What they liked. What they did. What sorts of presents might be suitable. He would have to point this out to her tomorrow, when she finally came home. He wrapped a bottle of gin for Guy and went to bed.

THE DOORBELL WOKE him on Christmas morning. A very insistent ringing. Like someone leaning on it for several seconds at a time. Killer was barking madly. Roger felt disorientated as he threw on yesterday's clothes and stumbled downstairs.

A thought now struck him. Of course. It was Jane! She'd come home. He threw himself down the final few stairs and scrabbled at the door. It took several seconds after he'd opened it for the full force of his disappointment to register.

Standing on the step were Andy and Sarah with Alfie. Andy was holding Alfie up to ring the doorbell. Killer bounded around them, still barking.

'Woger! Cwistmas! Happy Cwistmas!'

'Dad, are you okay?' Andy said. 'We thought we'd surprise you. Spend all day with you, rather than you being alone.' He turned and pointed at the pallets on the driveway. 'What the hell – I mean heck – is that?'

Roger blinked at him. His brain was taking a long time to process it all. No Jane. No one to help. What time was it, in fact? He glanced at his watch. Ten a.m. Why hadn't he set an alarm? Why had he drunk so much?

'Christ!' he said, and bolted back to the kitchen. Already he was hours behind on Mel's time plan. As the rest of the family came into the kitchen behind him, he grabbed the turkey and hauled it out of the fridge, dislodging the raspberries and a carton of cream, which fell onto the floor and burst. 'Shit!'

'Dad!' Andy said.

'Shit!' Alfie said.

Sarah glared at Roger and said, 'Alfie, let's go and look at the tree, shall we? I'm sure there's a present under it for you.' She grabbed Alfie by the hand and marched out.

'Is everything okay? You didn't just wake up, did you?' Andy said.

'I had a late night,' Roger said. He checked Mel's plan and put the oven on to warm up. She'd at least got the turkey ready to go, under foil. He just needed the oven to warm up.

'What is that stuff on the drive anyway?'

'It's a present for your mum.'

'Right. Do you want to get changed, then? Before Sam and Guy arrive?'

'They're coming early too?' Roger said.

'We thought you'd be pleased,' Andy said flatly. 'That we'd make sure you weren't lonely. And we can help.'

Roger knew that Alfie's presence was usually the opposite of helpful on days such as this. But Andy's face with its downturned mouth looked so like Alfie's at that moment that Roger put his arm around him. 'Thank you,' he said. 'I do appreciate it. I'll get changed.'

'I'll feed the dog, shall I?' Andy said. 'He looks hungry.'

By the time Roger had had a rapid shower and changed into something suitably smart and clean, the doorbell had gone again and he heard a hubbub of voices in the hall. He steeled himself and went downstairs.

Everyone had congregated in the sitting room because Alfie was as usual impatient to open his present. The year before, Roger had insisted Alfie should wait. He'd spoken over the tantrum and made everyone have 'a quiet drink' first. The drink had been anything but quiet with Alfie wailing away in the background. Sarah and Jane had both been icily cross about it. He now realised the futility of trying to contain Alfie's excitement about presents. Why not just get it over with?

Alfie had already handed everyone else's presents to them, with Sarah helping him read the labels.

'Woger's here! Wanna open my pwesent!'

Before anyone could stop him, he'd ripped open the wrapping paper. 'Lego!'

'Good present, Dad,' Andy said. He put the wrapping paper in a black bin liner for recycling. Jane usually did that. 'Why Thomas the Tank Engine?'

'I forgot to get Christmas wrapping paper,' Roger said.

Alfie asked Sarah to open the Lego box and was immediately engrossed in building something. Roger had made a good choice. It might give them a few minutes to unwrap everyone else's presents.

'Boys!' he said. 'Why don't you do yours? It will have to be at the same time.'

Andy and Sam both took the paper off their coffee machines. There was a silence. He'd expected a thrilled response. Possibly a sharp intake of awestruck breath. Instead there was a stunned blankness.

'Um, wow, thanks, Dad,' Andy said. He exchanged a glance with Sam.

'Thanks, Dad.'

'Isn't it the one you wanted?' Roger said. 'I thought this was the best one.'

'It's great, it's a really good one.' Andy wasn't smiling. Sam was shaking the wrapping paper, as though he expected something else to fall out of it. He picked up his phone, checked something on the box and tapped at his screen. He then showed it silently to Andy.

'Was it ... expensive, Dad?' Andy asked.

'Yes, quite.'

'Right.' Andy forced a smile. Exchanged another look with Sam. 'Thanks.'

'Mummy, Mummy, your pwesent!'

Sarah opened her present. She looked furious, but said, 'Thanks, they're lovely.' She showed the earrings to Andy, who frowned. What was going on? The only person who seemed happy was Alfie. What a spoilt lot they were. Roger had spent a fortune, he was cooking Christmas lunch for them ...

'Christ!' He shot to his feet and dashed back to the kitchen, registering as he fled that Sarah had her hands over Alfie's ears but the boy was asking, 'What's Cwist?'

He'd forgotten the turkey. It was sitting on the island, and the oven was now at the right temperature. He shoved it in and went back to the sitting room, where Guy was sitting with the bottle of gin in his hand. He looked irritated.

'Dad?' Sam was smiling, but the patronising smile of someone dealing with an elderly person. 'Thanks, but Guy doesn't drink. He gave up about two years ago.'

'I didn't realise,' Roger said. 'Sorry, Guy. Perhaps a voucher for something from John Lewis?'

Guy smiled thinly. 'Thanks, Roger.'

Roger wasn't even sure why Sam's flatmate always came to family events. Didn't the boy have family of his own? Friendship was all very well, but family events should really just be for family and partners.

He opened his own gift from everyone at that point. It was a gift voucher for golf equipment. 'Thank you all. Lovely.' He didn't point out that he had all the golfing equipment a man could wish for and hadn't in fact played golf since he'd retired. An atmosphere of disappointment mingled with intense irritation throughout the room. So much for the Christmas spirit. He got to his feet. 'I'd better get back to it. Andy, could you get everyone a drink?'

Back in the kitchen, he fixed Andy with a firm look. 'What's going on? The presents were obviously wrong but I don't know why. I thought you'd love the coffee machines.'

'Mum always gives us a cheque.' Andy got a bottle of champagne out of the fridge. 'She buys us something small and then gives us quite a large cheque. I put it towards the building work or a weekend away and Sam pays down his mortgage. And you spent a fortune on those coffee machines and I'm sure they're great but I already have one that's okay and I'd rather spend it on the extension.'

'They're from John Lewis, we can send them back,' Roger said. He felt exhausted already. 'Okay. What's the problem with Sarah's present?'

'We gave those earrings to Mum last Christmas,' Andy said.

Roger coloured. 'Sorry. I forgot about Sarah so I had to find something we already had.'

'We got married six years ago, Dad.' Andy was furiously ripping the foil off the champagne bottle as though he was wringing its neck. 'I know you don't like her but you can't forget her at Christmas.'

'I didn't. I just forgot when I was shopping.' Too late, Roger realised what he should have said. 'And I do like her. Of course I do.'

'And giving alcohol to Guy? Really?'

Roger shook his head at his son. 'Honestly! I'm doing my best here, with your mother away. Why on earth Sam's flatmate has to come with him to every family event, I just don't know.'

Sam's voice said from behind him, 'Fuck's sake, Dad. Work it out!'

Roger turned to see Sam, white-faced, in the kitchen doorway.

'I can't believe how little you know about me,' Sam said. 'I mean, seriously, what the fuck did you do with your time when we were kids and teenagers? Thank God for Mum who actually noticed us and supported us, because we're nothing like you, and thank Christ for that!' He looked as though anger had drained all the blood from his face. 'I'd like to really vent but Guy doesn't need this. His mum invited us over today but we thought you'd be lonely without Mum and we wanted to make it a good day for you.' Roger had never heard such fury in his younger son's voice. 'I think we'll take her up on it now. You bigoted old bastard.' He turned and left.

'Sam!' Roger was incredulous. He heard voices and quick, angry footsteps in the hall, and then a door slamming. 'What was that about?' he asked Andy.

'Dad, really?' Andy was cold. 'Why do you think Sam was bullied at school? Hey? Captain of the tennis team. Academic without being swotty. Good-looking.' True enough, Roger thought. 'The girls loved him. But Guy is Sam's *partner*. They've been together two years; they've been rock solid together since day one. They're trying to adopt. You are literally the only person who doesn't know because no one dared tell you. Gran knows and she's in a home and dementia-ridden. But she still gets it. You're the only one who doesn't.'

His partner? Roger's head hurt. Adoption? What was going on? When was Jane going to come home and help deal with this stuff? 'Does your mum know? About the adoption, I mean?'

'She's delighted. She said she's tried to talk to you about it but you're not very receptive.'

Roger thought back. It was true that he and Jane had had a strange chat a few months earlier about gay men adopting, and he'd been rather strident about it. He might have used the word *abhorrent*. He had definitely said it was unnatural and against the interests of the child. Jane had been unusually annoyed with him. Really quite cross. She'd gone to bed early in the spare room and hadn't been very friendly to him for several days. Now he understood. He also understood why he hadn't seen much of Sam for many years except at family events.

He checked his watch. It was eleven o'clock. He was well behind Mel's plan. He had no idea when he'd put the turkey in. He pushed a champagne glass towards Andy and said, 'I think I might need a glass.'

In silence, Andy filled up three of the five glasses and took Sarah hers. He came back and sat down at the island. He sighed. 'Dad, do you ever think that maybe Mum left because she was really angry with you? That you've let her down really badly too often?'

'Maybe.' Roger had got away with the affair all these years. He hadn't realised just how many other things Jane was cross about. So many areas of irritation. He drank his glass of champagne down in one long swallow and pushed it back. 'Fill me up. Then we'd better work on this bloody lunch.'

∼

THEY ATE AT THREE P.M. Andy had suggested a simplified version of Mel's plan: turkey, roast potatoes and some roast veggies plus one of the stuffings. The oven had been slower than either of them had envisaged and by the time they served the food, Alfie was behaving so appallingly that even Andy was cross with him. Roger's attempts to give him snacks were vetoed and he thought – but kept it to himself – that if he'd been on his own with Alfie, it would have been fine. He'd have given Alfie some biscuits or beans on toast and a glass of milk and put him to bed for a nap. He wouldn't have insisted on carrot sticks and 'waiting for a proper lunch'.

They ate in subdued silence, and for the first time Roger fervently hoped Jane would not reappear today. He'd annoyed everyone in the family except Alfie and Killer. Killer's stocking had gone down well. Too well. Roger hadn't anticipated that Alfie would feed the dog *all* the treats and that Killer would be quietly sick on the patio. After lunch, Roger hosed it away and then joined Andy at the sink to dry up. How was it possible that one meal had created so much fuss and washing up?

At five p.m. Andy announced they were going home. They all said stiff goodbyes and Roger noticed that Sarah left her earrings behind next to the boxes with the coffee machines in them and the bottle of gin. He'd only got Alfie's present right. Perhaps – Jane's voice in his head – because he'd spent time with Alfie and therefore understood him in a way he'd never understood his own children. He slumped down in the armchair and wondered what to do with the rest of his day. Had he ever felt more depressed? What a disastrous day it had been.

And Jane hadn't even sent him an email.

AN HOUR LATER, Mel rang him as he was carving the remains of the turkey and putting it into freezer bags.

'Wotcha, Mr. R.! Merry Christmas. How did it go?'

He couldn't bring himself to tell her. 'It went well, thanks, Mel. Really well.'

'No trouble with the turkey? All cooked okay?'

He tried to make his voice upbeat. 'It was delicious! Everything went like clockwork!'

'How about the beef?'

She'd see the beef in the freezer.

'Well, we decided there weren't that many of us. We kept the beef for another day.'

'Right.' She sounded hesitant.

'How's your day?' he asked.

'Brill. The best ever. I mean, me mum's smashed out of her mind now, but Treen and Gary loved it. Proper Chrissy lunch. Thanks, Mr. R. I really appreciate it.'

'My pleasure.' On impulse he said, 'It's not easy, is it? Family, I mean.'

She gulped, half-laugh, half-sob. 'Sure isn't. See you next week, Mr. R.'

BOXING DAY. No one was going to pop in. No one was going to invite him round for a lunch of leftovers. No one was going to ring him. Roger ate and took Killer for a walk in the drizzle, coat collar pulled up against the cold. He was genuinely grateful that he had a dog, for the first time in his life. A few other dog walkers said hello and he had to restrain himself from engaging them in long chats. They were only being polite. They didn't want to hear his life story.

On the 27th, he realised he should probably visit his mother. It was something Jane would have reminded him to do. He turned up at the nursing home with some chocolates and a card. His mother was slumped in a chair in the corner of a light-filled sitting room with shabby furniture. It was quiet; only four other people were in the room, all of them either asleep or staring blankly ahead. His mother looked shapeless under a checked blanket. Only her jumper – purple with a floral pattern on the sleeves – suggested she was female. He could see her pink scalp beneath her thin hair. She didn't recognise him. This was why he didn't visit her more often – it was too depressing. He talked at her for a few minutes and then one of the carers, a jovial lady originally from Zimbabwe, stopped by to say hello to him.

'Mrs. Kurmudge okay?'

He looked towards his mother before he understood what she meant. 'Oh, yes, Jane's fine.'

'We haven't seen her for a while,' she said brightly. 'Lovely lady.'

'Yes, she's away.'

'Where?' His mum's voice was cracked with age but she looked suddenly sharp. 'Where's Jane? I want to see Jane.'

'She's away, Mum. She'll be back soon,' Roger said.

His mother started to shake her head from side to side, faster and faster. She was getting agitated. 'I want to see her! Where is she? What have you done with her?'

The carer was making soothing noises. 'It's all right, Evelyn, it's okay. Try to stay calm, okay?' She looked over her shoulder at Roger. 'It might be time for you to go, Mr. Kurmudge. She's hard to calm down when she gets like this.'

He was relieved to leave. Trudging back to the car, he

wondered what would have happened if he'd been the one to disappear. Would anyone notice? Or even asked Jane where he was?

By the 30th December, he was feeling desperate for company. He'd returned both the coffee machines and organised refunds, then had sent both his sons a cheque for fifteen hundred pounds each. Both had sent a polite note back but Roger felt the ice beneath the words. He'd sent Sarah some earrings – small diamond studs from Malfields. If he'd been hoping for a discount, he didn't get it – and received a pleasant phone call from Sarah, who seemed genuinely delighted. But she didn't invite him over for New Year's Eve. And after quizzing her, he'd sent Guy a hamper from Fortnum & Mason. For which he also received a very polite thank-you email. But no invite.

Eventually, he emailed Tom. He was thrilled to receive an email back just a few hours later asking him when he was free for dinner. Roger wrote straight back suggesting New Year's Eve, and while it was clear that Tom was surprised by this date, as a man with two small children he was going to be at home and was 'delighted Roger could join them to bring in the new year!'

Slightly horrified by how delighted he himself was, Roger was about to go to bed when a final email came in. His heart leapt.

From: Janes Away Hurray
To: Roger Kurmudge
Subject: To do
Remember to renew the TV licence before the end of January. And MOT your car by Feb 10th.

24

The bunting outside was flapping jauntily in the wind. There was also a poster – *Alfie is 3 today!* Roger hoped his present had already been delivered. Sarah's face when she opened the door told him it had.

'Roger, thank you so much, it's a hit. And the green camel, too. Such a large one. Where did you find that?' She ushered him in and as he walked down the hall to the kitchen he could hear squeals coming from the garden. The kitchen extension had finally been finished, much to Roger's relief: he was tired of wearing his coat indoors.

Outside, in spite of the cold, Alfie was throwing himself around on the new trampoline. It had been far easier to source than the enormous green camel, which had come from China at great expense. The oval-shaped trampoline meant Alfie could run along it and perhaps, later, do cartwheels and maybe even some gymnastics. Perhaps that would be the boy's calling. Roger had seen him swimming – Sarah had been ill the first week of term and Roger had volunteered to take him. The boy was not going to be a swimmer. Some of the smaller children had disappeared behind the enormous plumes of water Alfie had kicked up while trying to impress Roberta.

Roger peered out of the window. There were four little boys on the trampoline and Alfie was shouting something at them before trying a very clumsy cartwheel. The trampoline seemed to have softened Sarah's feelings for Roger. She was also wearing the earrings. They sparkled in the January sunshine; as well they should, thought Roger. Malfields were doing well out of him.

He'd picked up Jane's ring the day before. They'd sized it and cleaned it so the shards of light it reflected gave him a headache. It was at home, in the safe in his office. He'd even increased the house insurance to cover it. All he needed now was his wife to come home. He was hoping today might be the day. It was Alfie's birthday; she adored him. The three months was up. Jane must be coming home.

Andy crossed the room and handed him a beer.

'Bit early, isn't it? Ten a.m.?' Roger said.

'When's the last time you came to a kids' party, Dad?' Andy said.

'I can't remember.'

'Trust me. Drink the beer.'

Andy was right, Roger concluded, as the party got into full swing. It was very loud. And set to get louder. After a rather enjoyable New Year's Eve with Tom, Roger had invited Ludo and Ricardo to Alfie's party. The following day, he'd had to ring Sarah and apologise for overstepping the mark.

It was an eye-opener for Roger to see that Alfie was in fact rather a well-behaved little boy. One of the others unzipped the trampoline net and deliberately threw himself out. He was encouraging the others to do the same even as his mum raced across the garden to scoop him up. A red-haired boy whose nose ran permanently was drawing on Andy and Sarah's bedroom wall with an equally permanent marker when his mother finally stopped chatting and went to see what he was up to.

An overweight boy in clothes a size too small positioned himself by the snacks table and shovelled crisps and sausage rolls into his mouth until the bowls were empty. Did he not see all the cucumber sticks and carrot batons laid out neatly, presumably just for him? (For Sarah, excess weight was akin to a moral flaw.) And Roger's least favourite child was the one that managed to wee all over the bathroom floor. Yes, he'd wiped some of it up. Unfortunately, though, he'd used the hand towel to do so before carefully hanging it back on the rail. Roger just wished he'd realised this before trying to wipe his own hands on it.

As for the parents, most of them had accepted a beer or wine with alacrity and then tried their hardest to ignore their offspring for as long as possible. Roger needed two beers to cope with the noise and the chaos and the general sense that no one was in charge. All the parents thought their children were gifted, despite all evidence to the contrary right in front of their eyes. It was actually funny to listen to them all:

'... and Oliver's reading skills are just crazily good; the pre-school teacher told me she'd never met such a deep, cerebral child ...': mother of the boy who'd thrown himself off the trampoline.

'... Jonah spends so much time colouring, his fine motor skills are exceptional ...': mother of the boy drawing on the walls.

'... in the hundredth percentile for weight and height, so clearly Barnaby will take after his old dad and play rugby ... For England, we're hoping ...': father of the fat boy.

'Where do all the gifted children go when they grow up?' a voice said behind him, and Roger turned to see Sam. He felt instantly awkward but Sam grinned at him and said, 'Thanks for the hamper, Dad. Guy loves Fortnums.'

'Glad he liked it,' Roger said. 'Is he with you?'

'Well, yes. I hoped you'd realised that over Christmas,' Sam said.

'I meant is he with you *today*. I did realise over Christmas. And I wanted to say that I'm sorry for being ... what did you call me? A bigoted old bastard?'

'Sorry,' Sam said, looking at his shoes.

'I think I may have been very bigoted,' Roger said. 'And I'm sorry. But I object to the old.'

Roger had never expected to have a gay son, but when he really thought about it, how did it affect him? All he had to do was accept his son's choice. And Guy was a pleasant sort of person who usually helped out with the washing up and liked to discuss the arts with Jane. If Roger just thought of him as the in-law Jane deserved (unlike Sarah, who was slightly spiky even at her best), then it was no problem at all.

Sam was beaming at him now. 'Another beer, Dad?' he said.

'No, thanks, I'm driving.' Roger regretted not being more reasonable over the years. It was nice to have his son so delighted with him. And maybe he'd get invited over again soon. Jane would be so happy about his change of heart. He couldn't wait to tell her.

Sam came back with another beer, managing to sidestep a boy with a pirate hat on and a wooden sword in his hand who was chasing after a terrified-looking smaller child. 'Have you got that studio base sorted yet?'

'No.' Roger had rung a few builders who'd all made it clear that what they wanted was to build a large extension.

Or a garage-slash-annex. Or a second home in the back garden. Not a small concrete base. Even the builder whose van stated *No Job Too Small!* in jaunty lettering said this job was too small for him.

'You could always try my mate. Back-Door Billy.'

Roger stared at Sam. It was one thing accepting his son was gay. It was quite another to be casually discussing the *mechanics* of it all. 'Back-Door ...? I'm not sure what you mean.'

Sam sighed. 'Back-Door because of the dodginess of his stuff, Dad. But he could probably build you a concrete slab without ripping off Homebase.'

'Do you think he'd be available?' Roger was past caring where the concrete came from. He just wanted it installed before Jane got home.

'I'll text him.' Sam got his phone out and tapped at it. A ping later, he said, 'Nope. Fully booked for months.' He carried on tapping at his screen. 'Maybe we could do it ourselves? There's something here called an Eze-Base, which we could install together. At least, according to this website. And it's more eco-friendly.'

Roger wanted to hug him. A project they could do together. Something to fill his time and to bring the two of them closer. 'Eze-Base sounds great. Let's do that.'

Tom arrived late with the twins and Roger was shocked by how pleased he was to see him.

'How are things?' Tom asked, accepting a beer. He looked visibly relieved as the twins ran outside and were instantly absorbed into the throng on the trampoline. 'It's so nice to get rid of them sometimes, isn't it?'

'It is,' Roger said with feeling. 'Looking after Alfie twice a week is fun, of course, but I'm always happy to get home to my nice calm house.'

'Twice a week? I'm impressed, Roger,' Tom said. He lowered his voice. 'Better not tell Elena that. She was rather taken by you that day at the soft-play place!' He threw his head back and laughed. There was a slight note of panic in it.

Roger almost told Tom how very safe he was. He couldn't think of anything worse than a high-maintenance younger wife. He just wanted Jane back. But he put on his best roguish face and said heartily, 'Better watch out, then, Tom! When you marry a beauty like Elena, it's always a risk!' He cleared his throat. 'I did want to chat to you about something worky. Is now a good time?'

Tom looked hesitant. 'Thinking of coming back as a contractor?' he said.

'No, nothing like that,' Roger said. 'I wanted to talk to you about diversity.'

Tom frowned. 'Diversifying our range, you mean? Moving into other categories?'

'No. Diversity in the workforce.'

Tom swallowed a long draught of beer and started to choke. Roger watched for a moment before gingerly patting him on the back.

'Sorry, just want to check I've got this right, Roger. *You'd like to talk about diversity*?'

'Yes.'

'It's just that you weren't sure about recruiting Mohammed. And you generally prefer to employ men rather than women, don't you? Because of the maternity leave?'

'I've been thinking. You know, Guildford has pockets of real deprivation, Tom. I didn't realise or do enough when I was working. And I thought we – Karter's – could try to help now.'

'Okay.' Tom was nodding. 'I don't disagree. We're a big local employer. What sort of thing did you have in mind?'

'Perhaps I could come in to chat with you next week? Run a few things by you?'

It wasn't until the party officially ended at twelve o'clock that Roger admitted to himself that Jane wasn't coming home that day. *MOT the car by Feb 10th* now took on a sinister implication and the teetering pile of unread *Guardian* newspapers lying in the porch were an all-too-painful reminder of his wife's absence as he put his key into the front door. The house felt quiet and cold. Killer was out with Hannah and he missed the joyful, slightly hysterical gambolling around his feet that he usually got from the dog when he returned. He didn't know what to do next. Ring the police again? Send Jane another email? It had been more than three months now. He couldn't believe she hadn't come home yet. And what did Nina think about it? Unless of course Jane had informed Nina of a change to the three-month plan.

On impulse, he put his coat on and got back in the car.

Nina was looking bored when he turned up. Her face brightened as he pushed the door open then fell again. 'No Killer with you?'

'He's at the dog walker's,' Roger said. 'I was at Alfie's birthday party.'

'Lovely,' Nina said vaguely.

'Everything okay?' Roger said.

'Yes. Well ... no. I could really do with more business coming in. Jane was so good at getting people to buy. So I'm slightly disappointed about her decision.'

'Her decision?'

'You know, to resign.'

'Resign?' For a moment, he couldn't understand the word.

'I'm really sad she won't be back.'

Roger swallowed. 'Me too. Did she tell you why?'

'No,' Nina said. 'Not really. Just that she was going to be too busy to come back to work here.' Her gaze sharpened. 'Why? Is there another reason?'

'No,' said Roger. 'How did she let you know?'

'Just an email.' She looked really curious now. 'You must be missing her a lot. Freya went away last month for four days on a course and I was so bored, I spent a fortune buying new art I didn't really need.'

Roger said, 'Yes.' He knew his voice sounded flat but he couldn't do much about it. It was all he could do to still talk. He'd been counting on Jane being back in January. On making plans and chatting in the evening, and having sex and doing all the things he'd been missing. Counting on getting his life back. On not being on his own. Now he saw how foolish he'd been. The truth smacked him in the face with the force of a brick.

She'd left him. Actually *left* him.

The dragging sensation in his stomach made him feel almost too weak to walk. Perhaps he should ring the solicitors and get his affairs in order. He muttered his excuses and left the gallery, aware that Nina was staring after him. He trudged back to the car and returned home. Killer was there, dropped off by Hannah, who had a key. There seemed to be no end to the number of people with a key to his house. And as he aged, he'd need more and more people to look after him and keep him company and do jobs around the house and garden, and all the time he'd be smiling and chatting while inside he'd be devastated. He'd lost the best thing that had ever happened to him because he just hadn't been sufficiently aware of her or how lucky he was.

He'd thought he was fortunate to be healthy and have a good career and plenty of money, but in fact the only bit of good luck that had really mattered in his life had been Jane. He should have been focusing on being grateful every single day that he'd managed to trick someone so fabulous into marrying him, and concentrating on keeping her right where she was. And ensuring that she never, *ever* found out about his betrayal in Sydney.

Roger could have wept. In fact, he was weeping. Leaning on the kitchen island and crying – blubbing – like a small boy. Like Alfie when deprived of the park or a Feast or a café trip. He leant his elbows on the counter and put his head in his hands and sobbed until he had no tears left. Outside, he could hear birdsong, and in the distance, a child shouting. He took a couple of deep, shaky breaths. Killer was looking up at him with eyes full of doggy sorrow.

'Good job you're here,' Roger said. He knelt down and stroked Killer. 'You're all I've got.'

His phone buzzed. He grabbed it from his coat pocket. But it was Sam.

R U in at 3 today?

He texted back instantly to say he would be, and went to wash his face.

∼

SAM ARRIVED at ten past three. Roger had to fight the urge to be too grateful for the visit. He offered him a beer but Sam waggled the car keys at him.

'Tea, then? Or coffee?'

'I've had three today,' Sam said. 'Better make it tea.'

'I went to the gallery today and saw Nina. Your mum has resigned. I don't think she's ever coming home.'

'Wait, what? Run that by me again.'

'Nina said your mum sent her an email resigning from her job.'

'Right. So?'

'So that might mean she isn't coming home at all.' Roger felt close to tears again. He couldn't cry in front of Sam. His sons were currently quite sorry for him but over time that sympathy would wane if he wasn't careful. Without Jane at home, would they still want to see him? Not if he started crying whenever they came over.

'But it might not,' Sam said. His calmness made Roger feel instantly better. 'Maybe she decided she wanted to pursue her own art instead of selling other people's.'

Roger liked this idea very much. 'Maybe.'

Sam lounged up against the kitchen island, stroking Killer with his foot. 'Anyway, I've had a better idea for the base, Dad. Might save us some work.'

'Okay.' Roger put tea bags in mugs. 'What were you thinking?'

Sam pointed to the garden. Beyond the formal part, with its neat flowerbeds and low hedge around the patio, lay the more rustic area. The boys had called it 'the wild bit' when they were growing up. It had a tiny copse of trees, a small triangle of open grass and a meandering stream. Jane and Gail had tried a wildflower meadow last year, and some of the flowers had done well, but it was mostly left to its own devices.

Backing onto it from the garden was the small shed that had originally been used for bikes and boogie-boards as well as the bird feed, until the insurance company had asked if it had a good lock on it. At that point Roger had brought the expensive bikes and surfing equipment into Jane's studio.

Roger was puzzled. 'What are you pointing at?' He handed Sam his tea.

'The shed has a base, Dad. It's concrete. Probably about the right size.'

'So?'

'We could knock it down and use the base for the studio. If it's still looking okay, I mean. You could put all the stuff in it into the garage instead.'

It wasn't a bad idea. The Eze-Base was almost certainly not easy at all to construct, and this base was already there.

'Will it be easy to knock down, do you think?'

Sam grinned. 'Only one way to find out.' He put his mug down. 'Come on.'

They went into the garden and walked down the neat lawn towards the shed.

Sam strode ahead. 'I think it's about the right size, Dad.' He tapped at his phone screen. 'Yeah, definitely, looking at this spec.' He held out his phone and tapped the screen before walking to the other side and tapping it again. 'Yeah, it's just right.'

'How can you be sure?' Roger said.

'Measuring app,' Sam said.

They both walked around the shed for a minute or two. The base was concrete, and from what Roger could see of the edges it was in good condition. The timber of the shed, on the other hand, was damp with rot.

Sam said, 'Have you got something to knock it down with?'

'Like what?'

'A crowbar to get the roof and sides off, maybe? Or a mallet?'

Roger tugged open the door. 'There's probably something in here.'

The smell of damp and neglect hit him. Once his eyes adjusted to the dim light, he saw there were still a few things stored in it, apart from the bird food. Some rusty tools lay in a corner, bound together with cobwebs. A pile of old welly boots. There was a tiny tricycle under a large piece of damp cardboard.

'Look!' Sam was delighted with the trike. 'I remember this! Mum used to push me around on it. I wonder if Alfie would like it?' He put his hands on the handlebars and wiggled them slightly. A squeaking noise, like a protest. 'Maybe not. It's a bit past it. I could do a tip run, if you like, Dad?'

'I can do it,' Roger said. Something else to fill a day. 'Let's get everything onto the grass and we can sort it after we've pulled the shed down. Then I can take all the rubbish to the tip.'

There was more in the shed than Roger had expected. An old terracotta plant pot, cracked, with some soil clinging to the base. A length of rope, which might actually come in handy. A few packs of seeds: ditto. Seeds lasted forever, didn't they? A bicycle with faded stickers on the frame that Roger didn't remember the boys having. An old scooter, scarred with rust.

Sam cooed over each discovery. 'Don't you remember,

Dad? I got this scar from falling off this bike.' He pulled up his jeans to show a puckered pink line on his left knee. 'It really hurt. I needed stitches. Came off on the road and skidded along for what felt like a mile. I was totally banged up afterwards. Grazes on my face even.'

'Where was I?' Roger said before he could stop himself. Why didn't he remember this stuff, too?

Sam shrugged and a look of grief crossed his face. 'In Australia, I guess. But Mum was there, of course.' He pulled at a length of clothesline. A forlorn-looking boy's sock was still attached. Sam threw it out onto the grass, along with two soggy cardboard boxes. A pile was building up. There were old gardening tools under the boxes, several gardening magazines, and a square, flat-looking cushion. Roger took a moment to recognise that it was a kneeling pad that Jane had used for weeding, to spare her knees.

He had a flash of memory: Jane working away on a flowerbed, creating a pile of unwanted green strands, while he sat inside watching sport. He wouldn't do that ever again. Why hadn't he been out here, helping her? Participating? Especially as in his memory, sun glinted off her hair as she pushed it behind her ears with a gloved hand and turned to smile at him, her teeth white against her tanned skin. She had waved at him as though inviting him to join her. Why had he just waved back and turned his face to the TV?

'Was it fun growing up here?' he asked Sam on a whim.

'Here?' Sam straightened and stretched his back out. His face was downcast. 'It was pretty good, actually. We used to play hide and seek in this bit,' he gestured to the trees beyond them, 'and often I hid in here.' He pointed to the shed. 'It's a bit sad to pull it down. Some good memories. But it's time to move on.'

Was that what Jane thought? Time to move on? Maybe,

as Roger's retirement had loomed, she couldn't bear the thought of him lying around watching Sky while she weeded? He really wouldn't do that now. He'd weed. Plant seedlings. Prune roses. Whatever she wanted him to do. And why hadn't he realised how sad his absence, both emotional and physical, had made his children?

'I'm sorry,' he said, clearing his throat, 'if I wasn't around enough for you when you were growing up.'

Sam was very still. 'I'm sorry I wouldn't play rugby. Or football. I won't apologise for being gay,' he said fiercely, 'but I am sorry I disappointed you.'

'I ... That's ... It's not *your* fault I wasn't around!' Roger said. 'I was too caught up in work. I should have paid more attention to you both. You have no need to apologise.' He coughed and blew his nose hard.

'I still need something to pull this down with,' Sam said after a brief moment. He rummaged around in the corner of the shed, deep in shadow. 'This might do it?' He brandished a crowbar, rusty but sturdy-looking.

'Roof first?' Roger said, relieved to get back to practical considerations.

'Yes. Just get the last few bits out and then I'll get it down.'

Killer was sniffing at the contents of the shed that were laid out on the grass. He followed a trail into the shed, weaving between Sam's feet and ending up in the farthest corner, where he started to sniff frantically, his neck fur on end.

'I hope it's not a hibernating hedgehog,' Sam said. 'We'd have to leave the shed right where it is. Guy would kill me if I disturbed one.'

Killer started to growl softly.

'What is it, Killer?' Roger said as Sam shouted, 'Look out!'

A mouse streaked out of the corner, past them and out of the shed, closely followed by Killer. Roger had never seen the dog move so fast. The rodent raced for the cover of the trees with Killer close behind. Roger hoped fervently that Killer didn't catch it. He'd have to dispose of the body.

'There's another one!' Sam shouted, and sure enough a second mouse ran straight towards Roger. With what he considered to be great presence of mind, Roger leapt into the air (banging his head on the low roof) and it ran under him, out of the shed door and into the nearest bushes.

'Gotcha!' Sam said, and Roger saw he'd taken a picture. 'Look!' His son showed him the phone screen: there he was, pale in the flash, mid-air, arms and legs flailing with a comical expression on his face and a tiny grey blurred shape below him. It wasn't the most flattering picture but Sam was laughing, so Roger laughed too and suddenly it was a shared experience. He hadn't had many of those with Sam.

'Send that picture to me, will you?' he said, and Sam grinned.

'I will. Killer! Come back!'

The dog reappeared from the trees, panting.

'No sign of the first mouse,' Sam said. 'Maybe he killed it?'

'I hope not, somehow,' Roger said. 'They've already lost their home.'

'Blimey, Dad, didn't think you were so wildlife friendly. You and Guy do have something in common, after all. He's always banging on about biodiversity.'

'Not sure that really covers mice,' Roger said. 'But still, I feel bad for them.' He knew what it was like to have his home life disrupted. He almost told Sam to leave the shed where it was. But even if the mice came back, would they ever feel the same about their old home? Could they go back to the way it had been? Could he and Jane? He yearned to be told he was looking a little too pleased with himself and be tapped playfully with *The Guardian*.

Sam smacked the crowbar into the palm of his hand. 'Here goes.'

Once the roof was off, the rest of the shed fell apart quickly. Several timbers collapsed inwards and the remaining ones that were still standing didn't put up much of a fight.

'We could pile these up under one of the trees,' Sam said. 'I'll pull the nails out and we can leave a pile for wildlife. Here, grab this, Dad.'

Roger took one of the pieces of timber and followed Sam to the nearest tree. 'Better go a bit further away,' he said. 'Your mum won't love mice near the studio.'

'Okay.'

They walked to the fence that divided Roger's house from the neighbour's. Tristan Golding was a truculent sort of person who never stopped complaining. He deserved mice.

'Here, Dad?' Sam asked.

'This should do it.' They put the timbers down, higgledy-piggledy, with gaps between them, then brought the rest of the shed walls over to pile on top. The roof would need to go to the tip, so Sam collected the corrugated sheets and put them in a neat heap by the back door. In no time they were left with a final pile of things that needed to go to the tip, and a concrete base.

'What do you think?' Sam said, staring down at it. 'I mean, I could give it a blast with the high-pressure hose. Clean it up a bit. But I think it looks okay.'

'It does. I think we need a spirit level to check it's suitable,' Roger said, thinking back to one of the many emails he'd received about the studio base.

'No worries, Dad,' Sam said. He tapped away on his phone for a few seconds. 'There's an app for that, too.' He put his phone down, landscape side down, on the base. 'Yeah, it's fine.'

'That was easier than building the base ourselves,' Roger said. 'Think we deserve a beer now, don't you?' It was almost dark and bitterly cold.

Back at the house, he tried to get Sam to stay for the evening but he and Guy had booked somewhere for dinner.

'Maybe one evening you could come for dinner here? Get Guy over, too?'

'Maybe, Dad.' Sam put on his coat. 'We'll see you soon.' Opening the front door, he said, 'You know, perhaps you should just cancel Mum's *Guardian* subscription. If we're not sure when she'll be back.' He leaned forward and hugged Roger: a proper hug that Roger could feel the love in. He hugged his son back, hard, before Sam wordlessly left.

Roger shut the door and went to renew the TV licence. Another long, lonely evening stretched ahead of him.

25

Only the thought of Killer forced Roger to drag himself downstairs the following day at ten am. He let the dog out and fed him before going back upstairs and falling into the still warm bed. A desperate feeling of isolation squeezed his chest. He needed company.

He sat up and called, 'Killer!' Nothing. He called again. 'Killer!' A few moments later, he could hear hesitant paws on the stair carpet. Killer had been shouted at so many times for trying to get upstairs that the habit was hard to break. But now the dog's white head peeked around the door.

Roger patted the bed. 'Come on, then!'

As if he couldn't believe his luck, Killer raced across the carpet and took a flying leap onto the bed. He didn't quite make it and Roger had to catch him and hoist him up.

'There. You sleep on that side. Good dog.'

Killer turned around several times before dropping heavily onto the duvet and sighing deeply.

Roger lay down again and stared at the ceiling. It was

comforting to have Killer's sturdy body stretched out where Jane used to be. The dog's breathing soon settled into a contented rhythm with an occasional snore. It did make Roger feel better, even if he couldn't drop off as easily as Killer had.

He stayed in bed for two more hours until he was able to force himself back down the stairs, dressed and functional, though stunned with misery. He took Killer out for a short walk around the block. At times like this, neighbours with driveways and houses set back from pavements were a definite negative. Roger needed to bump into people, to have a quick chat and interact with other humans. Killer was a good dog but a neighbour would be better.

When he glimpsed Cara on her doorstep, he shouted from across the road, 'Cara! Hello! Cup of tea?'

She looked mildly put out but agreed. 'As long as you leave Killer outside. Mathew's allergies are awful.' In her kitchen, she put the kettle on. 'How are things?'

'Terrible.' He knew he was supposed to say 'fine', but he couldn't. He sat down heavily on a chair at the kitchen table. 'Really awful. I expected Jane back by now but I don't think she's coming home. We might be getting a divorce.'

She looked shocked. 'Really? How did you find out she isn't coming home?'

'I asked her boss.'

'From the art gallery?' Cara asked.

'You knew she worked?'

'You didn't?'

'I had no idea. About a lot of things.'

'But surely she'll be home at some point? Won't she?' Cara sounded as perplexed as he felt.

He shrugged. 'Maybe not. She has her own money. She

doesn't need to come home, does she, at least not for a while: the children are grown up now.'

'But what about Alfie? She loves him. I can't believe she'd just leave without letting you all know. If she wanted to leave you then she could simply divorce you. Couldn't she?'

Roger scratched at his unshaven chin. 'I don't know much about divorce.'

'I do,' Cara said, 'and I think she'd just tell you she wanted one and move out. Or make you move out. It's not as though money's a problem, is it?'

'No. Money,' Roger said, 'isn't our problem.'

She smiled kindly at him. 'Well, then, I think something else is going on.'

'Like?' Roger said.

'Like ... revenge for you not being very involved in family life? Or an affair?'

He flushed scarlet. 'An affair? Oh, you mean *Jane*.'

Sorry, but it's possible.'

'I could overlook that,' Roger said. He'd be very jealous, of course, but he could overlook it, chalk it up to karma, as the boys would say. Provided she just came home and things were like they used to be. But better, because he'd be a much, much better husband. Kinder, more involved, more available, more appreciative.

Cara pushed a Karter's shortbread biscuit on a plate towards him. 'Have a biccie.'

He wasn't hungry but wanted to keep chatting so he nodded his thanks and nibbled at it as slowly as possible. He told her about the studio and dismantling the shed with Sam.

'What a nice project for the two of you,' she said. 'Fun to

do together as long, of course, that it's not too complex or tricky. That's when arguments start.'

'Sam's pretty good at this stuff,' Roger said. 'And I wouldn't argue with him, in any case.' He was enjoying their new relationship far too much. Nothing would make him argue with Sam. Or Andy. Or even Alfie, these days. Without Jane around, he had to count on the other relationships in his life. Would Tomasso expect to move into his lovely house with his lovely wife? How would Roger bear it? The house bit wasn't too bad. There were lots of lovely houses. But his lovely wife was a rarity. Most of the women he met were less lovely than Jane.

Take Cara. Perfectly nice, if a little brusque and starchy. The ideal person if you needed some hard-hitting practical advice. But none of Jane's calm kindness. People didn't warm to Cara. They respected her. Enjoyed the cut-and-thrust of conversation with her. But didn't think on a cold wintry evening, 'Let's spend some time with that charming woman, Cara, whose mere smile will make me feel better about all my worries.' And her dress sense? Just awful.

Whereas Elena had dress sense in spades. But she was far too worried about herself. How did she look? Did the men she was meeting find her attractive? Was Tom doing enough of the childcare? And earning enough to pay for the second house and two foreign trips a year and private schools? Of course, Roger did earn enough for all those things, but they hadn't been important to Jane. Something about Elena's overt materialism was very off-putting.

Now, Nina was warm. And could dress. And didn't seem materialistic. Concerned about sales, perhaps, but in a business-like way. In a Jane-free world, he'd certainly consider dating Nina. Or at least asking her to dinner. Except she was taken. And a lesbian. Highly unlikely to wake one morning and think, 'Perhaps I should take a closer look at that urbane and fascinating chap, Roger.'

Roger had never truly appreciated how incredibly rare his wife was. Like a two-carat flawless colourless diamond. Hard to find and extremely precious. How had he been so totally moronic as to overlook this prize of a woman?

He came to from this reverie to realise Cara was giving him a look. A look that said 'I know exactly why that charming woman left this gormless, pompous dullard. I hope she takes him for every penny!'

She didn't actually say that. She said, 'You seem very sad about Jane's departure, Roger. Have you told her how much you miss her? I mean, really told her nicely? Rather than a series of grumpy emails pointing out how cross you are with her for not being here?'

'Of course,' Roger said. 'Of course I have.'

Inside, he was having what that attractive Australian girl, Kate from Consumer Insight, would have called 'a light-bulb moment'. (Positives for Kate: sunny personality, lovely teeth. Negatives for Kate? Rather too convinced of what an intuitive marketing marvel she was, which, based on the last launch she'd worked on – Karter's Knobblies, their not-as-good answer to McVitie's Hobnobs – was not true.)

Of course he hadn't sent Jane nice messages. He'd sent emails that throbbed with resentment and irritation.

He left and started off home, forgetting Killer until the dog let out a howl that made an old lady in a too large raincoat on the other side of the road jump, put her hand to her heart and glare at him. Roger hurried back to untie the dog, and as soon as they got home he ran upstairs, Killer close behind him, to the study.

He logged on. Time to pour his heart out and bring Jane home.

My darling girl ... Too schmaltzy.

My love ... He'd never use that phrase.

Dear Jane ... Too much like any email she received from a friend.

He gave it some more thought. This was a critical moment.

He cracked his knuckles, took a deep breath and typed:

From: Roger Kurmudge
To: Janes Away Hurray
<u>Subject: I'm so sorry</u>
My lovely Janey,
I'm sorry. For not noticing you enough. For not noticing everything you do. I am totally at fault for you leaving and I know I haven't been the best husband to you. I had no right (ever!) to look so pleased with myself. Trust me, I'm not any more. But I've never ever been anything other than pleased – no, thrilled and amazed – that someone as fantastic as *you* agreed to marry *me*. Please come home so we can at least talk about what to do next. For the boys at least. And Alfie. And Killer.
I love you very much and I'm sorry I didn't make that clearer millions of times over the years.
Always yours,
Roger

He re-read it and made a few small tweaks. He hadn't called her Janey for a long time but it had been a frequent term of endearment in the early years when they'd fought, and he wanted to make up.

His email wouldn't win any literary awards. But it was as sincere as he could make it without actually admitting to the affair. He didn't dare do that. He still hoped she didn't know.

He read it through once more and pressed send.

HE WAS SO sure it would touch his wife that he fully expected to get a response in the next hour. Maybe with some details of her travel plans. A train arrival time or flight number.

Nothing.

A day went by. Then another. Then two more.

He began to think about the limits of his email. Grey clouds scudded across the sky and torrents of rain ran diagonally across his windows, matching his mood. He'd apologised for his sins of omission towards Jane herself. But what about his sons?

He sat down at his desk again.

From: Roger Kurmudge
To: Janes Away Hurray
Subject: Really utterly abjectly sorry
Dearest Janey,
I should also have said that I definitely approve of gay men adopting. Why did I ever have an issue with it? I'm not sure, but I don't anymore. And I will make much more effort with Sarah. She might be frosty but Andy loves her and that's enough for me. I promise to try harder.
I've changed. I really have.
Please come home.
All my love,
Rodge

Another three days went by without a word.

At the end of the third day, Roger realised: Jane wasn't coming back.

26

He kept going because he had no choice. Walking Killer. Taking Alfie on Mondays and Thursdays, (the best days of his week). Meeting other people in his situation at the GPPG at Cara's house. Chatting with Mel, avoiding Morwenna, sorting out a pile of washing and compiling shopping lists and filling recycling bins. Cara popped over from time to time. Tom invited him for a drink at the pub one evening and he accepted with enthusiasm. Vanessa even invited him to attend story-time at the library and he and Alfie went. She was warming to him, he thought. Perhaps because he was much better with Alfie now.

He filled his time as much as he could, to stop him thinking about Jane and where she was, who she was with. Sometimes, when Alfie ran to take his hand, or Killer panted up at him happily after a walk, or Mel gave him the spoon to taste a new recipe, or Cara came for tea, he felt something approaching happiness, or at least contentment, until he felt a thump of dread.

This was as good as life would get for him now.

He knew it wasn't bad. He wasn't living in poverty or

Syria or an old people's home full of dementia sufferers. But he had wasted his best years without even realising how lucky he was. He wanted to hit his stupid head against his Farrow & Ball-painted walls every time he thought of it.

THE DAYS PASSED. He sat down with Mel on a rainy Wednesday afternoon after she'd banged into the kitchen muttering about her mum's latest bender and how was Mel supposed to create a calm stable home with that witch drinking a bottle of vodka a day? He waved a packet of Karter's Chocowheels at her and gestured for her to come upstairs. Frowning, she'd followed him up the carpeted treads and sat down next to his desk. He offered her the biscuits but she shook her head.

'Mel, I want to have a chat with you,' Roger said. 'About your future.'

'My future?' She squinted at him. She looked anxious. 'Don't you need me no more?'

'No, I don't mean that, but you're wasted on helping me. You're a very bright girl,' he said. 'No, don't pretend you aren't. And I want to try to help you.'

'Help me how?' She looked truculent now.

'It's really important for you, Gary and Treen – and even your mum – that you get a good job. Probably something that means university.'

She started to protest about the cost, and he held his hand up. 'Just hear me out. What are you interested in, Mel?'

She glowered at him. 'Nights out away from the kids?'

'Well, maybe. But I meant something that might turn

into a job. Something similar to what you do here, for instance?'

'Cook? I can't be a chef, Mr. R. Late nights don't work for Gary and Treen.'

'I wasn't thinking of you being a chef, although you could.' He smiled. 'You might not be aware of all the options available to someone as bright and talented as you. How about becoming a food technologist?'

'A what?' She wrinkled her nose.

'Food technologist. There are lots of them at Karter's. They take a recipe from our home economist, something that can be made in a standard kitchen, and make it something we can do in a factory. It's a scientific sort of job but you need to love food. Sound like you?'

'I dunno.'

'Well, how about shadowing – following around – a food technologist at Karter's for a day or two? I could arrange it?'

'Thanks, Mr. R. Kind of you, but I can't afford uni fees; last thing I need is a massive debt hanging over me. And where would I live? Gary and Treen need me at home.'

'Not all universities are far away. There's Reading, which isn't far, and plenty of others. We can look at them together. But first, are you interested in spending some time shadowing the food technologist at Karter's? I can arrange it for half term even, so you don't miss school?'

She stood up. 'I need to get on. And I don't really see the point. I can't afford uni.'

'Please sit down, Mel. I wanted to explain that bit. If you like the idea of food science and are interested in doing the course at university, and if you get the right grades, I think Karter's would sponsor you. They've got a programme to try to increase diversity in the company and you'd be an ideal candidate for it. You'd have to work for Karter's afterwards for a couple of years to pay them back, but I promise it's a good place to work and you'd then have a guaranteed job. And perhaps Treen could help us a bit when she's older so she can earn some money that way? What do you think?'

Mel was blinking very fast at him. He couldn't read her expression. A few seconds passed. 'Okay, then. I'll see. After the half-term visit.'

'Of course.' He stood up and wondered whether to say anything else. She seemed upset but he knew enough not to pat her on the shoulder. 'I'd love some more of that chicken casserole for the freezer, if you don't mind?'

'Right-o, Mr. R.' She smiled; he could see she was trying to process what he'd said. She thumped off back down the stairs and he sent a quick note to Tom to ask him to arrange for Ed, the food technologist, to put some time aside during the February half term.

He had wondered about his own motivation. Why was he doing this? To help Mel and improve her life chances? No: he knew why he was doing this. He wanted to be able to tell Jane. Jane, who read *The Guardian,* baked for Macmillan coffee mornings, sponsored two children in Third World countries, volunteered at the local food bank, made monthly donations to the nearest wildlife sanctuary and had told Roger that he was rather low on empathy. He'd snorted and told her he was too busy making a living to be empathetic. She'd snapped that the two shouldn't be mutually exclusive.

She would surely appreciate what he was doing for Mel. Should he start writing an email to her now? Or would that look a bit blatant? He'd really prefer it to come out naturally, through someone else, but couldn't see how that would happen. Andy was hardly likely to email her and jauntily add a PS: *Dad is so much improved! Alfie loves him and he's being so kind to Mel. She comes to help him three times a week but he is helping her just as much!*

No. He'd wait. There would be a time to drop this nugget into communication. He didn't know when. But one day, surely Jane would ring. Surely she would. They'd have to sort things out, wouldn't they? People didn't just ... leave.

Even Morwenna was gradually warming to him. He overheard her on the phone one day as she was arriving. The words 'less of a tosser than I thought' echoed across the porch as he opened the door for her, and she flushed.

'Hello,' Roger said, 'how are you?' He almost asked her to email Jane. *Less of a tosser than I thought* could be the title of the email.

'Good,' she said and muttered into the phone, 'Call you back, yeah?'

He'd been heading upstairs to get out of her way when she shouted after him.

'I just wanted to say ... what you're doing helping our Mel? It's kind. Thanks.'

'She doesn't need help. She needs to see more of the options available. She's a very clever, talented girl and she deserves more opportunities,' Roger said. And he meant it. Mel did deserve more opportunities. He just hoped she decided she liked food technology. Or something else she could do at Karter's. Something he could help her with within his 'sphere of influence', as they used to say at work.

He now understood Jane's urge to get a job. It was dull, looking after the house and the garden and the dog and the emails about the French property. No wonder Jane had gone to the gallery. A chance to meet people and chat to Nina and get away from the drudgery and chores. He almost asked Nina if *he* could take the job. But he knew nothing about art. Except that her Jackson Pollock knock-off was rubbish.

In an effort to fill more time, he asked Sarah whether he could take Alfie for another day a week. 'Jane always took him on Wednesdays, too, didn't she? I'd love to have him then.'

'Really?' She frowned.

'Absolutely.'

'Well, in fact, I was going to tell you we don't really need you as much. He's off to pre-school now he's three, for three days a week. But if you'd like to take him and pick him up on those days, it would help. If you're sure?'

'I am.' Roger was appalled to learn that Alfie wouldn't need him as much. He was going to be so lonely. 'I'd also like to bring him home afterwards and keep him for tea on those days.'

'Great!' She smiled at him. A proper smile, with her teeth. It was slightly alarming.

STUDIO-INSTALLATION WEEKEND ARRIVED. Droopy Eyes was coming at ten. Sam was at the door at nine and naturally insisted on coffee first. He'd brought his own beans. He fussed around making it.

'Where do *you* think your mum is?' Roger asked him.

'Dunno.' Sam blew on his mug. He glanced at Roger, something in his expression that Roger couldn't decipher. Judgment? 'It's so unlike her, but she's been running after us for years, so I figure we need to give her some space.'

Perhaps Sam had a point. 'And how are things with the adoption?'

'Good.' Sam looked hesitant. 'We had a couple of months of filling in the paperwork about a year or so ago, and the last few months were more about assessing us and training us. That's pretty much finished. We're with this agency, and they look for children across the UK. So we're sort of waiting now, to see if a child comes up that we're compatible with.'

'Do you get to choose? I mean' – Roger searched for the right, non-offensive words – 'I mean, can you say that you'd like a particular type of child?'

'I suppose maybe some people might,' Sam said. 'But we haven't. We don't think we know enough to take a child with lots of special needs – we might not be the best people to manage – but apart from that we don't care about skin colour or gender or ethnicity or any of that stuff.' He jutted his jaw at Roger, looking very like Alfie for a moment, as though he expected Roger to protest. 'We just want to offer a child a loving home. Isn't that the point of being a good parent? Love the child you get, with all their quirks?'

A long silence drew out.

'Quite right, Sammy,' Roger said. He swallowed the lump in his throat – he hadn't used the name 'Sammy' in decades – leaned across the island and patted Sam's hand. 'Plenty of children out there who need exactly that.'

'It's hard, the waiting.'

'I know,' Roger said, perhaps with more feeling than he realised, because it was Sam's turn to grip his hand tightly.

Droopy Eyes arrived on the dot of ten a.m. He had also brought a rotund, bald man, who grunted when Roger greeted him. 'Can we drive into the back garden, then?' Droopy Eyes asked.

Roger would really have preferred them not to, but couldn't see any other way of getting the pallets into the right spot. 'Fine. But mind the lawn, if you can.'

He watched them pick the pallets back up with a crane and put them on the back of the truck. They disappeared around the side of the house and reappeared reversing at high speed across his lawn towards the base. It wasn't fun to watch the grass being churned up and tread-marks appearing. Gail would kill him.

'Think I might leave them to the installation,' he said to Sam.

'I'll give them a hand,' Sam said. 'Make it quicker.'

Droopy Eyes and his mate obviously thought Roger was a bit of a joke. It was easier not to be around. He popped out with tea mid-morning and left the mugs on the lawn, rather than staying to chat. But it was a shame to miss out on time with Sam. He peered out of the kitchen windows a couple of times. The modular pieces of the building were quite quickly slotted together and he could hear drilling and scraps of conversation. Sam had brought his own drill and Roger was rather impressed by his son's confidence with it. Perhaps they *should* have built the Eze-Base together. It would have been a reason for Sam to come over.

When lunchtime came, Roger heated up one of Mel's chicken casseroles.

'You know, you're doing all right, Dad,' Sam said. 'I'm quite impressed, actually.' He helped himself to a large portion of casserole and heaped it onto the brown rice Roger had managed to cook all by himself. Outside, Droopy Eyes and his mate were eating sandwiches, sitting on the bench and staring around them, clearly discussing the unfairness of a world that allowed a pillock like Roger to own such an amazing house. Roger could almost see their point.

'Well, I've had a lot of help,' Roger said. 'Mel's indispensable.' He told Sam about the idea of Mel becoming a food technologist with Karter's.

'That's great,' Sam said. 'Love the diversity stuff. I had no idea you were doing that sort of thing at work.'

Roger felt compelled to qualify the statement. 'I didn't do enough while I was there, but I wanted to do it now. Mel's a lovely girl who just needs someone to show her the door to a better life. She can walk through it and be successful on the other side all by herself.'

Sam was staring at him with something in his eyes that Roger struggled to name. Could it be *admiration*? Or maybe just relief that his father was more human than he'd thought? Whatever it was, Roger liked it.

After lunch Sam returned to the garden. A robin flew down to inspect the three men at one point and Roger noted that the bird feeders were empty again. It was a daily task to refill them. Along with all the other essential daily tasks he hadn't noticed before: unloading the dishwasher, making his own breakfast, putting the dirty dishes in the dishwasher, sorting the recycling, organising the washing, doing the odd bit of top-up shopping, emailing Victor about the French house (which was turning out to be like Roger's idea of a French mistress – easy on the eye but extremely high-maintenance), walking Killer, doing dental appointments and GP appointments and all the other things Jane had booked for him without him even thinking about it. Perhaps it was no wonder she didn't want to come home. The memory of what he'd done years earlier resurfaced queasily and he pushed it down hard.

Jane didn't know. She *couldn't*.

BY THE TIME the light was leeching from the sky, the garden studio was up. It looked amazing, Roger thought. Elegant, well positioned, with a view across the garden to the house. Droopy Eyes and his mate looked too tired to rib him about his lack of planning.

'It looks great,' Roger said, stepping in through the French doors. It was as good as his daydream had suggested. Fresh paint smell. Sharp corners. Very quiet.

'Yeah.' Droopy Eyes's mate stretched his back, releasing a strong odour of sweat. 'Nice buildings. If you have the space, like.'

Roger handed them both twenty quid. 'I appreciate all the work.'

'Thanks, lads,' Sam said, slightly self-consciously. 'I'll check out that show about tattoos you mentioned. What was it, again?'

ROGER ASKED Sam to stay for a beer and they took a couple of folding chairs from the garage into the new studio.

'Isn't this great?' Roger eased himself into one of the chairs and stared out over the garden. Lights from the kitchen at the back of the house made it look even more inviting than usual. 'Your mum will absolutely love this.'

'Yes.' Sam sounded hesitant. 'She will.'

'Don't you think so?' Roger demanded.

'Of course.'

'When she comes back. Which must be soon,' Roger said. Hope had risen in him as the studio had gone up. He was trying so hard to be a better dad and grandad. He *had* to believe his wife would come back. The alternative was just too grim.

'Hmm.' Sam drank his beer.

'I'll have to move her easel in here, once the electrician has been to install the power. She'll love it.'

'Dad?' Sam looked hesitant. 'I don't think we know enough about what Mum wants. Maybe that's why she left.'

'But she'll be able to paint. After her course in Italy, she'll be fired up again.'

'Maybe.'

It was unbearable to hear how unlikely Sam thought Jane's return was, so he changed the subject. 'Why don't you and Guy come over next weekend and we can set this up for your mum? The easel, and all her paints, and a kettle for tea, that sort of thing.'

Sam said again, 'Maybe. Let me check with Guy.' As if he realised how lonely the weekends were for Roger, he said, 'Any plans for tomorrow, Dad?'

'No. Nothing.' It sounded a bit too bleak. 'But it's a busy week coming up: Alfie starts pre-school.'

'Andy told me. Exciting.'

'I hope Alfie thinks so.' Roger wasn't sure about pre-school. Alfie was quite sensitive. The encounter in the soft-play centre with Chunky Boy had proved that there were some nasty types out there. Was Alfie really ready for them?

'He'll be fine, Dad.' Sam drained the beer bottle, picked up his coat and said, 'Better go.'

Roger had to restrain himself from begging Sam to stay longer. 'See you soon, I hope. Say hello to Guy for me.'

'Good luck with Alfie and pre-school,' Sam said, 'hope it goes well.'

27

From: Andy Kurmudge
To: Janes Away Hurray
cc: Sam Kurmudge
Subject: It's your birthday soon

Dear Mum,

Sammo and I really wish you'd consider coming home for your birthday. Dad seems really sad at the moment and he's trying so hard. Alfie loves 'Woger days' now and it's great to see them getting on so well. Like the relationship I'd always wanted them to have.

I know you're working on your exhibition paintings but surely you could paint at home? Even if you want Dad to move into the spare room, I'm sure he'd do that, while you try to work it out? You've been married almost 40 years, don't you think you should try to put this affair of Dad's all those years ago behind you?

I'm attaching a selfie Dad took at the park with Alfie last week. I think it's the first photo we've ever had of just the two of them.

Cute, isn't it? Apart from the chocolate smeared across Alfie's face – Sarah wasn't impressed.
Love,
Andy

From: Sam Kurmudge
To: Janes Away Hurray
cc: Andy Kurmudge
Subject: Please come home!
Hi Mum,
Everything's moving ahead with the adoption stuff. I'm really hoping we'll get some good news on it soon. I wish you'd come back. It's not the same here without you, although I have to say Dad's so much better. He knows he's been a bit crap and he's trying to think of ways to make it up to you (I won't spoil the surprise!) Please come home for your birthday. Like Anders said, you could always make Dad sleep in the spare room. He'd do whatever you asked, I know he would. Please think about it.
Love, Sam

From: Janes Away Hurray
To: Sam Kurmudge; Andy Kurmudge
Subject: I miss you too
Dear Boys,
It's so lovely to hear from you both and I'm happy to hear your dad is getting properly involved. I am planning to come home soon and sort out next steps with him – there's just one more thing I'm waiting for.

But I'm always here, you know. You can email or text and I could even FaceTime if you'd like to? I just won't speak to your dad, so please don't organise it with him in the background, will you?

I hope to see you both soon. Give Alfie a kiss and Killer a pat from me.
Love,
Mum

From: Janes Away Hurray
To: Pip Colbert
Subject: February trip

I don't want to pressure you into anything and I understand the reasons you gave for not wanting to join us – it will undoubtedly be awkward - but I wanted to ask you one last time. I think it would help Roger face facts and us all move forward. Don't you think it's time you met the family?
Please say you'll come.
Love,
Jane

28

'No pee-school.' Alfie glared mutinously at Roger as they got out of the car. 'Café.'

Roger wanted to say yes. They could see Bethany, eat something vegan, Killer could hoover crumbs off the floor. But then he remembered Sarah's face. That icy look when he'd tentatively said, 'Does he need to go to pre-school? I could just have him at home with me instead ...'

'Roger,' she'd said, 'it's important for Alfie to get used to a school environment. He's three now. And it's only three days a week. In fact it's only the mornings this week, please pick him up at twelve. If you can't manage it, of course ...'

'No problem,' he'd said. 'I can manage it.'

Now, as Alfie dragged at his hand and whined, Roger said firmly, 'Pre-school will be good for you, Alfie. It will be fun! There will be other children there!'

'Don't like uver childwen,' Alfie said.

'You like Roberta and Mathew.'

'Don't.'

'Your mum wants you to go.'

'Pease, Woger.' Alfie's eyes filled up and he tugged harder on Roger's hand. 'Wanna go home. Feel sick.'

Roger could now see why Sarah had been so pleased that he was dropping Alfie off. This was a hideous, stressful experience that might scar him, Roger, for life. He hardened his heart. 'Come on. Ludo and Ricardo are there, too, today.' Sarah and Tom had had a long conversation about the village pre-school at Alfie's party and Tom had been instantly persuaded that a small, cosy set-up was the way forward. He'd apparently rung and organised places for the twins the following week.

Roger could now see what he'd meant about the cosy aspect. The pre-school was more like a village hall, really, the kind that had one large room with a small kitchen and bathroom attached and a couple of storage cupboards. It reassured him: no dodgy types could hide here and ambush small children. He semi-dragged Alfie through the door and there was Tom. Was the man ever in the office? Roger hadn't ever made an excuse and ducked out to do this kind of thing when he was in charge.

'Roger! Hi, Alfie. Do you want to play with the boys?' Tom pointed to a corner, where the twins were wrestling over a piece of a jigsaw. Several other children were running around screaming. It was loud and too bright and Roger didn't think it was the right environment for Alfie. There was a faint smell of Play-Doh mixed with urine: pee-school indeed, Roger thought, his nose wrinkling.

Alfie clung more tightly to his hand.

'First-day nerves,' Roger said. 'He's usually so brave.'

A young woman in jeans and a necklace of huge coloured beads came across and knelt to speak to Alfie. She had the perky demeanour of a children's TV presenter. 'Hi, Alfie! I'm Terry. How lovely to see you this morning. Shall I show you where to put your coat and bag?' She held out her hand, and after a long pause Alfie took it. He threw an easily decodable look over his shoulder at Roger. *Am prisoner. Send help.*

'He'll be fine,' Tom said. 'How are you, by the way? When's Jane back?'

'Soon, I think.' Roger forced a laugh. 'Having too much fun away!' He'd have to come clean about it soon to Tom, but with the stress of seeing Alfie looking so withdrawn and scared, now wasn't the time. 'Are you picking up at twelve?'

'No. The boys love it and stay all day. Just dropping them off and they'll go through until three.'

'Off to the office now, then?' Roger said. How he envied the idea. All those people delighted to eat lunch with you.

'Yes.' Tom sighed. 'A few issues – you know: the usual with Tesco's payment terms, and the new wafer product is proving to be a nightmare on the line. Keeping up with orders is very hard.'

Roger nodded and tuned out. He didn't miss those things about work. Alfie was standing stiffly next to the young woman. He looked flushed and unhappy. Roger wanted to march across the room, pick his grandson up and inform Terry that he was going home. But Sarah would be furious. Terry glanced across at him and mouthed something.

'Think it's time for you to go,' Tom said. 'He'll be fine.'

'Can I just say goodbye to Alfie?'

'I'd keep it short,' Tom said, 'if I were you.'

HALF AN HOUR LATER, Roger sat in the car, breathing deeply. He hadn't expected quite the turn of emotion that Alfie had produced when he'd bent down to hug him goodbye. The boy really could be on the stage, with that dramatic range. The crying had been so loud that several of the other children had put their hands over their ears, and one boy – with headphones on, no less – had shouted, 'Stop! Too loud!'

But Roger hadn't been irritated. He'd felt a squeeze of his heart that hurt, and had stood wondering what to do until Terry, her arms firmly around Alfie's thrashing body, had said, 'Better go, if that's okay. He'll be fine when you've gone.'

'Do you know about the breath-holding?' Roger had said.

'Yes,' she said. 'He'll be okay. Come on, Alfie, sweetie! Let's do the welcome song with everyone, shall we?'

Roger exited the building with Alfie's wails ringing in his ears. Had his own sons been like this when Jane had taken them to pre-school? He couldn't remember at all. It didn't seem right to leave Alfie in such a state but what else could he do? He started the car and drove slowly home, wondering how to fill the day.

He was in the garden filling the bird feeders when his phone rang at eleven a.m. 'Sarah? Is everything okay?'

'Please can you go and get Alfie early? I'm afraid he's not well.'

'Not well?'

'Vomiting and headachy, apparently.'

'Of course!' Roger dusted seeds from his hands. 'I'll go right now. I'll bring him home and put him to bed.'

'Maybe give him some Calpol? They think he has a fever, too.'

'Of course.'

'It's just such a shame it's his first day.'

'He did say he wasn't feeling great when I dropped him off,' Roger said, 'but I thought it was just an excuse.'

'He was fine this morning,' Sarah said defensively, 'so it must have come on fast.'

Roger felt guilty now for overlooking Alfie's complaints. 'He can come straight home and go to bed in the spare room.' The one with the plastic undersheets on and the older carpet. He'd get a plastic bowl ready, too.

'Thanks, Roger. What would I do without you?' She hung up before he could answer.

Terry was frowning when he arrived to pick Alfie up. 'Thanks for coming so quickly.'

Alfie was lying on a mat on the floor. His eyes were shut and his face was flushed.

'When did he get sick?' Roger asked.

'Not long ago. He was very quiet to start with, totally normal on day one, but then he suddenly vomited – not *on* anyone, thank goodness – and said his head hurt. Probably just a virus.'

'Probably.' Roger knelt down stiffly next to his grandson. 'Alfs? I'm taking you home.' He expected the boy to sit up, grin victoriously and whisper the magic word: café. But Alfie's eyes didn't open.

Terry drew in a breath and said over his shoulder, 'He was talking to me just now ... Look, I'm no doctor, but he's very unresponsive and I don't know Alfie enough to say if that's very unusual ...'

'Highly,' Roger said.

'So I wonder ... I mean, I just wonder if you should go straight to hospital with him.'

'Hospital?' The word felt foreign in Roger's mouth. 'It's just a bug, isn't it?'

'I'm no doctor,' she said again, 'but he had a fever, a

headache, and now seems unresponsive. I'd want to check for ...' she paused then said, 'meningitis.' She bent down and pulled off Alfie's sock. Red dots were splashed around Alfie's skin as though flicked from a paintbrush. Flea bites? But he'd treated Killer so regularly.

'Right,' Roger said, 'is that a bug?' He'd heard of meningitis but couldn't remember much about it.

Terry had an empty glass in her hand. She ran it across Alfie's lower leg then took a sharp in-breath. 'That rash ... You need to go to the hospital. Right now. You'll be faster than an ambulance.' She'd lost the perky children's-presenter look.

Ambulance?

The world slowed down.

Roger scooped Alfie up, hurting his back in the process, and charged out of the door. Terry was saying something behind him but he didn't stop. He crossed the road to the car at a stiff trot, trying to cushion Alfie's head from the bouncing. He eased him into his car seat, wishing he could let him lie down. His back twinged with the effort of holding the boy out at arm's length. Alfie slumped sideways. He felt very hot to the touch and his breathing was now laboured. Someone was muttering something, and with a start Roger realised it was him.

'You're okay, Alfie, it's okay, sweetie, it's Roger, I'm taking you to the hospital ...'

He got in and fastened his seatbelt as he dialled Andy's number.

'Hey, Dad,' Andy said. 'How was the drop-off? I'm just about to start a meeting.'

'Alfie's sick. I'm taking him to the hospital.'

'Hospital?' Andy's voice sharpened. 'How sick is he?'

'The pre-school lady thinks it might be meningitis,'

Roger said, pulling out into the traffic. He needed to focus. Crashing would make things worse. 'He's got a rash.'

'I'm on my way,' Andy said. There was a swift screech from the phone and then the call ended.

Roger drove as fast as he dared. Alfie lolled sideways in his seat. He looked both pale and too red in the face. Roger's heart accelerated. Was this his fault? He shouldn't have left Alfie there this morning, should have trusted his instinct. If only Jane was here. She'd be so much better at this than him.

THE NHS, Roger later thought, was pretty terrible at stuff that didn't kill you. But by God they were good at emergencies. Alfie and Roger were lucky – it was morning. No drunks cluttering up A&E, just a few people in chairs. A child holding his elbow with a worried-looking woman next to him. An elderly man coughing into a hanky. Roger carried Alfie in after abandoning the car right in front of the door he'd staggered out of three months earlier. The nurse doing triage took one look at him with a limp Alfie in his arms and said, 'This way.'

After that it was a blur. So many people got involved. Their faces made Roger feel ill with anxiety. They asked him questions about Alfie, some of which he just didn't know the answers to, and when Andy turned up, he wasn't sure either. Questions that didn't seem relevant, like birth weight and how the birth had been. Then Sarah was there too, and before Roger could say anything she was hugging him and thanking him for bringing Alfie to the hospital and looking almost as though she might cry. A nurse asked Roger to go to the waiting room and he wanted to protest but meekly followed the instruction. He stood, dazed, next to the reception desk before he realised the car was still outside at a rakish angle. He pulled his coat around him and went to move it.

Back in the waiting room, the plastic chairs were uncomfortable. The utilitarian space had little to offer in terms of entertainment. He picked up an ancient copy of a cheap TV magazine and flicked through it. He couldn't concentrate. Last time he'd been here he'd been a different person. He'd expected to go home with Jane to his calm, orderly life. Instead, he'd stumbled out alone into a new world of female experiences: childcare, the dog, the house, the garden, domestic helpers. Looking after Alfie. The daily grind. This wasn't what he'd been expecting from his life, but he'd got used to it.

Now he yearned to be in Bethany's café with Killer and Alfie, at their usual table, ordering toast with butter, a babycino, a flat white and a flapjack. Why hadn't he realised how lucky he was to be doing that at that time? The old man across the way looked at him with sympathy. Had Roger groaned out loud?

The child holding his elbow was crying now, a whining noise that made Roger want to leap across the room and slap his hand across the boy's mouth. What stopped him was the look on his mother's face. A resigned endurance that spoke of putting herself last too many times. The woman reminded him of Jane. She hadn't expected her life to turn out like this either. She'd expected to be an artist; she was realistic enough to know she might not make much money out of it, but she hadn't cared. She just wanted to paint. But Andy had been a difficult baby, then a difficult toddler, and somehow he'd expanded to fill her time completely. The easel and palette had been set up in the studio on the day they'd moved in, and on a few occasions Jane had managed to start something. A painting of the apple tree at the edge of the 'wild bit' had been particularly promising, the blossom looking as light and fluffy as a wisp of cloud. It had made Roger reach out to touch it.

But Jane's painting was always interrupted. Problems at school or a tummy bug or a football tournament that needed parent volunteers to help organise it. Gradually, the studio filled up with junk and the paints and easel were lost behind it. Like Jane herself, lost behind the tasks of looking after everyone else until the person she'd been was almost obliterated. He shut his eyes. Too late now.

No wonder she'd left. He'd got away with doing something terrible – sheer luck she hadn't found out – but he hadn't got away with benignly neglecting her, year after year, decade after decade.

What was happening to Alfie now was something Roger didn't want to think about. Yet he drew his phone out of his coat pocket and googled 'meningitis'. He read through the symptoms. Couldn't it be something else? Something less frightening, like the flu? Or a breath-holding episode that had got out of hand? Anything but meningitis, which sounded so swift and terrifying. The Google links took him all too quickly to stories of families who one day had been living a normal life with all the minor stresses of getting to school on time and doing homework, and the next were facing a child on life support, followed by a tiny casket going into the ground. He was shivering, Roger realised. He rubbed his arms and huddled into his coat.

'Are you okay?' It was the mum with the child holding his elbow. She leaned across from her seat opposite him, her face concerned. Roger was glad he hadn't tried to stifle her son when the crying started. He'd almost got used to it now and it had subsided to a low intermittent moaning, which wasn't so bad.

'Fine, thank you.' Roger wondered what he even meant by the words. He wasn't fine. Why didn't he just tell her? He was terrible, and Alfie was very sick, and Roger wasn't sure he'd ever really told Alfie how much he loved him and what a special boy he was (even if he didn't have any particular talents). He was still special to Roger and always would be. Why had he never told anyone how special they were to him? Not Jane, not his sons, not Alfie. Not even Killer. Although at least Killer now slept on the bed every night. But people needed words.

He half stood, wondering if he could push his way back through the doors into the treatment areas, where Alfie was lying so sick on a bed somewhere, and tell him right now just how much he was loved. He sat back down again. The important thing was to treat Alfie.

Elbow Boy's mum gave him a sympathetic look. 'It's hard to wait, isn't it? Was that your grandson with you?'

'Yes.' Roger's vision blurred. 'He might have meningitis.'

'Oh.' That one word told Roger more about the risks than his Google search had. She stretched an unconvincing smile across her face. 'He's in good hands, here. He'll be okay.'

He smiled back and eased his back off the chair for a moment, wincing at another spasm of pain.

A nurse approached them and Roger felt hope flicker then die as she stopped next to Elbow Boy and said, 'Can you come with me, Tim?'

He and his mum stood up and Roger nodded to them as they shuffled off behind the nurse.

A couple of new people came in, a middle-aged woman walking stiffly, and a young man clutching a blood-soaked cloth to his arm. Roger heard him say something about landscaping to the nurse. He shut his eyes again. Perhaps it would make time go faster.

As the afternoon wore on, it became more crowded. After-school clubs were responsible at around five p.m. for a surge of children wearing sports apparel – netball in particular had a lot to answer for – with their anxious mothers in tow. Roger got up and walked around for a bit. Should he go home? Was there any point in sitting out here in this cold, sterile room when he couldn't help?

He wanted to text Andy but didn't want to add to the stress his son would be feeling. Sam had sent Roger a few texts, so he too had heard about Alfie. He asked Roger to keep him 'posted' and said he'd come to the hospital if it would help. Roger had told him to stay home and that he'd let him know if he got any updates. Tom had also texted after Elena had picked up the twins: could he help, did Roger need anything? Such a decent bloke.

Roger wondered now if he should ask someone for an update. Was that possible?

He waited until she was less busy before approaching the nurse at the reception desk. 'I'm sorry to bother you, but is there any update on my grandson? Alfie Kurmudge? I brought him in several hours ago.' It felt like days, not hours.

She looked up at him and then back at a screen. 'Let me check.' She tapped away. 'They moved him to Intensive Care a few hours ago.'

'Intensive Care?' Roger gripped the desk. 'Can I see him?'

She shook her head. 'We don't allow more than two visitors, and his parents are with him.'

'Has there been a diagnosis?' He almost didn't want to know.

'Let me see if I can find someone to talk to you.' Her eyes were kind. How had Roger thought, all those months ago, that the staff here weren't kind?

An Indian doctor – grey-faced with fatigue – came to talk to him a while later. Roger had no idea how much time had elapsed. The doctor told him that Alfie had bacterial meningitis; that despite being vaccinated he'd picked up a strain that the vaccine didn't protect against.

'What's the prognosis, Doctor?' Roger asked.

'Alfie's in the best possible place. We're doing everything we can. We've done a blood test and a lumbar puncture and started him on intravenous antibiotics ...'

The words stabbed at Roger's brain. Was the word 'puncture' absolutely necessary? Couldn't they have simply called it a test instead? It sounded as though Alfie was being tortured in there. And why hadn't the doctor answered his question? Roger fought the urge to shove the man aside and run through the doors to find his grandson. But the doctor's face was kind, too. Which was why he hadn't answered the question.

'We're doing everything we possibly can,' he repeated. 'And the whole family should take antibiotics, just in case. The local authority and the pre-school have been informed, but because your grandson had only just started, they're not concerned about their exposure.'

'Where would he have got this from?' Roger asked. He hadn't been cleaning much between Morwenna's visits. Should he have been using antibacterial spray? He would, from now on. The Dettol factory would need to take on more staff to cope with the surge in demand.

'He's three.' The doctor shrugged. 'A play-centre, a park, the GP surgery. Many places. And now I need to get back.'

Roger slumped back into his seat. People were looking at him. Sympathetic faces. He just wanted to hear from Andy and Sarah and see Alfie.

It was seven p.m. He'd been here for hours, but he felt incapable of deciding what to do next. Stay. Go. Text Andy. Text Sam. It was a struggle to think straight. Had he eaten since breakfast? He hadn't. Or had a drink. He fumbled in his pocket for change and went to the vending machine. He pushed the change into the slot and selected a black coffee. Too late for caffeine, really. But he needed to stay awake and alert in case they needed him. Which made him wonder: did Andy and Sarah need clothes and wash bags if they were staying the night? Or food? He could be useful, couldn't he?

Renewed purpose filled him. He gulped down the thin sour coffee and threw the cup in the bin. The nurse was dealing with the first drunk of the day, a painfully scrawny man with bad skin and deep cuts on his bare feet, who was making no sense at all in response to her questions and laughed wheezily at the end of each reply. It would be a relief to leave. Roger could text Andy and Sarah, ask what they needed. He started to tap at the screen as someone pushed through the entrance doors.

'Rodge?'

He looked up to see familiar eyes. Blue, clear, sharp, with thick black eyelashes and radiating smile lines around them. He knew these eyes.

He said slowly, 'Jane?'

29

Jane's eyes were the only part of her that still looked the same. Her haircut looked expensive: a shorter, blunter bob, just brushing her jawline. Her skin glowed. She had a suitcase and clothes he didn't recognise: a well-cut trench coat belted at the waist, jeans, and ankle boots with a wedge heel. They were clothes that seemed younger than the ones she usually wore, more carefree and less defining. Even her perfume was less familiar. This scent was spicier, darker.

He realised he was staring at her blankly. 'Where have you been?'

'Is Alfie okay?' She impatiently brushed off his question. 'Do you know anything more?'

'How did you hear?'

'I read my emails, Roger, as you know. Andy sent me one at lunchtime and … well, here I am.' She looked past him to the reception desk. 'Do I need to ask the nurse?'

'He's got bacterial meningitis,' Roger said. 'They've got him on intravenous antibiotics, and they've done a lumbar puncture.'

'Oh,' she said, almost to herself.

'We can't see him,' Roger said. 'Two visitors per patient in Intensive Care, and Andy and Sarah are there.'

She looked as lost as he felt.

'I wanted to go and get them some clothes and maybe some food,' he said. 'Do you want to come with me?' He didn't dare assume she would.

There was a long pause. 'Actually, if there's no point us being here, I might just go back to the house.' He noticed she didn't say home. 'I've really missed Killer.'

KILLER'S RESPONSE was like a scene from the end of a sentimental film when the star-crossed lovers finally reunite and the music swells to an emotional crescendo. He barked at first as Jane came through the front door, as though he, too, didn't recognise her. Then he whined. Then he cried, jumping up at her deliriously, leaping almost out of his skin, trying to get as close to her face as he could. Jane knelt down and hugged him fiercely as he licked her face, and Roger felt a wave of jealousy. He pursed his lips to stop himself from blurting out questions: *Where have you been? Why do you look so different? Why is Killer getting more affection than me?*

'There's a curry in the freezer,' he said instead. He took it out and put the container on the kitchen counter. 'Defrosts in about five minutes then you can zap it on high heat for one. You know where the rice is. I could do it but I'd better get over to Andy's and get some stuff. I'll get Bingo Bear for Alfie, too.'

'Okay.' She eased her coat off and hung it in the hall. There was a kind of isolation about her, as though being on her own for three months had turned her into a stranger.

She bent down to stroke Killer again. 'Have you been eating too much? You're quite chunky, aren't you?' She walked past Roger and into the kitchen, and he had to force himself not to reach for her as she passed. She seemed somehow untouchable.

'Can we talk later?' he said. 'Or tomorrow? I need to ask you some questions.' Were they getting divorced? Was she about to disappear again? 'You will be here tomorrow, won't you?'

'Did you make this?' she asked, looking at the curry. 'Even frozen, it looks great.'

'No,' he said. 'Mel. She's Morwenna's niece. Great girl who helps me. You'll like her.'

'I think I met her once,' Jane said, 'when her mum was sick and Morwenna brought her here.' Her smile was brittle. 'Go on, then. Go and get them some stuff.'

IT WAS hard to drive away, now that Jane was finally home. At Andy's house, he stood indecisively in the hallway. What would they need?

Upstairs, in Andy and Sarah's room, Roger opened a chest of drawers. Andy's, clearly. He took out a pair of pyjamas, some jeans and a fresh T-shirt and jumper. A pair of striped boxer shorts. It felt weird to be touching something so personal. Had he ever touched his son's clothes before? Probably not. Although he knew most of Alfie's clothes – the favourite T-shirt with the cartoon dinosaur on it; the jeans that were getting too small; and the woolly jumper that irritated Alfie's skin and had to be worn with a T-shirt under it, preferably the dinosaur one – as well as he did his own.

He felt even worse opening Sarah's cupboard with its

scarves and blouses wafting slightly in the gust of air. He pulled out a shirt and jumper combination he'd seen her wear several times, and a pair of jeans. Added a nightie from the top drawer. Putting his hand into her underwear drawer felt so uncomfortable that he wondered whether he should ignore that aspect of her clothing. He steeled himself and found some cotton knickers and a white bra, which he pushed into a bag that Andy had on the chair next to the bed. Socks? He found a pair for each of them and added them to the bag.

In the bathroom, he gathered together soap, shampoo, toothbrushes and paste and put them in a wash-bag. Flannels emerged from the airing cupboard, and two hand towels. He was putting off the worst bit.

It had to be done. He went into Alfie's neat little room. Navy-blue boats sailed jauntily across his duck-egg blue wall and a solitary soft toy lay on the carpet, looking forlorn and abandoned. It smelled of Alfie in here: baby shampoo and yeasty clothes. Roger sat down heavily on the bed with its Thomas the Tank Engine duvet cover. Next to the wardrobe was the green camel he'd given him for his birthday. It was the size of a Shetland pony and took up a lot of space. He hadn't noticed how lop-sided its face was before.

He wanted to lie down and shut his eyes. One problem had in theory been resolved, with Jane coming home. But he didn't know why she'd left or where she'd been, and he didn't want to risk losing her again by asking. It hadn't been anything like the reunion he'd been hoping for. It was as though an invisible force field was around her, keeping him out. In the meantime, his only grandchild lay in hospital fighting an infection that killed some kids. Why hadn't he appreciated Alfie more over the years? A world without Alfie in it was unimaginable.

His shoulders and back ached from carrying his grandson into hospital, and he had to force himself to focus. He pushed the camel out of the way and opened the doors. He took stock. What would he need? The tiger onesie that he loved to sleep in. His navy corduroy trousers, his blue Gap hoodie, the dinosaur T-shirt. Socks. Underwear. A vest. And Bingo Bear. Who was, of course, technically a sloth, but Alfie thought he was a bear, and frankly, what did it matter?

If Bingo got lost in the hospital, Roger was prepared to sell the French house to get an exact replica. He was sure there were people in China who could help, hand-stitching as many as required until they managed to recreate Bingo Bear. Right down to the small tear in Bingo's armpit that Sarah had mended badly with the wrong colour brown thread. Because Alfie would need Bingo to sleep with for many years to come. Of course he would.

Roger got out his phone and took photos of Bingo from various angles, just in case. Then he put the clothes in the bag, dropped Bingo on top and wearily shut the door to Alfie's room behind him, trying not to think about when – if – Alfie might come back to it.

BACK AT THE HOSPITAL, he asked the kind-eyed lady what to do with the bag.

'If you text your son, perhaps he can come and get it,' she said, looking harassed. Drunks were now filling the room, some bleeding, some slumped in their seats. He found himself a seat in the corner as far from the aggressive ones as he could. Two of them were yelling at each other and one woman in dirty clothes with hennaed hair who didn't seem to be with either of them kept trying to calm them down by shouting, 'Stop shouting! You're upsetting the kids!' in spite of the fortunate fact there were no children around.

Roger tuned out the shouting and texted Andy.

Got some stuff for you. Is Alfie okay? I'm in reception.

Ten minutes later, Andy appeared. He looked hollowed out, loose-skinned.

'Thanks for doing this, Dad.'

'I wanted to get you food, but wasn't sure what to get. I can go back out and get something?'

'We wouldn't eat it anyway.' Andy took the bag from Roger.

'Your mum's back,' Roger said.

'Yeah?' Andy didn't sound surprised.

'She came when you emailed her.'

'I need to get back.'

'What's going on with Alfie?'

'He's on antibiotics. A drip. We just have to wait now.' Andy's shoulders were stiff. 'He looks terrible, Dad. What if we ...?' He swallowed the rest of the unspeakable words.

'We won't,' Roger said, heartily. 'He's in good hands. This is the best place for him. He's a fighter.' *Christ, he was a walking cliché.* But Andy looked more cheerful for it. No wonder people used clichés: they gave comfort.

'Yeah. He is a fighter. I'll text you when we know more, okay?' Andy's back looked so vulnerable as he walked away that Roger had to swallow hard.

He drove home and let himself in. He could scarcely believe Jane was there but the proof was in the scented air itself. He couldn't bring himself to call out his usual 'I'm back!' *Was* she back? Properly, for good?

He stopped in the doorway to the sitting room and took a moment to really register her presence.

There she was, in her usual seat, on the left side of the sofa. Killer next to her, his head on her lap and his eyes shut in blissful sleep. The TV on: something about Brexit. On the coffee table, a plate with the remains of the curry. It was all so familiar, as though she'd never been away. Or perhaps he was dreaming her now.

He cleared his throat. 'Can I get you a drink? Wine?'

'Maybe just a half glass of something,' she said. 'Whatever you're having.'

In the kitchen he opened a bottle of Marlborough Pinot Noir and poured two glasses. He took them back to the sitting room and sat down next to her.

'Cheers,' he said, handing her a glass.

'Thank you.'

The formality of her words jarred him. He didn't know where to start, but he had to start somewhere. She'd disappeared for almost four months.

'Can I ask where you were?' He tried to make his tone as neutral as possible.

She took a large gulp of wine and swallowed it before looking at him. 'I know you had an affair. In Sydney – no, I don't want to hear all the lies! I really don't.' She held her hand up to him as he tried to speak, the classic *Stop* gesture that he used all the time with Alfie. 'I know you're an accomplished liar but I'm just not going to have it. In any case, this isn't the time. I'm here to see Alfie, that's all, and I'm staying here because, well, because I wanted to see Killer and it's as much my house as it is yours.'

He was battling to breathe. She *knew*. He didn't know how but she knew.

'But in answer to your questions, I did a few things. I

went to Paris, saw Sandrine and started painting again. It was bliss. And I spent Christmas in Bordeaux, on my own, just enjoying myself. Although that heating system really needs sorting out.' She lifted the corner of her mouth, remembering. 'I spent a lovely few days there, going to museums and restaurants and the Musée des Beaux Arts. Time spent being me again.'

He sipped his wine. He wanted to think very carefully about each word. He was terrified he'd be so grateful she was back that he'd end up confessing. 'And did you enjoy feeling like you again?'

'You know what? I really did.' She smiled properly for the first time. 'I loved it. I did what I wanted to do when I wanted to do it, and no one assumed I would pick up after them or shop or sort out the washing or get cash or make dinner or walk the dog or any of the things that have filled the past forty years. And it was bloody brilliant.'

'And now you're back,' he said, 'are you ... will you ...?'

She scoffed. 'I've never thought of you as a fool, Roger. Don't make me start now. I'm not *back*. I'm just here at the moment, that's all. Don't get too used to it.'

Killer yawned and stretched next to her as though he had never been so comfortable. A smattering of light rain hit the windows and a dog barked in the distance, making Killer's ears twitch forward.

Roger had always known he could talk people round to things, but it was hard to do that if he wasn't allowed to speak. He tried once more: 'Listen, I don't know what you think you've found out –'

She cut him off: 'Not now. We really have more urgent problems.'

'But, I mean, we can't just leave it like that. You've been gone for months and I have a right –'

Her eyebrows shot up. 'A *right*? After the way you have behaved? The utter mendacity of your behaviour for *years*? I'm only here because Alfie's sick. I didn't intend to come back yet. One more word and I'll book myself into a hotel.'

Jane had never spoken to him like this before. It took his breath away. She turned her head away from him, reached out for the remote control and turned the TV up. He went to the kitchen and found himself crackers and cheese for dinner. He had no appetite for anything more substantial. Back in the sitting room, he ate them and pretended to watch TV.

At ten p.m. he rang Andy. The perky ring tone buzzed in his ear but no one answered. He remembered too late that he hadn't taken a charger to the hospital. Stupid of him. They'd need one to stay in touch.

Jane was looking tired.

'Why don't you go to bed?' he asked her.

'How can I sleep?'

'There's little point us both staying up.'

'You'll stay awake?'

'Of course.'

Her face cleared. 'I might, then. It will be lovely to sleep in my own bed,' she said. She stopped as though the implications had just occurred to her.

'The sheets are fresh on,' he said. 'I'll sleep in the spare room.'

'Good.' She stood up, her expression cold. 'Before I go, what the hell is that in the garden?' She pointed out through the French doors into the darkness.

'It's a garden studio,' he said. 'For you. To paint in. I got it as your Christmas present.' He could hear the eagerness in his voice. He sounded slightly pathetic.

'Oh.' Her tone was indifferent. 'I'll see you in the morning, then. Unless there's news about Alfie that's urgent.'

HE SAT with the TV on quietly, waiting. Killer was lying next to him but eventually he yawned and pawed at Roger's leg: the signal to be let out. The dog trotted out into the cold night air, did what he needed to and ran, nose to the ground, along one of the flowerbeds for a second, as though he had caught the delicious smell of something nocturnal. Then he sneezed and raced back to the kitchen door.

'Time for bed?' Roger said. Was he going to let Killer sleep on the bed now that Jane was back? She had always wanted the dog to be closer, so with a mental shrug he let him go upstairs.

He heard the creak of their bedroom door and then Jane's sleepy voice: 'Hello, sweetie! Are you allowed up here now? How lovely. Up you come. Good dog.'

TIME PASSED. The room was very dark, in spite of the lamps. He sat without watching anything on TV, lost in his thoughts. The first time he'd looked after Alfie. The play-centre experience. Alfie grinning up at him last week after their café visit, a Joker-esque extended smile of chocolate either side of his mouth from the babycino's chocolate topping. The previous Christmas photo of the family on the mantelpiece had a light coating of dust on it. He stood and used a tissue to wipe it clean. The dust reminded him how long ago the photo had been taken.

He picked it up and really looked at it for the first time in ages. Jane had her head tipped slightly back as though she was about to laugh uproariously. Alfie had her chin, Roger realised. And perhaps her hair, although it was a bit too early to tell, because mostly Alfie's hair really did look like a toilet brush. It was impossible that either of them might not be here with him next Christmas, let alone both of them.

He put the photo back down and turned away. The mournful ticking of the clock on the mantelpiece made him want to itch. Half past eleven. What was happening in the Intensive Care unit? Was there someone he could call? He didn't want to be a nuisance: it was far more important that the doctors and nurses were looking after Alfie, not answering his questions.

His phone rang, loud in the silence. He sprang across the room to pick it up, knocking his glass off the table so blood-red wine gushed thickly onto the pale wool carpet.

'Hello?'

'Dad, it's me.'

His breath caught in his throat. 'Andy? How is he?' For a second, he wished he'd taken more time before asking the question because he wanted to stay in the safe space before Andy spoke. A precious space before he knew for sure if his grandson might no longer be with them.

'He's a little bit better. Might be turning a corner, they said.'

Roger dropped onto the sofa. 'Might be?'

'They think the antibiotics are working. He has to stay in here for another day or two because he hasn't actually woken up yet. But they look better than they did.'

'They?'

'The doctors. They all looked so grim before. It was ...' The phone went dead for a second and Roger realised his son was crying.

'Andy? Shall I come down? Can I help?'

There was a pause filled with sniffing sounds. 'Thanks, Dad. But it's okay now. I think it's okay.'

'Can we visit tomorrow?' He wanted to see Alfie for himself.

'Let me check in the morning. I'll call you. Better go. I need to ring Sarah's parents.' Andy hung up.

Roger looked at the wine stain on the carpet. It didn't seem very important in the great scheme of things. Alfie was going to be okay! He'd deal with the wine stain in the morning.

Upstairs, the light was off in their bedroom. He could hear the faint sounds of Killer snoring. Really, the dog needed another check up at the vet, unpleasant though the idea was. Was it normal for a relatively young beast to snore that badly? The vet would no doubt put it down to the extra weight he was carrying and deliver a lecture on cutting down on his food.

Standing on the landing, Roger wished he'd got his pyjamas from their room before Jane went to bed. Instead, he found a slightly too tight T-shirt from a pile he'd been building up for the charity shop. He cleaned his teeth in the family bathroom with a toothbrush Jane had bought for guests, and made his way to the spare room. The bed was nowhere near as comfortable as the one in the master bedroom. The curtains were thinner, too, and let in light from the streetlamp at the end of their drive.

You made your bed and now you must lie in it.

The phrase made him wince. She knew. After all these years, he had never expected the truth to catch up with him, especially given the distance involved. Back then, there hadn't been the technology for someone to haunt you: no texts or Facebook or FaceTime. He'd felt guilty, and still did, but he'd thought it was behind them. He hadn't thought Yvonne was the malicious type, but he'd obviously got that wrong. She must have contacted Jane.

He pulled back the duvet and got into bed. It was so strange being in a different room, like a trial run for divorce. They'd have to sell the house, divide up the assets and find new properties. Would Jane even stay near Guildford? He lay under the duvet, which smelled of dust, and tried to picture life as a single man. He'd be sad to say goodbye to the house but there was no doubt at all that it was far too large for one person.

Perhaps he could find a smaller place in Guildford so that he could stay close to the boys and Alfie. Sam and Guy were very close to finalising their adoption plans and Roger wanted to be involved in that, of course he did. He felt an ache of pride when Alfie ran up to him now or shouted, 'Look, Woger!' across the park as he did some new trick.

A new path was possible. But as he lay in a strange bed in his house, without even his dog to keep him company, Roger felt depressed enough about his future to weep.

30

Andy and Sarah stood in the hospital entrance like people who had survived a bombing: shell-shocked, exhausted, mute. Andy took one look at Jane and burst into tears. He put his arms around her, dwarfing her, and bent to sob into her scarf.

'It's okay,' Jane said. 'Go home and rest, we'll watch over Alfie.'

Andy nodded and sniffed, and he and Sarah left, clutching their coats around them against the biting cold.

A nurse showed them the way. Her shoes made a rubbery sound on the floor and her ankles were comfortingly solid. Someone to rely on. Her calmness and unflappability was in stark contrast to Roger's emotions. He felt churned up. The news was better for Alfie. There had been cautious smiles, Andy had reported on the phone earlier in the day. They could visit. Alfie looked better. But he wasn't going home just yet and they couldn't stay long. And Roger didn't trust the good news. He'd seen too much on Google. Read too many horror stories. And discovered something called Mollaret meningitis, which could recur. Yes, it was the viral kind, not the bacterial kind. But he wasn't banking on anything.

Intensive Care was not suited to anyone with sensory issues. You'd have to be pretty bloody sick, Roger thought, to be in here and manage to sleep. Lights flashed, there was bleeping at regular intervals, followed by a sort of sucking, hissing noise, and Roger felt overwhelmed within seconds.

The nurse made them both wash their hands thoroughly before leading them to a bed that looked as though NASA had constructed it to do something far more complex than support a small human body. On it, Alfie's small human body looked lost. There was a needle disappearing into one of his arms with a tube attached, snaking up to a bag of fluid hanging next to the bed. Alfie didn't like needles. Surely this was painful for him? He was breathing normally but his eyes were shut. Roger thought he was a healthier colour than he had been the day before at the preschool. Or was that wishful thinking?

'Can we wake him?' Roger asked the nurse.

Jane frowned.

'He needs his sleep,' the nurse said reprovingly.

She was peering at the screen showing Alfie's pulse and respiration. She paused for a second then smiled brightly at them. 'Do you want to sit with him for a while?'

'Please.' Jane looked around. There were no chairs to be seen.

'I can get you both a chair,' the nurse said and disappeared.

Roger found he was clinging to the rail on the side of Alfie's bed. Like a man on a life raft, gripping his last chance for survival. 'Do you think we should move him?' he asked Jane.

'Move him?'

'To a private hospital, a private ward.' There were lots of other children here and they all looked so sick. Immobile little forms with needles and tubes attached to them. What if they infected him with other diseases? 'Would Alfie be better in a room by himself?'

'They're not going to let you move him,' Jane said. 'He's still really sick.'

The nurse was back with two chairs. She shuffled along the ward and plonked them down next to Alfie. 'Here you are!' She walked off briskly, not waiting for their reply.

Roger motioned for Jane to sit and she did so. He sat next to her and put a cautious hand on Alfie's leg, under the blanket. It was very still. He'd never seen Alfie so still. Normally he was in motion, even when he was asleep, wriggling under the covers. Today he was as still as ... Roger grappled with the expressions that came to him, all of which revolved around death. No, the phrase was as still as a statue, wasn't it? That was it. As a statue.

To take his mind off Alfie, he said, 'Were you even here, in hospital, all those weeks ago? When you first left? Did you actually get a mole removed? Or go to Italy?'

'No.' She pulled her coat around her as though she was cold. 'But I had to catch a plane and needed to have a reason to leave the house with a suitcase. A hospital visit was a good excuse. And I had to tell Nina something. *My husband is a cheating bastard who deserves a good fright* didn't seem quite the right tone.'

Machines beeped and hissed. Lights flashed. Time moved along, one second at a time, more slowly than time had ever moved for Roger. A long moment passed before Jane spoke again.

'I really missed him.'

'Alfie?'

'I knew that even three months would be a long time to be away from him. No one else would really change. But he would. He'd learn new skills or stop doing something or saying something, like "I do it by my own".' Her lips twitched. 'I was worried that if you spent more time with him, he'd start calling you Grandad. I like him calling you Woger.'

'I don't think,' Roger said, 'he will ever stop calling me that. It has made life quite tricky.' He told her about his first day of looking after him.

'Naked? On the lawn?' Jane said. 'Really?'

'He reeked,' Roger said.

'And you took Bingo *out of the house*? That was brave.'

'I was an amateur back then.'

'Whereas now ...' she murmured.

'Well, I know a bit better. I still get it wrong a lot.'

'We all get it wrong a lot.' Jane shifted in her seat. 'Parenting – and grand-parenting – is tricky.'

A silence fell between them. There was so much he wanted to talk to her about but he didn't want to make things worse.

'How much do the boys know?' Roger asked.

'Well,' she said, 'Andy knows some of it.'

Roger shifted his chair slightly; the screech made the nearest nurse, a young man with ginger hair, look up from his patient and frown. 'How?'

'It's really his story to tell,' Jane said. 'Ask him.'

'I'm asking you,' Roger said.

'Shh. You'll wake Alfie.'

'How could Andy have known?' he said, more quietly, and she sighed.

'He used a private detective, apparently.'

'Why didn't he tell me?' Roger said.

'I told the boys not to. Andy found me, in Paris.' She glanced quickly sideways at him. 'He didn't understand why I'd left so I told him. Just that you'd had an affair.'

'I didn't know he was so good at lying,' Roger said bitterly.

She barked a laugh. 'That's a little rich coming from you, Roger, don't you think?'

'And Sam?'

'I told Andy he could tell Sam.'

'But not me.'

Her eyes were very cold. 'Roger, it wasn't the boys or Alfie I wanted to leave behind.'

A nurse bustled up and stared at Alfie's screen. Roger held his breath until she turned and trotted off. The little figure on the bed looked so helpless. He wanted Alfie to sit up and demand something, anything – two Feasts, a real giraffe, a working carousel in the garden – just to stop him feeling this helpless.

'Do you have any idea how resentful I feel? All those years of believing we were happy and to find out you did *that* ... It's just ...' For the first time, Jane looked grief-stricken. She closed her eyes for a second. 'So I thought it would be fitting revenge if you had to get on with it all on your own. Look after Alfie. Sort out the house. Do Christmas.'

'I did do all of those things,' Roger said. 'I did Christmas. The cooking, the presents.'

'Yes,' she said. 'The coffee machines were a great idea.'

'How was I to know that you always gave them money?'

'I know,' she said. 'How could you have realised what was in the envelope every year? I mean, it was such a *secret*. You'd have noticed if you'd really been present at all on Christmas Day.'

'I am now,' he said grumpily.

'Good.'

'And why didn't you tell me about your job?'

'I did.' Jane shifted her position in the uncomfortable chair. 'I met Nina when I went in just to have a look one day and we got chatting; she offered me some work. I came home and told you. You were reading the paper. I said, "I've been offered a job. Just a small local one. A few hours one day a week." You said, "Lovely idea." And then you turned the page and said something about the great opportunities Brexit had in store for us. So I started work and waited for you to ask me – *really* ask me – how my day had been. If you had, I'd have told you. But you never did. Not looking at me. Not without the TV on or the paper in your hand.'

Alfie stirred, one leg twitching under the sheet. For a second it looked as though he might open his eyes but instead he turned over, sighed and was still.

'I've organised a party for our wedding anniversary,' Roger said. 'It's our fortieth coming up.'

'I know.'

'In June.'

'Yes.'

'I've booked Watney Manor. The kind of big do we should have had for our wedding. Including the chairs with the big bows. We can have it now instead.'

Machines hissed and beeped around them.

'Roger, the one thing I'm sure of is that I won't be celebrating our anniversary in a few months' time.'

'But you love Watney Manor,' he said. 'And June would be ...' He felt close to weeping. 'We really need to discuss this, Jane, I don't what you heard but –'

'It was more something I saw,' she said. 'Like I said, I

don't want any more lies, Roger. There have been quite enough.'

He had no idea what she could be talking about. For once his usual confidence in his verbal skills was lacking. Without knowing what she'd seen, he was at a loss as to what to say in his defence; he might make things worse. So he did the only think he could think of doing. He shut up.

A second passed, filled only with the beeps and hisses, then Alfie shuffled in his sleep and turned back to face them. Consciousness spread rapidly across his face. He opened his eyes. They looked glazed for a moment but sharpened as he focused on them both. 'Gwamma, Woger did give me a camel. A big gween one.' He shut his eyes again.

'Hi, chickpea,' Jane said in a low voice, 'we're both here. You go back to sleep, sweetie. We'll see you when you wake up.'

Alfie's two front teeth appeared between his lips. A micro-smile. Then he was asleep again.

Roger sniffed back the emotion. 'Shall I call Andy, let him know he woke up?'

'You do that, I'll tell the nurse,' Jane said. 'I think it's a good sign. And he's still calling you Woger, too.'

31

'Wow, Mr. R., it looks fab in here!' Mel's eyes widened as she took in the dining room and the table set with the candlesticks, best cutlery and the hand-painted place mats they'd bought in Provence and rarely used.

'Does it look all right?' Roger said. 'I'm not sure – is it a bit fussy?'

'It's gorgeous,' Mel said firmly. 'Such a nice way to celebrate Mrs R.'s birthday.'

The words 'Mrs R.' made Roger squirm a little, although technically it was true. Jane was still his wife. Mel must surely have picked up on the intense awkwardness between them, not to mention the fact that he was sleeping in the spare room, but she was too tactful to mention it. Jane refused to discuss her accusation of him having had an affair unless he was prepared to be entirely truthful, and he was still trying to work out if that would be a good idea. In his experience, telling the unvarnished truth rarely improved matters. At work it had almost always resulted in someone being disciplined or sacked. Instead, his strategy so far had been to look bewildered and perplexed and simply hope that maybe time would heal the wound, if only he could keep her around long enough.

Fortunately for him, Alfie was the magnet that was keeping her in Guildford. A week after he'd been discharged from the hospital, he was back on form: demanding treats constantly, insisting on trips to the park after pre-school and asking Roger when they'd be going back to see the 'twucks'. He was clearly delighted to have Jane back, and would crawl into her lap for story-time after pre-school with his thumb in his mouth. Watching his wife read softly to his grandson, her chin resting lightly on top of his head, Roger felt his heart twist in his chest.

The closest thing to physical contact he had with Jane was offering to lift a sleepy Alfie from her arms and carry him up for his nap. The transfer allowed him to brush against her arms, and her scent – although still unfamiliar – reminded him of the things he still missed: lying in bed with her in the evenings, talking about the books they were reading or the TV show they'd just watched; turning the light out and feeling the mattress dip slightly as she moved closer to him and put her arms around him, the prelude to an intimacy that he now feared they would never get back.

Instead, he was carrying a toddler upstairs before returning to find that Jane was either in her studio or in the garden, digging up a browning plant or edging the beds with a ferocity that seemed pointed. If he tried to join her, to ask what needed to be done and how could he help, she would find an area as far from her as possible and suggest he start there.

'You could move some of those daffodils, perhaps? They're wasted behind the studio.' The dismissiveness of her tone suggested it was not her business, yet she was still trying to keep the garden looking neat and ready for spring. He thought it was a hopeful sign, but maybe that was wishful thinking; perhaps she just wanted it to look good for prospective buyers. She'd agreed to stay until after her birthday so she could spend it with the boys and Alfie. It was made abundantly clear that he was a downside to the bargain.

And as the day itself approached, he was concerned about the mystery guest she'd invited. Andy was, too.

'Dad, when I found Mum in Paris, it was a bit of a shock. I have to tell you, men were coming up to her in cafés or on the street and sort of flirting with her. I don't think you realise how attractive she is.'

'I do,' Roger said. 'Really, I *do*.'

'Well, this guest – what if it's a new man? Someone she's seeing? Someone she wants us to meet?'

'She wouldn't do that, would she?' Roger said. 'Not to ... me.'

Andy's pitying smile was answer enough. After all, Roger deserved it, didn't he? He had left his family for six months and gone to Australia when his mother-in-law wasn't well and his sons were both struggling, leaving his wife to cope alone. He'd then had an affair – a short, misjudged one, purely because of his loneliness, of course – and then lied about it through omission for another twenty-three years. Introducing a new partner would be fitting revenge for Jane to take. He just hoped she wouldn't. Maybe it was someone else, a friend she'd met. Sandrine herself, perhaps?

Mornings were rather different now. Jane was still up before him but there was never coffee standing ready for him in his *World's Best Dad* mug (which he'd found in the bin in bits a day after Jane got back). He had to make his own. Jane would take Killer out or go to the studio, or disappear off somewhere and wouldn't answer any questions about her return time. He'd stopped asking.

On days when they took care of Alfie before and after pre-school, she suggested they took it in turns to pick him up and take him to the park. Roger found this perhaps the most hurtful thing. He needed time with Alfie to feel useful and cheerful and part of society. Without it, he felt like a retiree on a slow declivity to infirmity and loneliness, especially now it was obvious that divorce was more likely than Jane forgiving him.

By returning, Jane had halved his time with Alfie, and he was almost resentful. His grandson just accepted it, although on the first day, as he headed out of the door with Jane and Killer, he had turned to Roger and asked, 'Woger come, too?' But once Jane had said firmly, 'No, just us!' he'd accepted it as just another example of adults behaving in slightly mystifying ways, had grinned up at Jane and swung her hand, and trotted off without him.

Roger had been left trying to fill his time. He managed to get a game of golf in with Frank one morning when a job had been cancelled and Frank was unexpectedly free, but he found the other man's coarse jokes suddenly unpleasant and was ashamed that he'd guffawed at them for years without understanding that it made him complicit in the coarseness. He hadn't suggested they meet again and Frank, openly contemptuous about how much Roger's golf handicap had deteriorated, hadn't called him either. It underlined to Roger just how friendless he was without Jane in his life. He had to make sure his relationship with his sons and Alfie was strong – he couldn't lose them just when he'd found them.

Today, Jane was up later than usual; he had already

showered and dressed. She came downstairs at nine a.m. and he asked if she wanted coffee.

'No, thank you.'

'I've arranged Mel to come over around ten thirty,' he said, 'to make your birthday lunch.'

'I know. She told me yesterday.'

'Right.'

There was an awkward silence. Roger sipped his coffee. It felt like the calm before a very large storm. The kind of storm in which you lost your house and wife to someone else.

'I'm going to pop over to see Cara,' she said after a few more moments of strained silence. 'She very kindly got me something for my birthday.'

Her words reminded Roger: he needed to organise his present. He'd contemplated giving it to her when they were alone but had decided perhaps there was some value in handing it over in front of the boys and the guest, whoever he might be. It would throw down the gauntlet to this new man. Show him the lengths Roger was prepared to go to in order to keep his wife.

Mel arrived promptly and went straight into the kitchen after hanging up her jacket.

'Such a great idea, Mr. R., to have a birthday lunch. I bought her something little,' she blushed, 'just as a small pressie, like.'

'That's too kind, Mel,' he said. 'She's just at Cara's, she'll be back shortly.'

'Right. I'll crack on, then,' Mel said cheerfully. 'Although to be honest it's just a roast; you'd be fine doing it.'

'I wouldn't do it as well as you,' Roger said, 'and it's nice to know it's in hand, rather than worrying about timings.' He'd heard her on the phone to Gary last week and judging from her end of the conversation, money was particularly tight after their mum had gone on another bender and spent the rent. He didn't want to give Mel charity. It was much easier to pay her for work she seemed to enjoy doing.

∼

WHEN JANE RETURNED, Mel gave her a card and a bath bomb from Lush.

'That's so sweet of you, Mel! None of the boys would ever *think* of getting me something like this,' Jane said, as though it was the best present she'd ever received, better than the Mulberry handbag Roger had given her the year before. She put her arm around Mel and gave her a warm hug. Mel flushed with pleasure.

Listening to his wife saying what a *luxury* it would be to use it in her bath later, Roger could hear how his wife naturally put people at ease and made them feel comfortable. He'd have to get better at that, especially if Jane was going to leave him for this new man. He'd have to learn to be kind and warm with people. He wondered again if he should take the opportunity to give her his gift before everyone else arrived. Just as he'd decided he would, Jane announced she was off to the station to pick up her guest.

'Shall I drive you?' Roger said.

'No.' She took her coat from the hall stand, picked up her keys and went out of the front door. He heard the garage door go up and her car start.

Who was this mysterious guest? How was Roger going to get through lunch with some man leering at his wife right in front of him? His shoulders ached with tension and he decided to go for a walk in the garden with Killer. He'd better enjoy it before he had to sell it.

He shrugged on a coat and called Killer, who leapt to his feet and trotted to the kitchen door. Outside, Roger sat on the bench near the studio. Jane had been pleased with it, he could tell, but it was now totally out of bounds to him. She often spent hours in there painting and he wanted to be invited in, to chat to her or sit silently drinking a cup of tea, watching her at work, the way he'd dreamed of when she was away and he'd optimistically hoped that all would be well when she returned. The studio was painful to contemplate, so he turned and stared at the house.

It was beautiful with its graceful Georgian proportions and elegant kitchen extension, like something out of an upmarket magazine. If he'd known when he was younger that he'd end up in a house like this, he would scarcely have believed it. He thought back to his time in Australia, to the loneliness he'd felt on his own every night. What had he been thinking of, risking everything like that? When Jane and his boys were waiting for him back here, in *this* house.

A light drizzle started, as though the weather knew the day wasn't going to turn out well. Killer huddled under the bench looking morose, and after a few minutes Roger said, 'Come on, then,' and they went back to the house.

He went upstairs and changed into a new long-sleeved maroon polo shirt which Sam had assured him suited him. He teamed it with a pair of jeans that Jane had helped him choose and which she particularly liked; he felt he was as well kitted-out as he could be. Andy had dropped plentiful hints about the groomed Frenchmen his mum had come into contact with while she was in Paris, and although Roger didn't feel up to competing with them, he needed to make sure he was at least 'presentable', as his mother would have said. He went downstairs and asked Mel what she thought.

'You look well smart,' she said, pausing as she basted the

chicken to give him the once-over. 'That colour goes with your hair.'

'What's left of it, you mean?' Roger said dryly, and she giggled.

The doorbell rang and he went to answer it. Andy, Sarah and Alfie were at the front door, and Sam and Guy were parking. He ushered them all into the sitting room and explained that Jane had gone to get her guest.

'Do we know yet who it is?' Andy said. 'It's just ...' He stopped.

'No,' Roger said. 'Can I get everyone drinks?'

'Lemon squash!' Alfie shouted, and Roger gave him a small frown.

'We don't drink squash, do we?' Sarah said. 'Water, Alfie.'

'I can get you some water,' Roger said. He threw Alfie a wink so rapid that no one else saw it, but Alfie's two front teeth appeared.

He went into the kitchen to get the drinks. 'Can I get you something to drink, Mel? Come and say hello to everyone when you get a chance.'

'No drink for me. I'll come and say hi in a sec, just need to get all the veggies prepped.'

Roger took in Alfie's sippy cup filled with water (and a drop of lemon barley water), some beers for his sons, and sparkling waters for Sarah and Guy. There was a small pile of presents in the corner of the room and he fetched his own from upstairs and added it to the pile carefully.

The front door opened.

'Here she is,' Roger said. His heart had started to race and his face felt flushed. Who was this mystery guest? Andy's face looked strained and he and Sam were exchanging glances which Roger didn't know how to interpret.

A second later, the door opened and his wife stepped in. She looked sharper than she usually did, as though a current of electricity was running through her veins. Her face was very calm, yet set.

Andy and Sam chorused: 'Happy birthday!'

Jane didn't acknowledge the greeting. Instead, she said, 'Oh good, everyone's here. I'd like you all to meet Pip.' She stepped to the side and gestured towards the person standing behind her.

Roger took in the guest. As far as he could assess, she looked to be in her twenties. She was a tall, well-built girl with warm amber eyes and chestnut hair that curled slightly and swung below her collarbones. She wore jeans and a striped long-sleeved top with a jumper draped over her shoulders, ankle boots and a plaited cotton bracelet around one wrist. Her lightly freckled face looked tired but she smiled around shyly.

Roger's first reaction was relief. This was so much better than a man, a competitor for Jane's affections. Hard on the heels of this reaction came puzzlement. Who was this person? Was it possible that he'd put his wife off men so completely that she had become a lesbian? The girl was staring at Roger. He stared back. There was something familiar about her. Something about her nose and the angle of her jaw. He couldn't put his finger on it but he wasn't the only one who'd spotted it. Andy and Sam were frowning, too.

It was Alfie who got there first. 'Woger!' He took Roger's hand and yanked it. 'She looks like you!'

'Well,' Jane said very calmly, 'she would.' She stared straight into Roger's eyes. 'Because she's your daughter.'

32

In the stunned silence that ensued, Jane decided the conversation would be easier if everyone sat down. She led by example, crossing over to the sofa and plonking herself down, gesturing to Pip to join her.

Everyone else apart from Alfie was frozen in a tableau of shock, as though her words had unleashed a sonic bomb, leaving them physically unscathed but mentally incapable of processing what had happened or deciding on the next move. Her husband's mouth was opening and closing but no words emerged.

'Dad?' Andy turned to him. 'What's going on?'

'You don't have a daughter,' Sam said, his brow creased. 'Although she does really look like you.'

'Woger!' Alfie was jumping up and down, still yanking on Roger's hand. 'What's a doorta?'

Sarah snapped out of her trance. 'Alfie, sweetie, why don't we take Killer outside into the garden with a ball?' As Alfie started to protest, Sarah added, 'And a chocolate biscuit?'

'I'd love a biscuit,' Guy said swiftly.

Once the door had closed firmly behind them, Jane turned back to Pip. 'Could I get you a drink or something?'

'No, I'm good,' Pip said.

Both Andy and Sam said simultaneously, 'You're Australian!'

'True blue,' she said. Her eyes were guarded but her voice was friendly.

'Pip has just flown in from Sydney,' Jane said. 'She's very tired and I don't intend her to have to listen to all of the drama that's about to happen, but I wanted her to meet everyone and, well, for you all to see her.' She gave both her sons her best, calmest mum stare. 'Boys, I'll talk to you about this properly later. For now, all you need to know is it was Pip's mum your dad had an affair with in Sydney all those years ago. He didn't know about Pip. But here she is.'

Now her sons were staring curiously at the girl, who met their eyes calmly. They were behaving well, Jane thought. She was proud of them for not making a scene, for sparing Pip's feelings. They were kind boys, and she'd always be grateful to them for not making a fuss now. Only Roger didn't know where to look. He dropped into a chair and started to breathe heavily. Was it possible he might have a heart attack? At least it would prove the bastard *had* a heart.

Andy sat down on the sofa opposite and said, 'So, um, what do you do, Pip?'

'I'm a doctor.'

'What kind?'

'Still training,' she said. 'Not entirely sure. I think maybe obstetrics? But maybe not.'

Jane felt a sense of unreality hit her. When was Roger going to say something?

Andy and Sam both shot a look at Roger and seemed to come to a silent agreement.

Andy said, 'How about we show you the garden, Pip? Or get you some breakfast?'

Pip's amber eyes met Jane's.

'Brekkie would be awesome,' she said. 'I could go for a coffee, too. After the dishwater on the plane.'

'Well,' Sam said wryly, 'looks like coffee addiction runs in the family. Let's see what beans Dad has in.'

They all stood and left the room.

Jane and Roger looked at each other. She wondered what his plan was to wriggle out of it.

'Jane ...' he said. 'I ... I ...'

'Think very, *very* carefully about your words, Roger,' she said. 'Please don't insult my intelligence.'

There was another long pause. The murmur of conversation from the kitchen seemed to indicate that Pip and the boys were coping with the bizarre situation they found themselves in.

'I didn't know. About a baby. I just can't b-believe it,' he said.

'Imagine how I felt when I found out,' Jane said. '*I* didn't know about the affair.'

Roger spoke slowly. 'She's called Yvonne. She was my assistant, PA, whatever you call it. She was kind to me, helped me sort stuff out. Explained how things worked over there and where to shop and eat, the best beaches to visit, where to go for weekends away.'

Jane was silent, listening, her legs and feet neatly pressed together, her hands in her lap. She knew her husband so well. She could see him now, weighing up his options: what could he say to placate her? If he lied to her now, concocted some elaborate fiction around stolen sperm, or 'I was too drunk to know what I'd done', she would make it her business to take everything else away from him: his sons, his grandson, his houses. The dog. The idea shocked her. She hadn't known she was capable of such vitriol.

Through the French doors, she could see her sons in the garden with Pip, who was wearing an old coat of hers against the cold and had her hands cupped around a mug. She brought her gaze back to Roger, who seemed to have come to a decision.

He cleared his throat. 'I was lonely. And stupid and selfish, of course. One evening, I invited her for dinner to thank her for all her work organising an event, and I had too much to drink and she was single and also, I think, lonely. Not married and no children, and, well ... I bitterly regretted it.'

'So it only happened once?' she asked, knowing what Yvonne had told Pip.

Roger took a long moment to respond. 'I want to say only once, but ... it happened more than once. Maybe three times? Then I told her that I couldn't possibly leave my wife, that I adored you, and that I was very sorry for my behaviour.'

'And then you came home,' Jane said.

'Yes. I came home.'

'And said nothing.'

'And said nothing.' He took a deep breath, like a drowning man grasping at the last air he'd ever have. 'I know it was wrong. But I thought you'd leave me.'

'I would have,' she said. Part of her wondered why she wasn't throwing things. That hideous clock from his mother, for instance. It would be quite satisfying to throw it at his head. But she was not a thrower of things and she had given him a deeply satisfactory shock. Her husband's usually ruddy face was blanched and pinched.

'Did you hear from Yvonne again?' she asked. She was

fact-checking now. Would he try to make himself sound better, tell some more convincing lies?

'I did. She sent me faxes at the office. The last one I got from her said that she had something important to tell me. She wanted to discuss it, on the phone, when I could be alone, not at work or ... with you.' Roger was rubbing his thumb along his opposite wrist, hard.

'Did you ask her what it was?' Jane said.

'No.' He shook his head. 'I sent money, because ... I thought ...'

'You thought she'd go away and leave you alone. Like a bribe.' Her tone was biting. 'She wanted to tell you she was pregnant. When you sent money, do you know what she actually thought? Do you?' Jane had promised herself she'd stay calm, but in spite of herself her voice started to rise. 'She thought you'd heard through the office grapevine that she was pregnant and that you wanted her to abort her child. She was forty and had always wanted kids and she thought you wanted her to terminate the baby. *Shame* on you.'

Roger started to scratch at his wrist, hard enough for her to see the raised welts. 'I am ashamed.' His voice was very low. 'I'm really, really ashamed.'

'So she stopped contacting you. She left Karter's and kept the baby and brought her up, and from what I've seen, she's done a very decent job.'

'I ... Maybe I can contact her now, make amends,' Roger said.

'You can't,' Jane said.

'Why not?' Roger's tone was meek, rather than imperious.

'Because,' Jane said, 'she's dead.'

Roger brought his hand up very slowly and rested it against his chest.

'She died three months before you retired. Cancer.'

Roger leaned back against the sofa and closed his eyes.

Jane paused before she spoke again. Should she test him one more time? If she did and he lied, she would absolutely take the nuclear option. She'd never be able to get past it. She grasped her left hand in her right, feeling her engagement ring beneath her fingers. 'Tell me: what did you tell Yvonne about us? About our relationship, when you got home?'

Roger opened his eyes. A long moment passed. He squared his shoulders and sat up straighter. 'I want you to know I'm not proud of this. I told her you knew. That you knew about the affair and had forgiven me, and I sent her the money. But I didn't know – I *promise* you – that she was pregnant. I don't know what I'd have done if I had,' he said, swallowing, 'but I didn't know.' He frowned. 'Do you think ...? If she wanted a baby, was it ...?'

'Does it matter?' Jane pushed her engagement ring up towards her knuckle. 'Let me tell you about Pip,' she said, into the silence. 'Unlike you, she seems to be brutally honest. She told me her mum never wanted her to contact you but Yvonne had always been very up front about how you were conceived, and once she'd gone, Pip was curious. She found me on Facebook. My account's not private and Kurmudge is a pretty unusual name and there are obviously photos of you on my account. She has no family left except an aunt she isn't close to, so she wanted to meet you, actually, but you're not on Facebook and she didn't want any more secrets, which is why she approached me directly.

'She sent me a message, a very nice one. Explained, apologised for giving me a shock, and sent a photo of herself. She really is the spitting image of you. Hard on her mum, to look at your face all those years. Perhaps for Pip, contacting me was revenge for what her mum went through. So I went to Sydney and met her and stayed for a few days and then went to see Anne.' She smiled. 'I think my sister rather enjoyed sending you that email. She said liars didn't deserve the truth.'

Mel opened the door and peered in. 'Hi, do you want me to put all the food on the table or plate up in the kitchen?' She saw their faces and her expression changed. 'Sorry, didn't mean to interrupt.'

'No, it's fine,' Jane said. 'Perhaps you could bring the food in and put it on the table? The boys can help. Alfie must be starving.'

'Okay,' Mel said cheerfully, but her eyes lingered on Roger's face for a moment.

'Are we really,' Roger said once Mel had backed out of the room, 'going to sit and eat lunch together as though this is all normal?'

'Yes,' Jane said, getting to her feet. 'You've had this secret for decades. Today's my birthday. As the boys would say – suck it up.'

LUNCH WAS REMARKABLY NORMAL, in fact. Mel refused to join them to eat, perhaps sensing that it wouldn't be a particularly relaxing place to be, and headed off home once all the food had been laid out. Alfie was at the tipping point but Jane noticed that Roger slid a plate of sliced-up roast chicken and roast potatoes in front of him just in time to head off the meltdown. Alfie sat swinging his legs in his booster seat, ate as though he was starving, and took little notice of the polite conversation around the table.

Pip was questioned at length and revealed that her mum had died recently (Andy and Sam exchanged shocked glances); that she was 'stoked' to get a coveted place on a training exchange programme and would be working at the Royal Brompton Hospital; that she was looking forward to spending time in the UK; that she had found a flat-share in Earl's Court and had a couple of mates who were also going to be in London. And that Jane had asked her to come and meet everyone. She delivered all this in very matter-of-fact tones.

She asked questions, too: what did Andy and Sam do, where did they live (she looked wistful when they revealed that they both lived within fifteen minutes of Roger and Jane). She was good with Alfie: leaning towards him as though confiding a secret, she said, 'Broccoli helps your brain grow, and I can tell you're super-brainy already, but it's always good to have more.' Alfie took another spoonful of broccoli and Sarah beamed at her. By the end of dessert (Eton Mess – such an appropriate choice, Jane thought) the atmosphere was almost light.

'Pwesents!' Alfie shouted, as he licked his spoon clean.

'I did tell him we'd do presents after dessert,' Sarah said, apologetically.

'Of course,' Roger said. It was the first thing he'd said since lunch had started.

'Mine!' Alfie said. He strained against the straps of his booster seat until Sarah undid them, before trotting over to the pile of brightly wrapped parcels. He found a cylindrical one with starry paper and brought it over to Jane.

'Thank you, sweetie,' she said. She unwrapped it to reveal a mug hand-painted with flowers, with the head of the flower represented by a yellow, slightly smudged fingerprint, obviously Alfie's. Delicate green lines had been carefully added to represent stems, clearly by someone other than Alfie. 'Did you make this at pre-school? I love it!'

'Look at the bottom!' Alfie demanded, turning it over to show the hand-painted words *With Love From Alfie*.

'Thank you so much,' Jane said, hugging him. 'Now, could you bring over another present for me to unwrap? I'll put this one here.' She put the mug carefully on the table. It really was rather lovely, she thought, in spite of the smudging. The pre-school were to be commended for their ambition in getting toddlers to put paint fingerprints on something.

Alfie brought over three more parcels: a new easel from Sarah and Andy; a new set of overalls to paint in from Sam and Guy, and finally a small bag, sealed at the top, from Roger.

'I'm so sorry,' Pip said. 'I didn't realise it was your birthday.'

'It's not a big deal,' Jane said. 'Honestly, at my age, it's hardly cause for elaborate celebrations, is it? We tend not to make much of a fuss about ... Oh.' As she was talking, she'd opened the bag and drawn out the small jewellery box inside. She lifted the lid, and there was an audible gasp from the rest of the table who were all craning their necks to look. She glanced up at her husband. 'Roger, it's ... huge.'

'Wow,' Guy said. 'Keeping up with the Kurmudges!'

'That's a *lot* of carats,' Sarah said.

The ring seemed to generate its own light. Jane took it out of the box and prised her small engagement ring off her finger, replacing it with the new one. It felt very heavy as it clicked gently against her wedding band. She wasn't really sure why she was still wearing her rings, but each time she'd considered removing them, she'd hesitated.

'What do you think?' Roger said, with an awkward laugh.

'I've never really been a fan,' Jane said, 'of cheap gestures.'

'The last thing that ring was,' he replied, 'is cheap.'

Jane glanced at Pip. It felt so wrong to be receiving an extravagant piece of jewellery from the man who'd left her mother in the lurch and hadn't provided any financial or emotional support for her. Yet Pip didn't seem to be at all bitter about the situation. She was a remarkably well-balanced girl, Jane thought. Yvonne had done a great job.

Roger leaned towards her. 'Do you like it?' he said.

'It's really not me,' Jane said honestly, feeling a savage pleasure in watching his face fall. 'It's beautiful, obviously, but not me.'

'I can take it back,' he said. 'Get you something you'd prefer. Anything.'

'We'll talk about it later,' Jane said. She took the ring off and put it carefully back in the box, and put the box back in the small bag. She picked her old engagement ring up and after a slight hesitation, she pushed it back onto her finger and heard the tiny metallic 'chink' sound as it settled into place. There was quite a groove around the base of her finger after so many years of wearing it. For the moment, at least, she'd continue to do so.

Jane made coffee for everyone and returned to the dining room with the tray.

Andy was asking, 'Why medicine?'

Pip took the coffee Jane offered her and said, 'I liked science at school and then Mum got sick.'

Roger blanched a little.

'She had cancer for quite a while – breast – so I saw how bad it was for her and also how great the doctors and nurses were. I wanted to do some good.' She shrugged.

'Have you always lived in Sydney?' Sam asked.

'Yeah. Such a great city, isn't it?' Pip directed the question at Jane.

'It is.' Jane nodded. 'I liked it a lot, and your house is beautiful. That view of the harbour.'

'Where do you live?' It was the first time Roger had spoken. Jane wasn't sure if he wanted to understand what she'd seen on her trip to Sydney or whether he was genuinely interested in his unknown daughter's life.

'Mosman,' Pip said. 'I'm lucky. Mum's parents bought several properties around Mosman, decades ago.'

'Mosman is a great area,' Roger said. 'Where did you go to school?'

It was incredible, Jane thought, how similar the well-off were, no matter what country they were in. Schools, universities, house prices. Surely the real point was that Pip was on her own in the world now?

'Queenwood,' Pip said.

'Good school,' Roger said. 'Several of the Karter's directors sent their children there.'

Pip turned to Alfie, who was starting to whine. 'Alfie, what do you want to be when you grow up?'

'A dinosaur,' he said.

'Great choice,' Pip said. 'T. rex? Iguanodon?'

'The biggest one.' Alfie made claws with his fingers and gave a sudden roar that made Jane jump slightly: she was more on edge than she'd thought. 'Pip, wanna see my Lego?'

'I really do,' she said, and he slipped off his booster seat and took her hand.

'Come!' He started to drag her out of the room.

'I'll come too,' said Sarah, and the rest of the family took the opportunity to leave the dining room.

Jane and Roger were left in a silence that hung over them. She didn't know what to do next. She'd almost hoped that he would try to lie to her about Yvonne so that she could unleash her utter fury on him, but he hadn't. He'd been honest, for once. He looked old as she stared across the table at him. His face was flushed from the wine with lunch. There were liver spots on his hands and he looked weary and sad. She hadn't registered how thin his hair was getting until she'd seen him at the hospital, wrung out with worry about Alfie.

Now he stared at her like a foreigner in trouble who doesn't speak the local language. 'Did you suggest Pip should come to the UK?' he said.

'Exchange programmes are not organised in a few months,' Jane said tartly. 'She told me when I met her that she'd be coming over here, and that she was looking forward to a change after her mum's death. I think she'd been hoping to meet you then. She really wasn't sure about coming today because she thought it would be so awkward, but I persuaded her. I wanted to put you on the spot so you couldn't lie to me. Seeing you both together, it's impossible to argue that she isn't related to you. It's just so obvious.'

It was. Pip looked more like her husband than either Andy or Sam did. In spite of their height, they'd both inherited Jane's lean build. Pip was sturdy and looked better able to cope with the world's stresses than Jane's sons did. She had the glorious mass of tumbling hair that Jane had seen in photos of Yvonne in Sydney, and Roger's eyes, slightly too close together. On her, Jane thought, they looked charming.

'If she's just arrived,' Roger said, 'where's she staying tonight?'

'Here,' Jane said. 'I asked her to. There's plenty of room and it's the least we can do.'

Roger was nodding vigorously. 'Of course!' He looked as though he wanted to say something else but stopped.

'Spit it out,' Jane said.

'What does this mean?' he asked. 'For us, I mean. Janey, I love you so much. I'm so sorry. It's been *torture* without you. Are you ... Will we ...'

'I don't know,' she said. 'I really don't. But I'm sure of one thing.'

'Which is?'

She stood and glared down at him. 'I expect you to make a fulsome apology to that girl. It's bad enough to be an absent father in spirit. To be one in person as well is unforgivable. I want you to ask her for a walk, maybe tomorrow, when she's had some sleep, and bloody well apologise.' She strode out of the room and slammed the door behind her.

33

From: Roger Kurmudge
To: Pip Colbert
Subject: Our chat, continued

Dear Pip,

After our walk last Sunday, I realised that there was a lot I hadn't covered. The rain didn't help, did it? And you felt so cold after the Sydney sunshine. Anyway, rather than wait until I next see you again (which I hope will be soon), I thought I'd email you so I can put my thoughts down properly.

I hope I did cover my guilt over not being there for your childhood and how much I want to atone for that now. I've been a looming absence for your entire life, but if it's any consolation, Sam and Andy received very little attention from me while they were growing up, too. I was a terrible dad and a hopeless grandad. Something for you all to bond over, perhaps! Jane vanishing forced me to really spend time with my children and Alfie and showed me what I've been missing. I have to hope I can do the same with you.

I'm not sure I said enough to you about your mum. I have great regrets over the way I treated her. I was firstly weak and then cowardly and I now have to live with that. I wanted to share with you my memories of her, which are entirely positive. Your mum was a truly warm, capable person, the kind of woman who got things done without hurting people's feelings. She made the office a better place to be every day. Such people are a rarity. As well as those rather dry-sounding words, she was funny and kind and a pleasure to be around; I can only imagine how much you miss her. She deserved to meet someone better than me but she also deserved to be a mum to someone as fantastic as you. I hope the latter was consolation for the former.

It's too late for me to atone with Yvonne. But I have just received the refund from that foolish ring. I'd like to donate it to Cancer Research in her name, unless you prefer the hospice in Sydney? Entirely up to you. Have a think and let me know what you decide.

I hope you know how welcome you are to come for the weekend whenever you can get away. Jane is rarely here, in fact, so it would probably just be me. I'm always available to pick you up from the station. In the meantime, make sure you buy a proper coat. You're in the Northern Hemisphere now! And the crime stats in London don't look good. I've ordered you one of those self-defence personal alarm things. I'll pop it in the post to you later this week.

With extremely belated love,
Roger

34

Watney Manor was glorious in early summer, Roger thought. Almost worth the extortionate cost of hosting a celebration here. There was a floral riot going on in the wide flowerbeds that hugged the main house, and the air was thick with their scent. The terraced lawns were so perfect, Roger imagined someone had measured the mown lines to ensure they were equal widths.

He took a glass of champagne from a wandering waiter and crossed the lawn to join Sarah, Andy and Alfie.

'Woger! Wanna touch your fower,' Alfie said, reaching up towards Roger's buttonhole.

'Of course.' Roger bent down to allow Alfie to reverently touch the white rose.

'You look smart, Dad,' Andy said. 'Groomed, even.'

'I tried,' Roger said. He'd spent quite a lot on a suit that really suited him. Although Sam and Guy hadn't wanted the wedding to be too formal, Andy had warned Roger: 'Make sure you buy something smart, Dad. What they say about gay men really knowing how to dress? Absolutely true.'

Roger also wanted Jane to notice him. After spending the last week in France, perhaps she'd be struck by his suaveness and decide once and for all to stay with him.

'Ready for your speech?' Sarah asked.

'As I'll ever be,' Roger said, taking a gulp of champagne. He wasn't really looking forward to it, but he'd been grateful to be asked. Guy's father was there in a slightly too small grey suit; he kept running a finger around the neck of his shirt and shifting from foot to foot. He looked too anxious to make the kind of speech Sam and Guy deserved.

'A shame Gran couldn't make it,' Andy said.

'I'm not sure it would have been a good idea,' Roger said. His mother had been unwell with a chest infection for a few weeks now. He'd gone to see her a few times and had stiffly suggested via email to Arthur that he should visit as well before it was too late. His brother had curtly emailed back to say he would, but there had been no mention of catching up with Roger at the same time. No invite to the wedding for him.

'Tween!' Alfie shouted and ran across the grass towards Treen and Mel, who had just arrived. Treen had started to babysit for him, and he adored her. He grabbed her hand and started to run laps with her around the lower terrace. Every now and then, he would pull a flower off as he raced past and throw it at Andy, who didn't seem to mind. The head gardener certainly would if he caught him at it, Roger thought.

'Hi guys. How ya going?' came a voice from behind him. He turned to see Pip. Her hair was swept up in a complicated style Roger wouldn't have known how to describe, and she was wearing a midnight-blue dress that set off her eyes.

He leaned forward and kissed her cheek. 'How lovely that you could make it.'

'Are you kidding? Such a good excuse to get off the rota for the weekend!' She laughed. 'Can't wait for a lie-in and a hotel brekkie tomorrow. Jane kindly said I could have the other bed in her room.' She turned to look around at the groups of people dotted around the lawn. 'What a great day for it. So lucky with the weather. Isn't this just beautiful?'

Roger experienced two emotions in rapid succession: relief that Jane wasn't sharing her room with a new man, followed by sadness that she wasn't sharing a room with him. He had to remind himself to be grateful that he and Pip were on good, if slightly guarded, terms and that she was willing to spend the occasional Sunday with him. Alfie thought she was marvellous and liked to hear gruesome tales of people's legs being cut off or necrotic kidneys being removed. She was gradually becoming one of the family, and the more time Roger spent with her, the more grateful he was for his new daughter. And a doctor, to boot! He'd have to find a way to let Arthur know.

'I'll just go and say hi to Jane,' Pip said, and patted Roger's arm. 'See you later.'

His wife was talking to Guy's mum. They were laughing at something, his elegant wife in her cool green lace dress and Guy's plump mum in a purple skirt and silver top, heads close together.

'Mum always gets on with everyone,' Andy said, following his gaze. 'How are *you* getting on?'

Roger drained his glass. 'I don't see much of her. She's in Paris a lot, of course, and I'm still in the spare room.'

'TMI, Dad,' Andy said, stepping back as though Roger had offered to show him a video of their sex life.

'Sorry. But I don't know what will happen. We're stuck in a holding pattern.' He took a fresh glass from a passing waiter and downed half of it to drown out the thought.

'I'd hate you to sell the house,' Andy said. 'It's home.'

'I know,' Roger said. 'If your mum wants to, though – to leave me and buy something else ...' He finished the glass. 'Do you think she's met someone?' Roger had lost count of the times he'd apologised to Jane since Pip's appearance at the birthday party. He'd ordered so many bouquets of flowers that he was now on extremely cordial terms with Sylvia from *Bloomin' Lovely* and he was fairly sure he and Alfie could trash her shop any time now without her turning a hair. He'd subscribed to a podcast Andy had suggested – *Building a Better Man* – hosted by two men whose virtuousness and what Andy called 'wokeness' made Roger feel mildly homicidal when he listened to it. But he was doing his best. His tidying, dog walking, cooking, dishwasher-unloading best.

'I don't know if she's met someone,' Andy said. 'I mean, I could find out. But I don't think it's a good idea.'

Just as Roger was about to ask Andy what on earth he meant, a voice rang out: 'Ladies and gentlemen, lunch is served!'

'Good luck, Dad,' Andy said. 'Break a leg.'

AN HOUR LATER, after tapping his knife against his wine-glass, Roger stood to make his speech. He had his notes on small cards and he'd practised several times, but as he looked at all the expectant faces, most of whom he didn't know as they were Sam and Guy's friends, he felt suddenly awash with anxiety (and perhaps a little too much champagne on an empty stomach).

He cleared his throat. 'Ladies and gentlemen, firstly, thank you all so much for coming, at such late notice. I booked this day initially to celebrate our fortieth wedding anniversary, but in fact we decided not to go ahead and I had to cancel all the invitations, but I couldn't cancel the booking without losing the deposit, which was quite hefty, and so it made sense to suggest that Sam and Guy should use it as a wedding day instead. And fortunately we were lucky enough to find a registrar who could make it today.'

What was he doing? This hadn't been on his first card. People were looking puzzled now. He'd have to explain.

'It was entirely my fault about the fortieth,' he said, with an expansive sweep of his arm. 'I'd kept a secret from my wife for over twenty years and she found out. I had a daughter, Pip, who I didn't even know I had, because of an affair – which obviously I, er, *did* know I'd had,' he chuckled nervously, 'and so she – that's Jane, not Pip – didn't feel like celebrating our fortieth, and frankly, who can blame her? But none of that's Pip's fault of course: she's here today and she's a wonderful girl, entirely thanks to her mother ...'

He looked around the room. Pip was unfazed – she'd be so good in a medical emergency, he thought – but other faces were puzzled or amused or shocked, all of which led to some sniggering. *Christ.* Not the effect he'd been after at all. Guy's parents were staring up at him in wide-eyed bemusement. Jane had a small smile on her face. Sam looked horrified, which reminded Roger of the point of his speech.

He turned back to the tables in front of him. 'If you don't mind, I think I'll start again. I'll look at my cards this time!'

A ripple of amusement ran through the room.

'Good idea. Stick to the script,' Sam hissed.

'Right.' Roger pulled the cards from his pocket. 'I wanted to speak about marriage. That reading you had earlier, the Shakespeare sonnet about love not being love which alters when it alteration finds. Those are lovely, lovely words.

Underlying them is the idea of communicating with each other when life changes, or you change. Telling the truth. Because lies are corrosive. They can lie dormant for years but they will come back to haunt you eventually.'

He swung his gaze around the room. Jane was frowning and Andy was tearing his name card into confetti bits.

Alfie said loudly, 'Cake!'

Roger cleared his throat. He'd gone off track yet again. He turned to look at Sam and Guy. Both looked apprehensive, he thought. They'd trusted him to do a solid, unremarkable job, and he was stuffing it up.

He glanced down at the white card in his hand. *Talk about Sh. marriage.* 'I often think about the Bard's marriage,' he said, as confidently as he could and caught a peripheral glimpse of Jane raising her eyebrows.

Roger rolled his shoulders, registering the sweat running down his back. He amended his words: 'Well, no. Not *often*.' A smattering of laughter. 'But when I started to write this, I looked him up and he was married for a long time: thirty-four years. I like to think that he would agree with me that marriage is a very long road, at least if you're lucky. Like a train journey that you start together. An "epic" one, as my sons might say. And you will both change during it. Physically, as well as mentally. I used to be quite fit, if you can believe it.' He patted his stomach and nodded at Guy. 'Perhaps it's just as well my new son-in-law is a personal trainer!' A few smiles. 'What we hope for in marriage is to grow and evolve together. But change is inevitable and you have to still love each other as your jobs alter or your circumstances become different. The important thing is to keep the line of communication always open, to make sure you both talk to each other all the time, even now you're about to be parents.

'That parental love,' he smiled across at Andy, who was clinging to Alfie to stop him getting off his seat and heading towards the cake, 'can surpass everything else. It can take up all your time and energy and passion. Sam and Guy, you're both about to get the biggest gift of your lives: a little boy to look after and make part of your lives. We're all really looking forward to Finn arriving.' Here, Alfie scowled, and Roger made a mental note to order something very large for Finn to give to Alfie as soon as he arrived. A pony, perhaps.

He turned to Sam. 'You have to *remember* each other. You have to make sure you're on the same train, on the same track, going in the same direction, always. Make sure that, at the end of the day, you come back to each other. Because a great marriage, as it turns out, is like oxygen or fresh water or the sun. Something you take for granted but which is really utterly essential for life. Never, *ever* forget that.' For a second, he thought he might cry. Celebrating the start of his son's marriage as his own ended felt like a punishment too far. 'It's also incredibly rare. Don't make the mistakes I made and ruin it.'

He sniffed back tears. Andy and Sarah were smiling at each other. Various people he didn't know, mainly men dressed more noticeably than he'd known men *could* dress – one in a shiny gold suit; several in shorts rather than trousers; scarlet waistcoat-ed, purple cravat-ed men with quite remarkable haircuts – were gazing into each other's eyes. Was it possible his speech had been well received after a rocky start? He should definitely quit while he was ahead, as the boys would say.

'I have more cards,' he went on, brandishing them at the audience, 'but I'm going to stop there.' He turned back to Sam and Guy. 'I'd welcome you to the family, Guy, except you've been part of it for years already. Congratulations to you both.' He reached for his glass and held it up. 'I'd like to finish with a toast. Could you all please stand and drink to the happy couple!'

A chorus of 'the happy couple' later, and Roger sat down.

Sam put an arm around him. 'Dad, that was lovely.'

'Glad you liked it,' Roger said. He had to clear his throat before he could speak.

'You can relax now,' Guy said.

'I will.' A sense of utter anticlimax hit him. The wedding had been the largest thing in his diary for the remainder of the year and now his part in it was over. He glanced around the room. Everyone else looked, to his mind, full of hope for the future. They'd have plans and people who wanted to spend time with them, jobs, hobbies, holidays booked. He felt bereft.

To hide it, he leant forward to pick up his wineglass and caught Jane's eye. She looked very, very serious and sad. She wouldn't leave him for good today, surely? He turned his head away sharply, and focused on the dessert being placed in front of him.

SAM AND GUY had decided on a disco rather than a band, and they'd chosen a DJ who knew how to get everyone up and dancing. Now Mel gave Roger a wave from the dance floor. She was quite the mover, Roger thought, waving back. It was just a pity she was unlikely to meet a nice boyfriend this evening. Although there were some nice girls here, if that was more Mel's thing. She was growing in confidence, he was pleased to see, especially since she'd enjoyed her time shadowing the food technologist and been offered sponsorship by Karter's. They'd looked at various universities and Reading was the best fit for her. He'd promised to keep an eye on Treen for her while she was away.

An influx of new people began to arrive for the evening reception, including Tom, Elena and the twins.

'We want Finn to go to the same pre-school as Alfie and we thought it would be nice for the twins and Finn to meet at the park a few times beforehand,' Sam had said as he'd told Roger about the invitation. 'Tom seems like a good bloke.'

'He really is,' Roger had said. 'And a good friend.'

Elena was wearing something – figure-skimming and very short, with an enormous bow at the neck – that wouldn't have been out of place on a catwalk. As she said hello to Jane, Roger could have sworn his wife's eyebrows lifted an almost imperceptible amount as she took in the outfit, although no one else would have noticed. Because no one else knew her like he did, he thought fiercely. Not even any smarmy well-dressed Frenchmen she might have met.

Tom came over to chat to him, holding both the twins' hands. 'How did the speech go?'

'Fine, fine,' he said. 'Well, I may have gone off on a tangent to start with, but I think I got it back on track.'

Ludo or Ricardo was whining, tugging at Tom's arm.

'Why don't you try to find Alfie?' Roger said to him. 'He's somewhere over there.' He pointed to the dance floor.

'Is it safe in there?' Tom asked.

'His dance moves are a bit wild,' Roger conceded. 'But apart from him almost taking out a couple of girls with those skyscraper shoes, it's pretty safe. Pip is keeping an eye on him.'

'Lovely girl,' Tom said, nodding, and Roger felt a rush of pride. 'I'd better get Elena a drink. I'll see you later.'

'Of course,' Roger said. He sat back down again, looking at his hands in his lap. They looked so old. How had he not noticed those liver spots before? He felt tired. They'd have to sell the house, and it was going to be a huge job. Possibly Jane was right when she said he was a hoarder. There was so much up in the attic and the garage was also full. Not Jane's fault; she'd asked him many a time to clear things out, and he just hadn't. Worse still, would she want to take Killer? He'd really miss the dog, he was such a good little –

'Penny for them?' came a clear voice and he looked up from his reverie to see Jane standing there. She looked so wonderful. As lovely as the day he'd met her, at that party; the memory came flooding back. Some posh London boy on his finance course had been throwing it at his parents' palatial home in Chelsea, and Jane had been there, along with a group of friends from the Royal College of Art. He'd caught sight of her across the room, lean, long-legged, in jeans and a wide-necked tunic top that revealed the beauty of her collarbones, and had bided his time until he saw her standing alone, contemplating a swirly, jagged painting on the wall. She'd had tiny flecks of paint in her long blonde hair, so he'd sidled up to her and asked the obvious chat-up question: 'Did you paint this?' She had laughed and laughed. It had taken her a few minutes to calm down and tell him it was by someone called Willem de Kooning and that he was 'quite famous'. Roger had asked how much the painting was worth and she'd told him that not everything was about money. It was, he realised, a debate they'd been having for forty years.

Now she was holding out her hand to him. 'Shall we?'

He scrambled to his feet. 'Of course. Although ... I'm not sure how to dance to this.'

It was a rather lively song, with someone warbling about 'coming here for love'.

'Come on,' she said, taking his hand and leading him to the middle of the floor to join Alfie, Sam, Guy, Andy, Sarah, Mel, Pip and even Tom. All of them smiled as he approached; would they have smiled at him like that six months ago? Not with such warmth, he thought. He felt a sudden rush of pleasure in their company that was so intense he found his feet moving of their own accord and his hips wiggling a bit, and even his sore knees ached less. Andy was laughing with him as his grandson spun in circles that came perilously close to flattening everyone nearby.

For the next three minutes, Roger forgot his troubles: the impending divorce, the house sale, the loneliness, the loss of Killer. He laughed at Alfie and grinned at Andy and swapped places with Pip when she shimmied across their little circle to do-si-do him, and bumped hips with Sam. He was enjoying himself. He even started to sing the chorus as he picked up more of the words. Jane was dancing near him and he felt good for the first time in weeks.

But all too soon, the track finished. Sam was saying something to the DJ, who nodded and said into his microphone, 'And now for a change of pace, folks.'

This song was much slower, in Spanish. All the younger guests recognised it and whooped; Sam and Guy took centre stage, arms around each other, the dance floor became quite crowded and Roger was about to leave them to it when Jane reached for his hand.

'I think it's your turn to ask me,' she said.

'Ask you?' Roger said.

'To dance,' Jane said.

'May I?' he asked, and she nodded.

He pulled her towards him and put his arms around her

waist as Jane put her arms around his neck.

'That was an interesting speech,' Jane said into his ear. It was the closest they'd been since she'd returned, and Roger was still trying to cope with the wave of emotions it produced in him. She felt light and lean in his arms, the way she had at their own wedding forty years earlier.

'Did you ...' he barely dared ask, 'like it?'

'Well,' she said, 'the first bit was slightly un-weddingy. You know, the bit about us not celebrating our fortieth. And the lying bit. It wasn't quite the tone people were expecting.'

'I know,' Roger said.

'We did some things well,' she said. 'Look at our lovely boys.'

Roger had a lump in his throat. Her comment was so clearly a summing-up of their relationship before it formally ended. He coughed and focused on his family.

Andy and Sarah were dancing in a circle, holding Alfie's hands. He was giggling in a slightly manic way and jumping up and down. He needed to go to bed soon, Roger thought, before the evening ended badly. Sam and Guy were smiling straight into each other's eyes, arms locked around each other.

'We did do some things well,' Roger said. His gaze slid to Pip, who was bending down to talk very seriously to Ludo and Ricardo as they stood next to the wedding cake. She had got to them just in time to stop Ludo or Ricardo (how Roger wished he could tell them apart) from trying to grab one of the figures from the top.

'She's a lovely person,' Jane said, nodding in Pip's direction.

'I know.'

'Nice that you sometimes get to spend weekends with her.'

'Yes, it is,' Roger said; but it wouldn't fill the void of Jane's absence. He wondered what *'despacito'* meant. Desperate? He certainly felt the melancholy of the song.

'Have you met anyone in Paris?' he asked. *Better to face the problem than ignore it.*

Jane made a non-committal face, which didn't mean no.

He felt weak with misery.

'There are some *very* attractive, cultured men in Paris,' Jane said, gazing away from him across the dance floor.

'Are you,' he said, scarcely able to form the words, 'in a relationship with one of them?'

A long moment drew out. Roger concentrated on keeping his feet moving. It took all of his energy.

'The thing is,' Jane said, 'the rest of your speech, once you got past that bit, was rather lovely. Particularly the "essential for life" bit. I liked it. When I first found out about Yvonne, I wanted public humiliation for you, and I got it tonight.' She leaned away from him and looked into his eyes. For the first time, Roger started to feel a fluttering of hope. 'I'm not going to lie, as the boys would say. I've thought about being with someone else but the trouble is they *all* need training. It might have taken me forty years to train you, but it's been a great success. Not to enjoy the results seems foolish. And strangely enough, I still love you.' She smiled at him: a glimpse of the old warmth. 'I think it would be a mistake to sell the house, or separate ... just yet. Let's see what happens, shall we?'

'I thought,' Roger said, 'when I saw your face after my speech, I thought ...'

She lifted a shoulder then dropped it. 'It's hard to find a great marriage. Ours was, once, wasn't it? Before the gender-traditional roles and the day-to-day drudgery and –'

'The massive lie I told?' Roger said.

'– the affair and then the outrageous lying that almost ruined everything,' Jane said.

'I really have changed. And I can do more.' Roger tried not to sound desperate.

'I hope so,' Jane said, 'because I want to paint and travel to Paris a bit. I've looked after you all for years; it's my turn to do what I want to do now. But someone will have to keep looking after Alfie and running the house, and I think Sam and Guy want us to help with Finn, too.'

'I'd love to,' Roger said, as breath filled his lungs. 'I'm very keen to help.'

'I thought this summer we might invite the whole family, including Pip, to Bordeaux? For a week or two? Maybe just one,' Jane qualified, as Alfie spun uncontrollably into a waitress, knocking her flying and smashing the glasses on her tray.

Sarah grabbed their grandson's arm. 'Time for bed, right now!' she said. Alfie's wails of protest drowned out the Spanish warbling.

'I think that's a truly fantastic idea,' Roger said to his wife. 'But now, I think the main thing I should do is to put Alfie to bed.'

'Do you need Andy's room key?'

'No, he can sleep in my room. Plenty of space in my bed. I'll get him now.'

He crossed the room and said, 'Alfs, do you want to come and see my bedroom with me?'

Alfie stopped sobbing and rubbed his eyes with his fists. 'I not *tired*.'

'Of course you aren't!' Roger bent down to pick him up, ignoring the ache in his knees. 'You're going to have a biscuit and jump on my bed for hours.'

Alfie's eyes were drooping. 'Biccit,' he said wanly. He

settled his head onto Roger's shoulder. Around them, everyone was dancing rather exuberantly, shouting tunelessly along to the words, and Roger felt a bit old for such partying. The music was loud and he was quite happy to have an excuse to leave, especially if his wife might feel the same.

'I don't suppose,' he said to Jane, 'you'd like to come with us? Have a cup of tea? I've got plenty of biscuits and there's a little sitting room, so we won't disturb Alfie.'

'Good biscuits?' Jane asked, narrowing her eyes.

'Karter's shortbread, and also those Knobblies. Not as good as Hobnobs, but they're okay.'

She looked steadily at him, then held up a finger. His heart fell as she disappeared into the throng of people on the dance floor – if only he'd brought the Karter's Christmas Selection box – but she came back a few seconds later.

'Andy will come and get Alfie from your room when he comes up to bed,' she said.

'He doesn't have to,' Roger said. 'I'm quite happy to have Alfie there.' Sleeping with Alfie would be an upgrade compared to sleeping with Killer.

'I'm not,' Jane said. 'He's such a wriggler.'

Roger tried to control his reaction. He didn't want to frighten her off. 'So you might ...?'

'I might,' she said, tilting her head. 'Come on, then.'

They walked side by side up the stairs, Alfie's head bouncing softly with each step Roger took, his breath in Roger's ear. The music receded behind them as they ascended.

When they reached his suite, Roger handed Jane the key and she pushed it into the slot. The light went green; Jane opened the door. They stepped over the threshold into the dimly lit room and the door slowly shut behind them.

AUTHOR'S NOTE

Thank you so much for reading *Jane's Away*. I am so grateful and I very much hope you enjoyed it. If you did, I'd be even more grateful if you could review it on Amazon or Goodreads or anywhere else readers look for information about books. Reviews benefit both readers and authors and they don't have to be long.

Secondly, if you enjoyed *Jane's Away* and would like to see what happens next to Roger, Jane and, of course, Alfie, please head to clarehawken.com where you can sign up for my mailing list and download a free short story, *Finn Arrives*. I promise not to bombard you with emails – I'll only use your details to tell you when my next book is available and perhaps send you the occasional blog post.

I'd also like to thank my family for their support and patience. Especially the dog. Many a walk has been missed because I can't tear myself away from my laptop. I just wish she was as forgiving as Killer.

Clare Hawken
Wiltshire, England

Printed in Great Britain
by Amazon